I0593766

Increase Niles Tarbox

Life of Israel Putnam

Increase Niles Tarbox

Life of Israel Putnam

ISBN/EAN: 9783744737883

Printed in Europe, USA, Canada, Australia, Japan

Cover: Foto ©Raphael Reischuk / pixelio.de

More available books at **www.hansebooks.com**

Isreal Putnam

[This fac-simile is from a bond given by Israel Putnam to his brother David, in 1743.]

LIFE

OF

ISRAEL PUTNAM

("OLD PUT"),

MAJOR-GENERAL IN THE CONTINENTAL ARMY.

BY

INCREASE N. TARBOX.

With Map and Illustrations.

BOSTON:
LOCKWOOD, BROOKS, AND COMPANY.
1876.

THOMAS TODD,
Stereotyper and Electrotyper,
1 Somerset St., Boston.

PREFACE.

It is not the aim of this volume to report any new historical discoveries, but simply to bring back to its old anchorage ground an important piece of American History, which, for a quarter of a century, by a subtle undertow, has been drifting from its place. I have attempted to write the Life of Major General Israel Putnam by the light and with the evidences of the last century, and not by the false lights of 1875. Whether I have succeeded in this purpose, the intelligent reader must judge.

In the preparation of this volume, I have had, for my assistance, first of all and chief of all, Force's "American Archives." Here we find the old revolutionary papers and documents, in every form and variety. To these volumes I have turned continually for original and reliable information. Next in importance has been the "Siege of Boston," by Richard Frothingham, Esq. This volume contains, unquestionably, the most full and careful collection of facts and incidents which we have, covering the period from the battle of Lexington, April 19th, 1775, to the Evacuation of Boston by the British troops, March 17th, 1776. For the early life of Putnam, most important information has been drawn from the volumes of Charles W. Upham, Esq., entitled "History of Witchcraft and Salem Village." Israel Putnam's birth-place was on the very ground covered by Mr. Upham's graphic narrative. In this same department, much valuable assistance has been gained from the "History of the Danvers Church," by Rev. Charles B. Rice. The "Life of General Israel Putnam," writ-

ten by General David Humphreys of New Haven, one of
General Putnam's Aids, has been constantly at hand, for reference. This work was first published about 1790, but was
afterwards brought out in a new edition in 1818, with an
Appendix by Colonel Samuel Swett of Boston. Colonel Daniel Putnam's vindication of his father, in his reply to General
Dearborn, as also his valuable paper published in the first
volume of the "Connecticut Historical Collections," have been
often consulted. For the period immediately after Putnam's
removal to Connecticut (1739), the writer has been greatly
assisted by Miss Ellen Larned's new "History of Windham
County," Connecticut. I have had, for constant reference,
the compilation of Bunker Hill authorities, found in the
"Historical Magazine" for June, 1868, prepared by its editor,
Henry B. Dawson, Esq. In the same connection, free use has
been made of the carefully prepared and extended list of authorities on this subject, recently furnished by Justin Winsor, Esq.,
Superintendent of the Boston Public Library. I have also
turned frequently to the smaller histories of the Battle
of Bunker Hill, by Rev. George E. Ellis, D.D.; Samuel A.
Drake, Esq.; W. W. Wheildon, Esq. ; and Col. Francis J. Parker. Valuable information has been gained from the published Memorial Address, by Rev. L. Grosvenor, given at the
gathering of the Putnam family at Putnam, Connecticut, in
1855. Bancroft's "History of the United States" has been all
the while near at hand, for reference.

But in addition to these helps, I have received valuable
hints and suggestions, as also more extended information, from
Miss Susan Putnam, who now owns and occupies the house at
Danvers where General Putnam was born ; from Prof. Benja-
min Silliman, of New Haven ; from J. Hammond Trumbull,
LL. D., of Hartford; from Hon. Daniel P. Tyler, late of
Brooklyn, Connecticut ; from E. P. Hayward, Esq., Town Clerk
of Pomfret, Connecticut ; from Rev. Edwin S. Beard, present
pastor of the church in Brooklyn, Connecticut ; from Rev.
Henry A. Hazen, of Billerica, Massachusetts ; and from John
Ward Dean, Esq., of Boston.

Chapter XI., entitled "The testimony of Bunker Hill Literature and Art," is *especially* devoted to the question, Who commanded in the Battle of Bunker Hill? The same question is raised and discussed at other points in the narrative, but not continuously — only partially, according to the suggestions made by passing facts and events.

I am well aware that this volume will disturb some of the modern literature pertaining to the Battle of Bunker Hill. It is not from delight in controversy for controversy's sake; but believing as I sincerely do, that this most important chapter in our revolutionary history has been gradually warped, and turned aside from truth and righteousness, I have sought simply to make "crooked things straight."

INCREASE N. TARBOX.

West Newton, Feb. 11th, 1876.

CONTENTS.

7

CHAPTER IV.
ELEVEN YEARS OF HOME LIFE.

CHAPTER V.
THE ARMY THAT GATHERED AT CAMBRIDGE.

CHAPTER VI.
LEADING OFFICERS OF THIS ARMY.

CHAPTER VII.
PREPARATIONS FOR THE BATTLE.

CHAPTER VIII.
THE FORENOON OF JUNE SEVENTEENTH.

CHAPTER XIII.

CLOSING YEARS.

CHAPTER XIV.

THE BUNKER HILL CENTENNIAL.

APPENDIX.

LIFE OF ISRAEL PUTNAM.

CHAPTER I.

HIS ANCESTRY AND EARLY HOME.

Ancient Salem. — Salem Village, now Danvers. — Mr. Upham's graphic Pictures of the early Society. — Character and Standing of the Putnam Family. — Customs among the early Settlers. — Birth-place of Israel Putnam. — History of the House. — Education and Schools in Salem Village. — Emigration from Massachusetts Towns to Connecticut. — Putnam prepares to remove. — His Marriage to Hannah Pope.

WITHIN the last few years, many signs have indicated that, for the interests of individual justice, as also for historical truth and accuracy, there is needed another biography of General Israel Putnam. No patriot soldier in our revolutionary struggle bore a better name for heroic courage and effective leadership than he. Though he was already fifty-seven years of age at the very beginning of that long contest, and had thus reached a period when most men begin to look about for rest and exemption from the hardships and toils which they are willing to encounter in their youth, yet the story of his prodigious activities and well-nigh superhuman endurance, in the early years of that war, reads to us now almost like the exploits of some of the demi-gods and mythical heroes of old. There was such an abundance of life in him, such an overflowing energy, that his very presence filled other men with a courage of which they had not before known themselves to be possessed. During the war and at its close he was the second in military rank in

the American army, Washington only before him; and as
he was second in military office and title, so was he in the
enthusiastic affections of his countrymen. In 1790, having
passed his " three-score years and ten," — full of days and
honors, he "slept with his fathers," and the grave closed
over as pure and unselfish a patriot as the world often knows.
Who could have surmised, at that time, that his name
would ever be drawn into angry disputes, and would become
a mark at which men would shoot their poisoned arrows?

What the particular occasion of controversy was, when
Michael the archangel contended with the devil about the
body of Moses, we are not very distinctly informed. But
the secret of that contention which has gone on over the
grave of General Putnam is not hard to guess. Little bitter-
nesses and jealousies among army officers were not a new
thing in 1775, and that they have not yet ceased from the
earth, our recent war of the Rebellion, and the still later
European wars, abundantly testify. There are always so
many men connected with an army that want honors and
offices that do not strictly belong to them, that they are
often quite unscrupulous in their methods of gaining them.
And when this jealous controversy has once been let loose
among men, it catches hold of new minds, where some
inflammable material is stored up, and it may be long before
the strife is stayed. In this general fact we have the
fountain-head of all difficulty in this particular case.

General Putnam, with his high and patriotic impulses,
and with his military ability, native originality and bold
leadership, carved out a large domain for himself in American history. But he never stopped to fence it in and call
it his own. He left it open and unprotected for others to
forage upon, and make out of it reputations for themselves
as best they could.

Israel Putnam was born in the ancient town of Salem,

Mass., on the 7th of January, 1718. The original territory of Salem was very large, embracing a tract of wild country, out of which many of the surrounding towns, as they now exist, have been organized. The first church in the Massachusetts Bay was planted at Salem in 1629, and this was the earliest centre of life and population opened under the Massachusetts Bay charter.

John Putnam and his wife Priscilla came from England in 1634, bringing with them three sons: Thomas, then twenty-four years old; Nathaniel, twenty; and John, twelve. They took their places in the early Salem society as among the most worthy, intelligent and enterprising citizens. All the records agree in ascribing to the Putnams from the first an uncommon amount of energy and force of character. They were thrifty, forehanded men, and had the art of making their way in the world by honest means.

In 1641, the head of this family had a grant made him of one hundred acres of land. Thomas, the eldest son, went for a time to reside at Lynn, and he appears in the Lynn records for a few years, as one of their most important citizens. Afterwards he came back to Salem, and through all his subsequent life acted a conspicuous part in the local affairs of the town, both civil and ecclesiastical.

The home of the Putnams was in what is now Danvers, anciently called Salem Village. This was the scene of the witchcraft delusion in 1692. We know of no more graphic picture of early New England life, than that which is presented in the opening part of Mr. Charles W. Upham's two volumes, entitled, "History of Witchcraft and Salem Village." While we should seriously dissent from some of the conclusions which he reached, at a later stage of the work, his description of that primitive society in the years before the outbreak, — its employments, its family histories, its institutions, its joys and sorrows, its fears and alarms, its strifes and divisions, — is more deep and subtle in its power over the reader than any other piece of writing in this line with which we are acquainted. The following brief passage may serve to show the picturesque beauty and searching force of this style. It must be borne in mind that he is all the while unfolding the causes which contributed to prepare the place for that dreadful experience of 1692.

"Cultivation had made but a slight encroachment upon the wilderness. Wide, dark, unexplored forests covered the hills, hung over the lonely roads, and frowned upon the scattered settlements. Persons whose lives have been passed where the surface has long been opened, and the land generally cleared, little know the power of a primitive wilderness upon the mind. There is nothing more impressive than its sombre shadows and gloomy recesses. The solitary wanderer is ever and anon startled by the strange mysterious sounds that issue from its hidden depths. The distant fall of an ancient and decayed trunk, or the tread of animals as they prowl over the mouldering branches with which the ground is strown; the fluttering of unseen birds brushing through the foliage, or the moaning of the wind sweeping over the topmost boughs, — these all tend to excite the imagination and solemnize the mind. But the stillness of a forest is more startling and awe-inspiring than its sounds. Its silence is so deep as itself to become audible to the inner soul. . . . . The forests which surrounded our ancestors were the abode of a mysterious race of men, of strange demeanor and unascertained origin. The aspects they presented, the stories told of them, and every thing connected with them served to awaken fear, bewilder the imagination, and aggravate the tendencies of the general condition of things to fanatical enthusiasm." *

* Upham. Vol. I. pp. 7 and 8.

In the natural unfolding of his plan of work, the Putnams of the early generations lie directly in his path and come very distinctly into our view, and no man need desire for his ancestry a more honorable record than Mr. Upham here gives them. When John Putnam, the founder, died in 1662, he left a large estate to be divided among his three sons. "Thomas, the eldest, as was then the custom, inherited a double share of his father's lands. He was of age when he came to America, and had received a good education." We have spoken of his residence for some years in Lynn. We find in the Massachusetts Colonial Records the following item for 1645, and substantially the same, year by year, for three years afterwards: "Thomas Layton, Edward Bircham and Thomas Putnam are chosen to end small controversies in Linn." His grandson was chosen to end a much larger controversy a hundred and thirty years later. But of this Thomas, Upham says: "Upon removing to Salem, he was chosen, as the town records show, to the office of constable. This was considered at that time, as quite a distinguished position, carrying with it a high authority, covering the whole executive local administration. . . . . He seems to have been a person of a quieter temperament than his younger brothers, and led a somewhat less stirring life. Possessing a large property by inheritance, he was not quite so active in increasing it, but enjoying the society and friendship of the leading men, lived a more retired life."

Nathaniel Putnam, the next son, had a fourth part of his father's estate, and his wife also brought him seventy-five acres of land. Mr. Upham says of him, "Nathaniel Putnam was a deputy to the General Court, and constantly connected with all the interests of the community. He had great business activity and ability, and was a person of extraordinary powers of mind, of great energy and skill in the management of affairs, and of singular sacagity, acumen and quickness of perception. He died July 23, 1700, leaving a numerous family and a large estate." *

Of John, the youngest son, he says, "John Putnam had the same indefatigable activity as Nathaniel. He was often deputy to the General Court, and accumulated a very great landed property." † To show the standing of these three men, as to property in 1681, he finds that of a tax levied that year in Salem Village, of £200 total, raised from ninety-four tax-payers, for the support of the local church, Thomas Putnam pays £10 6s. 3d., Nathaniel, £9 10s., and John, £8, so that these three pay nearly a seventh part of the whole tax.

A custom worthy to have been perpetuated prevailed among some of these early families of Salem Village, and is thus described by Mr. Upham:

"These brothers (Thomas, Nathaniel and John Putnam), as well as many others of the large land-holders in the village, adopted the practice of giving to their sons and sons-in-law, out-right, by deed, good farms, as soon as they became heads of families; so that as the fathers advanced in life, their own es-tates were gradually diminished; and when unable any longer to take an active part in managing their lands, they divided up their whole remaining real estate, making careful contracts with their children for an adequate maintenance, to the extent of their personal wants and comforts. . . . . In his last years, John Putnam (who, as we have seen, paid £8 tax in 1681) was on the rate-list for five shillings only, while all his sons and daughters were assessed severally in large sums. . . . . Where this practice was followed, there were few quarrels in families over the graves of parents, and controversies seldom arose about the provisions of wills. In some cases no wills were needed to be made. It is apparent, that, in many respects, this

* Upham. Vol. I. p. 157.   † Ibid.

was a wise and good practice.   It was moreover a strictly just
one.   As the sons were growing to an adult age they added by
their labors to the value of lands, inserted a property into them
that was truly their own ; and their title was duly recognized.
In a new country, land has but little value in itself ; the value is
imparted by the labor that clears it and prepares it to yield its
products." *

To go back now to Thomas Putnam.   After a few years'
residence in Lynn, he returned to Salem Village to dwell
among his kindred.   While living in Lynn he married his
first wife, Ann Holyoke.   She was of that family which,
two generations later, gave Edward Holyoke to be President of Harvard College, holding the office for the long
period of *thirty-two* years (1737–69).   This wife died in
1665, and in the following year he married the widow of
Nathaniel Veren.   This Nathaniel Veren had been a merchant trader, with business upon the sea, and his widow, in
her marriage to Thomas Putnam in 1666, brought to him a
large property to be added to his own landed estate.   She
had wealth in Jamaica and Barbadoes, and the union of these
two streams gave a real opulence for that generation to
this household.   Thomas Putnam had two sons by his first
wife, and one by his second.   These were Edward and
Joseph Putnam.   He died in 1686, leaving large estates to
each of these sons, and not forgetting a faithful servant, to
whom he gave fifteen acres of valuable land.

From the organization of the old church in Salem,
(the oldest in the Massachusetts Bay,) under the care of
Mr. Francis Higginson and Mr. Samuel Skelton, in
1629, down to the year 1671, all these scattered dwellers
for many miles around went through the forest by-paths
and over the stony hills to Salem harbor, to attend meeting.
Mr. Higginson died in one year after the founding of that

* Upham.   Vol. I. p. 158.

2

church, and Mr. Skelton in five years. But Mr. Roger Williams, and Hugh Peters and others, had preached there in the early years, and in 1660, Mr. John Higginson, son of the first minister, came back from Connecticut, where he had already been twenty-four years in the ministerial work, and was set over this ancient church, and continued in office forty-eight years, making his whole ministerial life *seventy-two* years. In 1671, the scattered population to the north and north-west, living upon the farms, had so increased that a branch church was opened at Salem Village, not far from the present church in Danvers. This continued as a branch church until 1689, when it was organized as an independent church. Of this branch church, Edward Putnam, son of Thomas, was the first deacon, holding office for forty years. In his eightieth year, he gave this comprehensive summary of the Putnam family, which we quote from Mr. Upham : " From the three brothers proceeded twelve males; from these twelve males, forty males; and from these forty males, eighty-two males ; there were none of the name of Putnam in New England, but those from this family. . . . . I can say with the Psalmist, I have been young and now am old ; yet have I not seen the righteous forsaken, nor their seed begging bread, except of God, who provides for all. For God hath given to the generation of my fathers a generous portion, neither poverty nor riches."

It does not consist with our plan that we should turn aside to depict the terrible scenes that agitated and afflicted these lonely and scattered homes in the year 1692. That story, one of the saddest in our New England annals, may be read elsewhere, and especially in this work of Mr. Upham. But we will give one fragment, not from Mr. Upham's volumes, but from the " History of the Danvers Church," by Rev. Charles B. Rice. As this concerns a member of the Putnam family, it will be akin to our general purpose.

At the 200th anniversary of this ancient church (reckoning from its first existence as a branch church) Mr. David Stiles of Middleton, one of the speakers, gave the following incident, which most forcibly illustrates these terrible scenes of 1692. He said:

" I will relate a little story that has never been in print, showing our intimate connection nearly two hundred years ago. At the time of the witchcraft excitement, in 1692, a sister of Joseph Putnam . . . . and aunt of the famous General Israel Putnam, had a wish, like many others at that time, to see the proceedings of the court, then held in the first meeting-house, a little east of where we are now assembled. But as she entered the house she was accused of witchcraft. The officers of the law were advised by Mr. Parris not to arrest her until the trial then going on was closed. Meanwhile the poor girl fled to the house of Bray Wilkins, living under the brow of Will's Hill. She took her weary and anxious way through the swamps, among the thorns of the wilderness, fording Ipswich River, leaving behind one or both shoes, lost in the mud ; and with her clothing nearly torn from her body, she entered the house of this well-known good man. But the officers were already on her track, and were soon seen on the plain land below. Again she ran with bleeding feet to the dismal locality at the head of Middleton Pond ; and there among the thorns and briers, wild beasts and reptiles, she secreted herself till the search was given up." *

We return now to the other son of Thomas, Joseph Putnam, who, like his brother Edward, had inherited a large estate from his father. Joseph Putnam was the son of the second wife, the Widow Veren. He was born in 1670, and at the age of twenty was married to Elizabeth Porter, daughter of Israel Porter, the bride being then sixteen

* Rice's " History of Danvers Church," p. 217.

years and six months old.   Upham says of this bridegroom
and bride, " We shall see what a valuable citizen he became ;
and she was worthy of him.   A large and noble family of
children grew up to honor them, one of the youngest of
whom was *Israel Putnam*, of illustrious revolutionary fame."

There has sometimes been a kind of slur or secret insinuation, that General Putnam was of plebeian origin and of
an obscure family.   But if there was any family in Massachusetts, at the beginning of the last century, more worthy to
give birth to one of the great revolutionary heroes than
this, we fail to discover where it had its dwelling-place.   By
that time the Putnams, having done a large share in breaking into the primitive wilderness, and subduing the rough
and rocky soil that lay about Salem, began, as Upham says,
"to give their sons to the general service of the country in
conspicuous public stations, and in the professional walks of
life.   Their names appear on the page of history and in the
catalogues of the colleges."   Daniel Putnam, a grandson of
Nathaniel, heads the list of college graduates of this name,
and he became the minister of North Reading.   The triennial catalogue of Harvard alone shows more than twenty-
five graduates from this stock, and other colleges would
swell this list very considerably.   If any other Massachusetts family can present from the early years a more honest
and solid basis of dignity than this, it has liberty to propose
its claim.

The house in which Israel Putnam was born, and where
his father Joseph lived, is fortunately still standing.   The
very chamber in which he first saw the light may still be
seen in something of its old-fashioned simplicity.   This
house is believed by Mr. Upham (who has explored the
antiquities of this locality as no other man has) to have
been built by Thomas Putnam in 1648, about the time of
his returning from Lynn to Salem.   Very large additions

ISRAEL PUTNAM'S BIRTHPLACE.

have since been made to it, but with rare good taste and judgment, the original structure has been kept in a great measure intact. One can easily trace the ancient dimen sions, and look upon the roughly hewn timbers of the prim itive frame. It stands only two or three minutes' walk from the " Swan's Crossing" depot, on the Salem and Law- rence Railroad. It is at the crossing of the roads, where the old Newburyport turnpike intersects one of the Dan vers roads. It is in the immediate vicinity of that immense and almost bewildering structure which the State of Massa chusetts is now erecting in Danvers, as a new and additional Insane Hospital. Looking from the door of this Putnam mansion, westerly, this gigantic construction nearly one- third of a mile in length, ranging along the crest of the ancient " Hathorne Hill," is in full view, less than half a mile distant.

But this ancient house received large additions in 1744, and again in 1831, so that now, while it is antique and venerable in its appearance, the rooms are numerous, spa cious and comfortable. The barns and outlying buildings show at once to the passer-by that this has long been a scene of thrift and industry. It is an ancient New Eng land farm-house of the better quality. But the interest of the visitor centres about that original structure, still so clearly traceable. And his wonder is excited, when he sees with his own eyes what was regarded as a house of a high class and order in New England, more than two hundred years ago. Hardly any man in Salem Village was in a con dition to build a better house than Thomas Putnam in 1648. Here he lived with his first wife, Ann Holyoke, and with his second wife, the rich widow of Nathaniel Veren, " en joying the society and friendship of the leading men" of Salem. And yet this ancient structure does not make cer tainly more than a third part, if even so much, of the present farm-house. It was called of two stories, and was so, but both stories would not make more than one in some of the palatial residences of the present day. It faced toward the east or north-east, while the present farm-house faces to the west or south-west, and as one passes along the present road, nothing is seen of the early structure. The region where this house stands is about six miles north-west of Salem Harbor, and about a mile and a half north of the old Salem Village (now Danvers) meeting-house. In this general locality in 1692, the year of the witchcraft outbreak, there were living upon their farms, and in separate houses, twelve families of the name of Putnam. And we cannot resist the temptation to copy one or two delightful passages from Mr. Upham, showing what kind of work the Putnams and their neighbors had wrought upon these lands.

"Among all the achievements of human labor and perseverance recorded in history, there is none more herculean than the opening of a New England forest to cultivation. The fables of antiquity are all suggestive of instruction, and infold wisdom. The earliest inhabitants of every wooded country, who subdued its wilderness, were truly a race of giants. Let any one try the experiment of felling and eradicating a single tree, and he will begin to approach an estimate of what the first English settler had before him, as he entered upon his work. It was not only a work of the greatest difficulty, calling for the greatest possible exercise of physical toil, strength, patience, and perseverance, but it was a work of years and generations. The axe swung by muscular arms, could one by one, fell the trees. There was no machinery to aid in extracting the tough roots, equal often, in size and spread, to the branches. The practice was to level by the axe a portion of the forest, managing so as to have the trees fall inward, early in the season. After the summer had passed and the fallen timber become dried, fire would be set to the whole tract covered by it. After it had smouldered out, there would be left charred trunks and stumps. The trunks would then be drawn together, piled in heaps, and burned again. Between the blackened stumps, barley or some other grain, and probably corn, would be planted, and the lapse of years waited for, before the roots would be sufficiently decayed to enable oxen with chains to extract them. Then the rocks and stones would have to be removed before the plough could, to any considerable extent, be applied. . . . .

"The opening of a wilderness combined circumstances of interest which are not, perhaps, equalled in any other occupation. It is impossible to imagine a more exhilarating or invigorating employment. It developed the muscular powers more equally and effectually than any other. The handling of the axe brought into exercise every part of the manly frame. . . . . He who best knew how to fell a tree was justly looked upon as the most valuable and leading man. To bring a tall giant of the woods to the ground was a noble and perilous achievement. . . . . Accidents often, deaths sometimes, occurred. A skilfull woodman, by a glance at the surrounding trees and their branches, could tell where the tree upon which he was about to operate should fall, and bring it unerringly to the ground in the right direction. . . . . There were elements also in the work that awakened the finer sentiments. The lonely and solemn woods are God's first temples. They are full of mystic influences ; they nourish the poetic nature ; they feed the imagination. The air is elastic, and every sound reverberates in broken, strange, and inexplicable intonations. The woods are impregnated with a health-giving and delightful fragrance nowhere else experienced. All the arts of modern luxury fail to produce an aroma like that which pervades a primitive forest of pines and spruces. Indeed, all trees in an original wilderness, where they exist in every stage of growth and decay, contribute to this peculiar charm of the woods. It was not only a manly but a most lively occupation. Where many were working near each other, the echoes of their voices of cheer, of the sharp and ringing tones of their axes, and of the heavy concussions of the falling timber, produced a music that filled the old forests with life, and made labor joyous and refreshing."

We have thus brought into view the birth-place of our subject with its primitive surroundings. He was of the fourth generation from the beginning, reckoning John Putnam the founder as the first. He was born not until twenty-eight years after the marriage of his father and mother, and was the youngest but one in a family of eleven children. At that time the opportunities for education were few. The college was doing its work at Cambridge. Ezekiel Cheever, the schoolmaster of seventy years' service, was busy in Connecticut and Massachusetts, especially in the department of classical instruction. *Others* followed his example. The better-educated ministers could also fit boys for college. But the common school system, as a system, had not borne its better fruits in Massachusetts in the days of Israel Putnam's childhood. The families were so scattered, and the ways so rough and lonely, that little children might not safely traverse them. Mr. Upham, speaking of the condition of things in this repect, in the early days of Salem Village, says: "Indeed, anything like regular schools was rendered impossible by the then existing circumstances. Clearings had made a very inconsiderable encroachment on the wilderness. There were here and there farm-houses with deep forests between. It was long before easily traversable roads could be made. A school-house placed permanently on any particular spot would be within the reach of but very few. Farmers most competent to the work, who had enjoyed the advantages of some degree of education, and could manage to set apart any time for the purpose, were, in some instances, prevailed upon to receive such children as were within reaching distance as pupils in their own houses, to be instructed by them at stated times, and for a limited period. Daniel Andrew rendered this service occasionally. At one period we find them (the people of Salem Village) practising the plan of a movable school and

schoolmaster. He would be stationed in the houses of particular persons, with whom the arrangement could be made,
a month at a time, in the different quarters of the village
from Will's Hill to Bass River. Of course there was a very
great lack of elementary education." All this refers to a
time antecedent to 1692. How great were the advances
which had been made between these times and the birth of
Israel Putnam in 1718, cannot very distinctly be told. It
is quite possible, if he had been born and reared in that
State which afterwards became his by adoption, he might
have been better off as to education than in his native
State. Before his birth, the laws in Connecticut required
that every town or ecclesiastical parish numbering seventy
families or upward should maintain a public school continuously the year round, for the instruction of all the children of the place ; and that a town or parish with less than
seventy families should maintain such a school for half the
year. Besides these schools there were by law maintained
four schools at the greater centres, to be called grammar
schools, in which Latin and Greek and some of the higher
English studies were to be taught. But beyond the mere
laws, there was at that time in Connecticut, as we read the
early records, a stronger public spirit in favor of universal
education than in Massachusetts. Laws are of little account, unless they are lifted up and borne out by the consenting and active spirit of the people.

We get some very distinct glimpses of the state of things
at Salem Village in the early times, as to this matter of
schools, from Rev. Charles B. Rice's history of the church.
He says : " The first reference to the subject which I have
noticed in the parish records is for the year 1701, when it was
voted : ' That Mr. Joseph Herrick and Mr. Joseph Putnam
and John Putnam, Jr., are chosen and empowered to agree
with some suitable person to be a schoolmaster among us,

in some convenient time ; and make returns therefor to the
people.' These men were the first school committee in
our town. It is doubtful, however, if with this committee
the 'convenient time' for hiring a teacher ever in fact
came. The passage of such a vote in one of these meetings, it must be said, does not of necessity signify accom-
plishment. Money was of right to be expected, and was
afterward received from the town of Salem, where their
taxes were paid. And the next mention of the matter is
eleven years later, at which time a committee was appointed
to receive whatever might be furnished by the selectmen
of Salem. And they were directed with this money to
make payment to 'ye Widow Daland of five pounds which
is her due for keeping school in ye village formerly;' and
also 'to invite her to come and keep school in ye village
again, and to engage her five pounds a year for two years,
or that money which is granted to us by the town for a
school.' Nearly a year later there is a receipt signed by
'Katharin Daland' for this five pounds, due 'for keeping
school at Salem Villig, at the school-house near Mr.
Green's.'"

This Mr. Green was then the minister of the parish, and
Mr. Rice has culled some extracts from a diary he kept,
which shows what was passing in his mind in these distant
years. Under date of March 22, 1708, he says :

"I went into ye Town Meeting [*i. e.* a meeting of the inhabitants of the village], and said to this effect : Neighbours, I am
about building a school-house for the good education of our children, and have spoken to several of our neighbours who are willing to help it forward, so that I hope we shall quickly finish it ;
and I speak of it here so that every one that can have any benefit may have opportunity for so good a service. Some replyed
that it was a new thing to them, and they desired to know where
it should stand, and what the design of it was. To them I

answered that Deacon Ingersoll would give land for it to stand on, at the upper end of the Training field, and that I designed to have a good schoolmaster to teach their children to read and write and cypher and every thing that is good. Many commended the design, and none objected to it.

"March 25. Began to get timber for school-house." *

Altogether, this is not a very promising outlook for popular education in the year 1708. Where the principles and habits for the general education of the children and youth have taken no deeper root than is here indicated, a boy born ten years later, a mile and a half away from the school-house which this good minister seems mainly to have built out of his own pocket, will not come under any very strong and constraining system of popular education.

But when we turn to the Massachusetts laws on this subject, the aspect is much better than in this actual view of the condition of the people at Salem Village. As early as 1642 it became a law in the Massachusetts Bay Colony that every township in the jurisdiction, after the Lord had increased it to fifty householders, shall appoint one within the town to teach such children as should resort thither, to read and write, etc. And it was made incumbent upon the town authorities to see that the children were not neglected in this matter of education. In 1683, it was provided that whenever a town has five hundred families, two grammar schools should be supported. In 1689, it became a law that all towns of fifty families should keep a school at least six months, and all towns of over two hundred families should have a grammar school. But we do not discover in the early laws of Massachusetts on this subject one provision that early in the last century was introduced in Connecticut, viz., that *parishes* should be reckoned in this respect as *towns*. This was the difficulty in the ancient Salem

* "History of Danvers Church," pp. 57 and 58.

Village. It did not become the *town* of Danvers until
1757. It was a part of Salem. Doubtless there was a good
school in Salem, but these people were too far away to be
able to avail themselves of it, and the law did not compel
them to maintain a separate school.

We will not, however, throw all the blame in the case of
Israel Putnam upon the Massachusetts laws, or upon the
spirit of the people. It is certain that the early education
of young Putnam was in some way sadly neglected, and
there was no one in after years, who more sincerely regretted this defect than himself. It is probable that Rev. L.
Grosvenor, one of General Putnam's descendants (who delivered the memorial address at Putnam, Connecticut, in
1855, at a meeting of the Putnam family), has given us the
essential truth on this point. He said:

"Putnam was a 'self-made man,' so far as that appellation
may be applied to any human being. He was not a product of
the schools. No schoolmaster or military chieftain could boast
of having made *him*. Like all such men he possessed individ-
uality and originality, for which he owed no debts, save to
nature. It is proof of his uncommon talents, that he acquired a
reputation so solid with the scantiest literary attainments ; it is
proof of his uncommon worth of character, that with all his ignorance of *belles lettres*, and all his lack of those graces which the
dancing-master contracts to furnish at so much per head, he
was able to maintain such influence and popularity among
officers accustomed to figure in the polite circles of society, and
possessing the highest scientific attainments. But a pearl is
precious, though encased in the roughest shell, and a diamond
is a diamond, without any polishing from the lapidary.

"It is altogether probable that he little valued learning in his
boyhood. A youth of his uncommon physical vigor is apt to
have too great a flow of animal spirits to submit cheerfully to
confinement to books, or to have any very profound respect for
the pedagogue. He likes the schoolmaster better when he is

abroad than when he is mousing round on tiptoe among the school benches. There is every reason to believe that the pecuniary circumstances of his family were sufficient to have given him a good education had he been disposed to study. [There is more of doubt in this last sentence than is needed. His father, Joseph Putnam, as we have seen was a man of large estate.] But he loved the tangled and howling forest, better than the tame and close-trimmed groves of the academy. His handwriting proves clearly that he left school forever just after manufacturing, with great labor, a few copies of the longest sized 'pot-hooks,' and long before he had attained the dignity of 'small-hand.' It is, like himself, remarkable for broad plainness rather than clerkly elegance. His spelling, too, is evidently all done upon the *phonographic* principle, entirely unhampered by the arbitrary rules of the dictionaries. He was consequently during all his military life conscious and ashamed of his ignorance of letters. He carried on all his military correspondence with the aid of amanuenses, that his ignorance might be exposed to the world as little as possible. He took care to impress on all his children the necessity of education, and gave them the best the country afforded."

It is impossible at this late day to gather out of the remote and misty past many incidents of Putnam's early childhood. We can infer from his very nature, that among the boys of the neighborhood he was the most active and daring, "ready," as was said of him afterward, "to lead where any would follow." General David Humphreys of New Haven, who was one of General Putnam's Aids in the war of the Revolution, and who wrote the earliest biography of him, has preserved one small anecdote which is highly natural and probable. He went to Boston, when a boy (probably with some of his kindred), and while there a bigger Boston boy began chaffing him on his rustic appearance, and seemed willing to pick a quarrel. Israel stood it for a while, but at length turned to and gave his insulter a sound flogging, to the great delight of the lookers-on.

Early marriages and the formation of new households were at that time in order. Land was abundant, and with resolute hearts and hands accustomed to toil, the young men of that day were encouraged to strike out for themselves and help to subdue and populate the country. We have seen that Israel's father was only twenty and his mother sixteen when they were married. And so, in turn, when Israel had reached the age of twenty he was united in marriage to Hannah Pope, daughter of Joseph Pope of Salem Village, she being but seventeen. This marriage took place in 1738.* He was the son of Joseph Putnam, and she was the daughter of Joseph Pope, so that it was necessary to go beyond the initials in indicating those names. In the very year of this marriage, Israel Putnam and his young wife were evidently getting ready to emigrate.† For in that year (1738) he sold to his brother

* There is some doubt about the date of Putnam's marriage. Upham puts it in 1739, and it is quite generally so stated. But the Putnam family have some records and traditions that point to 1738. It is not a matter of any special consequence in which year he was married.

† To show how the Putnams have abounded in this their ancestral home, a few striking facts may be given. Mr. Upham says: "Though there were descendants of this family in every company of emigrants that went from Salem Village, in all directions, in every generation, ... there is about as large a proportionate representation of the name within the precincts of Salem Village to-day as there ever was. Fifty Putnams are at present (1867) voters in Danvers, on a list of eight hundred names."

The following facts we compile from Rev. Mr. Rice's history of the church. In that volume, there came into view, in the years the history covers, 132 different persons, male and female, of the name Putnam. These, of course, are not all the residents of this place, bearing this name, but are such as the course of his narrative brought to the light. Of the 27 persons who united to form the regular church in 1689, 11 were Putnams, 7 men and 4 women. Of the 74 men who have been recording clerks in that parish, 24 were Putnams. Of the 23 men who have been deacons, 15 have been Putnams. Of the 26 treasurers, 12 have been Putnams. Of the 18 superintendents of the Sabbath school, 7 have been Putnams. Of the 92 pews in the meeting-house of 1786, 25 were bought by Putnams; and of the 92 pews sold in

David the interest he had in the landed estate of his father. We have seen the veritable quitclaim deed which passed from Israel to David.   It is a brown and rusty document, but exceedingly well-preserved.   For the sum of *seven hundred pounds and nineteen shillings*, he releases to David in part the title and interest in the real estate which came to him from his father.   We do not think that Mr. Grosvenor is quite borne out, in the passage quoted above, as to Putnam's handwriting.   The signature to that deed is apparently from a hand more accustomed to handle the axe than the pen; nevertheless it is a good, strong, fair signature, perfectly distinct, and as well written as though it had been executed by an average farmer of the present day.   Probably he was a little more at home in signing his own name, than in general writing.   But certainly that signature would not be called mean and coarse in any generation of New England common life.

In those years there was quite a wave of emigration from the towns of the Massachusetts Bay to Eastern Connecticut.   Traces of this movement can easily be found in all the records of that period.   Quite a large number of families went from Salem.   Lynn was also sending out little colonies.   The valley of the Connecticut River had been early occupied by movements from the Massachusetts Bay.   In 1635 and '36, the towns of Windsor, Hartford and Wethersfield were formed by colonies moving from Dorchester, Cambridge and Watertown.   The region along the shore of Long Island Sound was also taken possession of at an early date.   New Haven, Milford, Guilford and other shore towns are only a very few years younger than Salem and Boston and Charlestown.

the meeting-house of 1806, 21 were bought by Putnams.   Of the 11 persons who met to organize the first Sabbath school in 1818, and to become the first teachers, 6 were Putnams.

But in Eastern Connecticut, along the shores of the Quinebaug and its tributary streams, there was a region of fine farming land which had not so soon come into the market. If one rides at this day here and there through the ancient township of Pomfret when the summer glory is on those Connecticut hills, he will be impressed with the richness and beauty of those fields — mowing-lands and corn-lands — as they spread out in wide, sloping ranges before his eye. Probably no stranger ever rode from the present town of Putnam up to the old Pomfret Centre and through it without being surprised at finding among those hills farms so full of richness and so attractive to the eye.

This country was not exactly new in 1739. The lands which Putnam bought in that region in that year were not wild lands strictly speaking, as will be seen by the price which he paid for them. Woodstock, just to the north (anciently belonging to Massachusetts), had had a settled ministry since 1686. Pomfret had enjoyed preaching, with rude accommodations, since 1713, but its first meeting-house was erected in 1734. The lands in that general locality had acquired quite a marketable value before Putnam went there. But we will not in the present chapter speak particularly of them.

Before closing, however, we desire to make a somewhat fuller and more exact reference to the Pope family, out of which young Israel Putnam had selected his wife. The home of the Popes was some four miles away from his, to the south-west, toward Lynn, and not very far off from the border line. The house belonging to the Popes was originally occupied by Mr. Edward Norris, minister at Old Salem in 1640. Of this house Mr. Upham says: "Originally given as an ordination present to a minister of the old town, it has after the lapse of two hundred and twenty-six years come round into the hands of another. The house in which the Popes lived one hundred and twenty-nine years, and the families that succeeded them for about half a century more,— a venerable and picturesque specimen of the rural architecture in its best form of the earliest times, — has within the last ten years given place to a new one on the same spot. In that old house, besides unnumbered and unknown instances of the same sort, Israel Putnam conducted his courtship "

3

CHAPTER II.

REMOVES TO POMFRET, CT.

Settlement of Woodstock, Ct., by Colonists from Roxbury. — Land Purchases and Speculations. — Settlement of Pomfret. — Captain Blackwell. — Mortlake Manor. — Original Plan given up. — Gov. Belcher and his Purchase. — Israel Putnam and John Pope buy of Gov. Belcher. — Character of Pomfret Population. — The Wolf Story as told by Miss Larned. — Mortlake Parish. — Vigorous Farming.

IN the closing part of the last chapter we referred to Putnam's plan for emigration, about the time of his marriage to Hannah Pope. It was some fifty years before this, as early indeed as 1684, that there began to be a movement in the older portions of the Massachusetts Bay Colony to purchase and take possession of the wild lands of Eastern Connecticut. Almost at the same time the valley and shore towns of Connecticut were reaching eastward, as the Massachusetts towns were westward, to take up and occupy this wilderness tract. The first thoroughly organized plan started in Roxbury, Massachusetts, in 1683. The purpose of this volume will not permit us to go minutely into these matters, but if any one wishes to study all the details of these emigrations and their after results, he may find them most carefully and fully stated in Miss Ellen Larned's new "History of Windham County, Connecticut," — a volume that may be referred to as a model in the department of local histories. It took two or three years after the beginning of this organized movement, before the pioneers were ready to move in a body. But individuals had been back and forth from time to time;

the tract to be settled had been fixed upon, and in some
measure laid out; and in the year 1686, forty men, mostly
from the town of Roxbury, with their wives and children,
moved through the wilderness and appeared on the hills of
what is now the town of Woodstock, next north of Pomfret. When these pilgrims had passed the town of Med-
way, the rest of the way was a wilderness. About the
same time the present town of Windham, the county-seat
of Windham County, was settled by companies coming
from the older towns of Connecticut. Settlements were
made soon afterwards in districts now known as the towns
of Thompson, Killingly and Canterbury.

Not much progress was made in the settlement of Pomfret until the beginning of the last century, though as early
as 1684 Major Fitch, also of Roxbury, had purchased this
territory as wild land. After the Woodstock settlers had
planted themselves firmly in their new habitation, they
began to tell their old Massachusetts friends and neighbors
"of a fair land stretching southward into Connecticut," and
in 1686 Major Fitch sold to six men, all of Roxbury, 15,-
000 acres of wilderness land for the sum of £30. These
six purchasers immediately associated with themselves six
more, so that twelve men, all of Roxbury, then owned this
wild country. But this was not all the land included in the
purchase which Major Fitch had made two years before.
He still owned a large territory adjoining this, but farther
to the south.

In 1685, there came to Boston from England a Captain
John Blackwell. He was a noted Puritan and a man of
distinction. He was a son-in-law of General Lambert, who
was closely connected with Cromwell's army, and also a
member of Parliament during Cromwell's public administration. England was not a very comfortable place under
the restored Stuarts for a man with the associations of

Captain Blackwell. He had managed to keep out of the
way during the reign of Charles II.; but now with the coming in of James II. he did not object to have an ocean between him and the English throne. He came over commissioned by a company of English and Irish dissenters to
purchase a tract of country in America on which they
might settle in a body. He reached Boston just when these
land purchases and speculations in Eastern Connecticut
were greatly occupying the thoughts of men in the Massachusetts towns. That generation was not probably so very
different from some that have lived since, in respect to the
excitements that may be raised by land speculations. And
so Major Fitch traded with Captain Blackwell and sold
him, just south of the tract which the Roxbury men had
bought, 5,750 acres, which constituted the south-east corner
of his (Fitch's) original purchase. Captain Blackwell was
very desirous that this should be a territory by itself, separate and distinct, on which his colony might plant itself
without dispossessing or interfering with any one else. And
so he wished from the first to fix upon it a peculiar name
which would be a little romantic in that wilderness country,
and he called it Mortlake Manor, from the village Mortlake
in Surrey, England, where his father-in-law General Lambert lived, and where the men of Cromwell's party used much
to resort. Just after this purchase was completed, Sir Edmund Andros came over to New England, appointed by
that weak and gloomy tyrant James II. Andros was a man
exactly fit to do a tyrant's work in New England. His
arrival suddenly cut short all Captain Blackwell's plans.
But the reign of James was short, and when he was deposed
and Andros recalled, there was no longer any necessity for
Blackwell and his company to move into the western wilderness.

So matters lingered on. Years passed away. In 1707

Captain Blackwell died, and this great landed estate passed
to his son.   But this son did not wish to occupy it, and he
sold it to Jonathan Belcher of Cambridge.   This Jonathan
Belcher was a very conspicuous figure in New England,
from the beginning of the last century on for· fifty years.
Though of a humble family, he graduated at Harvard College in 1699, and soon rose into favor and success.   He was
fortunate in early winning, in some way, the smiles of the
royal family of England, the Princess Sophia and her son
George II.; and so in his lifetime he was Colonial Governor of Massachusetts, New Hampshire and New Jersey,
and in connection with his administration in the latter
State he became the founder of the College of New Jersey.
Wealth and honors rolled in upon him.   He appears to
have had no objection to the purchase of this wild country,
and probably it was a relief to the son of Captain Blackwell to have him take it off his hands.

Mr. Belcher through his agents undertook to break up
and subdue portions of this territory.   He also divided it
up and called a part of it Kingswood and a part Wiltshire.
In the course of this process of breaking and subduing,
and making small sales, he drew some settlers on to the
territory from whom afterwards he desired to be free.
There was one man by the name of Jabez Utter whom he
especially wished to have gone.   He bought him out fairly
and honestly, but just about that time Utter was arrested
for stealing.   The story of Mr. Belcher's troubles in clear-
ing this fellow out, and especially his wife (for she had
more power of cohesive attraction than her husband), is
amusing, but too long to be here told.

Not, however, to dwell upon these details at any greater
length, by 1714 Mr. Belcher had his matters so in hand
that he was able to sell portions of this territory to suit
purchasers.   But as the years went on, the improvements

that had been made in the lands themselves, and the population that was gathering in that general region, caused this tract to rise in value far beyond what it was worth when Mr. Belcher came into possession of it.

In 1739, Israel Putnam and John Pope (Putnam's wife's brother) bought of Gov. Belcher (he was made Governor of Massachusetts and New Hampshire in 1730) a portion of this old Mortlake district, in the part of it known as Wiltshire, five hundred and fourteen and a half acres, for which they were to pay £2,572 10s., about £5 an acre. But it must be borne in mind that these were not English pounds sterling. This debt was payable in bills of credit on the province of Massachusetts, and this was a sadly depreciated currency. The year following Putnam bought out his brother-in-law, and in one year more, 1741, he had paid for the whole tract, and the mortgage was raised. This is so like what we have seen of the Putnams in their old home in Salem Village! There was a family thrift . among them, from generation to generation, which no impediments seemed to hinder. We have seen that he had from his brother David £700 19s., and how much more may have come from the personal estate of his father we do not know. It is not likely that he had any great amount of property with his wife, for the Popes in Salem Village, though of good standing and fair property, were not wealthy as the Putnams were. At any rate, in 1741, Israel Putnam owned the whole tract of five hundred and fourteen acres without encumbrance.*

---

* Since writing the above we have received from a member of the Putnam family in Danvers, a statement based upon the careful examination of the old records, showing that between the years 1738–1743 seven different parcels of land were sold by Israel Putnam in Salem Village, for which he received the round sum of £1,920. It is not unlikely that his father had made him presents while he was yet in his minority, in accordance with that wise custom already spoken of, and as a reward for his strong and faithful industry.

This land lay in what was long known as a part of Pomfret, but is now the town of Brooklyn, Connecticut. The traveller who passes down the Norwich and Worcester Railroad, when he reaches Danielsonville, in South Killingly, is about three miles east from this purchase. We have already spoken of the beauty of the lands near the centre of ancient Pomfret. This Mortlake tract is perhaps not quite so fair and fertile, but is nevertheless of much the same general character. The old name Mortlake still lingers in that region, and is variously attached. The stranger stopping at the hotel in Brooklyn, Connecticut, finds himself at the Mortlake House.

Though, as we have said, this land which Putnam owned was not exactly wild land, it was not, after all, very far removed from that condition. The main work of subduing it and bringing it under easy culture was yet to be done. Forests were to be removed; and walls and fences were to be built. Much hard work was to be done, and hard work was what Putnam was used to, and in it he took delight. With his prodigious vigor, his physical strength and energy, obstacles that would have intimidated many quickly vanished before him. At this time Pomfret had made considerable progress. But he was in the outskirts of the town, some miles distant from the centre. It was indeed a matter of some uncertainty, in those early years, to what town this old Mortlake Manor of Captain Blackwell should belong. In his original purchase he had been particular to have it a region separate and distinct, for the sole occupation of his colony. This idea to some extent lingered about it long afterwards. In 1747 the people then living upon it petitioned the Legislature to be made into a separate town. But the request was not granted.

But before Putnam removed to Connecticut (as early as 1734), an ecclesiastical parish had been formed, covering not only the whole of the original Mortlake Manor, but reaching south and embracing essentially the same territory that is now included in the town of Brooklyn. This at the first was called Mortlake Parish. For more than twenty years it bore this name. In 1754 this name was dropped, and it became the Brooklyn Parish, and in 1786, when Brooklyn was incorporated as a separate township, the town took its name from the parish. In matters ecclesiastical, therefore, Putnam had a distinct centre ; but in matters pertaining to the town, he was at first almost the same as nowhere.

Rev. Mr. Grosvenor, to whose commemorative address we have already referred, thus describes the old Putnam farm in Pomfret, and the owner's early labors upon it :

"This farm is situated on the summit of the high hill between the villages of Pomfret and Brooklyn ; and the present line of separation between these townships passes through this tract. It is nearly all fertile soil, admirably adapted to cultivation, being level or gently sloping. The first house he built is not now standing, but the spot where it stood is pointed out. There still lie many of the stones of the old foundation ; there is the first well he dug, but covered now with the modern invention of a platform and a chain pump. There is an old pear tree, almost leafless and lifeless from old age, which it is said he planted. It stands about a hundred yards back of the house now occupied by Mr. Benjamin Brown. About a quarter of a mile south-east of this house is another* which he built, and in it is the long, narrow bed-room, ancient and comfortable in its appointments, in which he died. The main road from Pomfret to Brooklyn passes through the farm, and is planted on both sides for a long distance with very aged apple trees, which the old men of the neighborhood affirm were set out by the General. From the time of his arrival in Pomfret, even down to his death, he was

* From information received from Brooklyn we judge that Mr. Grosvenor may have been mistaken in some of his statements concerning this second house.

as fond of the peaceful pursuits of agriculture and horticulture, as of the excitement of hairbreadth escapes in the deadly breach, and by flood and field. He gave great, and at that time very unusual, attention to the cultivation of fruit trees. His neighbors give him the credit of introducing all the best varieties into Pomfret and Brooklyn, and especially the famous winter apple, the Roxbury Russet, now so abundant here, he is said to have brought with him from Salem, when he first settled in Pomfret."

For a new town planted at first in the wilderness, there was in Pomfret a very unusual degree of culture within a comparatively few years from the settlement. By the year 1731 there were over one hundred landed proprietors resident in the town, with an exceedingly fine range of family names. We have given some glimpses, showing the actual state of things in Salem Village in respect to the general education of the children in the early part of the last century. In contrast with what was there shown, mark the spirit of Pomfret. She had her public school from a very early date. But in consequence of the scattered condition of the families, it was provided by the town that any number of families might combine, according to the convenience of neighborhoods, and the selectmen had discretionary power to provide for them a separate school. In 1723 there were three, and in 1733 four, public schools sustained at the general expense. In the very year (1739) in which Putnam arrived in those parts, there had actually been formed among these people of Pomfret, a society with no less a name and aim than the following: "The United Society or Company for Propagating Christian and Useful Knowledge." And lest any should suppose that these people were merely amusing themselves with large words, let it be said that this association was in its first organization composed of thirty-five men, of whom no one paid in to the general fund less than £10, while quite a number

paid £15, £20, and even £30, and £40. The whole sum
subscribed by the thirty-five first members was £539.
Their plan included a library, which was soon put in operation, and furnished reading for these scattered families.
After a time all the leading men of the town became members and proprietors, and this institution had a vast influence in cultivating a taste for learning. As a remarkable
illustration of this spirit and tendency we give the following
sure and absolute fact, which cannot probably be matched
by any town of like age and circumstances in all the years
of New England history. There were at one time in Yale
College, from this remote and lonely township yet in its
comparative infancy, eleven young men. Ten of them
graduated in one class, that of 1759, and one of them in
that of 1760. Lest any should think there must be some
mistake here, we give their names. The first was a minister's son, bearing his father's peculiar name, Ebenezer
Devotion. The rest were Rev. Enoch Huntington, Mr.
John Chandler, Rev. Ebenezer Grosvenor, Rev. Ephraim
Hide, Mr. Ebenezer Craft, Rev. Abishai Sabin, Rev. Joshua
Paine, Rev. Joseph Dana, D. D., Rev. Ezra Weld and Rev.
Joseph Sumner, D. D., — eight ministers and three of other
professions,— and their names may all be seen on the Yale
triennial catalogue for 1759 and 1760.

If Israel Putnam's own early education had been neglected, he had at least now joined himself to a community
where there was all needed stimulus, and where there were
abundant advantages for the education of his children.
And they, as we have already had testimony, were all carefully educated.

We cannot very well pass over the early years of Putnam's residence in Pomfret without referring to the wolf
story. It is an old and familiar tale, but in narrating the
events of his life it would seem almost impossible to leave

this transaction out. And as we are quite sure that we cannot tell the story in so good a way as it stands narrated in Miss Larned's recent "History of Windham County," * we shall allow her to relate its incidents. She tells it with such an explanation of the outward circumstances, and such a minute detail of the internal facts, that it will be in some sense a new story to our readers. She says:

"At the time of the formation of the United Library Association, that famous historical personage known as 'Putnam's Wolf' was making much disturbance. No mythical phantom like the she-wolf of Roman tradition, but a veritable flesh and blood denizen of Windham County — the story of her exploits, pursuits and capture, is known to the whole civilized world, and her den in Pomfret included among the notable places in America. Part of her fame is doubtless due to the subsequent celebrity of her conqueror. Had Putnam remained obscure, his wolf might have been long ago forgotten, but she undoubtedly displayed great prowess and tenacity, and has fairly won a place in historic annals.

"Wolves had abounded in every Windham County town at their first settlement, but had gradually disappeared with advancing civilization. Indians Tom and Jeremy had routed them in Plainfield and Killingly; Woodstock's last reported wolf was shot by Pembascus in 1732; Ashford's succumbed in 1735, leaving Pomfret's in sole possession of the field. A craggy, precipitous hill range, bristling with jagged rocks and tangled forests, south of the Mashamoquet and between the Newichewanna and Blackwell's Brook, was her favorite place of residence, where she enjoyed the privilege of entire seclusion and easy access to the richest farms of Pomfret and Mortlake. The grave and reverend seigniors who met with Mr. Williams to devise means for propagating Christian and useful knowledge, were but half a mile from the lurking place of this surviving representative of barbarism, and doubtless discussed the exploits of the wolf as well as the projected library. For years this creature ranged and rav-

* P. 360.

aged the country. There was not a farm or door-yard safe from
her incursions. Innumerable sheep, lambs, kids and fowls had
fallen into her clutches. Little children were scared by her out
of sleep and senses; boys and girls feared to go to school or
drive the cows home, and lonely women trembled for absent hus-
bands and children. In summer she was wont to repair to wilder
regions northward, returning in autumn with a young family to
her favorite haunt in Pomfret. These cubs were soon shot by
watchful hunters, but the more wary mother resisted every effort.
She evaded traps, outwitted dogs, and made herself, in the words
of her biographer, ' an intolerable nuisance.'

"The great increase of stock following the sale and occupation of Belcher's tract opened a new source of supply to this
enterprising and keen-sighted animal. Israel Putnam's farm was
only separated by a deep, narrow valley from her favorite hillside. This young farmer had devoted himself to the cultivation
of his land with much skill and energy, and within two or three
years had erected a house and out-buildings, broken up land for
corn and grain, set out fruit trees and collected many valuable
cattle and sheep. This fine flock soon caught the fancy of his
appreciative neighbor, and one morning some ' seventy sheep and
goats were reported killed, besides many lambs and kids torn
and wounded.' Putnam was greatly exasperated by this loss and
butchery. He was not one to submit tamely to such inflictions.
From his boyhood he had been distinguished for courage and
reckless daring. He was a bold rider, a practised and successful hunter. He had a bloodhound of superior strength and
sagacity. His stock was very dear to him, and he at once
resolved to rid Pomfret of this nuisance. For books at this time
Putnam cared little. The United Library Association had no
attraction for him, but he was very eager to enter into combi-
nation with others for the destruction of this ' pernicious animal.'
With five of his neighbors he agreed to hunt the wolf continuously
by turns till they had caught and killed her.

"How long they watched and waited is not known. The final
hunt is believed to have occurred in the winter of 1742-3. A
light snow-fall the night preceding enabled the watchful hunters

to trace the wolf far westward over wood and valley, and thence back to her lair in Pomfret.

"The report of their success in tracking the enemy had preceded them, and men and boys with dogs and guns hurried out to meet the returning hunters, and join in the pursuit and capture. The track led onward into the heart of that savage fastness, never before penetrated by white men. John Sharpe, a lad of seventeen, grandson of the first William Sharpe of Mashamoquet, ran boy-like in advance of the others, following the trail up the icy crag as it wound on between overhanging rocks, gnarled stumps, and fallen tree trunks, to a small opening among the granite boulders on the hillside—the mouth apparently of a narrow cave or passage, tunnelling far down into the depths of the earth. A joyful shout from the lad announced the discovery of the wolf's hiding-place. The news soon spread throughout the neighborhood, bringing new actors and spectators. Great was the interest and excitement. The wolf was *trapped*, but how could she be *taken?* The day was spent in fruitless efforts to force her from her position. Hounds were sent in, but came back cowed and wounded. Straw and brimstone were burned in the cavern's mouth without effect. Secure in her rock-bound fortress, the enemy disdained to parley or surrender. Night brought with it new fears and anxieties. The cave might have some outlet by which the wolf might steal away in the darkness. After all their efforts and anticipated triumph, it was possible that their foe might even now escape them.

"It does not appear that Putnam had joined in the hunt, or seige, or that his absence was noted or regretted. The future world-renowned General was then a person of very little consequence. He was a young man and a stranger. He was not connected with any of Pomfret's old families. He lived in Mortlake, with whose inhabitants Pomfret had as little concern as possible. He was not a member of the church, School Committee, or Library Association. He was only a rough young farmer, making his own way in the world, with a good eye for stock and *a very superior bloodhound*, which in this moment of despondency was remembered, and summoned to the rescue.

"But the obscure young farmer of 1743 had every distinguishing characteristic of the brave 'Old Put of '76.' A crisis brought him at once 'to the front.' Emergency and peril proved him a leader. With dog and gun he instantly obeyed the summons. His coming changed the aspect of affairs. Doubt and fear vanished before his eagerness and impetuosity. Not a moment was to be lost. The wolf must be routed at once, whatever the hazard. If she would not come to them, they must go to her. The passage must be stormed and its hidden citadel carried. If dog and negro 'declined the hazardous service,' Putnam himself was ready for the onset. Remonstrance and representation of danger were unheeded. Divesting himself of coat and waistcoat, with a rope fastened around his body and a blazing torch in his hand, he slowly crawled down the black, icy, narrow passage,—'a mansion of horror,' unvisited before but by 'monsters of the desert,'—and at its farthest extremity descried the glaring eyeballs of his terrified adversary. Drawn back by those without, he descended a second time with torch and weapon, and with one dexterous shot brought down the wolf as she was preparing to take the offensive, 'and the people above, with no small exultation, dragged them both out together.' Pomfret's last wolf was destroyed, and her most famous hero was brought to her knowledge."

We have already spoken of the anomalous condition of things in the Mortlake parish, growing out of that peculiar charter originally given to Captain John Blackwell. All the rights and peculiarities of that charter descended with the property to his son in 1707, and were again transferred with the land to Governor Belcher. Though Mr. Belcher broke the property up, and by so doing seemed to scatter the ancient conditions belonging to it, yet this old network, though broken, still lingered. People who planted themselves on these lands thought they had some rights and privileges peculiar to themselves, though they did not very well know what they were; and the people round about thought the Mortlake folks were somehow a community by themselves. They tried, as we have stated, to get organized in 1747 into a town, but failed. But they had their parish and their church. The church was organized in 1734, five years before Putnam's arrival, and in 1735 Rev. Ephraim Avery was settled in the ministry, and continued till his death in 1754. Then Rev. Josiah Whitney, D. D., was settled for one of those very long ministries of which New England has a goodly number to show. His pastorate lasted from 1756 to 1824, a period of *sixty-eight* years, till his death. But ten years before his death he had a colleague, Rev. Luther Wilson, and through his agency Unitarianism was introduced into Brooklyn (it then was a town), and a small Unitarian parish sprung up, which is the only one that the State of Connecticut has ever been able steadily to maintain.

But we go back to Mortlake at the middle of the last century. Having failed in their efforts to become a town, in 1752, by act of the Legislature of Connecticut, these people and their territory were taken out of their uncertain state and condition, and made distinctly a part of the town of Pomfret. But the *parish* of Mortlake remained as before, and went on its own way. From 1752, then on till 1786, Putnam was a regular citizen of Pomfret. For the thirteen years before he had been only a *quasi* citizen.

In building the first meeting-houses in the old towns and parishes of Connecticut (and the same was true in other parts of New England), the structures were often exceedingly rude; sometimes unfurnished with seats of any kind, or if they had them, only of the roughest description. The process of building pews would generally be started by some enterprising young men, while the older and more conservative people looked on with not a little concern, and perhaps talked about the "fast generation" that was coming upon the stage. In the old Mortlake, meeting-house things were in this general condition when, soon after the wolf adventure, Israel Putnam, John Hubbard and Daniel Tyler, on condition that they would reset the squares of glass that were broken out of the meeting-house windows, should have the privilege of building pews for their own private use in the hinder part of the house, provided that "they spile not above two seats on a side." But awhile after, the glass having got broken out again, and no ambitious young men appearing who were willing to buy the privilege of building themselves pews by resetting the glass, it was voted by this parish "to board up the meeting-house windows," *i. e.* those which were broken. But Mortlake Centre even in those years had a good school and a school-house rather stylish for those times, and after its distinct assignment to the town of Pomfret in 1752, it was voted by the town that schools be kept at five places for the general accommodation of all the inhabitants.

In 1756, when the Rev. Josiah Whitney, a graduate of Yale College, was settled in the ministry in what was now Brooklyn Parish (the name Mortlake having been dropped with the action of the Legislature in 1752), the parish voted him £120 for settlement and £65 yearly salary.

Meanwhile the young farmer was getting his lands more and more under cultivation, and by hard work was laying the foundations of an ample fortune for those days of ancient simplicity. Children were growing up around him. His oldest child, named for himself, was born in 1740. This is the Captain Israel Putnam whom we shall meet thirty-five years later around Bunker Hill. His next son was David, born in 1742, and named from that brother whom he had left in the old homestead at Salem Village. But this David died in early life, as did also another son of the same name born years afterwards. His third child was

Hannah, bearing her mother's name. Then come Elizabeth, Mehitable, Molly, Eunice, till we reach Daniel, born
in 1759, who as a boy of fifteen years followed his father
to Cambridge in 1775, and was with him through all those
stirring scenes. After Daniel was born the second David,
of whom we have spoken as also dying in childhood, and
his last child, born in 1764, was named after one of his
compatriots in the French and Indian War, Peter Schuyler.
It was through the skilful agency of this Peter Schuyler, a
fellow-prisoner, that Putnam was delivered from captivity.
He was taken prisoner by the French and Indians, and had
been in imminent peril of his life. The services of Schuyler were gratefully remembered, and he attached his name
to his youngest boy. But as the eye ranges down the list
of those ten children, with their Scripture names given
after the old New England custom of his fathers, the last
one makes a sudden and unexpected contrast ; though even
here *Peter* redeems it and keeps it within the Scripture
enclosures.

We have made frequent references to the United Library Association. It may gratify the reader to know that
before Putnam ever went to the wars he became a member
of this society. Rev. Daniel Hunt, formerly pastor of the
church in Pomfret, in connection with its 150th anniversary, gives a little sketch of the history of the town and
says : " To this Association General Israel Putnam was admitted August 27th, 1753, and paid sixteen pounds 'old
tenor.'" His children were now coming forward into life,
and he meant they should have the opportunity of acquiring knowledge, and was all the more earnest because he
knew and felt his own deficiencies.

4

CHAPTER III.

GOES TO THE FRENCH WAR.

Bancroft's Idea of the French and Indian War.—Call for Men in 1755.—Putnam raises a Company and becomes its Captain.—Names of his Children. — Rendezvous at Albany.— Fort Edward.— First Battle.— One of the Rangers.—British Pride and Pomp.—Taken Prisoner.—Constant Exposures.—Is chosen Major.—Invasion of Canada.— West Indies.—Close of French War.—Returns to Pomfret in 1764, a Colonel.

BANCROFT in his "History of the United States" calls the French War the First Epoch of the American Revolution. It was a war for colonial independence against French aggression and interference. The American Colonies bore the great burdens of that war, fighting gallantly under the British standards. In a variety of ways the definition of Mr. Bancroft above given will hold good. Even if we leave the broader connections which he probably had in mind, and look at this French War simply as a grand field for the military training of men,— officers and soldiers, — nothing could have been more opportune in preparation for the scenes that were to be enacted a few years later. The young men of the country who displayed military genius in that war were all the while rising from the ranks of the common soldier to positions of military command. We had then no military school like our present West Point Academy for the training of officers, but this war of 1755, lasting several years, brought forward a large number of men who, instructed in the school of experience, knew how to guide an army and set its ranks in battle array. The great commanders in the revolutionary war were most

50

of them officers of lower or higher grades in the French
War.

Troubles between the French and English for the possession of this continent were not new in 1755. The story
reaches far back, but we cannot spend time to tell it. The
English General Braddock had suffered a most disastrous
defeat in this summer of 1755, and the remnant that remained of his boastful army was saved largely through the
military genius of that young provincial officer, George
Washington.

The special point for which the New England forces
were to rally was for the relief of Crown Point and the half
wilderness regions about Lake George, where the French
had gained a strong foothold. In the early part of 1755
the plan was adopted that the four New England Colonies
should raise a force of three thousand two hundred men, in
the following proportions: Massachusetts was to send twelve
hundred; Connecticut one thousand; New Hampshire six
hundred; and Rhode Island four hundred. It was noticed
that Massachusetts was drawn upon not so heavily in proportion to her population as the other colonies.* This
produced a slight current of discontent at the first in Connecticut. Massachusetts at that time included Maine, and
her population was far larger than that of Connecticut. But
Connecticut generously considered that Massachusetts was
much more exposed on her wide north-eastern borders, and
upon second thought, cordially raised the one thousand
men, and added to the number five hundred more for such
exigencies as might soon arise.

---

* Bancroft, in his history, gives the population of the New England States
in 1754 approximately as follows: Massachusetts, 207,000; Connecticut,
133,000; New Hampshire, 50,000; Rhode Island, 35,000. It will be seen
therefore, in this apportionment of men, Massachusetts furnished the least
number in proportion to her population, and New Hampshire and Rhode
Island the largest.

This call for a thousand men summoned Putnam from
the quiet labors of the farm into scenes of war. From
1739 to 1755 he had been most industriously occupied in
bringing his large landed estate under vigorous culture, and
he had wrought upon it a wonderful change. He had now
become a substantial and honored citizen of the quiet town
of Pomfret. He had grown rapidly in wealth, not by feed-
ing at any public treasury, but by hard, skilful, intelligent
industry upon the soil. Mr. Grosvenor says of him at
this period of his life: "Pursuing every branch of his
calling with all his native ardor and perseverance, his flocks
and herds increased around him, and his fields yielded
abundance, so that by the time of the opening of the
French War in 1755 he had acquired a handsome property,
and when he went out at the call of his country, he was
enabled to leave his wife and children in a comfortable
house and sufficiently provided for in case of his death." At
that time six of his ten children were born, but two of them
had died young, so that he left four at home with their
mother, the oldest of whom was Israel, a stout youth of
fifteen, and capable in some good measure of taking his
father's place in the management of the flocks and herds,
and in the cultivation of the lands.

The first glimpse we get of Putnam on this broader field
of action, is given us in Bancroft's "History of the United
States." He is describing the little army as it moves from
the southern end of Lake George to relieve Fort Edward
on the Hudson. He says: "Among them was Israel Putnam, then a private soldier." Now, it certainly serves to
show that Putnam's after life must have made a deep
impression upon the mind of the historian, that he should
pause at this stage of his narrative, and from those thousand *private soldiers* single out this one alone and call him
by his name. But we suspect that Mr. Bancroft has made

a mistake in speaking of him as a "private soldier." We have always understood that the first military service that Putnam ever performed was to raise a company of men in his own immediate neighborhood, of which he became captain. Mr. Grosvenor, a descendant, ought certainly to know about this, and he says: "He was appointed to a captaincy by the Legislature of Connecticut, before he had seen a single day's military service." And General David Humphreys ought also to know, who says: "His reputation must have been favorably known to the government, since among the first troops that were levied by Connecticut in 1755, he was appointed to the command of a company in Lyman's regiment of Provincials. . . . . As he was extremely popular he found no difficulty in enlisting his complement of recruits from the most hardy, enterprising and respectable young men of his neighborhood."

To understand the first warlike movements in which Putnam was engaged some few words of explanation are needed. Crown Point lies near the eastern boundary of New York, close upon the borders of Vermont, and about eighty miles north of Albany. It is on the southern waters of Lake Champlain, where the lake becomes narrow and is rapidly fading to a point. Lake George is between Crown Point and Albany, a little west of a straight line drawn between these two extremes. General William Johnson of New York, afterwards Sir William, was the commander-in-chief of the American forces in this expedition, and General Phinehas Lyman of Connecticut was the second in command, with the rank of Major General. The troops raised in New England joined those from other colonies, (especially New York) at Albany. That was the place of rendezvous during the summer of 1755. There was gathered here a force of 6,000 Americans, besides quite a large body of Mohawk Indians under the command of their chief

Hendrick. For though this is called the French and Indian
War, the name itself implying that the Indians were chiefly
on the French side, yet there were Indians also on the English side, and this force which Hendrick led consisted of
several hundred warriors. The country between Albany
and Canada was a wild border land, which very naturally
became a field of strife, as the two parties in the war were
then situated.

In leaving Albany to go northward the army could use
Hudson River for transport for a considerable distance, and
then it was necessary (in order to reach Lake George, which
was their first main destination) to leave the river and make
a path some ten or fifteen miles through the wilderness
to the southern end of the lake. But for the security of
their supplies it was needful to construct a fort at the junction of this road with the river. The building of the fort,
which was called Fort Edward, consumed some six weeks.
A garrison under the command of Colonel Blanchard was
left to man this fortification, and the main force under
General Johnson moved on to the southern end of Lake
George.

It was this Fort Edward which Putnam, at a later period,
with immense hazards and by almost superhuman exertions,
saved from being utterly destroyed by fire.

Before General Johnson had time to fortify himself in
his new position at Lake George, news arrived that Baron
Dieskau, the newly arrived French commander, was moving
to attack Fort Edward; and Colonel Ephraim Williams
from Massachusetts, with a thousand white soldiers and
some two hundred Indians, was sent back for the relief of
this fortress. But by a curious turn of affairs Baron Dieskau, having heard that Fort Edward was furnished with
mounted cannon and might prove a dangerous place to
attack, changed his plan and was moving to attack the main

PUTNAM SAVING FORT EDWARD.

body at Lake George. The two armies met in the forests, and before the Americans were aware of their danger, they were trapped in an ambush and a most deadly fire opened upon them, by which Colonel Williams, the Indian Sachem Hendrick, and many other subordinate officers, and a large number of the men, were almost immediately killed and wounded. It was in connection with this party that Bancroft names Israel Putnam. They were thrown into utter confusion and fell back, without keeping military order, to the main body at the lake. They came in as flying fugitives, each one escaping for his life. But the firing, only three or four miles distant, had been heard by General Johnson and his force, and it was noticed also that the guns were each moment drawing nearer and nearer. Putting themselves in battle array as well as they could, and receiving back to themselves their flying comrades, order was at length brought out of confusion, and the army of Baron Dieskau, composed of French, Canadians and Indians, met with a terrible repulse. Baron Dieskau was himself wounded and taken prisoner, and about seven hundred of his men were left dead upon the field. Thus a most mortifying and bloody repulse was turned into a decisive victory, which caused great rejoicings throughout the colonies. This was Israel Putnam's first baptism of fire and blood.

Colonel Williams, who commanded this relieving party, was an officer greatly trusted and beloved, and his name is destined to live in the quiet walks of learning through coming generations. Before setting out upon this campaign, while he was yet at Albany, knowing the uncertainties of the expedition upon which he was entering, he made a will, by which he bequeathed his property (which was considerable) for the founding of a free school in what was then a comparatively wild region. He had been in command of

Fort Massachusetts, which was in the region now covered by the town of Adams in Berkshire county. His school was to be in the town next west of that locality, then almost wild country, on condition that the place should be named Williamstown. For several years the funds were allowed to accumulate. But in 1785 trustees were appointed, and in 1791 the school was started, and in 1793 it was incorporated as Williams College.

Besides the one thousand men and the five hundred reserves which Connecticut had already raised, before this summer of 1755 was over she had also equipped and sent forward two regiments more, each numbering seven hundred and fifty men. But it became evident before advancing farther into that almost pathless wilderness, that several forts and strongholds should be built to keep a sure and safe connection with the more settled portions of the country. The autumn of 1755 was spent in this way, and when the winter set in, enough of the forces were kept to man these newly-built fortresses, and the rest allowed to return home to await the operations of another year.

Though France and England had been more or less at war on this continent for a long course of years, yet the real declaration of war in what is commonly called the French and Indian War was not made until 1756. In May of that year England openly declared war against France. To give dignity and force to her plans, she also sent over several English regiments, with General Abercrombie to be chief commander on the field, and the Earl of Loudoun to be Governor of Virginia and a sort of viceroy over all the colonies.

And now for a time, the Americans had to endure that peculiar English pride which showed itself in Braddock the summer before, who disdained the idea that a young American upstart in the person of George Washington could

teach a British General how to fight. In like manner
Abercrombie and Loudoun, despising all suggestions from
men born on this soil, proposed to astonish the provincials
at their methods of conducting a campaign. The consequence was that the summer of 1756 was used up in long
and tedious delays. Abercrombie had the idea of removing
the native officers from the regiments raised on these shores
and substituting Englishmen, so that the Americans would
be only of the rank and file. But he found that the men
of New England, and especially those from Connecticut,
who by their charter had never been ruled by foreign governors, would not submit to this measure. The season was
mainly used up in pompous nothings. Mr. Hollister in his
"History of Connecticut" says: "It was a sore affliction
that brought Abercrombie to Albany to delay the provincial
troops, who, had they been led on by Winslow, would probably have taken Crown Point without British aid." The
season ended with the defeat of the English and American
forces by Montcalm, which sent over the colonies a wave
of weariness and discouragement, in strong contrast with
that tide of rejoicing which followed the close of the campaign in 1755.

There are multitudes of people yet living who, in their
early life, used to hear the stories of this French War from
aged men who had been actors in it. It was a war of most
peculiar hardships and rough adventures. Carried on in
such wild and inaccessible regions, provisions often grew
short, and many a man spent days and weeks almost upon
the verge of starvation. Moreover, the operations that
went on in the winter months were attended with such
sharp exposures to the cold, that none but men of iron constitution could endure them.

But let us get such glimpses as we can of Putnam in

these scenes of 1755 and '6. When the army disbanded in
the autumn of 1755 (except such as were required to man
the northern fortresses which had been erected during the
summer), Putnam did not go home, but remained on the
field of action. He became one of that famous band of
Rangers, who employed their time most industriously in
picking up valuable information as to what was going on
in the French army, and at the same time annoying and
troubling the enemy in every way possible. General
Humphreys says on this point: "Soon after his arrival in
camp he became intimately acquainted with the famous
partisan Captain, afterwards Major, Rogers, with whom he
was frequently associated in traversing the wilderness, reconnoitering the enemy's lines, gaining intelligence, and
taking straggling prisoners, as well as in beating up the
quarters and surprising the advanced pickets of their army.
. . . . The first time Rogers and Putnam were detached with
a party of these light troops, it was the fortune of the latter
to preserve with his own hand the life of the former, and to
cèment their friendship with the blood of one of their
enemies."

Mr. Hollister, in a note on page 58, volume II. of his
history, has furnished the record of a vote passed in the
Connecticut Assembly in May, 1756. The Assembly
granted "to Captain Israel Putnam the number of fifty
Spanish milled dollars, and thirty such dollars to Captain
Noah Grant, as a gratuity for their extraordinary services
and good conduct in ranging and scouting, the winter past,
for the annoyance of the enemy near Crown Point." Mr.
Bancroft in his history thus describes Putnam: "There
was the generous, open-hearted Israel Putnam — a Connecticut Major — of a gentle disposition, brave, incapable
of disguise, fond of glorying, sincere and artless." Upon

this sentence Mr. Grosvenor in his memorial address, thus remarks:

" This is mostly a high eulogium, and it may seem ungrateful to find fault with it. But we must be allowed to repel with some warmth the charge of glorying, *i. e.* boasting of his exploits. We claim that whatever else might be lacking in Putnam's character he was every inch a soldier, and a boastful spirit is a very unsoldierly trait. We challenge Bancroft to produce from any living acquaintance of Putnam, or from any dead record that is worthy of credit, any the slightest proof that Putnam was ever a braggart. Here where he lived is the place to come and inquire the truth on this point. Here it can be learned that even in his old age, a time when most soldiers love to 'shoulder the crutch and show' how fields were won,' he instead of being boastful was a remarkably modest man. . . . . Judge Paine of the United States District Court of Vermont, who was Putnam's neighbor for thirty years, says, ' he was a modest, unassuming man, and had nothing of the braggadocio about him. . . . . Universally considered by all his neighbors a man of the strictest truth and veracity.' "

We cannot go over minutely the events of this French War. It would occupy space that we need for more important purposes. If any one wishes to know in detail the military history of Putnam through those years, he may find the story fully written out in General Humphreys' " Life of General Putnam," of which the first edition was published in about 1790. The French War was comparatively near to him in time, but distant from us. He had lived in General Putnam's society, and it was but natural that he should dwell upon the bold deeds and hairbreadth escapes of his hero. In that war Putnam passed through many an adventure, where he exhibited the same undaunted courage shown in his encounter with the wolf. He was often brought into the closest quarters where escape seemed impossible, but by his quick perceptions and amazing energy, — by keeping himself master of all his powers and faculties in the most critical moments, it was his habit, if we may so speak, to wrest his victory from what in others would have been sure defeat. As an *example* of what we mean (and there are many similar adventures) we will give one illustration in General Humphreys' own words. He says:

" As one day Major Putnam chanced to be with a bateau and five men, on the eastern shore of the Hudson near the rapids, contiguous to which Fort Miller stood, his men on the opposite bank had given him to understand that a large body of savages were in his rear and would be upon him in a moment. To stay and be sacrificed, to attempt crossing and be shot, or to go down the falls with an almost absolute certainty of being drowned; were the sole alternatives that presented themselves to his choice. So instantaneously was the latter adopted that one man who had rambled a little from the party was of necessity left, and fell a miserable victim of savage barbarity. The Indians arrived on the shore soon enough to fire many balls on the bateau before it could be got under way. No sooner had our bateau-men escaped by favor of the rapidity of the current beyond the reach of musket shot, than death seemed only to have been avoided in one form to be encountered in another not less terrible. Prominent rocks, latent shelves, absorbing eddies, and abrupt descents for a quarter of a mile, afforded scarcely the smallest chance of escaping without a miracle. Putnam, trusting himself to a good Providence whose kindness he had often experienced, rather than to men whose tenderest mercies are cruelty, was now seen to place himself sedately at the helm, and afford an astonishing spectacle of serenity. His companions, with a mixture of terror, admiration and wonder, saw him incessantly changing the course to avoid the jaws of ruin that seemed extended to swallow the whirling boat. Twice it turned fairly round to avoid the rifts of rocks. Amidst these eddies in which there was the greatest danger of its foundering, at one moment the sides were exposed to the fury of the waves, then the stern, and next the bow glanced obliquely onward with inconceivable velocity. With not less amazement the savages beheld him, sometimes mounting the billows, then plunging abruptly down, at other times skilfully veering from the rocks, and shooting through the only narrow passage; until at last they viewed the boat safely gliding on the smooth surface of the stream below. At this sight, it is asserted that these rude sons of nature were affected with the same kind of superstitious veneration which the Europeans in the dark ages entertained for some of their most valorous champions. They deemed the man invulnerable whom their balls, on his pushing from shore, could not touch, and whom they had seen steering in safety down the rapids that had never before been passed. They conceived it would be an affront to the *Great Spirit* to attempt to kill this favored mortal with powder and ball, if they should ever see and know him again."

No wonder these Indians thought that Putnam bore a charmed life, for it was no more than many white men thought. How he could always come out alive and generally unharmed from his many dangerous encounters, was a mystery. It is among the strange allotments of this life (some would say chances) that certain men can never seem to come even remotely into the region of danger, without a disastrous and often fatal issue; while other men all their lives long pass unscathed through the most perilous situations. From the day that Putnam entered the den at Pomfret till he rode down the steep declivity of stone steps at Greenwich, Connecticut (being then sixty years old, and weighing two hundred pounds), history hardly affords a parallel, in case of any one man, to the many places of imminent peril which he occupied. He did not indeed escape without wounds and scars, but he bore off his life, and died in old age in his own home.

General Humphreys says: " The active services of Captain Putnam on every occasion attracted the admiration of the public, and induced the Legislature of Connecticut to promote him to a majority in 1757;" which is the simple, old-fashioned way of telling us that he rose from the rank of Captain to that of Major in 1757.

The war dragged its weary length along. It is sometimes sportively said of certain physicians that they act and speak as if their patients ought to be willing to die if they can only die *scientifically*. And those great British Generals that came over in the early part of the French War, carried themselves with such lofty and pompous airs, that it seemed a matter of small consequence whether they led their armies to victory or defeat, provided they only exhibited before the untutored *provincials* the rules of scientific warfare. Too proud and haughty to receive suggestions from practical men who knew far better than they what needed to be done, they squandered the time through 1756 and '57 in the idleness of the camp, or if they made a military movement, it was almost sure to end disastrously. Mr. Hollister, speaking of the operations of 1756, says: "While this fine army was thus passing the summer in shameful inactivity, settling points of etiquette and waiting for leave from its officers to do what at an earlier day Major Treat, or at a later day Putnam, would have done in six weeks with six thousand effective men, the enemy was gaining every advantage by the delay."

After two years of this style of management under Loudoun and Abercrombie, but especially the former, as he was chief in authority, the colonies became disgusted and discouraged. And when in 1758 Loudoun called together the Colonial Governors to ask for more troops, and to block out the course of future action, he found them cold and formal, and in no hurry to comply with his requests. But fortunately just then William Pitt, the Earl of Chatham, had come again to the front in English politics, and Loudoun was recalled. A strong hand had now taken hold of the

helm of state, and there was to be a very different system
of operation.

In 1758, Putnam was taken prisoner by the Indians,
those savage allies of the French, and in this captivity he
suffered more horrible outrages, and was in more often and
imminent danger of losing his life than ever before or afterwards. All these painful and cruel details need not be
repeated, but he bore to his grave the huge scars from
wounds then inflicted. But at last he was passed along to
the French authorities, and was held as a prisoner of war,
awaiting exchange. We have before made reference to this
matter in connection with the name given by Putnam to his
youngest son, born in 1764. The story is pleasantly told
by General Humphreys, and as it is brief we quote it.

"The capture of Frontenac by General Bradstreet afforded
occasion for an exchange of prisoners. Colonel Schuyler was
comprehended in the cartel. A generous spirit can never be satisfied with imposing tasks for its generosity to accomplish.
Apprehensive if it should be known that Putnam was a distinguished partisan his liberation might be retarded, and knowing
there were officers who from the length of their captivity had a
claim to priority of exchange, he had by his happy address
induced the Governor to offer that whatever officer he might
think proper to nominate should be included in the present cartel. With great politeness of manner but seeming indifference
as to object, he expressed his warmest acknowledgements to the
Governor and said, 'There is an old man here who is a provincial Major and wishes to be at home with his wife and children ;
he can do no good here or any where else ; I believe your Excellency had better keep some of the young men who have no wife
or children to care for, and let the old fellow go home with me.'
This justifiable finesse had the desired effect."

We do not exactly vouch for the morality of this transaction, but it is an old adage that "all is fair in war." At any

rate one can easily see that Putnam, with his noble and mag-
nanimous nature, would never be likely to forget a friend
who had thus given him his liberty.

The year 1758 closed with failure again in the operations
around Ticonderoga and Crown Point, but with some grand
triumphs elsewhere which tended to encourage the army
and the people; but the year 1759 was to be memorable for
its successes, as it included among other victories the capture of Quebec by General Wolfe. This is one of those
battles that appeals strongly to the imaginations of men.
The preceding circumstances, as well as the issue of the
battle, give it a most romantic place in human annals. Not
even the flippant story, as told by the Irish driver who in
these modern days carries you out to the Plains of Abraham, and who has learned his lesson by rote, can wholly
destroy in your mind the romantic impressions of that
battle.

The success of Wolfe at Quebec opened the way in the
following year for the general conquest of Canada. Putnam, by this time had risen to the rank of Lieutenant-Colonel, and was rapidly acquiring skill and experience as a
leader of men. He was an important officer under General
Amherst in the completion of this Canadian campaign.

When these northern conquests were over, the scene
shifted to the French possessions in the West India Islands.
Fleets came out of England to co-operate with the land
forces, which were transferred to those heated regions, and
Putnam was put in command of General Lyman's regiment,
numbering one thousand men. Here success followed success in a very rapid manner, though this southern climate
was terribly destructive to men who had just been living
amid the cold of these northern regions. The war finally,
in its last act, passed from the French to the Spanish pos
sessions, and Havana the capital of Cuba was taken. Then

followed in 1763 the treaty of peace between Great Britain and France, and in 1764, after a brief expedition to our western borders, Putnam returned to his home with the title of Colonel.

We are aware that this is only the briefest outline sketch of the French and Indian War, and that is all that has been attempted. It serves to keep the succession of times and seasons, and to show the heroic proportions of this farmer from Connecticut. Putnam had acquired a very rare and unique reputation for the services he had thus rendered. His name and his deeds were everywhere upon the tongues of the people. Especially was he known for his new and original way of overcoming all obstacles and getting out of all difficulties. In the appendix may be found a larger reference to this trait of his genius, in which he was well-nigh unsurpassed. In any sharp, sudden and unexpected crisis his decisions were made with the quickness of instinct, but hours of the most sober reflection could hardly have improved them. He had gained too a character for courage and military ability which was not then trifled with. Men turned toward him as a tower of strength in any future complications that might arise.

5

CHAPTER IV.

ELEVEN YEARS OF HOME LIFE.

Death of his Wife. — Selectman and Moderator of Town-meeting. — Joins the Church. — Watching the Movements of the British Government. — The Stamp Act. — The Sugar Act. — The Boston Port Bill. — Early Remonstrances from Connecticut. — Growing Excitements. — False Alarm in September, 1774. — Colonel Deming's Oration. — News from Lexington. — Ride to Cambridge and Concord.

THE long war was at last over, and the American Colonies were free from French insult and interference. Putnam went out to this war in 1755, a plain, uneducated farmer. He came back in 1764, with large military knowledge gained in the rough school of practical experience. But like the officers and soldiers in our late war of the Rebellion, when his warlike service was ended he went back to the quiet pursuits of the farm just as naturally as he left them in 1755.

In the year 1765 two events occurred which deserve special notice. In that year, the wife of his youth and the mother of his ten children died, leaving her youngest son an infant of a year old. It added a pang to this affliction that now, after his long absence and painful separation from his family, this bereavement should fall just as he had come back to enjoy the rest and comfort of his substantial home. This was the Hannah Pope of Salem Village, with whom his destinies had been united for more than a quarter of a century.

In this year 1765 Putnam made a public profession of his Christian faith, and united with the church in Brooklyn, then

66

under the pastoral care of Dr. Josiah Whitney, whose long ministry has already been noticed. But in all the years before this, Putnam had walked strictly in the ways of his fathers. He came of a race, that in its several generations, from the beginning until now, had been a strongly religious race, as we have seen. In his life in Danvers and in Pomfret he was a regular attendant upon the worship of the sanctuary, and a firm supporter of religious institutions. There are no braver men on earth than those who humble themselves before God. History is full of its examples, showing us that the best soldiers are often the truest Christians. Many a godless scoffer has found to his cost that there are no more fearful men to encounter in the day of battle than those who have the fear of the Lord before their eyes. In the early days of our late Rebellion great stories were told as to the wonderful things those zouaves from the low purlieus of New York city were to do when they came in face of the enemy. But it was found when the trial was made, that they were as poor soldiers as they were citizens, and that no trust could be reposed in such men in the day of battle. In every long and trying war which this country has passed through, the burden has rested back at last upon solid character. And especially has it rested upon the Christian people — the ministers and churches of the country, without whose aid and support no one of our great wars seemingly could have been carried through.*

* The general spirit and position of the New England ministers in the war of the Revolution are pertinently illustrated by the following extract from a letter published in the "Independent Chronicle," May 29, 1777. The letter had been waylaid and so came to light. John Cochran, the writer, was a tory, then on Long Island. His wife, to whom the letter is addressed, is in New Hampshire, and he wants her to go from where she is to a place of more privacy and security. He says:

"I shall either hope to find you at the Isle Shoals or up at Londonderry. If you intend to tarry where you are, I pray for God's sake, that there be no CLERGYMAN in the house; if there is, your life is not worth a farthing."

It has sometimes been doubted whether Putnam ever was a member of the church. There need be no doubt whatever upon that point. The date of his admission to the church in Brooklyn is given us by Mr. Grosvenor, and is abundantly shown by many witnesses. He made this public profession May 19th, 1765, so that he was a communicant full twenty-five years.

The West India campaign, of which we spoke in the former chapter, was terribly destructive to life and health in those who took part in it, and the British government gave a tract of land to the men of Connecticut who survived those fearful exposures. This land was situated on the Mississippi River, near Natchez. In the winter of 1772-73 General Lyman, Colonel Putnam and others chartered a vessel, and made a voyage to examine this land tract with a view to the establishment of a colony upon it. They extended their voyage beyond the mere necessities of the case and visited the island of Jamaica, and also entered the harbor of Pensacola. Mr. Grosvenor tells us that in connection with this voyage Putnam kept a diary which is still in existence, and which is probably the longest piece of writing that he ever executed. This diary is valuable for the settling of a point about which there is some dispute. We call attention to this subject distinctly, because the matter will come up again in another form. Major Small, an English officer, was stationed at Pensacola as a subordinate of General Huldeman. Under date of March 8, 1773, Putnam records in his diary: "I went from the General's to see Major Small, who was not well. Stayed there all night." Again on the 13th of March he says: "Supped with Major Small; lodged at night." These items are of importance as showing that Putnam not only knew Major Small, but apparently knew him intimately, or he would not have been likely twice at least in this short visit to have spent the night with him.

It is not needful that we should attempt to expand to any great length the circumstances of his life, during the ten years and more that intervened between the close of the French War and the opening of the revolutionary drama. Our interest centres mainly about one feature of this life, viz., his intense indignation at that system of oppression which the mother country was trying to establish over these colonies. They had suffered and toiled and been impoverished by the burdens and hardships of the French War, which had just closed, and it seemed now that after all their faithful services, England was determined to extract from them the money wherewith to pay the expenses of this protracted conflict. Mr. Hollister says of the state of things at this period:

"An old national debt, by gradual accretions, had grown at last to the appalling sum of seven hundred millions of dollars. Even at the beginning of the last French War, the alarm of the government had been excited, and the Board of Trade had proposed a plan of taxing the American Colonies. But in the whirl of those exciting campaigns that followed each other like a succession of autumn gales upon an exposed ocean shore, the scheme had been allowed to slumber for about eight years. No sooner had the peace of 1763 given the nation an opportunity to look at its internal condition, than the British ministry again turned its eye toward the American Colonies as the proper field for financial experiment." *

England passed the Stamp Act in 1665. The excitement caused by this event, especially in the New England Colonies, was intense. As Massachusetts was the older and the larger colony, and had the chief seaport in New England, her course of action in those years has been more distinctly and largely written out, and many people suppose that it was mainly her influence that aroused the other

* Vol. I. p. 120.

New England Colonies, and that she did the chief work in
organizing opposition.   But Connecticut did not borrow
her indignation from Massachusetts.   From the earliest
dawn of this oppressive policy Connecticut was taking
action by herself.   Her peculiar charter made her the more
keenly alive to the dangers that threatened.   Hitherto she
had known far less of English rule and English interference than the other colonies.   Her charter exempted her.
She had chosen her own Governors, and lived in peace and
prosperity under them.   When the haughty Andros, the
minion of James II., undertook to be Governor of all New
England, 1686–89, and came to Hartford to demand
that charter which especially stood in his way, he went
back a wiser man than he came, but without the document.

Israel Putnam, though born in Massachusetts, had now
been a citizen of Connecticut for more than a quarter of a
century, and had thoroughly identified himself with her interests.   As we are writing his life, it becomes more natural that we should look at this opening strife preceding
the revolutionary struggle from the Connecticut standpoint.
Not that we would in any degree neglect or disparage the
course of Massachusetts.   Her record is clear and vigorous.   Her example was noble and inspiriting.   She has on
her historic rolls for those years the names of men whose
words and deeds will never be forgotten.   But Connecticut
was not the less bold, active, determined.   What was called
the Sugar Act was made a law in 1764, and the Stamp
Act was under discussion.   In that very year the Connecticut Assembly, when it came together in May, and before any other colony had taken public action, began to
move in this matter.   They appointed three men who, in
conference with Governor Fitch, should prepare a paper of
remonstrance against the policy of the British government.
The paper was finished and forwarded.   One of these three

men, Mr. Jared Ingersoll, soon after went to England, and though he did his duty faithfully in the way of remonstrance, yet when it was a foregone conclusion that the Stamp Act would pass, he unwisely (though it was done by the advice of the wise Doctor Franklin) allowed himself to be appointed Commissioner for Connecticut to sell this stamped paper.

When Mr. Ingersoll came back to this country with this commission in his pocket, the wrath of the people was kindled to a white heat. His residence was at New Haven, but not being able to stand the indignation of his townsmen, he set out for Hartford to consult the Connecticut Assembly and bring himself under the protection of Governor Fitch. His journey was nearly ended. He had reached the vicinity of Wethersfield, when he first met five men on horseback, who offered him no violence, but rode on in his company. Soon he met thirty more, who joined the procession and passed on with him towards Wethersfield. Then after a little he found himself received into the midst of a cavalcade of five hundred, who attended him into Wethersfield. The leader of this cohort was a man by the name of Durkee. Once in the street of Wethersfield they commanded him to resign his office of Stampmaster. He desired to parley, and wished to consult the Assembly and Governor Fitch, but they were not to be put off. He must resign then and there. It became more and more apparent to him each moment that these men meant all they said, and that he should never escape with his life from this company except by resigning the hated office. And he resigned. They had a form of resignation all ready for him, by which they made him say that he did this of his " own free will and accord."

Putnam was now a prominent member of the Connecticut Sons of Liberty. The stamped paper for Connecticut had been brought as far as New York, and it was uncertain what would happen. It was the Governor's place to appoint a Stamp-master in the room of Mr. Ingersoll, who had resigned of "his own free will and accord." Putnam called on the Governor as a deputy from the Sons of Liberty, on this Stamp Act business. The Governor said to him, "What shall I do if the stamped paper should be sent to me by the King's authority?" "Lock it up," said Putnam, "until we [the Sons of Liberty] shall visit you again." "And what will you do with it then?" Putnam's reply was, "We shall expect you to give us the key of the room where it is deposited; and if you think fit, in order to screen yourself from blame, you may forewarn us upon our peril not to enter the room." "And," asked the Governor, "what will you do afterwards?" "Send it safely back again." "But," said he, "if I should refuse admission?" "Your house will be leveled with the dust in five minutes." It must be borne in mind that Governor Fitch, in this colloquy, had no more love for stamped paper than Putnam himself. He was not a foreign appointee, but was elected Governor *by* the people and *for* the people. And it should be said also for Mr. Ingersoll, that he was an earnest friend of liberty, and fought against the Stamp Act at home and in England. And when he could not prevail to stop it, he did prevail to have the time of its enforcement put off, and this delay really caused the death of the bill. The stamped paper reached New York, but never got into Connecticut. The English ministry, finding what a furious storm they were raising, repealed the act in March, 1766, but superseded it by the Boston Port Bill, which was cunningly contrived to make a fair show, but upon close examination had the same essential elements of oppression in it that the Stamp Act had, though acting in quite a different way. This was especially fitted to rouse the indignation of

Boston, and it did thoroughly arouse it. The people took the matter in hand and on the 10th of June, 1768, the pent-up wrath broke out into open violence. Then came the tax on tea, and other arbitrary measures.

So passed these weary years of turmoil and excitement. The industry of the country was kept almost at a standstill by the wide preoccupation of the public mind, and by the immense uncertainties which overhung the future. England still held fast to her purpose, in one form or another, to tax America and raise her home revenues by sharp exactions upon her provinces. Men began to see that these matters would never end without the intervention of the sword. And yet this must be a struggle with many most painful features; officers and soldiers who had fought side by side through the French War, who had contracted close friendships, must now meet face to face upon the battle-field as mortal foes.

General Humphreys, in his " Life," etc., has given a kind of summary of Putnam's course of action during this period. It being settled in the minds of men that war must come, he says:

" All eyes were now turned to find the men who, possessed of military experience, would dare in the approaching hour of severest trial to lead their undisciplined fellow-citizens to battle. For none were so stupid as not to comprehend that want of success would involve the leaders in the punishment of rebellion. Putnam was among the first and most conspicuous who stepped forth. . . . . As he happened to be often at Boston, he held many conversations on these subjects with General Gage, the British commander-in-chief, Lord Percy, Colonel Sheriff, Colonel Small [here he saw Colonel Small again] and many officers with whom he had formerly served, who were now at the headquarters. Being often questioned, in case the dispute should proceed to hostilities, what part he should really take, he always answered, with his country, and that, let whatever might happen, he was prepared to abide the consequences. Being interrogated whether *he*, who had been a witness to the prowess and victories of the British fleets and armies, did not think them equal to the conquest of a country which was not the owner of a single ship, regiment, or magazine, he rejoined that he could only say justice would be on our side and the event with providence; but that he had calculated if it required six years for the combined forces of England and her colonies to conquer such a feeble country as Canada, it would at least take a very long time for England alone to overcome her own widely extended colonies, which were much stronger than Canada: that when men fought for everything dear, in what they believed to be the most sacred of all causes, and in their own native land, they would have great advantages over their enemies who were not in the same situation; and that having taken into view all circumstances, for his own part he fully believed that America would not be so easily conquered by England as those gentlemen seemed to expect. . . . . This was the tenor, our hero hath often told me, of those amicable interviews; and thus, as it commonly happens in disputes about future events which depend upon opinion, they parted without conviction, no more to meet in a friendly manner until after the appeal should have been made to heaven, and the issue confirmed by the sword." *

There is a man among us (we are happy in the belief that he was not born on our American soil) who has, within a comparatively few years, outraged history by repeated insinuations that Putnam was playing the part of a traitor in the opening scenes of the Revolution, especially in June, 1775. If a man ever lived, against whom these "fiery darts of the wicked" might be shot harmlessly, that man was General Putnam. With a character as transparent and open as the day, if the men of his own time did not know what he was about and what was the great current of his thought and feeling, then by all means let us have a for-

* Humphreys' "Life of Putnam," pp. 87-89.

eigner come a hundred years afterward and tell us. The man who makes these insinuations is one of large historical learning, and has greatly helped other men (even on this particular subject) by his immense accumulation of primary facts and documents. But if ever a theory defied the common sense of mankind, his theory does.

In violent contrast to this mean and skeptical philosophy, we propose to introduce a passage from the oration of Colonel Henry C. Deming * of Hartford (now deceased), delivered in 1859, on the occasion of the presentation of General Putnam's sword to the Connecticut Historical Society. He gives us one of the most graphic delineations of General Putnam's character that we have ever seen. He said:

" If Connecticut had foreseen her future from 1745 to the revolutionary period, and made for herself a hero, she would have forever forfeited her repute for practical common sense, if she had not made precisely such an one as General Putnam. The style of hero which those thirty years demanded was essentially military, for wars and convulsions decisive of our destiny were distinctly prognosticated; and yet a military hero that was adapted to our peculiar wants, graded to our scale, and willing to make himself generally useful. We were a feeble folk far away in the backwoods, just opening a stingy soil to tillage, just beginning to raise crops enough for home consumption, with naught but homespun manufactures, with meagerest foreign commerce, in wholesome fear of Indian massacres ; for in 1746 the tomahawk and scalping-knife had been freely used within a few hours' march of our borders ; environed with French settlements and posts, and at times in imminent danger of vassalage to the House of Bourbon, and liable to requisitions from our own sovereign liege, whenever the wars of European ambition kindled into flames his American dominions. What this little frugal colony could have done with a hero of more magnificent and

* Appendix A.

colossal proportions, an Alexander, a Cromwell, a Napoleon, except to offer up itself as one meal to his insatiable maw, it is impossible to conceive. We craved a hero of dauntless pluck, of unwearisome endurance, shrewd, generous, self-abnegating, fertile in expedients, with more genius for forest war than for pitched battles and complicated campaigns, a man of muscle and might and will, capable of intense wrath and inviolable obstinacy, who could bend or break into military subordination and trustful self-surrender the Connecticut levies, raw, verdant, awkward as soldiers, but independent and self-complacent as freeholders; while under his stubborn and imperious rule they were marched to Ticonderoga or Frontenac or Havana, or wherever else his Majesty chose to order them; and after the campaign was over and the troops discharged could render an exact and conceivable account of receipts and disbursements to the Commissioners of the Pay Table. We wanted a hero shaped more like a Cincinnatus than a Cæsar, who in the breathing times of peace could join his fellow-citizens in productive industry, and support the Gospel and sit in the General Assembly,— no useless drone in our hive, no barnacle on our poor treasury,— a hero, who in the fulness of time, when petitions, prayers and remonstrances had all failed, and our unborn rights and privileges were brought to the arbitrament of the battle-field, held in himself a sufficient volume of slumbering courage and martial enthusiasm to electrify our whole people, and dared to lead a sturdy yeomanry where any dared to follow. The model man which our era and our environments craved was none of your imperial spirits who bend all mankind into homage, and contemn the civil power and cross Rubicons and convulse the world; but a shield and sword to an untamed commonwealth in a steady struggle with untamed nature and with savage and civilized foes; the farmer that could subdue its stubbornest glebe; the hunter that could cope with its most formidable beasts of prey; the ranger that could banish the terror of the Indian and give security to the traveller in the forest, the laborer in the field, and the child in the cradle; the advanced guard on the Canadian war-path, behind whom women and chil-

dren could sleep secure ; the trusted leader who could hold our
untried ploughmen to a breastwork of hay through three assaults
from British grenadiers."

To illustrate this passage from Colonel Deming, and to
show the simple-hearted and serviceable spirit of this man,
take the following incident. In 1774 British troops were
gathering in Boston, and the business industry of the town
was almost paralyzed. Indeed the place began to be iso-
lated, cut off from the interior towns, and serving simply as
a British military post. There was distress among the loyal
inhabitants; and other parts of New England sent large
contributions for their relief. We copy the rest from
Bancroft (Vol. VII. p. 101) :

" Putnam of Connecticut, famous for service near Lake George
and Ticonderoga, before the walls of Havana and far up the lakes
against Pontiac, a pioneer of emigration to the southern banks of
the Mississippi ; the oracle of all patriot circles in his neighborhood, rode to Boston with one hundred and thirty sheep as a gift from
the parish of Brooklyn. The 'old hero' became Warren's guest
and every one's favorite. The officers (English) whom he visited
on Boston Common bantered him about coming down to fight.
'Twenty ships of the line and twenty regiments,' said Major
Small [notice that here he sees Major Small again], 'may be
expected from England in case a submission is not speedily made
in Boston.' ' If they come,' said the veteran, ' I am ready to
treat them as enemies.' "

Now, we may be sure, first of all, from the very nature of
the man, that his own flock was as heavily drawn upon to
make this contribution as that of any other person in Brooklyn parish. And besides, he volunteered his service to see
those sheep safely in Boston. A man of cold and aristocratic proprieties would have thought himself ruined for life
if he had been caught in such service as this, even though
it might be for the relief of suffering Boston. But we are

not aware that the man of cold and aristocratic proprieties is
any more beloved of God or men than one who exhibits a
spirit like this.

And we are the more ready to take passages like this
from the pages of Mr. Bancroft, because, as we shall see in
the later stages of his work, he is drawn into the acceptance
of theories, apparently without independent investigation,
which tend to dishonor this "old hero" of whom he here
speaks so nobly.

This was in August, 1774. Hardly had Putnam reached
his home again in Pomfret, when a rumor went through the
New England Colonies, which grew as it travelled, but which
was founded upon a small amount of fact. It stirred the
people of Connecticut from centre to circumference. This
excitement was caused by a movement in the British army
to seize the powder which had been gathered for future
exigencies, and which was stored in a magazine between
Cambridge and Medford. The British were successful in
this attempt. It caused a great stir about Boston, but the
proportions of the story, as was natural, were magnified as
it moved on into the interior. This event happened on the
first day of September, 1774, apparently toward night. The
news reached General Putnam as soon as it could be carried.
And we have the copy of the letter which he immediately
sent to Captain Aaron Cleaveland, with the endorsement of
Captain Cleaveland upon it, and a further endorsement by
some one in Norwich whose name is not given. The mis-
sive went like the war signals which the Highland Scotch
used to speed through their vales and mountains.

"POMFRET, Sept., 1774.

"CAPT. CLEAVELAND: Mr. Keys has this moment brought the
news that the men and troops begun to fire upon the people last
night at sunset at Boston, when a post was sent immediately off
to inform the country. He informs that the artillery played all

night; that the people were rallying universally from Boston as far as here and give all the assistance possible. The first was occasioned by the country being robbed of their powder from Boston as far as Framingham ; and when found out, the persons who went to take them were immediately fired upon. Six of our number were killed the first shot, and a number more wounded, and beg you will rally all the forces you can, and be upon the march immediately for the relief of Boston and the people that way. Israel Putnam."

" N. B.— Send an express along to Norwich.

"Aaron Cleaveland."

" Forwarded from Norwich."

Now it would be very easy for a grammarian to suggest several emendations in that letter in respect to style.* There are some awkward gaps in it, which the impetuous old warrior could not stop to fill up. He had to trust to the common sense of the man who received it to leap the chasms. But the man who received it took its whole meaning in an instant, and took it sooner than though the writer had stopped to fill his sentences and round out his periods.

The rumor thus set in motion travelled quickly across the little State even to the borders of New York. Hollister, in

---

* We have freely conceded that General Putnam greatly lacked literary culture, but compare him with Colonel James Reed of New Hampshire, who did heroic service in the battle of Bunker Hill, and he seems in contrast like a liberally educated man. Here are a few sentences from a letter of Colonel Reed, dated at Fitz William, N. H., June 8th, 1775, copied from the seventh volume of " New Hampshire Provincial Papers," p. 508.

" Honrad Sir, I bag Leve to Trobel you with one word in faver of the Barer Captain Colburn — that is to inform that he is one of the Siners of the paper of a greement to Rase a Regiment under command, and Sir as my Regiment is fit,d up with out him and as I had in Corigement that any officer that had got men should be taken Notis of, &c. &c. . . . . if your Honours the Committee would favor him in the next Regiment as a Major if a greeabel. . . . . would bag leve to subscribe myself &c."

Colonel Reed was afterwards Brigadier-General.

his history says (Vol. II. p. 158), " The whole colony was
in commotion, and it is believed that more than twenty
thousand men were on their march for Boston before they
were made aware that the story was without foundation."
Mr. Hollister says "without foundation." It had, as we
have seen, a germ of truth, but the story, in the proportions
with which it reached Connecticut, was essentially without
foundation.

From these warlike thoughts and associations we turn
now a moment to look upon Putnam amid the scenes of his
home life, and as a citizen of the goodly town of Pomfret.
It has been already explained how, owing to the complications of the Mortlake Manor, Putnam did not distinctly become a citizen of Pomfret until 1752. The interval between
that and 1755, when he went to the French War, was so short
that he would not naturally be much developed as a citizen
of the town. But after his return from that war, in the
eleven years that intervened before the opening of the revolutionary period, he was quite active as a citizen. Mr. E.
P. Hayward, the present Town Clerk of Pomfret, has furnished from the records a few items, which may illustrate
his standing and reputation in the town during this interval. He was first chosen one of the Selectmen of the town
in 1763. He was chosen to the same office again in 1765,
and still again in 1771. A Selectman in one of our old
New England towns was exactly what the word itself implies. It was the most important office which the town in
its municipal capacity had to bestow. It was given to men
of wisdom and uprightness. A rash, headlong, injudicious
man was not likely to be proposed for this office. A New
England *town* * is in itself one of the most remarkable

* We once heard an impressive remark in this connection from the lips of
the late Professor Agassiz. He had been out the evening before (this was
more than twenty years ago) to give a lecture in one of our Massachusetts
towns, and he was on the morning train returning to the city. The remark

products of our western civilization. Nothing like it is known in Europe nor even in large portions of the United States. We may hope that the present tendencies among us will bring the town system into use in States that have never had it. Indeed, we know that in one at least of the so-called Southern States that question is now under consideration.

We gather, from the fact that Putnam was three times chosen on the Board of Selectmen in Pomfret, that his neighbors and fellow-citizens regarded him as a safe and judicious man, wise in council as well as bold in action. In the year 1769 he was Moderator in Town Meeting, and this is another testimony not without significance. He was on the committee to rebuild the bridge over the Quinebaug River, near the present village of Danielsonville.

We adduce these little items, which may be deemed unimportant, simply to show what some are disposed to doubt, that along with his prodigious energy he had a well-balanced judgment and large practical knowledge. It is very easy by taking certain strong characteristics of Putnam and exaggerating them, at the same time leaving out of view his other qualities, to make him into a grotesque personality. It requires but little imagination or ingenuity to do this. But Putnam, while he impressed the men of his own times as a very unique character, did not impress them as a grotesque and ridiculous one. Would he have been " Warren's guest and every one's favorite," as Bancroft tells us, had he

was in substance that he could never cease to wonder at what he saw in New England. Said he, " I go in any direction among these towns in the valleys and on the hills, and I always find an intelligent audience gathered, prepared to listen attentively to the scientific subjects upon which I lecture. What an idea it would be for me to go out in this way and lecture among the peasantry of France ! At Paris, at Lyons, at Marseilles and such great centres, of course I could find audiences of the highest intelligence. But to go out into the open country of France to lecture in this way would be the height of folly."

6

been an outlandish boor? Doubtless he could not handle his knife and fork at Warren's table with the same grace as could the host, who nevertheless felt honored and gratified by his presence. Formal and fashionable proprieties are one thing ; and they are not by any means to be despised. They contribute greatly, if not run to excess, to the pleasures of life. But there are proprieties deeper than these. An unselfish and accommodating spirit, a noble heart, a mind free from all envy and hatred, a self-forgetfulness, a desire to give others pleasure,— these, in our real estimates of character, turn the scale very quickly when weighed against merely conventional proprieties. And these noble qualities Putnam had in large measure. The testimony in this respect is so well-nigh universal that it is needless to spread the proofs in detail. He had one of the kindest and most compassionate hearts that ever beat in a human bosom, and he made the men who were near him, whatever might be their culture, love him ; always excepting those who were moved with envy at his greater popularity and success.

We have already stated that Putnam lost his first wife in 1765. Two years later, in 1767, he was again united in marriage to Mrs. Deborah Gardiner of Gardiner's Island. He had no children by this marriage, and this wife died in 1777. She was at the time with him at his headquarters in the Highlands on the Hudson River.

We might introduce more details respecting this period from 1764 to 1775, but have perhaps done enough to bring the man into view, as he was known among his fellow-townsmen and the people of Connecticut. We must pass on to scenes immediately preceding and accompanying the revolutionary outbreak. We can desire no more evidence than we have now before us, that his mind and heart were most deeply interested and occupied with what was passing at

Boston. From those hills of Eastern Connecticut he watched all the signs of the times with intensest curiosity, and every important event reported itself to him as swiftly as couriers could bring the news.

The battles of Lexington and Concord took place on the 19th of April. Bancroft says (Vol. VII. p. 315), "On the morning of the 20th, Israel Putnam of Pomfret, in leathern frock and apron, was assisting hired men to build a stone wall on his farm when he heard the cry from Lexington. Leaving them to continue their task, he set off instantly to rouse the militia officers of the nearest towns. On his return he found hundreds who had mustered and chosen him their leader. Giving orders for them to follow, he himself pushed forward without changing the checked shirt he had worn in the field, and reached Cambridge at sunrise the next morning, having ridden the same horse a hundred miles within eighteen hours. He brought to the service of the country courage which during the war was never questioned, and a heart than which none throbbed more honestly or warmly for American freedom."

This is one form of the story, but the more common form is that he was ploughing at the time the news reached him. Daniel Putnam his son, who certainly ought to know, as he was then in his sixteenth year, says, "When this time came he loitered not, but left *me*, the driver of his team, to unyoke it in the furrow, and not many days after to follow him to camp." We have no doubt this is the truth.

But what he was doing at that time is of comparatively small consequence. What he did do under the circumstances will be told through all the future ages of our history. A straight line drawn from Pomfret, Connecticut, to Boston will measure not far from sixty miles. But no one travels through New England on straight lines even now, much less then. We know not precisely what route he took, but probably he did not reach Cambridge in less than sixty-five or seventy miles. But he had first been to the neighboring towns. Bancroft puts his ride, after he heard the news, at one hundred miles by sunrise next morning. This may be a little in excess of truth. Paul Revere's ride two nights before is made famous by its circumstances and the dangers that encompassed him, and especially by the pen of the poet who has glorified it. But here was a ride not attended with any such present dangers, but involving marvellous powers of endurance in a heavy man of fifty-seven years of age. And the story is not all told yet. The same day that he reached Cambridge he was also at Concord, and probably returned to Cambridge the same night. Governor Ingersoll of Connecticut, at the Concord Centennial Celebration, April 19th, 1875, in the speech he made, stated this fact, viz., that Putnam was at Concord on the 21st of April, 1775. The statement was doubted. Judge Hoar thought it could not be so. Governor Ingersoll rested for his authority upon Hollister's " History of Connecticut," but would not insist upon it in the presence of those who might be supposed to be better informed. He went home and applied to that indefatigable antiquarian, J. Hammond Trumbull, LL. D., of Hartford, and *he* found and produced a copy of an old Norwich paper containing Putnam's letter written at Concord on Friday, April 21st, and published in Norwich Sunday, April 23d. This whole matter is so interesting, as letting us directly into the life and stir of those momentous days, that we give in a note the whole account as prepared and published by Mr. Trumbull in the Hartford Daily " Courant," July 24, 1875.*

It may not be possible to tell certainly what route was taken by Putnam in this journey. The expresses that went out from Boston to that part of Connecticut seem to

---

* GENERAL PUTNAM'S RIDE TO CONCORD. — When news of the fight at Lexington and Concord reached Pomfret, Israel Putnam, says his biographer, Colonel Humphreys, "left his plough in the middle of the field, and without

have gone by Worcester, and we notice also that the Massachusetts Congress, May 13th, 1775, established the post-
road to Woodstock by Worcester. Woodstock joins Pomfret, and as Worcester was a local centre there was probably
a better road to Boston that way than by the more southern tier of towns. The distance to-day, on the New York
and New England Railroad, from Boston to Pomfret is given
in its time-tables, as sixty-six miles. But that road makes
some departures from a straight line for local accommoda-

waiting to change his clothes set out for the theatre of action." He was in
Concord on the second day after the battle, and the same day (April 21st),
after a conference with the Massachusetts Committee of Safety, he wrote to
Connecticut to advise the Governor and Council what was to be the colony's
quota for the army to be raised in New England. These facts seem to have
escaped the notice of our historians, and at the late Centennial Celebration in
Concord Governor Ingersoll's allusion to Putnam's visit in 1775 did not pass
unquestioned.

A despatch from the Committee of Safety at Watertown, dated at 10 A. M.
on the 19th, was received in Pomfret about 8 A. M. on the 20th, bringing news
that the British had fired on the people at Lexington, "killed six men and
wounded four others, and are on their march into the country." About
3 P. M. a second despatch came to Colonel Ebenezer Williams of Pomfret,
one of the Connecticut Committee of Safety, with an account of the fight at
Concord. Colonel Williams forwarded the news by express to Canterbury
and Norwich; writing under date of 3 P. M. (misprinted "A. M." in Force's
"Am. Archives," IV. p. 363), "I am this moment informed by express," etc.
The following letter from Putnam, dated in *Concord* on the 21st, shows that
he did not leave Connecticut until after the receipt of the *second* despatch, that
is, until after he had news "at Pomfret" of the battle at Concord. In the
interval, between the arrival of the first and second expresses, he was probably
in conference with the Windham County committees and military officers.
This letter was printed in Norwich, on Sunday the 23d, together with other
reports of the battle, in an extra from the office of the Norwich "Packet."

NORWICH, April 23, Sunday, 4 P. M.

A gentleman arrived here this Day, and has favoured us with the following particulars, which we think proper to communicate to the Public, who may
depend, that the most strenuous Exertion of Abilities, and unremitting Assid-
uity of the Publishers, shall never be wanting to give them satisfaction.

CONCORD, April 21.

To COLONEL E. WILLIAMS. Sir — I have waited on the Committee of the
Provincial Congress, and it is their Determination to have a standing Army
of 22,000 men from the New-England Colonies, of which, it is supposed, the

tion. The distance by Worcester is certainly not less than that.

Then we notice that Mr. Bancroft brings Putnam to *Cambridge* at sunrise June 21st, but Hollister takes him to *Concord* at the same hour. We think he went to Cambridge first. The letter was written from Concord; but before he wrote that he had seen the Committee of Safety. This committee held some of their meetings in those days at Menotomy, which was afterwards West Cambridge, but now Arlington. The committee probably met there or at Watertown on the 21st. These places would be on the way from Cambridge to Concord.

But put the matter as we will, this ride of General Putnam must ever stand as a most marvellous specimen of activity and endurance in a man of his years.

Colony of Connecticut must raise 6,000, and begs they would be at *Cambridge* as speedily as possible, with Conveniences; together with Provisions, and a Sufficiency of Ammunition for their own Use.

The Battle here is much as has been represented at Pomfret, except that there is more killed and a Number more taken Prisoners.

The Accounts at present are so confused that it is impossible to ascertain the number exact, but shall inform you of the Proceedings, from Time to Time, as we have new Occurrences; mean Time I am,

Sir, your humble servant,

ISRAEL PUTNAM.

N. B. The Troops of Horse are not expected to come until further notice.

A true copy E. WILLIAMS.

[The broadside has this imprint: "Printed by ROBERTSONS and TRUMBULL, who will, in a few Days have for Sale, THE CRISIS, number One and Two — A BLOODY COURT! a BLOODY MINISTRY! and a BLOODY PARLIAMENT!"]

At 9 o'clock in the evening of the 23d, a few hours after this sheet was printed, another letter from Putnam, dated at Cambridge, April 22, was received with despatches for the Committee of Correspondence. In this he urged immediate supplies of troops and provisions. [See Miss Caulkins's "History of Norwich," p. 381.]

The Windham County "troops of horse" — forty-five men, under command of Major Samuel McClellan (great-grandfather of Major-General George B. McClellan) — had marched for Lexington before the receipt of Putnam's letter of the 21st.

CHAPTER V.

THE ARMY THAT GATHERED AT CAMBRIDGE.

False and pernicious Conceptions of this Army.— Was it "Four Armies " or one "American Army "?— Assortment of Troops.— Putnam a Brigadier-General.— Exchange of Prisoners.— Battle of Chelsea.— March of the Army around Charlestown and over Bunker Hill.— What is a Council of War ? — Spirit of Massachusetts.— Generals and Colonels at Cambridge and Vicinity.

THERE is one fatal misconception as to the state of things between April 19th and June 17th, 1775, which has spread its disastrous trail over large portions of modern Bunker Hill literature. We cannot so well illustrate what we mean in any way as by taking the following extract from a letter of John Adams, written to George Brinley in 1818:

"The army at Cambridge was not a national army, for there was no nation. It was not a United States army, for there were no United Colonies ; and if it could be said in any sense that the colonies were united, the centre of their union — the Congress at Philadelphia — had not adopted nor acknowledged the army at Cambridge. It was not a New England army, for New England had not associated. New England had no legal Legislature, nor any common executive authority, even upon the principles of original authority or even of original power in the people. Massachusetts had her army, Connecticut her army, New Hampshire her army, and Rhode Island her army. These four armies met at Cambridge and imprisoned the British army in Boston. But who was the sovereign of this united or rather congregated army, and who was its commander-in-chief? It had none. Putnam, Poor and Greene were as independent of Ward as Ward was of them."

(1) We call attention to two or three important facts which
will serve to show that Mr. Adams was not fresh from his
revolutionary readings when he penned those sentences.
He was not over well informed about matters concerning
which he was writing. He introduces the name of Poor
with those of Greene and Putnam and Ward; whereas Poor
was not connected with the army at Cambridge at all until
after the battle of Bunker Hill. Then he introduces him
as though he were a General. The other three were Generals, and he is evidently thinking of Poor as a General
representing New Hampshire, and standing in the same
relations to his State as did Putnam to Connecticut and
Greene to Rhode Island. Poor *was* a General and a very
able one in 1777 (appointed Brigadier-General February
21, 1777). But he was only a Colonel up to that date, and
if Mr. Adams had intended to introduce a Colonel into his
category he would have named *Stark*, who was altogether
the leading man from New Hampshire at that time, with
that title. But he did not intend to speak of a Colonel; he
had his thought fixed upon a General, and unfortunately
selected a *Colonel*, who was not even about Boston in the
early weeks at all. But Mr. Adams was still more unfortunate in another respect. While Connecticut and Rhode
Island had not yet, by formal vote, helped to consolidate
this army, New Hampshire had taken official action and
had put her men upon the Massachusetts foundation. She
did this as early as May 20th. Mr. Frothingham quotes
the words on page 99, taken from the New Hampshire
record, that "the establishment of officers and soldiers
should be the same as in the Massachusetts Bay." Consequently, if Poor had been a General and had been at Cambridge before the battle (as he was not), he would have been
no more independent of Ward, than Thomas, or Heath, or any
other Massachusetts General. All this may serve to show

us that even a great man (as John Adams assuredly was) sometimes writes very much at random.

(2) Whatever truth there is in the quotation from Mr. Adams, it is a *rhetorical* and not a *historical* truth. It relates to the *legal* relations of the men from the different States and not their relations as a *matter of fact*. Between the 19th of April and the 17th of June, 1775, the men of that period, looking upon that gathering of patriot soldiers about Cambridge, did not speak of it as "four armies." When Massachusetts in her Provincial Assembly was raising her own troops and providing for them, she called them, as was entirely natural, the "Massachusetts army." Connecticut and New Hampshire and Rhode Island did the same. But when those soldiers were brought together and grouped around General Ward in the camps about Boston, they were no longer spoken of as four bodies independent of each other. It was true the contingency might arise when they might be so, but they never were so. The several States might recall them, or issue separate and independent orders to them; but the States did not issue such orders. It was *one army*, not so well organized and compacted as it might have been, and as it was destined to be, but still *one army*.

The common method of speaking of it in those days, was that which we find, for example, in Sparks's "Life of Washington," where he is describing the state of things after the battle of Lexington before Washington took command. He says (p. 135), "The Massachusetts militia convened at Cambridge. The plan of *the new army* was soon arranged, General Ward was placed at its head, and recruiting orders were sent out. The other three colonies agreed to furnish their proportion of troops, who were raised and sent forward with as much expedition as possible." With Sparks it was "the new army," and not "four armies."

We repeat that it was entirely foreign to all the habits of the men of that day, when looking upon those military camps, to be talking about the "army from New Hampshire," or the "army from Connecticut." We do not find this style of language in the writings of that period. And yet almost all writers upon the battle of Bunker Hill have naturally felt called upon to mention the fact that the four New England States were not at that time legally consolidated, and that in this circumstance lay a certain element of weakness. Important movements might be interfered with by counter orders from the several States. But as a matter of fact, the States never did during this period throw themselves back upon their reserved rights, but their soldiers grouped themselves into *one army* around General Artemas Ward, as commander-in-chief. The talk about four armies can only have reference to a possible contingency and not to a historical fact. It is like the "power of contrary choice" in the action of the human will. It resides simply in the consciousness, but is not used. And yet this condition of things has been spoken of so frequently and continuously as to produce upon the public mind an impression which is quite out of shape with the simple facts of those days.

It is a matter of the utmost importance that we should have right ideas upon this point, if we would understand the battle of Bunker Hill that follows. And for this reason we do not propose to leave the matter with this general statement, but to look carefully into the common facts of that day, that we may apprehend the real relations of State to State, and of man to man.

And first of all, it is to be noticed, as an open and outstanding fact, that the troops from the several New England States, gathering about Boston after the fight at Lexington, did not arrange themselves, and were not by any

one arranged, after the manner of "four armies" or
four State camps, but were mingled together and distributed as parts of one army. The first regiment from Connecticut, which was upon the ground by the 1st of May,
under the command of General Joseph Spencer, made a
part of the right wing of the American army under General John Thomas, which was stationed at Roxbury and
Dorchester and places adjacent. The standard number for
a Connecticut regiment at that time was a thousand men,
and the three Connecticut regiments first raised were commanded by Generals and not by Colonels. The second
regiment from Connecticut was General Israel Putnam's,
which was stationed at Inman's Farm, now Cambridgeport,
making a part of the centre of the American army, under
General Ward the commander-in-chief. The troops from
New Hampshire made Medford their rallying point, where
Colonel Stark had his headquarters, and they composed a
part of the left wing of the army. The troops from Rhode
Island were at Jamaica Plain under General Nathaniel
Greene, making a part of General Thomas's right wing.
This very distribution of the troops signified but one grand
army, composed of the men from the four States. The
other theory should show us a Connecticut encampment
distinct and by itself, a New Hampshire encampment, and
so on. But nothing of the kind appears.

Then again it is to be remembered, that very many of
the officers commanding these troops, especially those above
the rank of Captain, had seen service *as officers* in the
French and Indian War, which closed only twelve years
before. Generals Ward, Putnam, Thomas, Spencer, and
Pomeroy had all served in that war. The only Generals,
so far as we remember, connected with the American army
before the fight at Bunker Hill who had not been in the
French War, were General Joseph Warren, General Wil-

liam Heath, and General Nathaniel Greene. They were younger men, General Greene being thirty-three years old in 1775, General Warren thirty-four, and General Heath thirty-eight. Strictly speaking, General Warren was not connected with the army in any active way before the day of the battle. In revolutionary matters his department had been that of civil affairs rather than military. He was made Major-General of Massachusetts troops three days before the battle, and died at Bunker Hill as a volunteer soldier. But with the exception of Warren and Greene and Heath, all the rest of the general officers in the camp about Boston were old soldiers, with their military ideas and habits already acquired.

The same was true quite largely of the Colonels. Prescott, Nixon, Brewer, Learned, Stark, Whitcomb, Reed, Frye, Gridley and others, had received more or less military training in the war of 1755. These men, whether from Massachusetts, Connecticut, New Hampshire or Rhode Island, gathered about Boston in 1775 to repel a common foe. From the three last named States they came at the call of Massachusetts, urgently imploring help in her great exigency. Now, whatever may have been the relations of the four States from which they came in a legal point of view, provided there were no positive orders to the contrary, these old soldiers and military leaders would gravitate toward *one organization* as naturally as the rain falls from heaven. Massachusetts had already taken the initiatory steps for the organization of an army. A camp had been formed at Cambridge with General Artemas Ward at its head. On the 20th of May he was duly commissioned as commander-in-chief of Massachusetts troops. When the patriot soldiers came in, some in regiments, some in companies, and some as individuals, they reported themselves at headquarters and had their places assigned them, not in four separate armies, but as parts and parcels of *one American army*. If a hundred men of the Anglo-Saxon race cannot be thrown together in an unoccupied spot anywhere upon the face of the earth without immediately creating a government for themselves, by a still stronger instinct do Anglo-Saxon soldiers gathering in this way gravitate toward organization and subordination. It is the first law of military life. And although time is required to make this organization compact and strong, the earliest movements will all be in the direction of order and unity.

Look at the case also in another point of view. Massachusetts had asked, even with an earnest and imploring cry, that these men from the other States should come to her help. Would she not treat them as the equals of her own men when they came? They had gathered from long distances, had separated themselves farther from their homes, had overcome greater obstacles in reaching the scene of action, than had her own soldiers. Would she seek to impress upon them, when they arrived, that they had been called to share in the labors but not in the honors of the common enterprise? We may be very sure that Massachusetts exhibited no such spirit in those days of danger and distress, and there is no occasion now for any of her sons to try and prove that she did; or that she sought to rank herself, by any action of hers, above her sister colonies. The army that gathered within her borders in 1775 was the American army, not legally consolidated, but actually one by the drift and pressure of the times, and by all soldierly instincts. The General from Connecticut was entitled, in this common army, to the honors and distinctions that belonged to the rank of a General. Colonel Stark from New Hampshire, in this American army, was not one whit below Colonel Prescott or Nixon or Brewer from Massachusetts. The assumption by which Massachusetts, greatly to her injury, is made to appear aristocratic in this gathering of soldiers upon her soil for a common cause, belongs to a later day, and was not a fact of those times. It is the privilege of writers, a hundred years after, to see how easy and natural it was for *Colonel* Prescott of Massachusetts to command Connecticut troops, but how improper and impossible even for *General* Putnam to command Massachusetts troops. Such theories found no place in the American army besieging Boston in 1775.

But far more convincing than any mere statements of this kind, are actions and events occurring from day to day, between the 19th of April and the 17th of June.

In the month of May an affair took place which clearly illustrates the point now before us, and shows that there were not "four armies" besieging Boston, but one army. We will quote a few sentences from the "Circumstantial Account of the Battle of Chelsea, Hog Island," etc., which may be found in Force's "Archives," Vol. II., 4th series, p. 719.

"On Saturday, May 27th, 1775, a party of the *American army* at Cambridge, to the number of between two and three hundred men, had orders to drive off the live stock from Hog and Noddle Islands, which lie near Chelsea. . . . . About eleven o'clock A. M., between twenty and thirty men went from Chelsea to Hog Island, and from thence to Noddle Island, to drive off the stock which was there, but were interrupted by a schooner and sloop, despatched from the fleet in Boston Harbor, and forty marines, who had been stationed on the island to protect the live stock. . . . . Having cleared Hog Island, the provincials drew up on Chelsea Neck and sent for a reinforcement of three hundred men and two pieces of cannon (four-pounders), which arrived about nine o'clock in the evening; soon after which General Putnam went down and hailed the schooner, and told the people that if they would submit they should have good quarters, which the schooner returned with two cannon shot; this was immediately

answered with two cannon from the provincials. Upon this a
very heavy fire ensued from both sides, which lasted until eleven
o'clock at night, when the fire from the schooner ceased ; the fire
from the shore being so hot that her people were obliged to leave
her and take to the boats, a great number of which had been sent
from the ships to their assistance. . . . . Thus ended this long
action without the loss of one provincial, and only four wounded.
. . . . The loss of the enemy amounted to twenty killed and fifty
wounded."

It is implied of course, in the above extract, that Putnam
was the commander in this expedition, and a letter of General Ward's settles it that Putnam was commander. In his
letter to John Adams the following October he expressly
states this fact. But who were the men whom he commanded ? The account tells us that they were a "party of
the American army at Cambridge" — not a party of the
Massachusetts army, or the Connecticut army, or the New
Hampshire army, but of the American army. The narrator from whom we have thus far quoted, writing in the
spirit of 1775, does not even have a care to tell us whether
these troops came from Massachusetts or Connecticut or
New Hampshire. It is sufficient for him that they came
from the American army, or from the provincials, as he
sometimes calls them. But other histories and narratives
tell us that some of them were from Massachusetts and
some from New Hampshire, and apparently none from Connecticut.

And there is a sequel to this story which is told us by
Daniel Putnam, son of General Putnam, and which is quite
as important for us to notice, as what has gone before.

"When he [General Putnam] returned to his quarters, wet,
and covered to the waist with marsh mud, contracted by wading
over the flats to burn the vessel, he met there General Ward and
Doctor Warren. Without stopping to change his dress he related

to them the events of the day, and added, 'I wish we could have
something of the kind to do every day; it would teach our men
how little danger there is from cannon balls, for though they have
sent a great many at us, nobody has been hurt by them. I would
that Gage and his troops were within our reach, for we would be
like hornets about their ears; as little birds follow and tease the
eagle in his flight, we would every day contrive to make them
uneasy.' Warren smiled and said nothing, but General Ward
replied, 'As peace and reconciliation is what we seek for, would
it not be better to act only on the defensive and give no unnecessary provocation?'" *

The point to be especially noted in this last extract is,
that General Putnam reports himself to General Ward as
his commanding officer and says, "I wish we could have
something of this kind to do every day;" which is the same
as though he had said, "If we are to have such work to do,
you must order it." If General Putnam and the independent "army from Connecticut" had alone been responsible
for this action, there was slight need for any such remark.
They could, according to the theory, go and come at their
own pleasure. But it was an American army, and General

---

* In Sumner's "History of East Boston," there is a much fuller account of
this battle than the one here given. The following passage may be found on
pp. 374–5:

"Putnam, inspired with the same dauntless courage with which he entered
the den of the wolf, heading his men, and wading up to his middle in mud and
water, poured so hot a fire upon the sloop that, very much crippled and with
many of her men killed, she was obliged to be towed off by the boats. It is
a striking illustration of the courage and impetuosity of Putnam, that he and
his brave followers attacked and crippled this sloop with small arms; that
leaving their cannon they waded within musket distance, and there fought the
heavy armed vessel, heedless of the great disparity of weapons and of their
dangerous position. Putnam's spirit animated the provincials, and foremost
in the fight himself, he was nobly sustained by his brave followers. The
spirited words of the poet will almost literally apply to the dauntless bravery
of Putnam in this engagement,—

"'There the old-fashioned Colonel galloped through the white infernal
Powder cloud:
And his broad sword was swinging, and his brazen throat was ringing
Trumpet loud.'"

Ward was at its head, and Putnam was a subordinate officer and recognized his place. And it is a fact not denied, that in this expedition he led Massachusetts and New Hampshire troops.

Now, just at this point, to show how entirely this history of 1775 has been turned aside from truth by certain Massachusetts writers of the present day, we give a sentence from the recent little book of Colonel Francis J. Parker of Boston. He is giving his reasons for the belief that Colonel Prescott was the chief commander in the battle of Bunker Hill, and his last reason is the following :

"*Fourth.*— That General Putnam, owing no obedience to the commanding General and having no claim to rank in the Massachusetts army, could not have commanded Massachusetts soldiers on Massachusetts soil."

We take this sentence for illustration, because it is such a bold, open statement of a theory entirely unsupported by facts, which in more disguised forms mingles largely in much Bunker Hill literature from Massachusetts writers in these latter days, and renders what they say of small historical value. In the light of what has gone before and what will follow after, it is not hard to perceive that this sentence of Colonel Parker and all kindred ones, wherever found, betray a great misconception of history in 1775. As we have said before, these writers find no difficulty in having Colonel Prescott command Connecticut troops, but General Putnam cannot command Massachusetts troops. There is a haughty Massachusetts assumption here, which, when drawn from its concealment and openly brought to view, has a very ungraceful look.

We have had a plain historical fact before us, and by its light we have seen that General Putnam *did* owe "obedience to the commanding General," and *did* "command Massachusetts soldiers on Massachusetts soil."

7

But let us take still other incidents from the records of those days, showing what Putnam's position was in this combined American army. In the affair at Lexington, April 19th, some prisoners had been taken from us, and we had taken some from the British. It may be that here and there a prisoner had been taken at other times. It matters not, for our purpose, when or where these prisoners were taken. The 6th of June, 1775, was fixed upon as a day for the exchange of prisoners. The whole account of the proceedings of that day may be found in Force's "Archives," Vol. II., 4th series, p. 920. In this transaction, Doctor Joseph Warren was appointed to represent the civil authorities, and Brigadier-General Putnam acted for the army. Doctor Warren, confessedly one of the most cultivated and scholarly men of that day, seems to have had no aversion to this companionship, any more than Washington had a month later, and through the following years of the war. The friendly relations of Warren and Putnam have been previously noticed. General Putnam and Doctor Warren rode in a carriage together from Cambridge to Charlestown, escorted by Captain Chester's company from Connecticut, and attended by the nine prisoners that were to be delivered to the British. There they met Major Moncrief with the nine American prisoners that were to be restored, and a very pleasant interview took place between the two parties, for Moncrief and Putnam were old companions in arms in the French War. "After which," as the account states, "General Putnam with the prisoners that had been delivered to him, etc., returned to Cambridge, escorted in the same manner as before."

Now, to gain the full significance of this transaction in a military point of view, let it be borne in mind that these prisoners whom General Putnam received from the British authorities were all of them Massachusetts men, taken prisoners probably before ever General Putnam came upon the ground. Four of them belonged in Boston, two in Cambridge, one in Danvers, one in Roxbury, and one in Dorchester. We have here a General from Connecticut, escorted by a Connecticut company, transacting very important business, not for Massachusetts (though it chiefly concerned that colony), but for the American army. And it would seem as though a man from Connecticut high enough in military rank and authority, as well as in social standing, to be entrusted with such honorable and at the same time delicate negotiations as these, might possibly command even Massachusetts men in battle, without causing any great shock to the feelings.

Take still another transaction in the illustration of this same point. Mr. Frothingham, in his "Siege of Boston," (p. 107), has given us a specific account of it. He says, "On the 13th [May], in the afternoon, all the troops at Cambridge, except those on guard, marched under General Putnam into Charlestown. They were twenty-two hundred in number, and their line of march was made to extend a mile and a half. They went over Bunker Hill and also over Breed's Hill, came out by Captain Henley's still-house, and passed into the main street by the fish-market, near the old ferry where Charles River bridge is. They then returned to Cambridge. It was done to inspire the army with confidence. Though they went within reach of the guns of the enemy, both from Boston and the shipping, no attempt was made to molest them."

Colonel Swett, in his "Sketch of Bunker Hill Battle," makes a similar statement, but places the march in June. He says, "General Putnam, to encourage discipline and emulation and brave the enemy, marched in the face of them with all the troops from Cambridge to Charlestown about the 10th day of June. And about the same time, to support the policy of engaging the enemy in an affair, he attentively reconnoitered the country with other officers."

Whether these two accounts refer to one and the same transaction, differing only in their dates, it matters not. There is no doubt there was a movement of this kind either in May or June, and if there were two, all the better. Both writers make General Putnam the commanding officer, and the troops he led must have been mainly Massachusetts troops. They were not marching to battle, as it proved, and yet they were marching where it could not well be told beforehand what might happen. They were going within reach of the enemy, and going there with something of a defiant air and manner. And General Putnam led and commanded them, because he and they alike belonged to the one American army. Mr. Frothingham tells the story without the slightest hint or apparent suspicion that General Putnam was not as fully entitled to lead these Massachusetts troops on that occasion as General Thomas or General Ward himself.

We dwell upon this point because, as we have already suggested, it is a vital one in any just comprehension of the battle of Bunker Hill. Few writers have ever dared to state the opposing idea or theory in language so direct and blunt as that which we have copied from Colonel Parker; but in a more subtle and concealed form this opposing theory thrusts itself in here and there in many writings, to disturb the reason and turn aside the natural flow of historical events. It is the vitiating quality in many labored essays and orations from the pens and lips of eminent men. This opposing theory all the while puts a *might be* in place of what *was;* a *possible contingency* in the room of *solid fact.*

We come now to other important items, all looking in the

same direction. In all the accounts of what took place in
those days just preceding the battle, frequent references
are made to the Provincial Congress, to the Committee of
Safety, and to the council of war. The Provincial Congress of Massachusetts was, of course, composed wholly of
Massachusetts men. There were similar bodies in Connecticut, New Hampshire and the other States generally. So
the Committee of Safety in Massachusetts was composed
wholly of Massachusetts men. There were similar committees in the other States. But what was a council of
war? Was this a Massachusetts body also? or were there
four councils of war, corresponding to the four States whose
troops were gathered about Boston in June, 1775? Nay,
there was but one council of war, composed of the higher
officers of the American army. It mattered not from which
one of the four States these officers might come. Their
rank and not their *locality* entitled them to membership; and
in this council one man's voice and vote were as good as
another's. It would have been the strangest assumption in
those days if any one had thought or dared to urge, that
General Nathaniel Greene because he came from Rhode
Island, or General Israel Putnam because he came from
Connecticut, could only speak and act in these councils
of war by Massachusetts sufferance.

   In the council held on the 16th of June, when it was
decided to go forward immediately and take possession of
the Charlestown heights, no man certainly was more prominent than Putnam. No writer of any repute denies his
presence in that body. All authors of every shade of opinion recognize his activity there, and his great influence.
He was without much doubt the leading man there, in that
his plans and purposes prevailed over strong opposition.
Through all the dusky years of a century intervening, no
figure is so distinctly seen in that conference as that of Gen-

eral Putnam. We may have occasion to refer to this council again, but we instance it now to show that no State lines shut men out from it, for it was a body representing not the "army of Massachusetts," or the "army of Connecticut," but the one American army, whose lines were coiled about Boston to hold the British' troops securely within their narrow confines. Now, the greater includes the less. If General Putnam, by his rank, could act in a council of war, and help to decide (and in a divided council, perhaps, by his vote actually decide) that Massachusetts soldiers and New Hampshire soldiers and Connecticut soldiers should together go into battle, how preposterous the idea that he could not command those very men in battle! It might be that in this very crisis an order would come from the State of Connecticut forbidding him, and forbidding the Connecticut troops from taking any part in the battle; but no such orders ever came, and none were expected. And in the absence of all such mandates the form and constitution of the army, in all essential points, were practically just the same as they were after the several States by their express votes were consolidated. The *contingent weakness* was taken away by that later action, and the army was made legally one. Soon it came to pass that the several States did so act and vote, and the army was thereby secured against those possible contingencies that might otherwise have occurred. But it was not changed at all in its original constitution. It was one American army before, crude, as all armies hastily called together are in their beginnings, greatly needing time and discipline for the development of soldierly qualities,— but one army, grouped around General Artemas Ward of Cambridge.

If any more proof is needed that General Putnam could command "Massachusetts soldiers on Massachusetts soil," it may be mentioned as one of the simple outstanding facts

of those days before the battle, that it was a part of his
daily life to command Massachusetts soldiers and New
Hampshire soldiers.   Colonel Daniel Putnam, his son, who
was with him daily in his life at Cambridge, makes the following statement ("Connecticut Historical Collections," Vol.
I. p. 232): "It is true there was at that time no other Connecticut troops at Cambridge but Putnam's regiment and
two or three independent companies; but Sargeant's regiment (his men were from New Hampshire), posted at
Inman's house, and Patterson's, still farther advanced towards
Lechmere's Point (a Massachusetts regiment), were placed
under his immediate orders.   I know this fact from having
often myself in the night season accompanied the officers
who performed the "grand rounds" for General Putnam's
command; and also that the selection of officers for this
duty was made alternately from those regiments and his
own."

This force, which General Putnam thus commanded day
by day, was the advanced guard of the American centre.
It held the post of honor and of danger.   These troops
were at Cambridgeport and parts adjacent.   They were
nearest the enemy, and there was good reason in General
Ward's mind why Putnam should be the man to have charge
of this advanced post, nor was there the slightest question
with him as to the right of General Putnam to command
Massachusetts troops.   That is a difficulty encountered
only by men a century afterwards, who write history according to their ideals, and not according to plain and open
facts.

We have been minute on this point, for it was needful to
be so.   The moral of the whole is obvious.   In this American army, nothing hinders a General or a Colonel from New
Hampshire, Rhode Island or Connecticut from doing precisely what a General or a Colonel from Massachusetts can

do. In the battle of Bunker Hill, which is soon to come, it is not of the slightest consequence from what State the chief commander comes. All that is wanted is the right man in the right place. If from either of the four States, he will still be subordinate to General Ward at Cambridge.

CHAPTER VI.

LEADING OFFICERS OF THIS ARMY.

Artemas Ward. — John Thomas. — Joseph Spencer. — Seth Pomeroy. — William Heath. — Nathaniel Greene. — Joseph Warren. — Israel Putnam. — The Colonels and their subsequent Promotions. — Who was the most popular Officer? — Who would most naturally lead in any bold Military Enterprise?

IT will be an instructive record, and will throw light upon certain historical problems, if we pass rapidly in review the chief officers directly and indirectly connected with this army about Boston in the spring and early summer of 1775, or till July 3d, when Washington took command.

General Artemas Ward, its commander-in-chief, was a native of Shrewsbury, born in 1727, and graduated at Harvard College in 1748. He was a man of good culture, and had already acted a creditable part as a member of the Provincial Assembly of Massachusetts. He had served under Abercrombie in the French War, but seems to have been placed at the head of the army at Cambridge rather as a civilian than as having any special military history. Bancroft says of him (Vol. VII. p. 324), "Ward, the General who was at Cambridge, had the virtues of a magistrate rather than a soldier. He was old, unused to a separate military command, and so infirm that he was not fit to appear on horseback, and he never could introduce exact discipline among free men, whom even the utmost vigor and ability might have failed to control, and who owned no superiority but that of merit, no obedience but that of will-

105

ing minds." Mr. Bancroft calls him old, but he was only forty-eight, which certainly cannot be called old for a man in his position. Several of the Generals about him were older than he. He was commissioned as commander-in-chief of the Massachusetts troops on the 20th of May, and the officers from the other colonies, without dispute, accepted as their commander-in-chief the man whom Massachusetts had appointed before their coming.

General John Thomas, commanding the right wing at Roxbury, was a soldier of a very different stamp and character from General Ward. Born at Marshfield in 1725, he was educated as a physician, and became an army surgeon in 1746. Showing soldierly qualities, he was taken from his place as a surgeon to become a military leader. He was made a Colonel in the French War in 1759, and commanded a regiment at Crown Point. In February, 1775, he was made Brigadier-General of Massachusetts troops. He was a man with the true proportions of a soldier. He was two years older than Ward.

General Joseph Spencer, born in East Haddam, Connecticut, in 1714, was thirteen years older than Ward. He was a man of good culture and of good military abilities, perhaps not a great General, but one much trusted and honored. He, also, had been a Colonel in the French War, and had seen much hard service. He was made second Brigadier-General of Connecticut troops, April 26th, 1775, and was stationed at Roxbury in command of a Connecticut regiment of one thousand men, as an under officer of General Thomas.

General Seth Pomeroy, from Northampton, was a veteran soldier of sixty years, a man of unquestionable courage and force. He was a Captain in the colonial army as early as 1744, a Major in 1745, and a Lieutenant-Colonel in the French War in the campaign of 1755. Bancroft quotes him as sending back a message to Massachusetts from the depths of the northern wilderness, where he was employed in that memorable summer of 1755, "Come to the help of the Lord against the mighty; you that value our holy religion and our liberties will spare nothing, even to the one-half of your estate." He was made a Brigadier-General of Massachusetts troops in February, 1775.

General William Heath was a younger officer, though not so young as Greene or Warren. He was born in Roxbury in 1737, and displaying military talents and tendencies, was in 1770 made commander of the Ancient and Honorable Artillery Company. Early in 1775 he was chosen Brigadier-General of Massachusetts troops, and was stationed at Roxbury under General Thomas.

General Joseph Warren has a story which is familiar to almost every one. We shall not repeat it here in full, as he will be noticed from time to time at a later stage. But the outline of his history is briefly this : He was born at Roxbury in 1741, was a graduate of Harvard, a skilful physician and an accomplished scholar. He was exceedingly active and courageous in the stirring scenes in Boston just before the revolutionary outbreak. He was a man greatly beloved by all classes of the people, high and low, rich and poor. His sphere had been especially that of civil affairs and not military. But so popular was he, that on the 14th of June he was chosen by the Massachusetts Assembly Major-General of her troops. He had not been regularly commissioned on the 17th, when the battle was fought, and for still other reasons refused to take command. He died on Bunker Hill simply as a volunteer.

General Nathaniel Greene of Rhode Island, under Thomas on the right wing, was the youngest man bearing the title of General in the army about Boston. He was only thirty-three years old, but of great promise, and this

promise was amply fulfilled during the years of the war.
He was the son of a Quaker preacher in Rhode Island, but
his early life had been one of labor and hardship. He had
an insatiable thirst for knowledge. The schools in Rhode
Island were poor, but he managed to find books and pick
up learning by instinct. The story is told in his "Life"
how, when a youth, he visited Newport with some articles
which he had manufactured for sale, and when he had sold
them and obtained the money, going out into the street he
met a man whose appearance attracted him, and he said to
him, "I want to buy a book." This man proved to be no
other than the Congregational minister of Newport, Rev.
afterwards Dr. Ezra Stiles, for eighteen years President of
Yale College. He took interest in the young man, went
with him and helped him to make the purchase, and the
book that was bought was no other than "Locke on the
Human Understanding."

When the alarm sounded from Lexington little Rhode
Island voted fifteen hundred men, to be organized in three
regiments, with Greene for Brigadier-General. The Rhode
Island troops as fast as they were enlisted were forwarded
to Jamaica Plain, and when Greene came to take command
he found turmoil and disorder. But after a time he brought
order out of confusion, and became subsequently one of the
most brilliant commanders in the war, and a great favorite
of Washington.

General Israel Putnam being the subject of this volume,
we need not enlarge here upon his previous history, which
has been already given. It is well, however, simply to
recall the fact that he went through the whole of the French
War, and came out from it with the title of Colonel. He
was made third Brigadier-General of Connecticut troops,
April 26th, 1775.

Colonel John Whitcomb was chosen Major-General of

Massachusetts troops June 13th, four days before the battle, but, like Warren, had not been commissioned.

Having given this rapid outline sketch of the previous history of these general officers, it may be well also to cast a rapid glance over their future career.

General Artemas Ward was chosen first Major-General of the Continental army by the Congress at Philadelphia on the very day of the Bunker Hill battle. Being already put forward by Massachusetts as commander-in-chief of the patriot army about Boston, the Congress at Philadelphia very naturally elected him to this highest place. But he resigned in the following April, and returned to civil life. What General Washington thought of him as a military man after he came to be acquainted with him, is made known very clearly by a letter* which he wrote to General Charles Lee in May, 1776, in reference to this resignation. There is a certain element in the letter not often found in Washington's writings.

"General Ward, upon the evacuation of Boston, and finding that there was a possibility of his removing from the smoke of his own chimney, applied to me, and wrote to Congress for leave to resign. A few days afterward some of the officers, as he says, getting *uneasy* at the prospect of his leaving them, he applied for his letter of resignation which had been committed to my care; but behold! it had been carefully forwarded to Congress, and, as I have since learned, judged so reasonable (*want of health* being the plea), that it was instantly complied with." †

He was a valuable man in civil life, and was at a later

* " Lee Papers," Vol. II. p. 13.

† " CONTINENTAL CONGRESS, Tuesday, April 23, 1776. — A letter of the 12th, from Major-General *Ward,* being received and read, repeating his desire for leave to resign,

" *Resolved,* That the resignation of Major-General *Ward* and of Brigadier-General *Frye* be accepted, and that the President inform them by letter."

period for several years Member of Congress. But in the management of armies he was utterly out of place. He died in 1800.

General John Thomas was made Continental Brigadier-General in June, 1775, and Major-General in March, 1776. He was the chief military leader under Washington in taking possession of Dorchester Heights, and was soon after sent upon a military expedition to Canada, and died there of small-pox, May 30th, 1776.

General Joseph Spencer was made Continental Brigadier-General in June, 1775, and Major-General in 1776. In certain matters of a general nature Spencer was much employed by Washington. We have seen the parole written by his own hand, when Major-General Richard Prescot of the British army was a prisoner entrusted to his care. It is a well worded, handsomely written paper, which General Prescot was to sign, promising to keep himself, until his exchange, under the eye of Governor Trumbull of Connecticut, and not to go beyond the bounds of the "First Parish of Lebanon." He promised also, upon his honor as a man and a soldier, to reveal nothing to the prejudice of the patriot cause which might come to his knowledge during his confinement. General Prescot's signature to this paper is in striking contrast to Spencer's writing. It is extremely shaggy and rough, though not uncultivated.

General Heath became Major-General of Massachusetts troops June 21st, 1775, then Continental Brigadier-General, and in 1776 Major-General. He was an able officer.

General Nathaniel Greene, before the close of the war, rose to a high position in the esteem of Washington and the country.

General Warren's untimely death will be noticed elsewhere.

Though Israel Putnam was outranked in this army at the

time of the battle by Thomas, Spencer, Pomeroy, Heath, and Whitcomb, yet the Congress at Philadelphia had such an opinion of him that, passing by all these Generals, they raised him at once to the high position of Continental Major-General, June 19th, 1775.   On June 17th, Artemas Ward and Charles Lee were chosen to this office, and on June 19th, Philip Schuyler and Israel Putnam ; and of the four, Putnam only was chosen *unanimously.*

It may be well to trace here, in few words, the subsequent military career of these four Major-Generals first chosen.   General Ward, as we have already shown, resigned in the April following, and his resignation was cheerfully accepted.

Charles Lee, the second Major-General, was a man of genius, literary and military, but a strange character.   He was a Welshman, and a kind of knight-errant adventurer. He had served in the European wars, and in the French and Indian War.   He had a very high opinion of himself, and did not hesitate in his correspondence to criticise severely the conduct of Washington.   He undertook to teach Major-General Heath to obey *him*, without much regard to Washington's instructions; tells him, "For the future I must and will be obeyed."   So he went on for a time, performing some excellent service, but being restless, ungovernable, domineering.   In 1778, he was "arrested for disobedience of orders, for misbehavior before the enemy, and for disrespect to the commander-in-chief."   These charges were sustained.   He was found guilty and left the service.

Dr. Belknap, in his journal, thus describes General Lee as he appeared when connected with the army at Cambridge : "General Lee is a perfect original, a good scholar and an odd genius; full of fire and passion, and but little good manners, a great sloven, wretchedly profane, and a great admirer of dogs."

James Warren, who succeeded Joseph Warren as President of the Massachusetts Provincial Congress, writing to Samuel Adams, July 9th, 1775, thus describes General Lee: "I know not what to say of your friend Lee. I believe he is a soldier, and a very industrious, active one; he came in just before dinner, drank some punch, said he wanted no dinner, took no notice of the company, mounted his horse, and went off again to the lines. I admire the soldier, but think civility or even politeness not incompatible with his character." (Wells's "Life of Samuel Adams," Vol. II. p. 316.) Mrs. Warren, on the same page, adds her opinion, and describes him as "plain in his person to a degree of ugliness; careless even to impoliteness; his garb ordinary; his voice rough; his manners rather morose; yet sensible, learned, judicious and penetrating."

Philip Schuyler, the third Major-General, for reasons not so plain,— indeed some have thought him very unjustly treated,— was superseded in 1777 by General Horatio Gates.

Putnam, as we have seen, was chosen last and alone *unanimously*, and it happened that he received his commission as Major-General before any of the others. Such objections were raised to the others when Washington reached the camp, that there was a delay in giving them their commissions. We are not sufficiently versed in military matters to know precisely what the official ruling in this case would be. Some writers speak of Putnam as *second in command* from the very day when Washington reached Cambridge, because he first received his commission; and certainly Washington treated him as his second self immediately, and in the years following. He kept him at the centre near his own person, placing Artemas Ward over the right wing, and Charles Lee over the left.

But at any rate he was second to Washington after the

year 1778, for the three elected before him were by that
time all laid aside. When Putnam was compelled to leave
the army in 1779, he did not lose his rank. Had he been
able to return, as he sometimes hoped, he would have gone
back to the same standing.

Before enumerating the Colonels connected with this
patriot army, it may be well to recall the fact that several
of the regiments were commanded by Generals. General
Ward had a regiment of which Jonathan Ward was Lieutenant-Colonel. General Pomeroy had a regiment of which
Colonel John Fellows was next in command. General
Thomas had a regiment of which John Bailey was Lieutenant-Colonel. General Heath also had a regiment. The
two regiments from Connecticut, of one thousand men
each, were commanded by Generals Spencer and Putnam.

But of Colonels, the list will include the following names :
John Stark, James Reed and Enoch Poor from New Hamp-
shire (Poor joined the army the day after the battle). The
Massachusetts Colonels were Asa Whitcomb,* James Frye,
Joseph Frye, Ebenezer Bridge, John Whitcomb, William

---

* We find the following incident of Colonel Asa Whitcomb in the New
England "Chronicle" for January 11th, 1776, copied from the New London
"Gazette" :

"Deacon Whitcomb of Lancaster, who was a member of the Assembly of
Massachusetts Bay till the present war commenced, had served in former
wars, and been in different engagements, served as a Colonel in the Continental army; but on account of his age was left out upon the new regulation.
His men highly resented it, and declared they would not list again after their
time was out. The Colonel told them he did not doubt there were sufficient
reasons for the regulation, and he was satisfied with it ; he then blamed them
for their conduct, and said he would enlist as a private. Colonel Brewer
heard of it, and offered to resign in favor of Colonel Whitcomb. The whole
coming to General Washington's ears he allowed of Colonel Brewer's resignation in Colonel Whitcomb's favor, appointed the former Barrack-Master
till he could further promote him, and acquainted the army with the whole
affair in general orders. Let antiquity produce a more striking instance of
true greatness of soul."

8

Prescott, John Glover, John Fellows, Ebenezer Learned, James Read, John Nixon, Theophilus Cotton, Moses Little, Ephraim Doolittle, Samuel Gerrish, Thomas Gardner, Richard Gridley, James Scammans, John Mansfield, Timothy Walker, Timothy Danielson, John Patterson, Jonathan Brewer, Benjamin R. Woodbridge, and David Brewer. Besides these, Massachusetts had several Colonels which were early employed more in a civil capacity, as members of Committee of Safety, etc., but afterwards figured in military affairs, such as Azor Orne, Joseph Palmer, and Benjamin Lincoln. There were three Colonels from Rhode Island, Thomas Church, Daniel Hitchcock and James Mitchell Varnum.

Here were thirty-four men, with the title of Colonel, connected directly or indirectly with the American army before the arrival of Washington, and there may have been one or two others with the same rank. It was altogether natural that these officers, the heads of regiments earliest in the field, showing a prompt devotion to the patriot cause, should, if they displayed even a fair military ability, be promoted as time passed on. For the war was to be long, and there would be ample time for real merit to be rewarded. If one were to ask certain men who have studiously read some of the modern histories, and neglected the old, what Colonel from all this list would be first singled out for immediate promotion, they would answer unhesitatingly that it would be Colonel William Prescott of course, that his great and heroic services at the battle of Bunker Hill entitled him to the first consideration of the military authorities. But how very, very different this happens to be from the historical facts. Let us study attentively this remarkable record.

Of the Colonels contemporary with him in this patriot army of 1775, John Nixon, Ebenezer Learned, John Fellows, John Glover, Joseph Palmer, John Patterson, John Stark, James Reed, Benjamin Lincoln, James M. Varnum, Enoch Poor, Azor Orne, John Whitcomb, Joseph Frye, Richard Gridley and Daniel Hitchcock, sixteen of them, became Brigadier-Generals or Major-Generals; some of them speedily, and some at later stages during the progress of the war.

The last named, Daniel Hitchcock, was only an acting Brigadier, but would doubtless soon have received a commission except for his untimely death in 1777. So eminent were his services at the battle of Princeton, where he commanded a brigade, that Washington, with his large and generous nature, led him before the army after the battle, and taking him by the hand, publicly thanked him in that presence.*

But the promotions out of this patriot army do not stop here. Men from lower grades of military rank also rose to these honorable places and distinctions. Lieutenant-Colonel Brickett, of Frye's regiment, and one of Prescott's under officers in that night expedition, June 16th, became Brigadier-General in the following year. John Greaton, a militia officer in Roxbury before the war, was afterwards made Brigadier-General. Rufus Putnam, Lieutenant-Colonel of David Brewer's regiment, rose to the rank of Colonel very speedily, and was made Brigadier-General before the war ended. Eleazer Brooks, only a Captain of militia before the war, also became Briga-

---

* In the life of General Nathaniel Greene, by George Washington Greene, his grandson, there is a reference to this Colonel Hitchcock connected with the event of his death in 1777. It may be found Vol. I. p. 312. The author says, "I have already had occasion to mention more than once the name of Daniel Hitchcock, who had accompanied Greene to Boston as Colonel of one of the three regiments which formed the Rhode Island contingent. From that time to this (Jan. 1777), he has continued with the army, performing during the last few weeks the duties of a Brigadier, winning honor wherever honor was to be won, much loved by his own men and respected by all."

dier-General. Samuel B. Webb, simply a Lieutenant of a
company among those Connecticut men by the fence, was
made soon after one of Putnam's Aids, and subsequently
Washington's Aid, with the title of General. Captain
Knowlton, commanding those Connecticut men in the battle, was soon chosen Major, then Lieutenant-Colonel, and
was as clearly on the upward road to honors as any man in
the army, when his course was cut short in 1776, by his
death at Harlem Heights. Of him it was said, " He would
have been an honor to any country." Lieutenant Thomas
Grosvenor (another Lieutenant of a company by that fence)
afterwards became Colonel. . Captains James Clark, John
Chester, George Reid and Henry Dearborn (the two last
named of Stark's regiment), all rose to the rank of Colonel.
Major John Brooks, another of Prescott's under officers in
that night march, was promoted to be Lieutenant-Colonel,
then Colonel, then Acting Adjutant-General at the battle
of Monmouth, and afterwards Governor of the Commonwealth of Massachusetts.

It will be seen by this rapid review that some of the
most marked cases of promotion above enumerated were
for services rendered at the battle of Bunker Hill, showing
that our fathers in 1775 were not oblivious to merit, but on
the other hand that they sought to foster and encourage it.

And Colonel William Prescott was never promoted. He
remained in the army until 1777, while these men around
him — his contemporaries in the spring and summer of
1775 — were rising up to take these higher places, but he
remained stationary, keeping the same military title which
he brought with him from Pepperell on that historic 19th
of April. What shall we say to these things ? In the eye
of our revolutionary fathers, was he the same man that is now
paraded before us in Bunker Hill orations, in some of the
Boston newspapers, and in many modern books and pamphlets ? Did the men of 1775 think of him as a soldier of

any special military ability? Is it not apparent, that from what they saw and knew of him at the battle of Bunker Hill, where he was for the first time in his life tested in his military capacity, they looked upon him as a man "weighed in the balances and found wanting." *   And we may have some further glimpses of him, before the volume closes, which will help us to the same conclusions. It is next to a certainty, if he had acquitted himself well in that action, he would have been speedily promoted. He was of good family and of good estate, holding a most honorable position in society, and it was as natural for him, other things being equal, to take these steps upward as for any man in that army. We cannot resist the conclusion that this silence and neglect on the part of the military authorities, in his case, was a verdict of military incapacity.

* We place here in a note an item of evidence, that may not impress others as it does the writer, but it certainly seems to show that there was no very great enthusiasm over Colonel Prescott in the days immediately following the battle. We ·copy from " American Archives," 4th Series, Vol. II. pp. 1119-20.

"MASSACHUSETTS PROVINCIAL CONGRESS.—The petition of officers belonging to Colonels Prescott, Frye and Bridges's Regiments, humbly sheweth,— "That whereas in the late Battle of *Charlestown* on the 17th of this instant, *June,* a number of things belonging to us fell into the enemy's hands, whereby we are deprived of some necessary clothing, arms, etc. : As the loss is considerable, we beg that (if it may be consistent with the honor and dignity of the Congress, and the good of the country), they have an allowance for the same as your Honors shall see fit ; and your petitioners as in duty bound, will ever pray.

"[Signed by William Prescott, who heads the list, and seventeen other officers of the three regiments.]

"June 27th, 1775."

Upon this the following action was taken :
                                    "WATERTOWN, June 29th, 1775.
" The Committee appointed to consider the within Petition beg leave to report that the petitioners have leave to withdraw their petition."

New Hampshire rewarded her men for their losses in this battle, though poorly able to do so in comparison with Massachusetts. We cannot but think if Colonel Prescott had just performed such great and heroic services as now claimed, this petition, with his name heading it, would not have been so coolly bowed out of the Massachusetts Assembly.

But leaving now the subject of military promotions, let us turn to a more general consideration.

Of all the military men gathered about Boston in that early summer of 1775 (Generals and Colonels), who was the man attracting chief attention, the most acknowledged leader, the most popular man among both citizens and soldiers? We answer unhesitatingly, General Israel Putnam. By all the historical lights shed over those times, there would seem to be room but for one answer to that question. We have already seen how popular he was about Boston in the year before, what a magic influence stood connected with his name and his presence. Bancroft has told us that when he came to Boston in August, 1774, he "was Warren's guest and every one's favorite." And Mr. Frothingham, referring to this same visit, in his "Life and Times of Joseph Warren" (p. 341), says, "Warren's guest, Colonel Putnam, remained in town several days. 'The old hero, Putnam,' Dr. Young writes, 'arrived in town on Monday, bringing with him one hundred and thirty sheep from the little parish of Brooklyn. He cannot get away, he is so much caressed both by the officers and the citizens.'"

The same universal favor and admiration attended him when he came in 1775 to join the army, and followed him all through those exciting days. The facts already brought to view in the previous narrative are conclusive enough in this direction. He is the man sent to represent the army when the Massachusetts prisoners are to be received back from the British. He is the general officer to lead the troops in Cambridge almost *en masse* around the peninsula of Charlestown and over the heights of Bunker Hill. He goes as commander of the force of Massachusetts and New Hampshire men, to fight the battle of Chelsea, in which they beat the British and burned their ship. He is the man of all others whom General Ward chooses to set

in his own front, at the point nearest and most exposed to
the enemy.   If General Putnam with his Connecticut regiment is at Inman's farm, a mile in advance of his own
headquarters, he, in his extreme timidity, can rest more securely than under any other disposition he can make.   In
all those weeks, between April 19th and June 17th, the
figure of old General Putnam in that camp at Cambridge
is the one which confronts the student of history more
frequently, and in sharper, bolder outlines than any other.
Colonel Samuel Swett, a Massachusetts man, in his essay
written in 1850, says, " No military despot ever was obeyed
with more implicit subjection than Putnam was, ... by
every one, officers and men, from their enthusiastic love
and admiration of him, and boundless confidence in him as
a great, experienced and fortunate hero and patriot."

It is easy to multiply these evidences of Putnam's popularity, as he figured in the army about Boston in the spring
and summer of 1775.   Mr. Frothingham helps us to illustrations, for he is always faithful in gathering the primary
facts on which judgments may be formed.   On page 165,
in a note, he gives us two brief extracts from the letter
which the Committee of Safety wrote to Putnam in 1776,
in which they tell him that his conduct, " while in Cambridge, in every respect, and more especially as a General,
. . . . we hold in the highest veneration, and ever shall."
And again, in the same letter, they speak of " the extraordinary services you have done to this town, which must
always be acknowledged with the highest gratitude, not
only by us, but by rising generations."

And he has preserved the letter which Captain Chester
wrote to Connecticut, two days after the battle, in which he
said, " Head-officers is what we stand greatly in need of;
we have no acting head here but Putnam; he acts nobly in
everything."

When the battle of Bunker Hill was fought, Silas Deane of Connecticut was at Philadelphia, a member of the Continental Congress. His letters ("Connecticut Historical Collections," Vol. II.) will show us what was passing in the minds of men in that memorable summer of 1775. The news of the battle reached Philadelphia on the morning of June 22d. It took nearly five days at that period to convey this exciting intelligence from Boston to Philadelphia. On that day he writes to his wife, "We this moment received advice of a battle at Bunker Hill, but the account is very confused." On the 9th of July he writes again, "New England, with all its foibles, must be the glory and defence of America, and the cry here is, Connecticut forever! so high has the universally applauded conduct of our Governor, and the brave intrepidity of old General Putnam and his troops, raised our colony in the estimation of the whole continent."

Then we have a letter written about this time to Mr. Deane from Samuel B. Webb in the camp at Cambridge, in which he says, "You'll find the Generals Washington and Lee are vastly fonder and think higher of Putnam than any man in the army; and he truly is the hero of the day. . . . . Better for us to lose four Spencers than half a Putnam."

Very soon Mr. Deane writes again to his wife, and speaks of "Putnam, on whom by every account the whole army has depended ever since the battle of Lexington." And again, July 20th, he says, "Putnam's merit rung through this continent, his fame still increases, and every day justifies the unanimous applause of the continent. Let it be remembered he had every vote of the Congress, and his health has been the second or third at almost all our tables in this city. But it seems he does not wear a large wig nor screw his countenance into a form that belies the sentiments of his generous soul."

Now, let it be remembered that this is not the language of a great oration an hundred years afterward. It is contemporary language, describing the passing emotions of men in regard to matters then transpiring. And it is very remarkable language, such as men of Mr. Deane's standing and character do not use except in connection with events very important and exciting.

But if we want any more evidence of Putnam's fame and popularity in 1775, take the following odd letter from Major-General Lee, introducing to Putnam an Episcopal minister. We find this letter in the diary of Dr. Belknap, as published in one of the volumes of the Massachusetts Historical Society (1858–1860, p. 83).

> "HOBGOBLIN HALL, Oct. 19th, 1775.
>
> "DEAR GENERAL: Mr. Page, the bearer of this, is a Mr. Page. He has a laudable ambition of seeing the great General Putnam. I therefore desire that you would array yourself in all your majesty and terrors for his reception. Your blue and gold must be mounted, your pistols stuck in your girdle ; and it would not be amiss if you should black one half of your face.
>
> "I am, dear General, with fear and trembling, your humble servant,   CHARLES LEE."

At the very time when this patriot army was operating about Boston in the summer of 1775, John Trumbull was writing his somewhat famous poem, " McFingal," in Four cantos. Drawing illustrations from passing events, and showing how easy it is for men, in certain circumstances, not to keep their promises, he says, —

> " So Gage, of late, agreed you know,
>   To let the Boston people go,
>   Yet when he saw, 'gainst troops that braved him,
>   They were the only guards that saved him,—
>   Kept off that Satan of a Putnam

From breaking in to maul and mutt'n him ;
He'd too much wit such league to observe,
And shut them in again to starve."

One who signs himself "A Friend to Truth," writing from
Watertown August 10th, 1775 (see "American Archives,"
4th Series, Vol. III. p. 84), in pointing out men from Connecticut who did meritorious service in the battle of Bunker
Hill, says, " In this list of heroes it is needless to expatiate
on the character and bravery of Major-General *Putnam*,
whose capacity to form and execute great designs is known
through *Europe.*"

Indeed, if we have rightly studied the history of those
days, it was out of this very popularity as before suggested
that the trouble has since arisen. Human nature was not
materially different then from what it is now. It was but
natural, taking mankind as they average, that among the
higher officers of that army there should be feelings of
jealousy that a General from another province should so
carry all before him, and rise in popularity to such a height
above them.* Envy and dislike were thus secretly scattered abroad, which, like the seeds under the mud of the
Nile, were destined long afterwards to spring up and bear
their evil fruit. When General Dearborn took up his pen,
forty-three years after the battle, and more than twenty-five
years after Putnam was in his grave, to revile the old hero,
" whose courage," Bancroft says, " was never questioned
during the war," he let us, without thinking of it, at once
into the secret motives that animated him. It was Putnam's " remarkable popularity " and " unaccountable popularity " that troubled him. He is also witness that this

---

* These envious feelings are easily traced in Heath's memoirs, published
in 1798, as also in General Ward's letter to John Adams, written Oct. 30th,
1775, in which he says, " Some have said hard things of the officers belonging
to this Colony and despised them."

popularity once existed as we have claimed ; but he proposes
in 1818 to explain it all away, and show that there was no
ground for it, and that people were deluded. Like "the
atrocious crime of being a young man," so Putnam's "atrocious crime " was, that he did not let some man from Massachusetts or New Hampshire have his "popularity." And
yet, as we have said in the opening part of this volume,
Putnam was not running round to look after his reputation.
He was not courting popularity. He was prodigiously
busy as a soldier and patriot, and he furnishes a noble illustration of that great saying of the Master, "Whosoever
shall seek to save his life shall lose it, and whosoever shall
lose his life shall preserve it." General Dearborn calls this
popularity of General Putnam "ephemeral," but he might
with much more propriety have called his own influence
to destroy it ephemeral, for it has already come to pass,
that his natural successors in this work of disparagement
no longer dare to make much use of anything which he
ever said or wrote.

But to return to the fact itself. We may consider that
Putnam's friends and enemies agree in saying that he was
the most *popular* military officer about Boston, from April
19th on to the arrival of Washington. No military movement of any great importance could take place in those
weeks, which would be likely to leave him out. So far
from this, no such movement, if an offensive one, would
naturally occur in which he would not be found in close
connection with it, if not at the head of it. All witnesses
agree that General Ward had no genius or disposition for
any bold adventures. His only "strength was to sit still."
General Pomeroy had a spirit kindred to that of Putnam,
but he chose rather to be an aider than an originator of
offensive measures. Colonel Prescott was also restless
under the long delays, but he was too inexperienced a man to

lead off in a daring military movement, though willing to play a part in it.   Besides, his military rank naturally precluded him from leadership in such enterprises.   He was simply Colonel of a regiment, waiting to receive orders from his superiors.   There is no doubt, we think, that General Putnam and he had talked over this Bunker Hill plan, and that Prescott was thoroughly sympathetic with him in it. Nor do we doubt that Putnam had asked and obtained leave of General Ward, that Prescott should be the man to go with that night detachment to fortify Bunker Hill, and so take the first steps which would be likely to bring on an engagement.   But there was a larger and stronger man than Prescott behind that night movement.   We shall hereafter have occasion to notice more at length the fact, that Prescott's record as a military hero begins and ends here, and that record is very largely a production of modern times.   It will be difficult to find his name in any prominent connection with the French War, or with his remaining years of service in the revolutionary army.

Take any general history covering this period, like Bancroft's, or Irving's "Life of Washington," and try this experiment.   Following (as both these writers have) Mr. Frothingham as authority in relation to this battle, you will find a few pages relating to the 17th of June, 1775, that bristle with Colonel Prescott's name and heroic acts.   But you have heard little of him before, and you will hear just as little afterwards.

That we may not seem to be dealing in assertions, we have culled from Bancroft's ten volumes every item we can discover relating to Colonel Prescott, aside from this battle.   The three first items speak of him before, and the three last after, the battle.

Vol. VI. p. 447.— "With one voice they (the people of Pepperell) named Captain William Prescott to be the chief of their

Committee of Correspondence, and no braver heart beat in Middlesex than his."

Vol. VII. p. 99.— "In the coming storm they clustered round
William Prescott of Pepperell, who stood firm as Monadnock, that
rose in sight of his homestead."

Vol. VII. p. 307.— "That morning (April 19th) William Prescott mustered his regiment, and though Pepperell was so remote
that he could not be in season for the pursuit, he hastened down
with five companies of guards."

These are good words and full of promise. The last
chapter of the seventh volume is devoted to Bunker Hill.

In the eighth volume nothing whatever is said of Prescott
except in the opening sentences, referring back to Bunker
Hill.

In the ninth volume there are three items.

Vol. IX. p. 82.— "Two regiments, one of which was Prescott's,
were all that could be spared to garrison Governor's Island."

Vol. IX. p. 109.— "The dilatoriness of his antagonist [Lord
Howe] left him [Washington] leisure to withdraw the garrison
from Governor's Island, where Prescott ran almost as great risk of
captivity as at Bunker Hill."

Vol. IX. p. 175.— "Washington, who had foreseen this attempt
to gain his rear, seasonably occupied the causeway and bridge
which led from Frog's Neck by Hand's riflemen, a New York
regmient, the regiment of Prescott of Pepperell, and an artillery
company."

The reader may think there was no particular reason for
mentioning him by name in either of these three cases,
except that the historian had a hero left on his hands, whom
he was bound to nurse upon the slightest opportunity.

It is not claimed, so far as we are aware, by any writer,
that Thomas, or Spencer, or Heath, or Greene, originated
this Bunker Hill movement. They were all able officers,
and were doing their duty faithfully over at Roxbury and

Dorchester. By their position they were not drawn into this action. Nor is it claimed that it originated with any of the Colonels. Colonel Stark over at Medford was heroic and daring enough to have conceived it, but no one claims this honor for him, for he was not in such relations to Cambridge as to have been father of the scheme, though he bore a very important part in giving the movement the measure of success it achieved. We know that neither Ward nor Warren contrived the plan. It must naturally lie between Pomeroy and Putnam. And as General Pomeroy did not take command of the expedition, but insisted upon serving as a volunteer, it is made sufficiently plain that he was not the foremost man in the case, though he heartily approved it, and gave it all the assistance in his power. If we had no later historical evidences whatever, we should be driven to the conclusion that the man who had most to do in unlocking those Bunker Hill thunders was General Putnam.

Here were eight Generals connected with this army, of whom Pomeroy, Thomas, Spencer and Putnam had all seen long service in the former wars, most of them as Colonels. They were men of age and experience, and knew how to set an army in battle array. The idea that these men should all be passed by, and that the general oversight and control of an enterprise so vastly important should be entrusted to any one of the Colonels about Cambridge, would be to the average soldier mind of that period a subject for derisive laughter. If it had been only some slight affair, some small military errand, not likely to involve any material consequences, then a Colonel or a Major or a Captain, with a detachment of men, might have been sent to attend to it, and to finish it. But this was a movement of such exceeding importance that General Ward would never give his assent to it till he was pushed forward by the Committee of

Safety. Even General Warren, young and heroic as he was, and full of the patriotic fire, stood trembling in the presence of such an enterprise, and never gave his public approval.

And can we be made to believe that the chief directors of affairs in 1775, passing by these Generals of large experience, gave the supreme oversight and command in that momentous expedition into the hands of a Colonel who never, so far as we can discover, had seen a field battle in his life, who probably never saw a man killed in action till that day? Is this reasonable? Is it according to the laws of common prudence and common sense? Does any one know of any other important piece of military history which reads after this fashion?

The evidence, at the outset, is well nigh irresistible that Colonel Prescott was a subordinate officer in this enterprise. Instead of leaping to the conclusion that he was chief, the historical student ought to be pushed by the strongest documentary evidence before he should ever accept a theory so utterly improbable.

And in reference to this question of command, has there not been a needless cloud of mystery thrown about a very simple matter? Would it not be just as easy to raise doubts about Colonel Prescott's command, as about that of Putnam's? Mr. Frothingham tells us (p. 122) that Prescott "had orders in writing from General Ward, to proceed that evening to Bunker Hill, and build fortifications to be planned by Colonel Richard Gridley, the chief engineer, and defend them until he should be relieved." No one need have the slightest objection to that order. It is no broader or stronger than it ought to be to cover the action of any subordinate officer sent on such an errand. He is to hold the command till "he should be relieved." That is about the way such military orders usually run. It con-

templates the *possibility*, at least, that he will be relieved of
that command, and even the *probability*.   But does any man
of this living generation know certainly that those orders
were written ?   Colonel Prescott, in his letter to John
Adams, says, "I received orders," but he does not say,
"written orders."   It was a night expedition, and a very
secret one.   It is hardly probable that they would wish to
strike a light after passing Charlestown Neck, to read those
orders, and if not, they might as well have been verbal as
written.   As we understand it, the claim that they were
written is gratuitous.*

But it is an old adage that "actions speak louder than
words," and if we study the facts of the case, it is as plain
that Putnam was acting under Ward's orders as that Prescott was.   What does it mean that Putnam could not have
his own regiment to go with him ?   Does not that imply
that Ward and Putnam were in conference on this subject,
and that Putnam was acting under Ward's direction ?   What
does it mean that he goes back to Ward's headquarters
early next morning, and again during the forenoon ?   By
these very circumstances and a great many others of like
character, it is just as apparent that Putnam is a man
clothed with authority from headquarters as that Prescott

---

* "General Ward was the general-in-chief of 'the army of Massachusetts,'
and the immediate commander of Colonel Prescott.   His orderly book, therefore, would have contained the order which he issued to the latter, had he
really issued any ; but no such order appears there, and it is a fair inference,
therefore, that none was issued in writing." — Mr. Dawson, in "Historical
Magazine," June, 1868, p. 330.

"On the contrary, no such orders were really issued, nor any other, except
those reckless verbal directions to the Colonels of the fatigue parties." — Ibid,
p. 323.

In Sumner's "History of East Boston," p. 371, is a note in reference to the
battle of Chelsea, in which the following statement is made :

"There is no written order to this effect, which gives reason to believe that
at, and previous to, the battle of Bunker Hill, the 'orders' were given ver-
bally and not in writing."

is. No written authority from Ward can be produced in either case. And when you add to all the little outstanding circumstances, the broad and open fact that Putnam was a Brigadier-General, and was pointed out in the sight of all men as the most natural military leader in those camps, a man toward whom all eyes turned to head such expeditions, we should say that the claim of Colonel William Prescott to the supreme command the next day, as set over against Putnam's, is as shadowy as the stuff that dreams are made of. We have not the slightest idea that Ward ever thought of him for one moment as the man to take the supreme command in that battle.

9

CHAPTER VII.

PREPARATIONS FOR THE BATTLE.

Action of Committee of Safety.— Council of War.— Relations of Putnam and Prescott to the projected Movement.— Night Detachment.— Night Council.— Forces detailed to take Part in the Battle the next Day.— From Connecticut.— From New Hampshire.— From Massachusetts.

THE last two chapters, though not designed to follow the history of affairs about Boston day by day, have so brought the general condition of things to light, that it is hardly necessary to go back and trace the succession of events with more particularity, until we reach the few days immediately preceding the battle.

It was on the 15th of June that the Massachusetts Committee of Safety, having become satisfied that the British were planning a movement, either to take possession of Charlestown or Dorchester Heights, recommended that decisive action should be taken.

The step they advised was so important that we give the record of their action, in full, as follows :

" Whereas, it appears of importance to the safety of this colony that possession of the hill called *Bunker's Hill* in *Charlestown* be securely kept and defended, and also some one hill or hills on *Dorchester Neck* be likewise secured : therefore

" Resolved, unanimously, that it be recommended to the *council of war*, that the above mentioned Bunker Hill be maintained by sufficient force being posted there ; and as the particular situation of *Dorchester Neck* is unknown to this Committee, they desire that the council of war take and pursue such steps re-

specting the same as to them shall appear to be for the security
of this colony.

"Ordered, That Colonel *Benjamin White* and Colonel *Joseph
Palmer* be a committee to join with a committee from the council of war, to proceed to *Roxbury* camp, there to consult with the
general officers on matters of importance, and to communicate
to them a resolve this day passed in this committee respecting
Bunker Hill, Charlestown and *Dorchester Neck.*"

What was this Committee of Safety? and who constituted
it? It was first appointed in October, 1774, by the Massachusetts Provincial Assembly, and was then to consist of nine
members, *three* from Boston (which seems to mean Boston
and immediate vicinity), and *six* from the country towns.
The nine first members were John Hancock, Joseph Warren and Benjamin Church, as representing Boston, Benjamin White, Joseph Palmer, Morton Quincy, Richard Devens, Abraham Watson and Colonel Azor Orne, as representing the country towns. But before June 17th, 1775,
the committee had been at different times enlarged, and
the number was a variable one. At a meeting of the committee April 17th, 1775, there were present John Hancock,
J. Pigeon, Colonel Gardner, Colonel Heath, Colonel Joseph
Palmer, Benjamin White, Mr. Watson, Mr. Devens and
Colonel Orne — nine members; but new names have come
in, and Warren and Church are not present, though still
members. At some of the meetings of the committee before the time of the battle, a still larger number, ten or
eleven, were present.

This action of the committee was a recommendation to
the council of war. The committee did not intend to override this council, but to urge this matter upon their prompt
attention. The council of war speedily met to consider
this subject. Perhaps some one knows all the persons who
took part in that council of war, June 16th. We do not

claim such knowledge, but we conclude it was composed
only of general officers. Four persons are quite distinctly
seen to have been present, viz., Ward, Warren, Putnam and
Pomeroy. In this immediate connection Mr. Frothingham
uses the name of Prescott. He says, "General Putnam,
Colonel Prescott, and other veteran officers were strongly in
favor of it," *i. e.*, the proposed movement to take possession
of Bunker Hill. Is there any evidence of Colonel Prescott's
presence in that council? A few weeks later we have
records of these councils of war, and they are composed
only of the general officers.

As we understand the matter, there is no fixed rule about
a council of war. If a General is sent on an expedition
away from the main body of the army, as the time draws
near for action, he will naturally call his Colonels, or even
officers of lower grade, into council. But in the main army
a council of war is not likely to embrace any but the general officers. We can see with tolerable distinctness in that
council of June 16th, the four men above mentioned,— the
two former holding back, and the two latter urging matters
forward. There were probably other Generals there, from
the right wing of the army at Roxbury,— Thomas, or Spencer, or Heath, and perhaps all three of them. If Colonel
Prescott was present, which we do not believe, he was there
doubtless by special invitation, as one upon whom Putnam
had already fixed his thoughts to bear an important part in
the expedition. It is very certain that the Colonels generally were not in that council, and the putting of Prescott
there we take it to be of the imagination, and not by any
historical authority.

In the Committee of Safety this general measure had
been urged *unanimously.* In the *fac simile* transcript of
a portion of that document, which may be found in Mr.
Frothingham's "Siege of Boston" (facing p. 116), in Ben-

jamin White's handwriting, the word "unanimously" is
above the line, showing that the writer went back to put it
in, as a word that ought not to be omitted.   But the council of war was not unanimous, though the major vote was
for action, and preparations were promptly made to put the
decision of the council into execution.   The meeting of the
Committee of Safety as before stated, was on Thursday, the
15th, and by Friday night, the 16th, the council of war had
uttered its voice.

This council decided in favor of a plan, which in its general features was undoubtedly Putnam's, a plan which he
had revolved in his mind, and talked about for days and
weeks before.   His *aggressive* policy had at last prevailed
over Ward's *do nothing* policy.*

The way in which Prescott's name has been in these
modern times adroitly substituted for that of Putnam, may
be conceived to be the following : This was the first great
offensive movement of the war, and that night expedition
on the 16th of June, in which Prescott had an important
part, was in itself a romantic affair, and in after times
strongly touched the imaginations of the people.   Prescott's
name therefore became linked indissolubly with that first
bold act of aggression, and in later times it was comparatively easy to shift his name along to the next day, and to
pass him forward from a subordinate to a chief.   But in
reality, what Prescott did is no more than is likely to be
done, in some form or other, in every offensive movement
in any army.   It usually happens that some leading steps
are taken, some preliminary work is done, and almost
invariably by a subordinate officer.   Before the battle of
Waterloo, because Napoleon sends Marshal Ney with

* "If General Putnam is to be believed, *he first proposed* the taking possession of Bunker Hill, and was detached for the purpose of fortifying it ; and
Colonel Prescott was placed under his orders. . . . . . It was for a *second post
of danger* that the gallant Prescott was aspiring." — Hon. John Lowell, 1818.

40,000 men to hold a pass, and if possible prevent the junction of Blucher's army with the allied forces, does any reader ever become confused, and doubt who was commander-in-chief on the French side in that battle? If one were to go over all the great battles of the world, he would find as a common and almost universal fact, that the movement of an army on the offensive, toward a battle, shows itself first in local and subordinate movements of the under officers. And this was the movement of Colonel Prescott. Had the battle of Bunker Hill been the *last* instead of the *first* of the revolutionary period, what Prescott did would never have been set in such a conspicuous light. But it was something new and strange. That prayer on Cambridge Common, that silent march beneath the stars, that midnight toil close to the ships of the enemy, when men spoke one to another in hushed voices,— all this played upon the thoughts and imaginations of men in a fresh and original way. But Prescott was simply an under officer sent that night to do a preliminary work.

That this was his place and no other, that he had no special military reputation, either before that battle or after, evidences already adduced, and subsequent events, sufficiently show.

As we draw near this battle, it is proper to say that we do not undertake to give a full history and description of all its minute parts and belongings. That has been often done, and it is not necessary that we should burden ourselves specially with this duty. We are writing the Life of General Putnam, and our purpose is to trace his footsteps as carefully as we can through these exciting scenes ; and in doing so the outlines of the contest itself will come into view with sufficient clearness. In reference to what may be called the primary facts of the battle, we give full honor to Mr. Frothingham's celebrated work, the " Siege of Boston." We still regard that as the most complete book we have, as to the details of the battle, the forces employed on both sides, and the various movements and fortunes of the day. But we are obliged to differ very widely from him in the interpretation of the facts, and in the conclusions drawn.

In reference to the number of men that went from Cambridge on the night of June 16th, it will be noticed that different writers are quite at variance. Colonel John Trumbull says 1,200 or 1,500, Stark says 1,500, Chester says 2,000, and others still 800, while some rate the number as high as 2,500. Prescott himself says 1,000, and Daniel Putnam says 1,000. The last named gives the following very natural reason why this was the number. He says, " It was finally agreed that 2,000 men should be employed in the undertaking. . . . . The reason why the whole number contemplated for the expedition was not all ordered at once, General Putnam stated to be this. It was found that intrenching tools could not be had for more than about 1,000 men, and he agreed to go on with that number over night, and return in the morning for refreshments and a reinforcement or relief for those who were expected to toil all the night." In the unpublished writings of Colonel John Trumbull,* the painter, now in the hands of Professor Benjamin Silliman of New Haven (to which we shall have occasion to refer by-and-by), we find the best statement of this night movement that we have anywhere seen. This body of men, according to him, was " commanded by General Putnam and Colonel Prescott." That we conceive to be the just and exact truth, putting the whole matter into its proper historical and military shape. The relations of those two men are precisely the same in a military point of view as though it had been General Pomeroy, or General Thomas and Colonel Prescott. In Chapter V. we have shown, we trust, with suf-

* Appendix D.

ficient clearness, that State lines had nothing whatever to do with such matters. It might be Heath, or Spencer, or Thomas along with Prescott in that night movement, and it would have been all just the same.

In each case one would have been a Brigadier-General and one a Colonel, and the latter would of course have had a subordinate command to the other. If Putnam was in command that night or the next day, who gave him the right to command? is a question that has been many times asked with an air of triumph, with a tone of assurance, as if it were the end of all strife. There is a haughty assumption in the very asking of the question. It is based upon that pretentious claim which we have fully discussed in Chapter V. We can with equal propriety ask, If Colonel Prescott was in command even that night, to say nothing of next day, who gave him the right to command? Is there one particle of evidence bringing Prescott into direct personal relations to General Ward touching this movement, which does not exist still more clearly in the case of Putnam? If we will once go back of modern asseveration and reiteration and the talk about "written orders,"* when none can be shown, nor substantial proof given that any ever existed,— if we can once clear our ears of the perpetual *ding-dong* of modern days, we shall find, on a calm survey, far more evidence that Putnam came out of that place of majesty and power, Artemas Ward's headquarters, to enter upon that expedition, than that Prescott did.†

* Let it be understood, however, that we have no objection to "written orders," if any can be produced, or if evidence can be shown that such orders in writing ever existed. They would cover only a subordinate command. No one will dare pretend that Prescott ever received "written orders" authorizing him, a Colonel, to take supreme command the next day, against general officers who might be upon that field.

† We are not sure but the facts concerning Colonel Prescott, in connection with this battle, might be summed up in the following proposition, viz., That Prescott had no orders written or verbal, directly from Ward; that this expe-

If Warren had chosen to take the command next day, when it was offered to him, would he have been asked who gave him the right to command ?   Yet he would not technically have been nearly so well entitled to that command as Putnam, for he had not been commissioned.   But would he have been obliged to produce from his pocket a written order to show Prescott or any body else that Ward had sent him there, before he could have assumed command ?   Warren, when he came to that field, did not probably come from Ward's headquarters.   General Ward did not even know of his going, so far as appears.   He had not expected to go. And yet he might have commanded, and all parties would have acquiesced.

If General Putnam had been asked that night or the next day, by what right he commanded, and in whose name, setting aside technics, he *might* have answered with less impiety and with far more propriety than did a son of Connecticut, Ethan Allen, six weeks before, at Ticonderoga, " In the name of the Great Jehovah and the Continental Congress," for the Lord had evidently given him the spirit and power to command, as he gave to Joshua of old ; and as for the Continental Congress, though Putnam knew it not, it was hastening to clothe him with ample authority, and forty-eight hours later he was one of the four Major-Generals of the Continental army.

These two men, Putnam and Prescott, are to be seen on that night of June 16th, under the sheltering darkness, going on that momentous errand to Bunker Hill.

dition being known and publicly recognized as of Putnam's devising, Ward gave into his hands the management of it on the field, and Prescott was the Colonel that Putnam chose as his principal subordinate officer, whose movements he directed.   We do not recall any sure and well-established historical fact that is inconsistent with this theory, and it is certainly far more defensible than the statement that Prescott's movements were directed by the *written* orders of Ward.

Arrived at that hill, there was a long parley. General Pomeroy was probably there, Colonel Gridley was there, Colonel Bridge was there, and Putnam and Prescott were there. These, at least, can be distinguished through the shadows. We notice that Mr. Frothingham, in his "Siege of Boston" (p. 123), says, "The order was explicit as to Bunker Hill, and yet a position nearer Boston, now known as Breed's Hill, seemed better adapted to the objects of the expedition, and better suited the daring spirit of the officers." But Colonel Prescott, in his letter to John Adams, says it was Breed's Hill to which he was sent. "On the 16th of June I received orders to march to Breed's Hill in Charlestown." We have no disposition whatever to rely unduly upon this authority, for we shall have occasion hereafter to comment freely upon this letter, but let it be borne in mind that Prescott says "Breed's Hill." *   Then as to that "daring spirit of the officers." We think we discover in these words an insinuation against General Putnam, as if he were a rash man and would disobey orders.

There is no one thing about this battle concerning which there has been more loose and rambling speculation than this night council on the Charlestown heights. No man can unveil the secrets of that conference. Who it was that first proposed to build the redoubt on Breed's Hill cannot be told. There was evidently a difference of opinion, causing quite a long delay, when time was very precious. The question was not decided so that the men could begin their work

---

* We notice that Mr. Frothingham tries to help Colonel Prescott out, in his saying "Breed's Hill," by the suggestion that there was no place in Charlestown then called Breed's Hill, and that he inadvertently used the name given after the battle. But this letter of Colonel Prescott's was not written till the 25th of August following, and we should conclude by that time that the supposed commander-in-chief would have learned the difference between Breed's Hill and Bunker Hill, for there certainly was a place called Bunker Hill long before that battle. We prefer that Colonel Prescott should be left to tell his own story.

until nearly twelve o'clock. We have the impression that military engineers in our own day, looking over the ground, are generally agreed that Breed's Hill was the best place for the main redoubt. Many writers have sagaciously shown the utter folly of building such works anywhere upon that peninsula, because the British could so easily bring their ships of war up the Charles and Mystic rivers, and shell them out or cut them off, without losing a man. That kind of wisdom comes altogether too late for practical use. We set the actual results over against these theories and possibilities and probabilities, and can reasonably ask if somebody else had not thought of all those things before. A point so easy to be thought of by a modern man, had probably received the attention of the man who planned this expedition. Putnam had fought alongside of Englishmen for ten years, and he knew well enough that English pluck would say, " Those rustics have thrown down the gauntlet, and for us not to take it up promptly and boldly, but to fight them only with our ships at a safe distance, would be a kind of sneaking and cowardly way of doing the business. We will teach them a lesson on the spot."

But as to the position of those earthworks, it seems as rational a supposition as any that can be made, that Colonel Gridley's judgment was followed. He was the engineer, and deference would naturally be paid to his opinion. Whether Putnam coincided with that opinion can never be accurately told. In reference to this point, certain writers are in the most curious antagonism with themselves. For the purpose of showing Putnam a rash, headlong man, full of bluster and noise, they make him in that night-work preparatory to the battle override everybody else, and have his own way, in spite of all opposition. He breaks through orders from headquarters and majorities on the spot. But the next day he has no proper command at all, and is only a kind of volunteer assistant of Colonel Prescott. It would have been well for any such writer to have followed the wise precaution of John Gilpin, and

> " . . . . hung a bottle on each side
> To make his balance true."

And there is still another thing which seems to have been strangely overlooked or perverted. It may be that Putnam thought it best, on the whole, that the chief earthworks should be at Breed's Hill, though we do not know that he thought so. But one thing we do know, that he wanted to fortify Bunker Hill also. We *know* this of him, and we do not know it of any other one who took part in that night council.

If Mr. Frothingham is sure that the order said Bunker Hill, we are equally sure that Putnam wanted to fortify that hill, and so obey orders. The facts of the next day seem to show conclusively that he could not rest until intrenchments were begun on Bunker Hill. Dr. George E. Ellis, in his "History of the Battle," etc., published in 1875, confirms this view of Putnam's wishes and plans, in language which will show at once that he is not a friend to him. The passage may be found on p. 49. "So completely was he [Putnam] identified with the consuming zeal for fortifying the higher hill in the rear [Bunker Hill], that the traditionary rehearsals from the life of some survivors represented him as on horseback, buried under and surrounded by heaps of intrenching tools, enough for a cart load." By the testimony of one of his most vigorous opposers, therefore, Putnam wanted to fortify Bunker Hill, and Mr. Frothingham says that was the hill they were ordered to fortify.

And if Putnam had had his own Connecticut regiment on the ground that night or early in the morning, composed

of men who would obey military orders without being constantly watched, that second line of defense would have
been completely finished long before the British attack at
3 o'clock the next afternoon.   And instead of seeing a rash
and headlong man in all this, we see only a man who, though
bold in action, was careful and judicious ; and if he had
had the cordial co-operation of General Ward and the
Massachusetts regiments, he would completely have saved
the day (supposing that the British should have pursued
the same essential mode of attack they did).   From the
actual result secured, as the case was, we have no reasonable doubt, if Putnam could have had the whole of his own
regiment, with Chester's company and the two regiments
from New Hampshire, and had them in the morning, he
would have carried that battle to a perfectly triumphant
conclusion.   He would then have had almost exactly 2,000
men, and they would have been all he needed.

But to return to this night council.   Mr. Frothingham
says (p. 123), that " The veteran Colonel Gridley and two
Generals, one of whom was General Putnam, took part in
it."   Perhaps no one absolutely knows who that other General was, but there is no real doubt it was General Pomeroy.

After the parley was ended, and the men were at work,
it being now near midnight, Mr. Frothingham says, " General Putnam . . . . returned to Cambridge."   It is implied,
of course, in this sentence, that Putnam returned to Cambridge at midnight, and he helps the reader to have the
passing thought that other men are awake and hard at
work, but he has gone to take his rest.   Mr. Frothingham
gives no sufficient authority for this, and has he any?   It
is in direct contradiction to Daniel Putnam's circumstantial
account of what was passing in those exciting hours.   Anxious about his father, Daniel Putnam tells us that early on
the morning of the 17th, he hastened to Putnam's regiment

and asked Major Durkee (the same man that escorted Mr. Jared Ingersoll into Wethersfield) where his father was. He pointed with his sword to Charlestown, and confirmed the gesture with words. Then he ran to Putnam's head-quarters and found the Adjutant of the regiment, and he answered that his father "had been there but for a moment, and had returned to Charlestown as soon as the firing began." Then he went to what we now call Old Cam-bridge to General Ward's headquarters. General Ward was out, but he found his secretary, Joseph Ward. His answer was, "Your father was here before dawn of day this morning, but has gone back to Charlestown." By this explicit and most circumstantial testimony we conclude that Putnam remained at Charlestown till early dawn, near the time that the British ships in the harbor made their first discovery of the redoubt. Then he went back to Cambridge for the reinforcements and the refreshments ; but the firing from the ships hastened his return, and he only left directions there for that *to be done*, which he was intending personally to superintend and *see done*.

In the enumeration of the officers and soldiers of the American army, who were detailed to take part in the eventful struggle of the 17th of June, we will begin with Connecticut, whose record in this respect is very plain and simple. Putnam was sorely disappointed that he could not move his own regiment to the scene of action. We are not aware that any writer ever doubted that he wished those men to be there, longed for their presence, as men whom he knew would obey his orders. The simple fact that this regiment was only represented by two companies, and these obtained after earnest solicitation, is one of the most vital and satisfactory proofs that Putnam was acting under General Ward's orders that day, and that there was not "an army of Connecticut" separate and distinct from "an

army of Massachusetts," but that both of them were only
parts of one " American army," in which General Ward was
acknowledged and treated as commander-in-chief.

Two hundred men from the Connecticut forces went on
to the ground with Prescott's detachment that night. We
need not suppose that two companies were taken entire,
though in the constitution of a Connecticut regiment, two
would make two hundred men. But the detachment for
that night's service was made up by drafts from four companies of Putnam's regiment, and the men were placed under
the subordinate command of the brave Captain Knowlton.
Besides Putnam's full regiment, there were two other companies of Connecticut troops at Cambridge, which were
called *independent.* And yet they were not what we now
should understand by an " independent company." They
were simply detached and away from their own regiments.
Captain Chester's company of one hundred men belonged
to General Spencer's regiment over at Roxbury. Captain
Coit's company belonged to Colonel Parsons' regiment (the
sixth Connecticut), which (except this company) was at New
London, Connecticut. In making up this detachment, a
part of Chester's company was certainly taken. We have
not been able fully to satisfy ourselves whether a draft was
made from Coit's company for that night detachment, or
whether his company went on the next day, just before
the close of the battle. It is evident that Coit's company,
in whole or part, participated in the battle, and we believe,
from all we can discover, that a draft was made from it
for the original two hundred. There is a kind of by-play
between the numbers one hundred and twenty and two
hundred for the Connecticut troops often met with in different accounts of the battle. This fact is probably to be
explained as follows : Lieutenant (afterwards Colonel)
Thomas Grosvenor, in his letter to Daniel Putnam, in 1818,

says, " A detachment of four Lieutenants (of which I was
one) and one hundred and twenty men, selected the previous day from General Putnam's regiment," etc.   We know
these four Lieutenants, and can easily fix the four compa-
panies.   Thirty men were probably taken from each company, for Mr. Grosvenor speaks of his own immediate command as consisting of "thirty men and one subaltern."
From Putnam's regiment proper, therefore, one hundred
and twenty men were taken, and the drafts from Chester's
and Coit's companies probably made up the two hundred.
Colonel Prescott says two hundred, and Daniel Putnam
says two hundred, and we rest quite securely upon those
figures.

The next day, just as the battle was beginning, General
Putnam sent a hasty summons by his son, Captain Israel
Putnam, for the rest of Chester's company to come (and
some include Coit's company in this call) ; but whoever
went in answer to that call could only reach the field near
the close of the battle.   Captain Chester tells us distinctly
that, making all haste, he was able to reach the front only
a few moments before the battle was ended.

This Chester's company, it will be remembered, was the
one that did escort duty when Putnam and Warren went to
exchange those prisoners.   It was a company fit for even
British disciplinarians to see.   Hollister in his history
(Vol. II. p. 180), after enumerating some of the notable persons and military bodies from Connecticut, says, " Chester's company was by far the most accomplished body of
men in the whole American army."

Adding these to those who went the night before, we conclude that Connecticut may have had two hundred and seventy-five or three hundred men in the battle; only it must
be remembered, as already suggested, that whatever the
number of the reinforcement, the men connected with it

were in the battle but a few moments. Through the two
first repulses Connecticut had but two hundred men there.

Fortunately we have the means of tracing the New
Hampshire men almost as closely as the Connecticut.
We say, *fortunately*, for this point has been somewhat in
dispute. The recently published seventh volume of the
"New Hampshire Provincial Papers," gives us data whereby
the case can be narrowed down very closely to the actual
facts. We shall see in the sequel what many of the New
Hampshire men have for years claimed, that the battle of
Bunker Hill was very largely fought by her men. Let us
attend carefully to the records gathered from the volume
mentioned.

On the 14th of June, 1775, only three days before the
battle, we have an exact return of Colonel James Reed's
New Hampshire regiment. There were ten companies,
and the regiment was reported by Stephen Peabody, Adjutant, under two heads, "effective men for duty," and "sick,
absent, unfit and on command." Under the first head are
returned four hundred and ninety men. Under the second
head the number is one hundred and forty-nine, making the
whole regiment six hundred and thirty-seven. From returns
after the battle, we find that of these ten companies, Captain John Marcy's (which in the above enumeration has
forty-eight "effective men") was not in the battle, and was
probably left to guard the camp. Taking these out, we
conclude that Colonel Reed led four hundred and forty-two
men to Bunker Hill. We do not find any such exact enumeration of Colonel Stark's regiment; but he too led nine
companies to battle, leaving one, probably, to guard the
camp, and as his regiment was the older, and his name was
immensely popular, it was doubtless not less in number than
Reed's. Even as early as May 18th, Stark had five hundred and eighty-four under his command. We judge it

10

safe to say that Stark and Reed brought nine hundred men
to Bunker Hill.

By Colonel Stark's letter, written after the battle (June
19th), it appears that he first sent forward two hundred
men under Lieutenant-Colonel Wyman. "About 2 o'clock
in the afternoon express orders came for the whole of my
regiment." So says Colonel Stark, and he obeyed that
order, only, as we suppose, he left one company to guard
the camp. He led nine companies into the battle. We
know this by the following documentary evidence. In this
seventh volume, beginning at page 586, and onward for several pages, we have a list of the New Hampshire men in
this battle, who were afterwards reimbursed for their losses
on that day.* In this enumeration *nine* companies are
brought to light in each regiment, and it is not likely that
there should be just one company in each regiment that
lost nothing. We regard this important document as
settling the question, and showing conclusively enough that
Colonels Stark and Reed each led nine companies of their
respective regiments to the battle. In some of these companies the losses of property for which the men were paid
were few. In one of Stark's only two men were remunerated, in another only seven; but generally the number was
much larger. The whole number remunerated in the two
regiments was four hundred and fifty-two; and this would

* The day was very hot, and before these troops went into battle they seem
to have deposited some of their luggage on the ground back of them, the
northerly slope of Bunker Hill. If everybody on that field had done his duty
as well as they, this luggage would have been taken again, each man taking
his own, as they went off. But when that break came at the redoubt, it
came suddenly, and amid the dust and smoke that enveloped the scene,
these New Hampshire men that were farthest away did not know what had
happened till some few minutes afterwards, when they found that the British
had broken through the lines, and they were flanked. So they had to beat a
hasty retreat. Hence these losses.

confirm, in a general way, the conclusion already reached, that New Hampshire had as many as nine hundred men at Bunker Hill under Stark and Reed. (These are the " party of Hampshire," that Prescott casually mentions as a quite unimportant matter in his letter to John Adams.)

But besides these, New Hampshire had other men in the battle. Captain Dow's company in Prescott's own regiment were from Hollis, New Hampshire, and twenty-eight men of this company were also reimbursed for losses by the New Hampshire generosity, notwithstanding they were enrolled and serving in a Massachusetts regiment. By the best judgment we can form, we set Captain Dow's company in Prescott's regiment at fifty men. But Prescott had New Hampshire men (scattering cases) in his other companies. As he lived at Pepperell, on the borders of New Hampshire, men from over the line came and joined the companies enlisting for his regiment. We have tried faithfully to find the part which New Hampshire played in this battle, and after sifting the evidence carefully, we are satisfied that she had not less than nine hundred and sixty men on that field. Some would place the number higher. What is of vastly greater importance, they were men who knew how to find their way to the front, and did not run away. They fought it out to the last moment.

In our further references to the New Hampshire men, we shall not include Captain Dow's company, as that was in a Massachusetts regiment, and will have its place and its reckoning there. Only we will not forget the fact that about sixty (it may be more) of Prescott's men were from New Hampshire. But we call the others nine hundred, which is probably a close approximation to the real truth, and the balance may be one way or the other.

Besides these, that fragment of a regiment (Sargeant's, with only four companies in the Massachusetts service, but recruited in New Hampshire, and which had been under General Putnam's command at the Inman farm) begged to be allowed to go into the battle, but General Ward would not give his consent. The Committee of Safety a few days before had advised the Massachusetts Congress that this regiment was not likely to be full, and that it be disbanded. That work had not yet been done.* Herein may be found some source of confusion among New Hampshire writers. Stark had thirteen companies at Medford;† and this may have occasioned the supposition, sometimes made, that these New Hampshire companies of Sargeant's had gone over to the Medford camp. But they were still at Cambridgeport when the battle of Bunker Hill was fought, making a part of General Ward's front body guard. Patterson's Massachusetts regiment, which had been also under General Putnam's command, as a part of this front guard, though more to the north, toward Lechmere Point, did not have any part in the battle. We give therefore for Connecticut two hundred (with an uncertain number in the reinforcement, but too late for service), and for New Hampshire nine hundred.

And now we have to make a very miscellaneous reckoning for Massachusetts. A standard Massachusetts regiment, when full, was at that time five hundred and ninety-eight men; but none of her regiments were full. She had

---

* A few months later, this Colonel Paul Dudley Sargeant is found on the muster-rolls at the head of a full regiment.

† This we learn from General Folsom's letter, in the " New Hampshire Provincial Papers," Vol VII. p. 529, written June 23d, six days after the battle. There is a difficulty between Folsom and Stark, but that is of no consequence now. General Folsom says, " I have since made enquiry and find that he [Stark] would not be able to lead off many more than the supernumerors [*sic*] of his regiment, it still consisting of thirteen companys." But in the battle, Stark probably went with only his own proper regiment, leaving one company, as before stated, to keep guard, and these three companies were treated as the nucleus of another regiment.

many more regiments than any other colony, and a much larger number of men. There were fifteen Massachusetts regiments in Cambridge and vicinity, around the centre of the American army, besides Gridley's regiment of artillery. Mr. Frothingham estimates that these sixteen regiments (including Gridley's) had at that time six thousand and sixty-three men, besides the accessories in the shape of drummers, etc., which would make one thousand five hundred and eighty-one more, in all, seven thousand six hundred and forty-four, and Mr. Frothingham is very exact and careful in such computations. Massachusetts had also nine regiments in the right wing under Thomas, about Roxbury and Dorchester. But neither these nor General Spencer's men, that were at Roxbury, nor General Greene's men, took any part in the battle.

Of the Massachusetts men Prescott led eight hundred of them on to the ground on the night of June 16th. These were taken from his own regiment, from Colonel Frye's and Colonel Bridge's. It is generally estimated that he had three hundred from his own, which would leave five hundred, or two hundred and fifty apiece, to come from the other two. But the next day, just before the battle and in the midst of the battle, there were sent forward as reinforcements portions of ten other regiments, Little's, Gerrish's, Doolittle's, Gardner's, Ward's, Nixon's, Whitcomb's, Mansfield's, Woodbridge's, and Scammons's, besides Gridley's artillery. In some cases the numbers were comparatively few, perhaps one, two, or three companies. In other cases the regiments went with a good degree of fulness. We are very sure we shall not overstate the case if we say that one hundred and forty men, on the average, went or started to go from each of these ten regiments, which, added to the eight hundred that marched with Prescott the night before, would make two thousand and two hundred men that Massachusetts undertook in some sort to contribute to the active forces of that day. But the manner of this contribution, as we shall see, greatly impaired, yea, almost destroyed its value. The facts which go to show this will come to light in the next chapter.

CHAPTER VIII.

THE FORENOON OF JUNE SEVENTEENTH.

Putnam's Desire to fortify Bunker Hill. — Ward does not send the promised Reinforcements. — Scene at the Redoubt, and its Moral. — Construction of the Fence Line. — Arrival of two hundred New Hampshire Men. — Stark's and Reed's Regiments. — Coming of Warren upon the Field. — Lateness of the Massachusetts Reinforcements.

LET it be understood that we use the word *forenoon* in this chapter, for that part of the day which passed before the action began.

It is plain, as already shown from a great variety of witnesses, friendly and unfriendly to General Putnam, that he was possessed with a strong desire to throw a line of entrenchments across Bunker Hill, at some distance back from the actual line where the battle was fought; and without doubt he intended to man them, before the battle begun, with a sufficient force of men. It is not likely that the fence arrangement was in his early morning thoughts at all — that this was an after plan — a make-shift for something better. Mr. Drake says that "The mistake of the day appears to have been the omission to throw up some defences on Bunker Hill. Putnam, who seems to have appreciated the importance of a supporting line to raw militia, exerted himself to little purpose for this end."

Dr. Ellis says (p. 24), "Probably if both summits could have been simultaneously intrenched and defended by troops well supplied with ammunition and artillery, the provincials might have maintained their ground."

Whose "mistake" was it that Bunker Hill was not intrenched? We wish to show under what conditions General Putnam wrought that forenoon to get this work done He intended, doubtless, to have that second line of fortifications all completed in the early morning hours. If the second detachment of one thousand men, agreed upon the day before, could have been brought on to the ground in the cool of that summer day, fresh from the rest of the night, and animated by the sight of what their brethren had done while they were permitted to sleep, it would not have been a long task to throw that girdle of intrenchments across the peninsula, narrow as it there is and tapering towards the neck. Was it an easy thing for such a man as General Putnam, with his strong will and prodigious powers of execution, to wait, and look, and wait, hour after hour, when he knew how precious every moment was? Was it a remarkable fact that he should lose patience and grow so nervous that he could hardly contain himself, and that he should go dashing again across that neck, without ever stopping to think whether the British had a dozen batteries throwing chain-shot at him, or none at all?

One writer says, "His furious ardor may or may not have needed the control of a cool deliberating judgment, and of that prime essential of the soldier which is called 'conduct.' His courage was unquestionable. He is here fairly presented by the writer, according as a careful examination of authorities, and a review of widely different estimates and judgments of him by others, assign to him his share in inspiriting a patriotic enterprise."

And on the same page as the above, it is said, "Putnam pleaded and cursed, a misuse of emphasis for which he afterwards humbled himself before his Puritan church." Some efforts have been made to discover whether, as a matter of fact, the Brooklyn church ever disciplined him for swearing. We have not been able to find any evidence of it, but rather evidence to the contrary. But if they did, it shows us one or two things not unworthy of our notice. It shows us a little New England country church sturdily maintaining its rules of discipline without "respect of persons." It was something for such a church to bring to its bar of censure a Major-General of the Continental army. On the other hand, it shows us a man of the very strongest will, high in office and popularity, bowing before that plain and humble tribunal, and confessing his fault. We should want no better evidence that General Putnam was a humble-hearted, Christian man. It is an example which a Christian minister ought naturally enough to respect.*

But to be true and exact about this, it must be said that one to whom application was made for information, and who has access to the sources of information, frankly answered in substance that Putnam swore that day without much doubt, but he did not find evidence that the church ever disciplined him for it. They regarded it probably as a case of extreme provocation, where Uncle Toby's recording angel would be likely to wipe the record out if it were written against his name, and so it was not entered.

---

* That church certainly, according to the writer quoted, came off better than another country church in Connecticut, of which the following story is told : When General William Eaton, a native of Woodstock, Connecticut, but living in Brimfield, Massachusetts, came back to his native country in 1805, after successfully fighting the Algerine pirates, he was making his way as fast as he could to his home in Brimfield. He left Hartford, Connecticut, on horseback, Sunday morning, wrapped in a cloak that concealed his uniform, and was jogging on his way, when he reached Vernon, Connecticut, while the people were standing about the meeting-house, at the noon intermission. They, seeing a stranger journeying on the road, thought it their duty to stop him. Some of the official men went out to the road, and inquired the occasion of his travelling on the Sabbath. Up to that moment, the General apparently had not stopped to inquire whether it was Sunday, or some other day. It required a moment to enable him to take in the situation. Then he threw open his cloak, and began to draw his sword from the scabbard, whereupon they went back to the meeting-house, and he on his journey.

We shall all have to confess probably that General Putnam had not a very quiet temperament during that summer
forenoon.　His

> ".... manners had not that repose
> That marks the caste of Vere de Vere."

General Ward had what might be called "conduct" in
an eminent degree, and in a military view, *very bad conduct.*
His failure to carry out the plan and keep his own promises
was enough to disgust and infuriate any man who was competent to be left in charge of so important an enterprise.
And yet these immense activities of his, on this wearisome
summer day, to save the expedition from utter failure, are
treated as though he were an amateur rider, racing here and
there to show his horsemanship, and work off his superflu-
ous physical energies.　A man approaching threescore
years, who had known little sleep for thirty hours, and was
to know little for thirty hours to come,— left in this critical period by his military superior, who had become half
frightened to death out at Cambridge at the noise of the
cannon, and had utterly failed to keep his promises,— seems
deserving of sympathy rather than ridicule.

This prodigious activity with which some writers choose
to credit General Putnam, and at the same time turn it into
ridicule, or deny him all the honors belonging to it, reminds
one of an old and simple story that used to be told.　A
farmer who had several sons went from home one day, and
left the boys to hoe a field of corn.　When he came back
he found much bad hoeing, but the other boys laid it all to
John.　Wherever the work was faulty, "John did it."　"You
rogues," said the old man, "it seems that John did it all,
and I am going to give the rest of you a whipping!"

One may read page after page in many recent books and
pamphlets, in which the confusions and disorders around

that hill are somehow allowed to rest on Putnam's shoulders, even though these writers at the same time imply that
he was not the commander, and had no right to command.
This is the old story of Pharaoh over again, who would
have his "tale of brick," straw or no straw.

No careful reader of modern Bunker Hill literature can
have failed to notice this quiet and adroit way of shifting
General Ward's delinquencies, and all the disorders that
came in consequence, over on to General Putnam. This
is a far heavier load than that with which Doctor Ellis has
weighed him down, in his graphic picture of those intrenching tools. Putnam, with his old white horse, could bear that
burden very comfortably. But to charge General Ward
and his doings to Putnam, is the height of cruelty. The
old hero would rather have gone through again the Indian
tortures he endured in the French War, than to bear that
imputation. We shall see, as we go on, how General Ward
kept his promises and furnished his reinforcements.

The hours passed away, while no reinforcements came.
And now comes a little episode of that forenoon which we
desire to open up to view until we see and understand it.
We copy a passage from the " Siege of Boston" (pp. 129–
30) which will bring the matters directly before us. "About
11 o'clock, the men had mostly ceased labor on the works;
the intrenching tools had been piled in the rear, and all
were anxiously awaiting the arrival of refreshments and
reinforcements. No works, however, had been commenced
on Bunker Hill, regarded as of great importance in case of
a retreat. General Putnam, who was on his way to the
heights when Major Brooks was going to Cambridge, rode
on horseback to the redoubt, 'and told Colonel Prescott,' as
General Heath first relates the circumstance, 'that the
intrenching tools must be sent off, or they would be lost.'
The Colonel replied, 'that if he sent any of the men away

with the tools not one of them would return.' To this the
General answered, 'They shall every man return.' A large
party was then sent off with the tools, and not one of them
returned. In this instance the Colonel was the best judge
of human nature."

We have read this passage many times, and have often
thought we could draw some more useful and legitimate
inferences from it than the very tame one which General
Heath drew.

(1) It shows us that General Putnam on this field was
clearly the military superior of Colonel Prescott. He was
the man to command what should be done with those tools,
and Prescott was the man to obey.

(2) It shows us that Colonel Prescott had already been
losing his men, or he would not so speedily have jumped
to the conclusion that these soldiers would run away if
they were once allowed to go out of his sight. This confirms his own statement in general, in his letter to John
Adams.

(3) It shows us that Putnam, with his generous nature,
attributed to those soldiers the same faithfulness and spirit
of obedience that he would to his own. He knew that the
men of his regiment would not run away from their post
of duty the moment his eye was off them. Those two
hundred men that came from his own command were not
eye-servants. They never left that field, not a man of
them, till the British broke through at the redoubt. General Putnam, full of heroic devotion to the cause that
brought them on to that field, though he was from another
colony, willing to endure labor and danger and heat for
the general good, really thought and believed that those
Massachusetts men on their own soil felt as he did and
would endure to the end.

(4) It is rather evident from this incident that those

two hundred Connecticut men were not at that time at the redoubt. If they had been there, Putnam would have been likely (especially after Prescott's expression of his want of confidence in his own men) to have told *them* to convey the tools to Bunker Hill. Indeed, had they been there, he would probably have done so in any event. As the time had not yet come for Prescott to send these Connecticut men to support the artillery, as he says he afterwards did (that event could not happen until the British landed), one can discover some evidence here that they were busy in the construction of that fence. Probably they had been already detailed by Putnam for that duty. They had wrought all night and through the morning hours as the others had done. Now the others were resting, and the Connecticut men were probably at work to construct that extemporized line, which Putnam felt it was time to begin, in the absence of the promised reinforcements. One need not be dogmatic about this opinion, but it looks very much like the truth. Still Putnam wanted those tools up at Bunker Hill, for he kept hoping that General Ward would get over his great apprehensions, and find time to send along some of those men he had promised.

(5) If General Heath had repeated this story with its momentous inference to General Putnam himself, we can imagine that the old hero would have replied somewhat as follows : " When I made that promise I thought those men were soldiers, attached to Colonel Prescott, the commander at the redoubt; that out of their personal devotion to him they would return and see him through this business. I did not keep my eye on them very closely. I had a great many cares on my mind, and lo! 'while thy servant was busy here and there, they were gone.' But pray do not be so cruel as to attribute *their* shameful desertion to *my* want of a knowledge of human nature."

Perhaps that speech has been drawn too finely and at too great length to suit the way and style of General Putnam, for there is an anecdote carefully preserved in the "Prescott Memorial" (p. 58) which tells us exactly what he did say. The passage reads in this way: "But the men did not return, nor was a reinforcement sent. Colonel Prescott met General Putnam after the action near Charlestown Neck, and inquired the cause of his failing to fulfil his engagement. General Putnam replied, 'I could not make the dogs *go*.' Colonel Prescott then stated, 'If you had said to them *come*, you would have found men enough.' 'This statement,' writes Doctor O. Prescott, Jr., 'I received from Colonel Prescott himself, who never forgave Putnam for this breach of promise.'"

Now, first of all, how any man could record or read that anecdote without seeing in it that Prescott is made subordinate to, and dependent upon, Putnam as his military superior, is a marvel. Certainly the General Putnam of this story is not the man described by one of the modern writers from whom we have quoted. He is not the man who had no right "to command Massachusetts soldiers on Massachusetts soil." Colonel Prescott held him responsible, even to the extent of never forgiving him, we are told, for not sending back those Massachusetts men to the redoubt, whether they would or no. He held him responsible, too, for not supplying him with reinforcements, when Putnam could not possibly get them from General Ward, and when Prescott was losing the men he already had. Those whom Putnam took out for that temporary service were not the first ones he had lost, according to his own story.

What was the underlying meaning of the last sentence in this anecdote? Could it be possible Prescott meant to imply that General Putnam had not courage enough to go to that redoubt, which everybody supposed to be the safest place on that whole field, and *was* the safest place so long as it was held? It would not seem that Prescott could make such an insinuation as that to such a man. Or did he mean that his men were more used to the moral suasion system in military affairs, and if Putnam had only said, " Come, now, let us reason together," they would have been convinced, and would have returned directly to their duty? One or the other of these two inferences must apparently be drawn from this anecdote, which is so carefully laid up.

It is obvious, from a great variety of testimonies and inci-dental facts, that the reinforcements were expected to march from Cambridge to the field of action, early on the morning of June 17th. That was the arrangement of the day before. That was Putnam's expectation and Prescott's expectation. The men, weary with their night toil, were looking early in the morning for the coming of their breth-ren with provisions, and with strong arms to take up the intrenching tools, and complete the unfinished fortifica-tions.

At what time did those reinforcements come? When that question is adequately answered, we shall have such a vivid idea of General Ward's imbecility as a military com-mander, that we shall no longer wonder at that letter of Washington to General Lee, already quoted.

And it is suitable to remark at this point, that had the reinforcements gone early in the day, they would have found a perfectly open and safe path across Charlestown Neck. It was not till well on in the forenoon that the Brit-ish brought their floating batteries up the Charles River and the Mystic River, to rake that neck and make all pass-ing extremely dangerous.

Individual men went back and forth between Cambridge and Charlestown all through those morning hours. There has just been published, in an elegant pamphlet, the paper which Mr. Frothingham read last summer before the Massachusetts Historical Society, and in the appendix some extracts are given from the diary of Lieutenant-Colonel Ephraim Storrs of Mansfield, Connecticut, belonging to General Putnam's regiment. In these extracts the author of the pamphlet is faithful to record the following item, though in doing so he is like that good man spoken of in the Scriptures, "that sweareth to his own hurt and changeth not:" June 17th, "At sunrise this morning a fire began from the ships; about 10, went down to General Putnam's post, who has the command; some shot whistled around us."

One can catch sight, by one light and another, of quite a number of individuals that went back and forth that forenoon, and doubtless there were many more of whom we know nothing. But the first military body that moved on to that hill in the way of a reinforcement, so far as appears, was the detachment of two hundred from Stark's regiment, under Lieutenant-Colonel Wyman. No signs are discovered of any earlier arrival of men in a military body, and from the best light afforded, it does not appear that those men came until full 12 o'clock. A forenoon of June 17th, when the sun rises at 4 o'clock and 23 minutes, is a very long one to weary and hungry soldiers. It was a most severe trial of faith and patience for those men who went there the night before, and many of the eight hundred Massachusetts men under Colonel Prescott did not stand this tremendous strain upon their sensibilities. They deserted in large numbers. If we are to believe Colonel Prescott's own statement in his letter to John Adams, they deserted in very large numbers. He says that when the action began, he was left "with perhaps one hundred and fifty men." And this was at the very moment when the British columns were moving up those slopes to give battle

He had sent out some small detachments under Robinson
and Woods, to flank the enemy, which means, probably,
that they were to post themselves around the village of
Charlestown and harass the British left wing.   But we presume these companies did not number over *one hundred.*

Do we accept this statement of Colonel Prescott?   Nay,
we do not accept it.   We will not be so unjust to Massachusetts as to give credence to such a statement; besides,
there is satisfactory proof to the contrary.   The " Siege of
Boston" helps us to prove these sentences from that letter
incorrect.   Colonel Prescott certainly leaves the impression
on all readers that those men from Bridge's and Frye's
regiments left him early in the morning, and never came
back.   But when the British broke into the redoubt, the
men from those two regiments were there to be " killed
and wounded," in about the same proportion to their original numbers as the men in Prescott's own regiment.   The
killed and wounded in the latter were seventy, in Bridge's
forty-four, and in Frye's forty-six.   Total, one hundred and
sixty.

It is to be noticed that the heaviest slaughter on our
side fell upon those three regiments, because they were directly in the path where the British broke through.   Up
to that moment it is not likely that many men had been
killed or wounded in this fortress, for so long as it remained unbroken, the men were sheltered as they were nowhere else along the lines.   This slaughter took place in a
very few moments.   The British were terribly exasperated
at the repulses they had received and the dreadful losses
that had come upon them ; and they used the bayonets
which they had (and which our own men had not) with the
greatest fury.   Some of the British accounts of the battle
describe this fearful slaughter, when our men were huddled
together and could not escape.

11

Adjutant Waller, of the Royal Marines, says, "I was with those two companies who drove their bayonets into all that opposed them. Nothing could be more shocking than the carnage that followed the storming this work. We tumbled over the dead to get at the living, who were crowding out of the gorge of the redoubt."

But our object just now is to show that the impression which Prescott makes in his letter to John Adams, as to the wholesale desertion of the men of Bridge's and Frye's regiments, as also of the very small number of men he had with him when the British came up to attack, is unreliable. And the very fact that this slaughter fell in such nearly equal proportions upon these three regiments, serves to show that they were near together, involved in a common fate, and without any reasonable doubt they were all within those earthworks, and that there was no other regiment with them.

We do not, then, by any means accept Colonel Prescott's statement, that out of his original eight hundred Massachusetts troops, when the battle began he had but about one hundred and fifty men in the fort. But we do accept it to this extent, that he had had large desertions, that his men had been dropping off one by one, or in little companies, and that he had not been reinforced. Mr. Frothingham says (p. 136), "They were joined just previous to the action by portions of Massachusetts regiments, under Colonels Brewer, Nixon, Woodbridge, Little, and Major Moore." Long search has been made to find clear and reliable proof that any Massachusetts regiment in the way of reinforcements reached that battle line before the action began. If we can credit Prescott's own statements, quoted above, he had not been reinforced at that time, nor does it appear that he was to any extent reinforced during the battle. The moral of that anecdote which we have copied from the "Prescott Memorial" would all fade out, if it could be proved that he was reinforced even during the action to any substantial degree. We have before us the diary of a soldier in Colonel Little's regiment, from which we shall make some fuller quotations by-and-by. But a few words here will serve to show at what time Colonel Little's regiment reached the field. He says, "We were alarmed at Cambridge. [Notice that he was at Cambridge.] The army set out. [He moved with the main body of the Massachusetts reinforcements.] We found the town in flames, and the regulars ascending the hill. [The second attack of the British was now coming on.]" That serves to mark the time of the arrival of Little's regiment.

As to those desertions during that long forenoon, it may naturally be said that men left in that way were under peculiar temptations. They had toiled all night, the sun was beating heavily upon them in the morning, they were hungry and thirsty, and refreshments did not come, the promised reinforcements did not come, and it began to seem to them, untried soldiers as many of them were, that they had been brought on to that hill only to be left uncared for and to be sacrificed.* All these thoughts and many more went coursing through their excited minds, while the cannon from the British ships kept up their thunder, and sent their missiles against the earthworks, or whistling through the air over their heads. It was enough, we admit, to make raw soldiers nervous, and under sore temptations to run away; and they did run away, very many of them. If Prescott had said that when the attack began he had not more than three hundred of his original eight hundred Massachusetts men (allowing one hundred more for the

---

* "Nothing like discipline had entered our army at that time. General Ward, then commander-in-chief, remained at his quarters in Cambridge, and apparently took no interest or part in the transactions of the day." — General Dearborn, in "Port Folio," March, 1818.

flanking party, so as to make in all four hundred), we should feel inclined to believe him. But it must be remembered that those two hundred men from Connecticut had also toiled all night, and felt upon their heads the hot sun of the morning. They were hungry and thirsty like the rest, and there is no evidence that a single man of them ran away. Colonel Prescott found it far easier, that long, hot, weary forenoon, to command those men from another State than his own, for they had been under a disciplinarian, and had learned the principle of military obedience.

But we return now to the reinforcements. Those two hundred New Hampshire men probably arrived about noon, and it is seen by various accounts that they were received by General Putnam as the commander on that field, and were set to work under his directions.

We are inclined to the belief that the very next reinforcements did not come till more than two hours afterwards, and that they, also, were New Hampshire men. We have briefly referred before to Colonel Stark's statement, but it is best here to quote it in full. This statement he sent to New Hampshire immediately after the battle. Mr. Frothingham says the order went to Colonel Stark about 11 o'clock, but this is what Stark himself says: "I was required by the General to send a party consisting of two hundred men with officers to their assistance, which order I readily obeyed, and appointed and sent [Lieutenant-] Colonel *Wyman*, commander of the same, and about 2 o'clock in the afternoon express orders came for the whole of my regiment to proceed to *Charlestown* to oppose the enemy who were landing on *Charlestown Point*. Accordingly we proceeded, and the battle soon came on, in which a number of officers belonging to my regiment were killed, and many privates killed and wounded. . . . . But we remain in good spirits as yet, being well satisfied that where we have lost one, they have lost three."

Just before the battle, Colonel Reed's regiment had been moved from Medford to Charlestown Neck, as will clearly appear by the following letter of the Colonel, contained in "American Archives" (4th Series, Vol. II. p. 1006) :

"Then I was informed by Colonel *Stark* that *Medford* was so full of soldiers that it was necessary for some to take other quarters. Then I applied to General *Ward* and received orders in these words :

"(GENERAL ORDERS.)   HEADQUARTERS, June 12th, 1775.

"That Colonel *Reed* quarter his regiment in the houses near Charlestown Neck, and keep all necessary guards between his barracks and the ferry, and on *Bunker Hill.*"

The order going from Cambridge to the New Hampshire regiments would naturally reach Colonel Reed twenty minutes or half an hour earlier than Colonel Stark, and there would have been the same difference in the time required by the two regiments to reach the field from their starting-points. We conclude that Colonel Reed's regiment came on first, and took station next to the Connecticut troops behind the rail fence, and when Stark arrived three-fourths of an hour later, he filled out the line down to the Mystic River. But Stark could not possibly get there much before 3 o'clock.

We do not discover that any Massachusetts reinforcements were there by the time when Reed would naturally arrive. They were probably just beginning to come at the time of Stark's arrival, but did not, like his regiment, march straight to their post of duty. They lingered, as we shall see, about the neck and on the back side of Bunker Hill.

With regard to the intrenchments, it is probable Putnam found that he could not properly complete them, and it was doubtful whether he was to have any forces to man them if he did, so that more and more he turned his thoughts toward that line of fence. But it is to be noticed that

whatever men from New Hampshire were set. to intrenching, were set to it by Putnam's order. Mr. Frothingham,
in his "Siege of Boston" (p. 134), makes this company of
New Hampshire men come from Stark's regiment, and it
is implied that they were taken out of the regiment by
General Putnam, after Stark himself was upon the ground.
This may be so, but they could only labor a short time.
We must think the two hundred who came earlier did most
of the intrenching and fence building. But Mr. Frothingham says, " General Putnam ordered part of these troops
to labor on the works begun on Bunker Hill." Little
glimpses which we catch all along through that weary forenoon show how strongly Putnam's mind was set upon these
intrenchments on Bunker Hill. The removal of the tools
thither, and the turning aside of men from all the parties
that came earliest upon the ground, distinctly indicate how
earnestly his mind was fixed upon this purpose, which after
all, by the long delays of Ward, he was obliged to abandon.

It was no slight work to prepare that fence line, fifteen
hundred feet in length. It does not appear, moreover, that
Colonel Gridley, the engineer, had anything specially to
do in the tracing and construction of this peculiar system
of fortifications. This idea probably came from the active
and fertile brain of General Putnam himself,* when he found

---

* How remarkably fertile his mind was for such expedients is made
plain by the following item, which we copy from the " New England Chronicle," August 31st, 1775, relating to the French and Indian War. In such
contrivances Putnam was always noted for his ingenuity.

"ANECDOTE OF GENERAL PUTNAM.—During the late war, when General
Amherst was marching across the country of Canada, the army coming to one
of the lakes which they were obliged to pass, found the French had a vessel
of twelve guns upon it. He was in great distress. His guns were no match
for her, and she alone was capable of sinking his whole army in that situation.
While he was pondering what should be done, Putnam came up to him and
said, ' *General, that ship must be taken.*' 'Aye,' said Amherst, ' I would give
the world she was taken.' ' I'll take her,' says Putnam. Amherst smiled and
asked ' How?' ' Give me some wedges, a beetle, ... and a few men of

he must give up his line of intrenchments on Bunker Hill. Or, if some one else first suggested it, it is plain that he heartily adopted it as the best thing that could be done.

The actual time when this fence was begun is made indefinite in most of the narratives of the battle. But the impression generally left upon the reader is that it was hastily constructed just on the eve of the battle. There seems to be reason for supposing that it was begun some three or four hours before the battle. In its very nature it was not the work of a few moments. Almost all accounts agree that it was built, or at least begun, by the men of Connecticut, and it has already been suggested that the apparent absence from the fort of those Connecticut troops at 11 o'clock, is to be explained by this circumstance.

It doubtless went sorely against the feelings of General Putnam to call upon men who had toiled all night. But he was driven by a kind of necessity, and it would be altogether like him to say within himself, I will take only those men from my own regiment for this new work. It is hard, but they will not complain. It will be noticed that the Massachusetts men who were asked to go with those tools were not to be set at work with them, much as he wanted that work done. It was only to convey them to Bunker Hill, and he hoped that fresh men would soon appear, who might be set using them. Our theory, then, is (it is not a pet theory nor an important one, only as explaining the probable succession of events) that the fence line was begun before 11 o'clock, and that the New Hampshire

my own choice.' Amherst could not perceive how an armed vessel was to be taken by four or five men, a beetle and some wedges. However, he granted Putnam's request. When night came, Putnam with his materials and men went in a boat under the vessel's stern, and in an instant drove in the wedges behind the rudder, in the little space between the rudder and ship, and left her. In the morning the sails were seen fluttering about ; she was adrift in the middle of the lake ; and being presently blown ashore, was easily taken."

men that came with Lieutenant Wyman helped to build it;
and when Stark and Reed came with their regiments, it
was essentially complete, though they probably made some
slight additions near the Mystic River.

And now we come to another most interesting scene that
happened just before the battle; this was the unexpected
coming of General Joseph Warren upon that field. In
order to understand the full meaning of this event, it is
necessary to go back a few days, and know some things that
had taken place at Cambridge. We cannot better set forth
the scene than in the simple and touching words of Daniel
Putnam.

"He [General Putnam] had soon afterwards a spirited conversation with General Ward, Dr. Warren, and Colonel Joseph
Palmer,* a member of the Committee of Safety, who inclined to
favor the measure, but Ward and Warren both opposed it, alleg-
ing that as we had no powder to spare, and no battering cannon,
it would be idle to make approaches on the town. He told them
they had entirely mistaken his views, that it was not for the purpose of battering the town, but to draw the enemy from it, where
we might meet them on equal terms, and that Charlestown and
Dorchester were the only points where this could be done; that
the army wished to be employed, and the country was growing
dissatisfied with the inactivity of it.

"It was objected again that it might bring on a general battle,
and that, in our situation, it was neither politic or safe to risk
one. He replied, 'Two thousand men will be enough to risk, and
with that number, we will go on and defend ourselves as long as
we can, and then give the ground.' 'But suppose your retreat
should be intercepted?' 'We will guard against that and run
when we can no longer contend with advantage; we can outrun

---

* Colonel Daniel Putnam, in his article in the "Connecticut Historical
Collections" (Vol. I. p. 243), says that General Joseph Palmer in later
years purchased a large tract of land in Pomfret, Connecticut, "and in 1782,
while on a visit here, he called on General Putnam, and recurring to the time,
recapitulated to him with great minuteness the details of that conversation."

them, and behind every wall rally and oppose their progress till
we join our friends again. But suppose the worst, suppose us
hemmed in, and no retreat ; we know what we are contending
for, we will set our country an example of which it shall not be
ashamed, and show men who seek to oppress us what men can
do who are determined to live *free* or not live at all.'

"Warren, he said, rose and walked several times across the
room, leaned a few moments over the back of a chair in a
thoughtful attitude and said, '*Almost thou persuadest me, General
Putnam*, but I must still think the project a rash one. Nevertheless, if it should ever be adopted, and the strife becomes hard,
you must not be surprised to find me with you in the midst of it.'
' I hope not, sir,' said Putnam, 'you are yet but a young man, and
our country has much to hope from you, both in council and in
war. It is only a little brush we have been contemplating ; let
some of us who are older and can well enough be spared *begin*
the fray ; there will be time enough for you hereafter, for it will
not soon be ended.'"

The import of this conversation will be better understood
by the general reader if we recall somewhat more fully who
General Warren was and what he was. Born at Roxbury
in 1741, he was at this time only thirty-four years old, in the
very promise of a glorious life. Highly educated and accomplished, with refined tastes and habits, moving in the most
cultured circles of society, he had nevertheless gone down
among the workingmen, identified himself with their socie-
ties and associations, not for any low, selfish, personal ends,
but to help form their minds and hearts, and shape their
thoughts to this great struggle that was coming upon the
land. He was universally beloved and admired. It has
already been shown in this volume, and is pointed out by
many signs, that Putnam and Warren, unlike as they were
to each other in culture and outward manners, were bound
to each other by peculiar ties of affection and brotherhood.
To show how high this man stood in the love and confi-

dence of his fellow-men, it is simply needful to recall that he was Chairman of the Massachusetts Committee of Safety, President of the Massachusetts Provincial Congress, and three days before, though he had had but little military experience, had been made a Major-General of the Massachusetts troops.

He had not intended to go to that battle-field. He had not given his personal consent that the battle should be fought. He had an invitation to dine that day with some family in Cambridge. He dressed for this dinner-party, wearing the full and elaborate suit such as the most refined gentlemen of that generation wore on these occasions of politeness and ceremony. It was a far more elaborate and showy dress than any now known among us on similiar occasions. He set out to go to the house where he was to dine. On his way he heard the guns from Boston as he had heard them at intervals all that morning. A tide of patriotic feeling apparently came over him, and he said within himself, Here am I, after having talked as much patriotic talk as any other man, going to-day on an errand of pleasure, to dine with a select party of friends; and yonder, under this burning sky, are my brethren, perilling their lives in the high places of the field. I will not go on this errand of pleasure. Come life or come death, I will go to those heights of Charlestown, and share the fortunes of those men that are fighting for their homes and their native soil. And without returning to change his dress he went to the battle-field. (A description of the dress he had on when he was killed will be found in a later chapter, as given by one of the British officers.)

Now, in some of the modern accounts of the battle no one would ever know that Warren met Putnam as he went on to that field.* Putnam's name is conveniently slipped

* Mr. Devens, in his oration last June at Bunker Hill, entirely forgot this

out and laid aside. But Mr. Frothingham is guilty of no such rudeness and historical untruth. On page 170 he thus describes the interview which took place between these two men that day on the battle-field :

" A short time before the action commenced, he [Warren] was seen in conversation with General Putnam at the rail fence, who offered to receive his orders. . General Warren declined to give any, but asked where he could be most useful. Putnam directed him to the redoubt, remarking there he would be covered. ' Don't think,' said Warren, ' I come to seek a place of safety ; but tell me where the onset will be most furious.' Putnam still pointed to the redoubt. ' That is the enemy's object, and if that can be defended the day is ours.' General Warren passed to the redoubt, where the men received him with enthusiastic cheers. Here again he was tendered the command by Colonel Prescott. But Warren declined it."

A very natural question certainly to ask just here after this quotation is, Did Colonel Prescott tender to General Warren precisely the same command that Putnam had just before tendered ? If so, there must have been a curious state of things on that field. Warren talked first with Putnam, and Putnam, without any consultation, offered to lay down his command. What was the nature of that offer ? Was it simply that Warren might take direction of those two hundred Connecticut troops ? Did any one ever so understand the record ? Prescott was the commander at the redoubt. What was the command which he proposed to put into Warren's hands ?

But leaving this point, we return to the interview itself. Daniel Putnam has given a more lifelike picture of it. He

circumstance, which Mr. Frothingham faithfully records. Perhaps he did not wish to trouble his hearers with perplexing questions. If he had told this story about Warren and Putnam, they might have asked inwardly, Was not Putnam a General, and if he offered to Warren the command, would he not have to offer him a General's command ?

had often heard the story from his father. It was just as
the battle was about to open that Warren met him, and as
he had come on horseback to the neck, he had passed the
Massachusetts regiments on their march from Cambridge.

"Alluding to a former conversation he [Putnam] said, 'I am
sorry to see you here, General Warren; I wish you had taken
my advice and left this day to us, for from appearances we shall
have a sharp time of it, and since you are here I am ready to
submit to your orders.' Warren replied, 'I came only as a volunteer; I know nothing of your dispositions, nor will I interfere
with them. Tell me where I can be most useful.' Putnam
pointed to the redoubt, and intent on his safety said, 'You will
be covered there.' 'Don't think,' said Warren, 'I came here to
seek a place of *safety*, but tell me where the onset will be most
furious.' Putnam pointed again to the redoubt. '*That*,' said he,
'is the enemy's object; Prescott is there and will do *his* duty,
and if it can be defended the day will be ours.' Warren left
him and walked quickly toward the redoubt. The rest, alas, is
too well known."

Let us now return again to the subject of the Massachusetts reinforcements. It is generally agreed that Warren
reached that field only just before the battle opened, and
that he passed the men who were on their way as reinforcements. This and many other little items of evidence make
it sufficiently plain that very few, if any, Massachusetts
reinforcements had reached that hill when the action
began.*

Now let it be understood that while we are trying to discover the actual condition of things around that battle-

* Some brief editorial remarks (very likely by Colonel Scammans himself)
in the "New England Chronicle" for February 21st, 1776, based upon the court-
martial to try Colonel Scammans, are very instructive in this connection. As this
paper was published at Cambridge, it may be believed that the writer knew
whereof he affirmed. He says, "It is observable that the Adjutant would
insinuate that the regiment (Colonel Scammans's) arrived at Bunker Hill time
enough to reinforce the breastwork before it was forced by the enemy, but if

ground at that late hour of the day, we are not endeavoring to prove that the men of Massachusetts were not just as courageous, just as patriotic, just as good material for soldiers, as the men from the other colonies. Nothing of the kind. But what we are seeking to show is, that up to that time her regiments had not been brought up to that standard of drill and military discipline which had been reached by the men of New Hampshire and Connecticut. The trouble was primarily in General Artemas Ward himself.

It will be well for us, at this point, to take a look at Cambridge around General Ward's headquarters, and try to discover what was passing in his mind.

Mr. Bancroft has before told us, as will be remembered, that General Ward "never could introduce exact discipline among free men," and it was but natural that the Massachusetts Colonels should not rise in their methods and plans above the standard set them by their commander-in-chief. The confusion, timidity, hesitation, desertion, among those Massachusetts regiments on the day of the battle, was only a more general manifestation of the confusion, timidity, hesitation and *desertion* (we include this last word deliberately) of General Ward himself.

For notice, by way of recapitulation, the plan of action was fixed upon the day before. Putnam was to have two thousand troops for the expedition. Some accounts lead us to believe that those two thousand men were all selected

the public will only consider that those regiments which were stationed only two miles distance [at Cambridge] did not arrive seasonable enough," etc.

What the Adjutant [Marsden] had said was, " I went half way up Bunker Hill with Colonel Scammans, where I left him and went to the breastwork, where I got before the enemy forced it. The confusion was so great when we got to Bunker Hill we could not form the regiment."

The following item from the testimony also helps to fix times and seasons :

"Lieutenant James Donnell deposed, about noon we marched to Lechmere's Point, where we remained one quarter of an hour. Going from the point, Charlestown was set on fire."

and set apart for this purpose in the afternoon of the 16th, and that they were actually together on Cambridge Common that evening, to have God's blessing invoked upon them, and his fatherly care and protection sought, in that prayer of President Langdon.

As already explained, it was thought best that only one thousand should go that night, as there were not intrenching tools enough, so that more than that number could work to advantage. The remainder were to stay in Cambridge and have the refreshment of sleep, and be ready to march early in the morning. Many signs show that this was the impression of the men who had toiled all night at the fort. Prescott and the men with him expected that early reinforcement. Putnam went to Cambridge at the dawn of the morning to bring on refreshments and these reserves, so that the men on the hill should be kept in good courage and cheer. But the firing brought him back personally, with instructions left for the refreshments and the other forces to follow. If Ward had been a general commander of any military force, he would certainly have seen that the other thousand men should have been provided with everything needful for an early morning start. But when the morning came, nothing had apparently been done, and what was far worse, the work of the day before had been apparently undone. The one thousand men selected for the reinforcement seem to have been resolved back into their original elements. Ward's vacillating mind as soon as he heard those cannon, was whispering inwardly, It will never do to let *these* men go, nor *these*, nor *these*, till I understand better what is going to happen. The British will certainly burst out on some side track and attack Cambridge. So when the sun rose that morning, the arrangements of the afternoon before had vanished, and it was a totally unsettled question who should go and who not.

Hours passed on, and the question was still unsettled. Putnam and Prescott, who had both been up all night, were looking anxiously through the morning hours for those reinforcements to come. Putnam had been to Cambridge once, and now he went again straight across that neck where the British had brought their batteries to play. Prescott also sent Major Brooks on the same errand. Late in the forenoon Ward had that very happy thought, that though he ought not to spare any of the six or seven thousand men round about Cambridge, there was that "party of Hampshire" out at Medford and vicinity, that might go. That was the best thought he had all that trembling forenoon. But the New Hampshire men had not expected this order, and they were not ready, and had to get ready with all haste. Their muskets were not of the same bore, and into many of them their bullets would not go ; so they had to pound them down and elongate them. These were probably those "poisoned and chewed bullets" which some of the British officers complained were fired at them.

Through all those long, hot, weary hours, Putnam could not help thinking and saying to himself, There is my own regiment at Inman's farm, well provided with powder and ball, ready to obey my word even to the death. I could have them on the ground in an hour. O, if I only had them here I could do everything I wish ! And yet so true a soldier was he, so accustomed to pay obedience on the one hand, and to demand obedience on the other, that he would not stir to break through General Ward's official command. No matter if even John Adams did say that in that early summer of 1775, Putnam was as independent of Ward as Ward was of him. They were among the most poorly considered words he ever uttered. It was not so.

There has never been, so far as we are aware, any charges that the New Hampshire and Connecticut troops in this battle did not do their duty faithfully and entirely. Mr. Frothingham says of the New Hampshire men, " They fought with great bravery;" and of the others, " The conduct of the Connecticut troops is mentioned in terms of high commendation in the private letters and journals of the time." The deficiencies and disorders of that day, and the courts-martial that followed, were confined wholly to the Massachusetts regiments.

We will now proceed to give some illustrations from eye witnesses, showing what these disorders were. The large desertions from the fort we have already referred to. But on the other point we will first give the following graphic extract from a letter of Captain Chester. He was the very last sent for to come to the battle, and he managed to overcome all obstacles and break through all the hindrances of the crowds he encountered, and reach the front line before the battle was over. And this is what he saw on his way :

" I waited not, but ran and got my arms and ammunition, and hasted to my company (who were in the church for barracks), and found them nearly ready to march. We soon marched, with our frocks and trousers on over our other clothes (for our company is in uniform wholly blue turned up with red), for we were loath to expose ourselves by our dress, and down we marched. I imagined we arrived at the hill near the close of the battle. When we arrived there was not a company with us in any kind of order, although when we first set out perhaps three regiments were by our side and near us ; but here they were scattered, some behind rocks and hay-cocks, and thirty men perhaps behind an apple tree, and frequently twenty men round a wounded man, retreating, when not more than three or four could touch him to advantage ; others were retreating seemingly without any excuse, and some said they had left the fort with leave of the officers because they had been all night and day on fatigue duty, without sleep, victuals or drink, and some said they had no officers to head them, which indeed, seemed to be the case.

"At last I met a considerable company who were going off rank and file. I called to the officer that led them, and asked why he retreated. He made me no answer. I halted my men, and told him if he went on it should be at his peril. He still seemed regardless of me. I then ordered my men to make ready. They immediately cocked, and declared if I ordered they would fire. Upon that they stopped short, tried to excuse themselves, but I could not tarry to hear him, but ordered him forward, and he complied.

"We were then very soon in the heat of action. Before we reached the summit of Bunker Hill, and while we were going over the neck, we were in imminent danger from the cannon shot which buzzed around us like hail. The musketry began before we passed the neck [*i. e.* they heard it in the distance] ; and when we were on the top of the hill, and during our descent to the foot of it on the south, the small as well as cannon shot were incessantly whistling by us. We joined our army on the right of the centre [*i. e.* behind the fence line nearest to the fort], just by a poor stone fence two or three feet high, and very thin, so that the bullets came through. Here we lost our regularity, as every company had done before us, and fought as they did, every man loading and firing as fast as he could. As near as I could guess we fought standing about six minutes."

And then the crash came, the British had mounted the parapet, the fortress was carried, and the centre and left wings had to retreat.

This is one vivid picture of what was going on that day, on the back of Bunker Hill, around the neck, and along the road to Cambridge. Massachusetts writers have, very naturally, not cared to tell their readers that these disorders were confined to the Massachusetts regiments, nor should we wish to dwell upon this subject now, in this centennial year of joy and good feeling, except for the ends of justice and historical truth.

Take another picture given us by General Dearborn, at

12

that time a Captain of a company in Stark's regiment. It relates to the march of the regiment from Medford to Bunker Hill. He says,—

" When it reached Charlestown Neck we found two regiments halted, in consequence of a heavy enfilading fire thrown across it of round, bar, and chain shot from the *Lively* frigate, and the floating batteries anchored in Charles River, and a floating battery laying in the Mystic. Major McClary went forward and observed to the commanders, that if they did not intend to move on he wished them to open and let our regiment pass ; the latter was immediately done. My company being in front, I marched by the side of Colonel Stark, who moving with a very deliberate pace, I suggested the propriety of quickening the march of the regiment that it might sooner be relieved from this galling crossfire of the enemy. With a look peculiar to himself he fixed his eyes upon me, and observed with great composure, ' Dearborn, one fresh man in action is worth ten fatigued ones,' and continued to advance in the same cool and collected manner. When we reached the top of Bunker Hill, where General Putnam had taken his station, the regiment halted for a few moments for the rear to come up."

The reader will take notice that the narrator here saw General Putnam, and he was on the top of Bunker Hill. That was ground where he could overlook the redoubt, and the whole field of operations, and see whether troops were coming from Cambridge. But the battle had not yet begun. In a subsequent chapter of this volume the reader will find that General Dearborn tried to make Putnam a coward, because, as he thinks, he did not come forward into the fighting lines. In this he was mistaken. But if General Putnam had kept that position on the top of Bunker Hill, after the British lines came up and began their firing, his chances of being killed would have been at least ten times greater than though he had been in the redoubt. It is a

notorious fact in this battle, that the British fired over the
heads of our men who were in the front of the fight.   Captain Chester has just told us how the cannon and musket
shot whistled past him, from the moment he reached the
top of Bunker Hill and began to descend.   It was a very
poor place for a coward to take refuge.   The men who
really kept out of danger were over on the back side of the
hill, and around the neck.   General Dearborn, therefore,
when he brought his calumnious charges against General
Putnam for cowardice, fixed upon an exceedingly undesira-
ble place for a coward to tarry in order to keep out of danger.   Colonel Swett, in his history of the battle, speaks of
the top of Bunker Hill in these words : " The battle indeed
appeared here in all its horrors.   The British musketry
fired high and took effect on this elevated hill, and it was
completely exposed to the combined fire from their ships,
batteries and field pieces."

   In the distribution of the forces from these three States,
it fell to the lot of the New Hampshire men to guard the
fence line at the northern extremity, near the Mystic River.
It fell to the Connecticut men to guard the same line
nearer to the redoubt, and by them this fence line had been
mainly constructed.   The operations of the Massachusetts
men circled chiefly about the redoubt, inside or out, where
Prescott was stationed.   Some of them were along the fence
line, but not a great number.   Some were in the half-open
space between the southerly end of the fence line and the
redoubt.   Some were behind the earthwork which extended
out from the redoubt northward, and which was, if not a
part of the redoubt, an appendage of it.   A few were down
by the road running through the village of Charlestown.

   Let it be further borne in mind that this redoubt, on
the morning of the 17th of June, was regarded, both by the
Americans and the British, as the stronghold on those

Charlestown Heights. Later in the day, when that fence line had been hastily constructed out of the frail and chance materials that came to hand, it was looked upon both by the Americans and. the British as a very fragile affair compared with the fortress on the top of Breed's Hill. The Massachusetts men were not asked in any considerable numbers to guard that weak line of the fence. They were allowed to make Prescott in the redoubt the central figure around whom they should rally, and the Connecticut and New Hampshire men would take what every one on both sides would say was the place of chief danger. The British certainly thought the fence line the easiest place for them to break through ; and when Putnam, sorry to see Warren on that field, advised him to go to the redoubt, unquestionably he was seeking for him the place of greatest security. Warren at least surmised this was in Putnam's mind, and answered that he did not come there to find a place of safety. Putnam was too noble and generous-hearted to tell Warren, under these conditions, that the redoubt was the safest place, so he told him *that was the object* at which the enemy aimed, and still advised him to go there, as he did. It is clear, by a great volume of concurrent testimony from both sides, that the redoubt was regarded as the stronghold to which one might fly and be comparatively safe.

These two thousand men of Massachusetts were allowed, if they would come to the front, to be stationed mainly in and immediately around that redoubt, but the great body of them managed, or were so managed, as never to get there.*

---

* " There may have been a very few volunteers from various regiments of the Massachusetts army scattered over the entire field, but theirs was the spirit of enthusiasm which needed no orders, and would have paid little attention to them had any been issued. There is little doubt, however, that the number of these zealous ones is greatly exaggerated, and that the mention of single members of a company or of single companies of a regiment is too often

In concluding this chapter, there is one general suggestion which we do not remember to have seen distinctly
made, and which will probably explain, in some measure,
the backwardness of Massachusetts soldiers that day. They
knew that General Ward did not approve of the battle.
They knew that Warren did not approve of it. The Committee of Safety had urged the movement, and the council
of war by a major vote had ordered it. But the Massachusetts troops were doubtless well aware that Ward, to
whom they looked up as head commander, did not want it.
If one could report to us to-day what was heard among
those regiments, in conversations between man and man,
he would probably bring us many expressions of dislike,
that a General from another colony should prevail to make
them do what their own commander did not wish them to
do. This vitiating influence, without much doubt, spread
itself more or less through those troops, and took away
all their force as soldiers. They saw how slow General
Ward had been to send them at all; and they thought
they might hang back and be just as slow as he. Raw
troops have motives enough for a kind of cowardly conduct
in themselves, without having this tendency so directly ministered to as it was in this case by General Ward himself.

We have referred to the confusion and want of organization and co-operation among the Massachusetts regiments.
Some may think we are writing in a partisan spirit, and coloring the facts too highly. We will take a passage then from
Doctor Ellis (p. 41), and let him tell us some of the facts.

" Now it was that our troops and our cause suffered from the

received as evidence of the presence *in the battle* of the entire bodies to which
they respectively belonged ; indeed, it is said by a respectable writer, who has
investigated the subject, that in addition to the New Hampshire not more
than a hundred and fifty men reached the peninsula and actually participated
in the action during the whole of this notable Saturday."— Mr. Dawson, in
" Historical Magazine," June, 1868.

want of discipline, and from the confusion apparent in the whole
management of the action, originating in the extemporized and
imperfect preparation, and in the baffling secrecy of the purposes
of the enemy.   The neck of land, ploughed by the incessant
volleys from the ships, and clouded by the dust thus raised, was
an almost insuperable barrier to the bringing on of reinforcements.   Major Gridley, wholly lacking in spirit and skill, had
been put in command of a battalion of infantry, in compliment
to his father.   He lost, and could not recover, his self-possession
and courage.   Though ordered to the hill, he advanced towards
Charlestown slowly and timidly ; and though urged by Colonel
Frye to hasten, he was satisfied with the scant service of firing
three-pounders from Cobble Hill upon the 'Glasgow' frigate.
His Captain, Trevett, refused obedience to such weakness, and
ordered his men to follow him to the works.   Colonel Gerrish,
with his artillery on Bunker's Hill, could neither be urged nor
intimidated by Putnam to bring his pieces to the rail fence.   He
was unwieldy by corpulence, and overcome with heat and fatigue.
His men had been scattered from the summit of Bunker's Hill,
where the enemy's shot had taken tremendous effect, as it was
supposed to be strongly fortified."

(Notice in this last sentence what Doctor Ellis thinks of
the safety of remaining on the top of Bunker Hill, where
General Dearborn says Putnam stayed in order to be out
of danger.)

CHAPTER IX.

THE BATTLE.

Description of Bunker Hill and its Surroundings.— Landing of the British,
and Plan of Attack.— First Assault and its Consequences.— Burning of
Charlestown.— Second Assault.— Interval.— Change of Plan.— Reinforcements.— The Redoubt Carried.— The Retreat.— Killed and Wounded.

BUNKER HILL is on a peninsula nearly a mile long
in its longest part, and about half a mile wide in its
widest part. This peninsula is now almost entirely covered
with buildings. But in 1775 it was mostly open country.
Here were pastures and mowing-grounds, and lands devoted to various forms of farm culture. The village of
Charlestown stood near its south-eastern extremity, looking
directly across the wide mouth of the Charles River over
upon Boston, or what would now be called the North End
of Boston, which embraces mainly what was called the
town of Boston in 1775.

For the sake of readers unfamiliar with the ground, it is
desirable to give as clear and minute a description as possible of this peninsula as it appeared one hundred years ago.
Its neck where it connected with the main land was a narrow passage-way, over which all travellers coming in from
Cambridge, Lexington, Concord, and the country generally west and north-west, must pass if they wished to go
to Charlestown, or to Boston by the way of Charlestown.
The present causeways and bridges connecting Cambridge
with Boston had then no existence. As one came in from
the open country and was passing this neck toward Charles-

183

town, he was moving almost directly south-east. The water on the left or northerly side of him was the Mystic River, so called, which here near its mouth is an arm of the sea of considerable width and depth. The water on his right hand was the Charles River, also an arm of the sea, the tide-water setting inland for some seven miles. As soon as the traveller passed the neck, he began to ascend. Bearing slightly to the left, and going on about one-third of a mile, he would find himself on the very top of the real Bunker Hill, about one hundred and ten feet above the sea level, the highest land on the peninsula. On his left he would then look down on the waters of Mystic River or Bay, the land falling off in that direction in a somewhat steep declivity. The peninsula is not so wide here as farther on, perhaps not more than a quarter of a mile. But the traveller would be much nearer here to the Mystic River than to the Charles. Standing on Bunker Hill and looking nearly east, to the very end of the peninsula where it meets the waters of Boston Bay, he would see the land falling off rapidly immediately before him, till it came down to a spot low and marshy, and then it would begin to rise moderately. At the very end of this land view, his eye would rest upon a small elevation called Morton's Point. Turning now more to the right, or south-east, he would look down a slope to this same marshy land before spoken of, but higher above the sea level here than that lying more towards the Mystic River; and when this was passed he would see the land again ascending until it reached the top of Breed's Hill, some sixty or seventy feet above the tide-water, where the redoubt was built, and where the monument now stands. From the top of Bunker Hill to the top of Breed's Hill, the distance was about a third of a mile. Turning now still more to the right and going on a little distance farther, still descending, the traveller would find himself in the village of

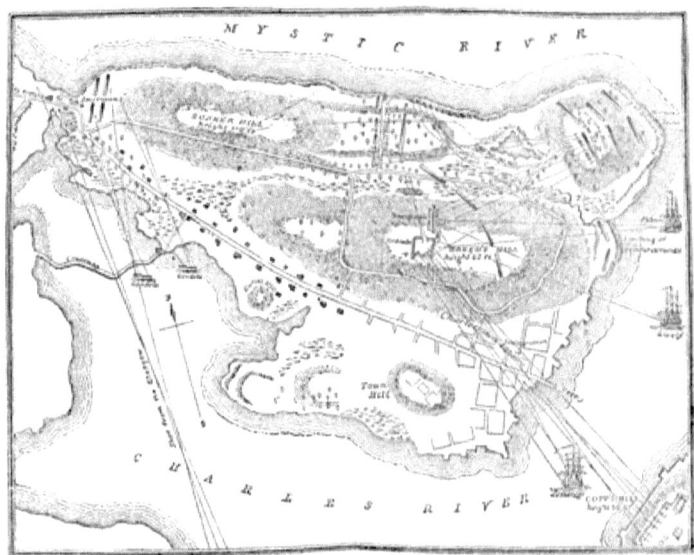

PLAN OF THE BATTLE OF BUNKER HILL, JUNE 17TH, 1775.

Charlestown among the houses and shops and stores nestled close along the shore. Some of these houses and barns on the upper slope came near the top of Breed's Hill. It is not nearly so far to the water's edge in a line drawn straight from Bunker Hill, across the top of Breed's Hill, as when a line is drawn from Bunker Hill to Morton's Point. In other words, the land pushes out farther into the water at Morton's Point, than anywhere else on the south-easterly end of the peninsula.

The British began to take their men over from Boston to Morton's Point in boats about 12 o'clock, and they completed this business of transportation about 2 o'clock. The reinforcements afterwards brought over were landed at a place lying midway between Morton's Point and the village of Charlestown.

On the top of Breed's Hill, lying near the village of Charlestown, a redoubt about eight rods square had been constructed during the night of June 16th, facing easterly; and in the morning a line of embankment had been carried north from the front corner about twenty rods. So silently had this work been done, beneath the waning moon, that the British sentries pacing along the shore of Charles River, and the night guards on the ships anchored near by in the bay, knew nothing of it till the morning dawned. The dawn, however, comes early in the middle of June.

Going now to the northern end of this twenty-rod embankment, and passing around the corner, then turning to the north-west (with a little open space left between), the fence line, so called, began. It first ran about six hundred feet in the direction just named (to the north-west) till it struck the lower slopes of Bunker Hill; then turning at an obtuse angle, it went in a straight line along these lower slopes, dropping down gradually till it reached the Mystic River. This last section of fence was about nine hundred feet in length, making that of the whole fence line fifteen hundred feet.

When the British officers took a survey of these lines of defence from Morton's Point, they saw at the extreme left, as they were facing this redoubt, which, with the embankment running out from it, presented to them a front line of earthworks measuring a little more than four hundred and fifty feet in length. Then from near the corner of these earthworks, they saw the fence line running in a diagonal, six hundred feet. Then turning, it ran nine hundred feet, in a way to meet their eye almost as a front facing line. This last line thrown back, as it was some four hundred or four hundred and fifty feet beyond the face line of the redoubt, was not exactly parallel with it, and yet it approached a parallel. As the British officers looked upon this extended arrangement, the redoubt at the left, on the high land, probably gained from them a degree of serious respect. But as to that low, fragile fence line, it was without much doubt treated by them with a kind of contemptuous laughter. They naturally enough thought that British soldiers would walk over that impediment as easily as sheep in search of water or fresh grass would go over a tumble-down stone wall. And they laid their plan of battle accordingly. That plan we will not now explain, as it comes up naturally later in the chapter. But this was the aspect of things which met their eyes just before the battle, as they looked upon what the Americans had been about during the night and forenoon. And in reference to the *forenoon* let it be understood, as already suggested, that we call the part of the day by this name which passed before the beginning of the battle.

Seldom does it happen that a battle-ground is so set that the action can be watched from so many directions, and by so many people, as in this case. All Boston could flock to

the steeples and house-tops, and without any help from
field-glasses, could see the main part of what was occurring. From many of the high lands about the town
south-westerly, northerly, easterly, spectators could have a
more distant view of the scene. What was passing close
down by the Mystic River could not be seen very well
except from the north and north-east. But the redoubt
stood in open sight from many points of observation.

Cambridge could not see the battle; she could only hear
its noise. Bunker Hill cut off her view. But from the high
lands of Brookline and Roxbury the distant view would be
excellent. The look-out places about the town were many,
and numerous eyes watched the progress of the fight, British
and American alike.

When the action began, a little after 3 o'clock, such
troops as Massachusetts had in the fighting lines, as before
stated, were mainly in and about the redoubt, though some
few were behind the fence. The Connecticut men came
next along the fence line, and the New Hampshire men
filled out that line down to the river.

As the British moved up to the attack, they came in
three columns. It would be easy to tell the assortment of
the British forces, showing what regiments were in this
column, and what in that. This has been often told, and it
would be easy to repeat the enumeration. But it matters
little to us now what the names and modes of designation
were for these troops, or how they were sorted and arranged.
It is rather confusing than otherwise to the average reader.
Suffice it to say, they were among the best troops which
England had to send. It is computed that she then had in
and about Boston ten thousand men. She anticipated serious business, and had sent here her most renowned battalions.

Mr. Frothingham computes the American forces at that
time as follows (p. 101): "Massachusetts furnished eleven

thousand five hundred; Connecticut two thousand three hundred; New Hampshire one thousand two hundred; and Rhode Island one thousand."

After the British ranks were arranged, and the columns were ready to move forward, Howe sent over to Boston for reinforcements. He told the soldiers to halt and eat their dinners, while he dispatched messengers for additional troops. When these were added, and they moved up to battle, they were doubtless between two and three thousand strong. We have said that they moved in three columns, and yet the two northerly columns nearest the Mystic were parts of one whole, and these two constituted together the right wing of the army, under the special command of Howe, who was also chief commander on the field. The other column constituted the left wing, under General Pigot's special command.*

A word more as to these two columns composing the right wing. Some of the finest companies in the whole British army had been selected to make a column which should move close along the Mystic River, and while the other column of the right wing should move up and engage the fortress and that part of the fence line nearest to the fortress, this column by the Mystic (when the attention of the American lines would naturally be called away, to some extent, by the firing which would begin near the redoubt) should make a bold push and go over that fence at a point near the river, rush up the sides of Bunker Hill, and flank the redoubt on Breed's Hill.

---

* "Opposing these (the British troops) were the raw, undisciplined bodies of insurgents posted behind the rail fence and the unfinished breastwork, and in the earthen redoubt on Breed's Hill, numbering together not more than fifteen hundred men, while those who were skulking on the slopes of Bunker Hill, afraid either to fight or to run over 'the neck,' and numbering in the aggregate nearly the same number, were neither useful nor ornamental for the purposes of the expedition." — Mr. Dawson in "Historical Magazine," June, 1868.

Captain Dearborn, who was with Stark by the Mystic, tells us that the attack first began by the firing of Howe's column upon the redoubt, which was answered. He says, "At the moment our regiment was formed in the rear of the rail fence, with one other small regiment from New Hampshire [this remark of his about the other regiment as *small*, implies that Stark's was larger, and shows that we have not probably overestimated the number from New Hampshire] under the command of Colonel Reed, the fire commenced between the left wing of the British army, commanded by General Howe, and the troops in the redoubt under Colonel Prescott, while a column of the enemy was advancing on our left on the shore of Mystic River, with an evident intention of turning our left wing."

This firing upon the redoubt then was only a feint. They regarded this as the stronghold, and they meant to take it by flanking it, and not by storming it. The *animus* of that first attack was in that column of picked companies, making a force of several hundred men, that was creeping stealthily along by the banks of the Mystic. Howe had sagaciously, as he thought, acted upon the idea that raw troops fresh from the farm would be so excited, and have their attention so drawn to the point where the firing began, that this column would break through almost without hindrance. But in this he had made a great mistake. The New Hampshire troops, withholding their fire till the column was near, poured such a deadly volley upon it, directed with the aim of hunters, that its front lines went down as grass before the mower's scythe. Dearborn says, "In the course of ten or fifteen minutes the enemy gave way at all points, and retreated in great disorder, leaving a large number of dead and wounded on the field." (We shall elsewhere show how terribly destructive that fire of the New Hampshire men was upon the front ranks of this column.) Without materially changing his plan of attack, Howe tried this experiment the second time, only now a new element of excitement was mingled with the scene. Charlestown was on fire. In the first attack, Pigot found that his left wing, which swung round near to the village of Charlestown, was played upon seriously by sharp-shooters, who made the houses and barns of that village nests and hiding-places for their operations. As a war measure, the British troops were doubtless right in burning the village. If they were justified in making the attack at all, they were justified in this expedient to give it success. As the British lines closed in the second time, the smoke and flames were rolling fiercely up from the burning vil-lage. Pigot's left wing was seemingly thrown more exclu-sively against the redoubt than even the left-hand column of Howe. The latter began the firing in the first attack upon the redoubt, but the column, as we understand the order of the movement, was centrally thrown more upon the upper lines of the fence than upon the redoubt. The second attack, based upon the same general idea as the first, was alike unsuccessful. The New Hampshire and Con-necticut men, with such Massachusetts forces as were with them, rolled back both those columns of Howe with heavy slaughter.

Now, let it be borne in mind that up to this time there had been no really earnest and hearty attack upon the re-doubt. The firing upon it had been very considerable, both with cannon and with musketry, at long range, for the Brit-ish were plying their cannon as well as their small arms. But they had not in either case really tried to take it. That was not the order of their plan. They wanted to *seem* to be trying to take it, both for engaging the men in and about it, and also drawing off the attention of the other American troops. But the real brunt of the two first onsets was against the fence line, and reaching all along that line from one end to the other, though sharpest near the river. Mr. Dawson's account of this battle, contained in the " Historical Magazine " for June, 1868, is fuller and better in some respects than any we know, and we quote the following graphic passages from him. He calls the repulses at the fence *three* instead of *two*.

" The rail fence, on the high bank against which the grenadiers and their flank company were moving in a parallel column, was manned with the remainder of the New Hampshire troops commanded by Colonel Stark ; by those from the same colony commanded by Colonel Reed ; and by the four incomplete companies of Connecticut men, commanded by Captain Knowlton. . . . . Colonel Stark in person commanded on the extreme left of this rail fence, directly above the temporary wall on the beach, ... and he is said to have ordered his men at the fence to reserve their fire until the half-gaiters of the approaching grenadiers should become distinctly visible. The Connecticut men, who occupied the rail fence on the right of the New Hampshire men, are said to have been instructed in like manner by their officers, to withhold their fire also until they could see the whites of the grenadiers' eyes. When the grenadiers and light infantry reached the points which had been thus designated as the ' deadlines ' of their respective lines of march, the insurgents opened upon them a well-directed and rapid fire ; and entire ranks were mowed down in an instant with terrible accuracy. Both the grenadiers on the bank, and the light infantry on the beach, of course, were instantly thrown into the utmost disorder, and fell back discomfited, beyond the range of the insurgents' fire ; and there, under cover of an unevenness in the ground, the former were rallied, and soon after returned to the attack, the light infantry also re-forming and co-operating with them on the bank as far as they were able to do so. The grenadiers and the light infantry, thus re-formed, with singular bravery moved against the fence and wall a second time ; but the insurgents concentrated their defence, and with the same steadiness and accuracy as before, poured upon the shortened line of their assailants another fire which was as murderous as the first. Again the royal troops were repulsed, and a second time they fell back, scathed, but not dishonored. But the end of this terrible slaughter was not yet. The pride of the officers and the obstinacy of the troops could not quietly submit to even this renewed disaster, and again the shattered companies of grenadiers and light infantry were re-formed, and with a still more shortened line than they had previously presented, and with depressed spirits, they approached the fence a third time. They were repulsed the third time. . . . .

" During the continuance of this stubborn contest on the left of the insurgents' position, which occupied upwards of an hour, there seems to have been no serious attempt by the left wing of the royal troops to carry either the redoubt or the breastwork, although a vigorous fire had been kept up in order to employ the insurgents who were posted behind those earthworks, but the third repulse of the grenadiers and light infantry probably convinced General Howe of the hopelessness of his original undertaking, and led him to make an entirely new disposition of his command. He accordingly allowed the shattered fragments of the eleven companies of light troops — those which had escaped from the terrible ordeal to which they had been exposed in front of the rail fence and stone wall on the extreme right of his line of attack — to amuse and hold in check those whom they had recently assaulted, while he should direct his attention to the right of the insurgents' position, the redoubt and the breastwork, in which were only the handful of Massachusetts men commanded by Colonel Prescott, and the very few stragglers who had ventured to assist them." *

* If any one doubts whether this was the real plan or order of the battle at its opening, we commend to his perusal the long and able note in fine type on page 347 of the " Historical Magazine," from which we have quoted. In this note Mr. Dawson cites his authorities and arranges his evidences in a very admirable manner. He quotes, from English and American officers, little passages just to the point. He takes a sentence from Gage's dispatch to his Government, which of itself is sufficient authority on a matter like this. He

After the second repulse (we reckon as two what Mr. D. calls three), there was a pause of considerable length. The British troops found they had very heavy and serious work on their hands. More reinforcements came over from Boston. General Clinton also came. These things necessarily required time. There was a breathing spell. If those Massachusetts regiments which Ward had despatched at the last moment, and who might reasonably urge that they did not have time to get there before the battle began, had wished to bear a hand in this action, here was a fine opportunity for them to come forward and fill that redoubt with fresh men and fresh ammunition to its utmost limit of accommodation. There were Massachusetts soldiers enough about that hill, doing nothing, to have crowded this fortress beyond its proper capacity. The very fact of these two repulses would seem to have been enough to put courage into men that had not had it before, and there was powder enough on that field, if it could only be got to the front where it was wanted. It would certainly have been the height of folly for General Ward to send soldiers to that field without powder, and there were in that immediate vicinity doubtless a thousand Massachusetts soldiers who had hardly fired a gun.

We will copy now a brief passage from the "Siege of Boston" (p. 147), descriptive of the state of things at this point of time. "While such was the confusion at Bunker Hill, good order prevailed at the redoubt. Colonel Prescott

says, "The light infantry was directed to force the left point of the breastwork [Gage calls the whole fence line a breastwork] to take the rebel line in flank ; the grenadiers to attack in front, supported by the fifth and fifty-second battalions." He refers also to General Wilkinson as saying, on the authority of Stark, that at first "the fire on the redoubt was feeble and at long range, '*apparently with a design to draw the attention of Colonel Prescott*,'" and also in the last attack that Stark's men were "*unassailed and unoccupied.*"

13

remained at his post, determined in his purpose, undaunted
in his bearing, inspiring his command with hope and confidence, and yet chagrined that in this hour of peril and
glory adequate support had not reached him."

But at page 136 of the "Siege of Boston," the reader
will find that the redoubt had been reinforced "just previous to the action, by portions of Massachusetts regiments
under Colonels Brewer, Nixon, Woodbridge, Little and
Major Moore, and one company of artillery." That would
seem to be "adequate support." With any such numbers
as this mention of five regiments naturally suggests, there
would then have been in the redoubt (including those who
were there before) not less than eight or nine hundred men,
about as many as could have been efficiently employed on
that front line. But were those reinforcements on hand
"just previous to the action"? Or did they ever get there?
It does not seem fair nor symmetrical, that the Massachusetts regiments, on the one hand, should have the credit of
reinforcing Prescott, and that Prescott, on the other, should
be chagrined and indignant that he was not reinforced.

We have already alluded to a species of ridicule cast upon
General Putnam, because he was riding around so furiously
on the back side of Bunker Hill urging forward these reinforcements. In some of these passages, the fact is made to
hold, and to discharge upon the mind of the reader, the
insinuation that he preferred to be over there about such
business, out of harm's way, rather than to mingle in the
fury of the fray, where the bullets were flying. But in his
immense activities that day we have never been able to see
either the *cowardly* or the *ridiculous*. We see only an
elderly man, putting in exercise every power of his mind
and body to make up for other men's deficiences, and to
save from ignominious failure an enterprise of vast importance to the common cause. We are all ready to admit

now that the moral consequences of this first great battle of the Revolution were very weighty, and that is why men want the honors of the enterprise who are not entitled to them. General Putnam had from the first some clear fore-shadowings of what the result would be, if a reasonable amount of success could be secured that day ; and no man ever went through more prodigious toil than he to make the enterprise a success. And while upon this point, we may call attention to a direct antagonism among those writers who would take the honors of that day from him. General Dearborn would have it that Putnam kept essentially in one place on the top of Bunker Hill, out of the way of danger, by the side of Colonel Gerrish. It helped to lend a nice sting to the charge, to put him in concert with, and by the side of, Colonel Gerrish, whose regiment that day only managed to get *three* men killed and *two* wounded. This association would seem at once to give him the companionship of cowards. But another writer, not friendly to General Putnam, keeps him in a kind of perpetual motion, for idle or ignoble ends. With him, General Putnam that day was "well-nigh ubiquitous." This last testimony is undoubtedly correct, but Putnam would have been far more quiet and near one place, if General Ward and the Massachusetts regiments had only done their duty.

As one studies his movements during those battle hours, this appears to be the law that governed them. When the British were making their desperate onsets to break our line (call them *two*, *three*, or *four*, as you please, for writers differ, not substantially but technically), Putnam was always near the front in the very thickest of the fray. But the moment there was a respite, and he could be spared, he rushed up Bunker Hill and over the back side of it to see if he could not put some courage into those halting Massachusetts regiments, and move them forward to reinforce

Colonel Prescott.　But those hasty journeys seem to have been of no great use.　He ran against a mass of *inertia* that he could not overcome.　He could tarry often but a few moments, for he must hasten and be back in his place. We accept the words "well-nigh ubiquitous" as exactly meeting the case, for he was trying to do his own work and that which belonged to others, but which by them was left undone.

We can, with the most perfect confidence, challenge any man to bring real proof, such as will stand close examination, showing that Putnam was ever away for five minutes from the fighting line while the sharp fighting was going on.　Mr. Frothingham is authority for his being there when the action began.　"General Putnam was here [by the fence line] when the action commenced."　Major Small (as we shall hereafter show) is authority that he was on hand at a later point, where the fight was hottest.　Mr. Frothingham and Dr. Ellis are both witnesses that he was close at hand when the redoubt was finally carried.　He was "well-nigh ubiquitous," but it was not to his dishonor, nor for Massachusetts' glory, that he had to be so.

We turned aside in the pause of the battle.　Let us now come back and look at its closing act.　That redoubt was not filled with fresh troops and fresh ammunition in the interval of delay, at least not to any great extent.　There were men enough, but the Committee of Safety, General Putnam, and many others, say that there were never over fifteen hundred men in that fighting line, and knowing what we do of the New Hampshire and Connecticut men, it is easy to complete the enumeration.　No notice we have ever seen, no light we can gain, make it appear that the forces at the redoubt were materially increased during this pause in the battle.　The British were bringing over, even from Boston, fresh troops, but those regiments on the

American side which had kept clear of danger up to this time, still managed by one excuse and another to hold themselves in a great measure aloof. It would not do to reinforce the redoubt from the fence line. Hitherto that had been the chief object of attack, and what the next move of the British would be could not then be told.

Let us try at this point to fathom the thoughts of the British officers, especially Howe, causing him materially to change his plan of attack. Did he not say within himself, We began this battle under the strong impression that the redoubt itself would be very hard to carry, but the fence line would be easily broken. We have made two advances along the whole line under this impression, and it has been a very costly operation. I never could persuade my men to try that experiment over again. Besides, we have felt the fire of the enemy twice along the whole battle line, and to our surprise have found that the parts of their line.which we supposed to be the weakest are the strongest, and those which we supposed to be the strongest are the weakest. We will leave the fence and push now for the redoubt. It must, we think, be apparent to all, that something like this train of thought went through his mind. The battle began with the intention of flanking the redoubt by breaking the fence line. It ended by flanking the fence line by carrying the redoubt. The New Hampshire and Connecticut men, with such Massachusetts men as were with them, were not beaten that day; they were simply flanked. The weakness, inefficiency and disorders of that day were in connection with the Massachusetts troops. Yet we will never accuse Colonel Prescott of a want of personal courage and personal faithfulness according to the measure of his military ability. Nor have we any but words of high honor and praise for those Massachusetts men of the original detachment, who stayed by, and did their duty faithfully to the end.* The test they passed through was extremely trying, for they had seen at least half of their original number (Prescott makes it more) drop off by desertions, and they knew that there were multitudes of their Massachusetts brethren near at hand, who could, but would not, come to their relief. The men of Prescott's, Frye's and Bridge's regiments who stayed to the last, deserve to be crowned as heroes ; but it was shameful that they were so left by their companions, and equally shameful that they were not reinforced.

General Ward is more to be blamed for this than Colonel Prescott ; and if the one local commander, who did not hold his line, were not pushed upon the modern public as the great military hero. and leader of that day, we should feel inclined to sympathize with him, to pity and excuse him. But we cannot hide the historical fact that the weaknesses and disorders of that action circled around that portion of the battle line where he was the central figure. Heroic as he personally was, and faithful to the last, he showed himself lacking in some of the prime qualities of a military commander. It is too much to ask that he, in spite of these things, should be exalted into the chief man of all, to gratify any one's private wishes. Brought down to the basis of hard and stubborn facts, the case stands thus: Eleven hundred men from New Hampshire and Connecticut, with a few Massachusetts men added, had successfully kept a slight and hastily-built line of defences of fifteen hundred feet in length, against two desperate attacks of the British army, and had rolled that army back with great slaughter. Then came a crisis when Massachu-

---

* " Previous to that [the arrival of Stark's regiment] there were many who left the ground at the fort, particularly at the landing of the British troops ; but after the commencement of the battle with small arms, I know of no man leaving his post until the order to retreat was given by Colonel Prescott." — Letter of Abel Parker, in Prescott's regiment.

setts, with two thousand men, more or less, was called upon
to defend in like manner a *strongly-built* line of about four
hundred and fifty feet in length.   If she could defend that
for fifteen minutes, the day would be ours.   She failed, and
the British broke through.   Colonel Prescott and the men
of his original command did all they could under the circumstances.   We see no real evidence that he was reinforced,
except by individuals.   It would appear that he had with
him in that final resistance about four hundred men, of
whom one hundred and sixty were killed or wounded.   We
have searched in vain to find satisfactory evidence that any
Massachusetts regiment marched into that redoubt to his
help.   If the anecdote already given is authentic, as to
what took place at Charlestown Neck after the battle, between Prescott and Putnam, it would seem quite conclusive,
as showing that Prescott was not reinforced.   Putnam tried
hard enough to reinforce him, but as he told Prescott, " I
could not make the dogs go."   The " Prescott Memorial "
says expressly, " Nor was any reinforcement sent."

Looking upon the killed and wounded on the American
side, one might naturally enough think, as before suggested,
that the Massachusetts men did the hardest part of the
fighting ; but the law which underlies that list of casualties
has already been noticed.   The British broke through where
the Massachusetts men guarded the line ; and when that
wrathful current was once in motion, it was terrific in its
sweep.   It dealt out destruction without mercy.   Massachusetts lost in the battle one hundred and five killed, and
one hundred and seventy-five wounded ; New Hampshire,
twenty killed, and sixty-six wounded ; Connecticut, fifteen
killed, and thirty wounded.   But of the Massachusetts
losses, a large proportion occurred within the space of ten
or fifteen minutes at the very close of the battle, and
then because the redoubt was not held.

Gage admitted a loss of one thousand and fifty-four on
his side, while he claimed that the men in the battle on the
British side made "a body of something above two thousand men;" in other words, taking his report according to
the apparent sense of the language, the killed and wounded
made about half the whole force employed. Lieutenant
Clarke, a British officer, speaks of the marvellous losses
of the British that day. He says, "From calculations of
most pitched battles, the proportion of the number of
killed and wounded is only every eighth man." In all
her long wars, reaching over hundreds of years, England
hardly ever fought a battle in which she lost so large a
portion of the men engaged.* But we do not accept
General Gage's estimate, either of the men employed or
the losses. The British probably had not less than from
three to four thousand men on the ground, and the Americans estimated the British loss at one thousand five hundred. Their men were far away from home, and it was
easy to put in false estimates; but there could be no such
deceptions on our side. The men who were killed and
wounded all had their homes not far away, and doubtless
every man of them was noted and enumerated. If the
British could only have been repulsed on the third attack,
our loss would have been a comparatively trifling one,

* *Thaddeus Burr to General Wooster.* — "General Howe says you may talk
of your *Mindens* and *Fontenoys,* but he never saw or heard of such carnage
in so short a time."

General Greene to Jacob Green. — "The Welsh fusileers, the finest regiment in the English establishment, is ruined. There are but one Captain and
eleven privates left in the regiment."

General Greene put that case too strongly, but the destruction in this regiment was frightful, by many accounts.

"Such a slaughter was perhaps never before made upon British troops in
the space of about an hour, during which the heat of the engagement lasted,
by about fifteen hundred men, which were the most that were at any time
engaged on the American side." — Account of Committee of Safety.

while theirs would have been greater than it was. They would not have been likely to make a fourth attempt.

There were some incidents of special interest in the course of the battle, little episodes of a strange and half-romantic character, that might be related, of which we take a single one. Lieutenant Clarke, from the British point of view, tells the following story:

" Before the intrenchments were forced, a man whom the Americans called a marksman, or rifleman, was seen standing upon something, near three feet higher than the rest of the troops, as their hats were not visible. This man had no sooner discharged one musket than another was handed to him, and continued firing in that manner for ten or twelve minutes. And in that small space of time, by their handing to him fresh-loaded muskets, it is supposed that he could not kill or wound less than twenty officers, for it was at them particularly that he directed his aim, as was afterwards confirmed by the prisoners. But he soon paid his tribute, for upon being noticed he was killed by the grenadiers of the Royal Welsh fusileers."

But we cannot close this account of the battle without describing more fully what took place at the very last. And we purposely take Mr. Frothingham for our authority. We might bring other witnesses, but we are entirely satisfied with his statement. He says (" Siege of Boston," p. 152), " The whole body of Americans were now in full retreat, the greater part over the top of Bunker Hill. The brow of Bunker Hill was a place of great slaughter. General Putnam here rode to the rear of the retreating troops, and regardless of the balls flying about him, with his sword drawn, and still undaunted in his bearing, urged them to renew the fight in the unfinished works. 'Make a stand here,' he exclaimed ; 'we can stop them yet! In God's name, form, and give them one shot more!' It was here that he stood by an artillery piece until the enemy's bayonets were almost upon him."

Now let us remember that these troops which Putnam was thus addressing were largely, if not entirely, that routed mass in and about the redoubt, Massachusetts troops, to whom, just before, Prescott (feeling that the redoubt was lost) had given the order to retreat. As soon as possible after that rush began, Putnam hastens to put himself *behind* this flying column,— between it and the British troops,— and assuming the command from that post of greatest danger, calls upon the fugitives to stop. He reverses, on the spot, the order which Prescott had just given. He takes possession in a military way of the very men whom Prescott had just had under his subordinate command.

And what Putnam did here, he might just as naturally have done anywhere along that whole line. If the break had occurred among the New Hampshire men, and Stark or Reed had sounded a retreat, Putnam, as commander over the whole field, would have seen it, just as he saw this giving way at the redoubt. In that case he would doubtless have rushed to that point, and have attempted to do the same things he was doing here. He was exercising, in other words, the functions of a common commander, and how any one can pen such a passage as we have just quoted, and many others of the same general import, and not see in General Putnam something more than a mere assistant of Colonel Prescott, passes our comprehension. Besides, what folly once to think of Colonel Prescott as the commander on that broad field, while he has been shut up in the redoubt and does not even know what has been happening away from that fortress! Mr. Frothingham says (p. 166), "Colonel Prescott was left in uncontrolled possession of his post. Nor is there any proof that he gave an order at the rail fence or on Bunker Hill." To that statement no objection need be made, but the chief commander does not make his appearance in it.* Mr. Frothingham goes on to say, " He remained at the redoubt, and there fought the battle with such coolness, bravery and discretion as to win the unbounded applause of his contemporaries." The student of history will probably search the records of 1775 in vain to find evidence such as will fairly and naturally sustain that last assertion. We have turned over within the past year a great many books and records bearing upon this period and upon this battle, and we do not find this " unbounded applause of his contemporaries." The facts given in Chapter VI. have a different complexion. Nay, the only way in which any true glory can be saved for Prescott out of this battle, is by regarding him simply as a commander of the redoubt, who was faithful and heroic to his trust, who stayed to the last and did all he could with his military experience and ability. We are as willing as any one to make him a hero, if the case can be put reasonably; but the moment he is exalted as the commanding head over that field, his deficiencies of action are so glaring, his ignorance of details is so amazing, that he is only covered with disgrace in being made to occupy such a position.

Of the killed and wounded on our side we have taken our summary from Mr. Frothingham's account. We have no

* In the April number of the "North American Review" for 1826 (p. 466), we find a notice of Colonel Swett's writings. He had brought forward a witness who testified to Putnam's presence in the redoubt ; upon which the editor remarks,—

"This was a little before the battle ; during the battle the distinguished hero and patriot, Colonel Prescott, had the entire and uncontrolled command in the redoubt."

That is a perfectly rational and safe position to take. Prescott was placed there to do just that, and no claim is made that Putnam gave orders *within* the redoubt during the action. But he overlooked it, and watched its fortunes with intense interest till the break came, and then he speedily appeared on the scene.

doubt that he sifted all the evidence carefully, and has given
the list as accurately as it can be made. But it may interest
the reader to see other computations, not differing largely
from his, but showing slight variations. We give first Mr.
Frothingham's figures, as distributed among the different
military bodies.

The following list of killed and wounded is taken from
the "Siege of Boston," p. 193:

	Killed.	Wounded.
Prescott's regiment	42	28
Bridge's regiment	15	29
Frye's regiment	15	31
Brewer's regiment	7	11
Little's regiment	7	23
Gardner's regiment	6	7
Nixon's regiment	3	10
Woodbridge's regiment	1	5
Doolittle's regiment	0	9
Gridley's regiment	0	4
Ward's regiment	1	6
Scammons's regiment	0	2
Gerrish's regiment	3	2
Whitcomb's regiment	5	8
Stark's regiment	15	45
Reed's regiment	5	21
Putnam's and Coit's regiment	11	26
Chester's company	4	4

Killed, 140; wounded, 271; captured, 30; making a total of
441.

From Force's "American Archives" (4th Series, Vol. II. p.
1628), we take this statement. No date is given with the document, but surrounding ones would place it July 9th or 10th, 1775.

	Killed and Missing.	Wounded.
Colonel Frye's regiment	14	38
Colonel Little's regiment	7	23
Colonel Brewer's regiment	12	22

	Killed and Missing.	Wounded.
Colonel Gridley's regiment	0	4
Colonel Stark's regiment	15	45
Colonel Woodbridge's regiment	0	5
Colonel Scammons's regiment	0	2
Colonel Bridge's regiment	17	25
Colonel Whitcomb's regiment	7	8
General Ward's regiment	1	6
Colonel Gerrish's regiment	3	5
Colonel Reed's (Reid's) regiment	4	29
Colonel Prescott's regiment	43	46
Colonel Doolittle's regiment	6	9
Colonel Gardner's regiment	0	7
Colonel Patterson's regiment	0	1
Colonel Nixon's regiment	3	0
Connecticut	13	26

Total, killed and missing, 145 ; wounded, 301 ; making a total of 446.

The record says 304 wounded, but simple addition gives 301. Ward's orderly book, as quoted by Mr. Frothingham, makes, killed, 115 ; wounded, 305 ; captured, 30 ; total, 450.

The diary of Mr. Haskell, from which some quotations will be made in the next chapter, gives, killed, 138 ; wounded, 292 ; total, 430.

The six killed in Gardner's regiment, as reported in Mr. Frothingham's list, stand connected with Doolittle's regiment in the "Archives." In Reed's New Hampshire regiment, Mr. Frothingham gives five killed, the "Archives" four. By Mr. Frothingham, Connecticut had fifteen killed, and thirty wounded. By the "Archives," thirteen killed, and twenty-six wounded, and there are other slight variations. In Ward's orderly book the wounded are more numerous and the killed less in number than in the other accounts. Doubtless quite a number entered by him as "wounded" soon died of their wounds, and their names were carried over to the list of the killed. But the four statements above given do not differ greatly in the total results.

One general fact already mentioned about the killed and wounded should not be forgotten. Probably no regiment that went over to Bunker Hill in that early afternoon and back again, escaped without having some of their men killed and wounded. Stark's Major, the heroic McClary, was killed here. The fact that a regiment reported a considerable number of casualties, was no sure sign in itself that it had actually taken any part whatever in the battle proper, though we do not doubt that several of the Massachusetts regiments like Little's, Gardner's, Brewer's, Nixon's, Whitcomb's, etc., did go over the top of Bunker Hill and down toward the redoubt, and so brought themselves into that storm of missiles already described. But that any one of these regiments, in a body, went fully to the front, where their own guns could materially harm the British, we doubt. Individuals went, and some companies apparently, but those who halted and retreated even out of these regiments, were vastly more numerous than those who went forward to fight. There were several other regiments that kept themselves in a remarkably safe condition, regarded as men supposed to have fought at Bunker Hill. There were five Massachusetts regiments, the total of whose accidents are summed up in two killed and twenty-six wounded.

CHAPTER X.

Condition of a defeated Army — What became of the American Army after the Battle.— Prescott goes to Cambridge.— Fortifications on Prospect Hill.— Daniel Putnam and Mrs. Inman.— Diary of Mr. Haskell.

AN army is not annihilated when it is defeated. It is to be carefully guarded and kept for future use. And yet there is no time when the powers and capacities of a military leader are more thoroughly tested than immediately after a defeat. The first question that arises is, how to conduct these soldiers securely out from the dangers that press immediately upon them. And when that is accomplished, other cares arise. Here is a body of men, weary with watching, toil and conflict, chagrined and disappointed in their hopes, smarting under wounds that are not severe enough to consign them to the hospital, mourning for comrades that have fallen by their side, the familiar faces of the drill, the tent, the mess-room : how shall these men be lifted over these hours of despondency ? A military commander often reveals his greatest and noblest qualities in such times as these.

There is one clear and well-attested historical fact which has never apparently been brought to bear much upon the questions now before us ; but which, when set in its true relations, would of itself, standing alone, show with sufficient clearness who was the chief field officer of the forces who fought the battle of Bunker Hill. No one can know all the details respecting the movement of those troops that Saturday evening. Most of the Massachusetts regiments, it is likely, were led off in sections by their regimental officers, and taken back to their respective encampments. Some of them had not been near enough to the real battle to receive any damage from it, and such casualties as had happened were received in the tumults of the crowd, or by missiles thrown from the British batteries across the neck. Others of them had been nearer and had borne losses. Such of those three regiments first detailed as had remained, and fought the battle through, were badly cut up.

But who identified himself with this defeated army, and took care of it and kept with it? Prescott certainly did not. He at once separated himself from it and went back to Cambridge, apparently not even in connection with the remains of his own regiment, though he may have marched in their company. But such descriptions as we have, make it appear that he went as an individual and not in command of, or in connection with, any military body or bodies whatever.* Colonel Swett, in his "History of the Battle of Bunker Hill" (p. 49), gives the following graphic description of Prescott's movements that night. He says, " Prescott repaired to Cambridge, furious as a lion driven from his lair, foaming with indignation at the want of support

---

* In the "Prescott Memorial" the story is told how, as Prescott was returning to Cambridge that night, he went into an inn, where some soldiers had just had a bowl of punch mixed. Seeing him they naturally passed the bowl to him to take the first drink. Just as the cup reached his hands, a cannon ball came ploughing its way through the house, whereat the men were so frightened that they ran away with all haste. Prescott remained, cool and collected, and as there was no one else to drink with him, he had the punch to himself. This cool personal courage Prescott exhibited in a high degree, through the whole expedition. He never ran from that redoubt, though many of his men did. There had been a tremendous strain upon his nerves from the moment the British ships began their cannonading in the morning. But *personally* he never flinched.

when victory was in his grasp,—a victory dearly purchased with the precious blood of his soldiers, family and friends." We do not care how fierce the rhetoric was with which he plied General Ward. He deserved it all. But in these very complaints we have the evidence of what we have all along claimed, that Ward was shamefully remiss in duty, and that he (Prescott) was not reinforced.

Mr. Frothingham, in the "Siege of Boston" (p. 153), gives us a still clearer and more detailed picture. He says, "Colonel Prescott, indignant at the absence of support when victory was within his grasp, repaired to headquarters, reported the issue of the battle, already too well known, and received the thanks of the commander-in-chief.* He found General Ward under great apprehensions lest the enemy, encouraged by success, should advance on Cambridge, where he had neither disciplined troops nor an adequate supply of ammunition to receive him. Colonel Prescott, however, assured him that the confidence of the British would not be increased by the result of the battle."

This was all right and proper so long as we regard Prescott as the local and subordinate commander of that redoubt. He was nominated and appointed for that particular duty. He had done all he could personally, and here was the result. His task was ended, and he might go back to Cambridge alone, or in company with the troops marching to their quarters, and no fault is to be found with him.

But if he had been chief commander on that field, and left the army in this way, his conduct would have been strange and inexcusable. General Putnam certainly did not go to Cambridge that night. He kept with the men

---

* "The thanks of the commander-in-chief!" that is one of those neat and decorous arrangements of words which helps to dress a paragraph, but the historical facts which support it are of the *minus* quantity. The very next sentence will show General Ward in too great a state of perturbation to be paying formal thanks to anybody.

14

who had done the chief portion of the fighting. He led them across the neck to what is now Somerville, and at once began intrenchments on Winter and Prospect Hills. Mr. Frothingham, on the same page with the last quotation, gives us these facts plainly. He says, "The Americans at Winter and Prospect Hills lay on their arms while the British, reinforced by additional troops from Boston, threw up during the night a line of breastwork on the northern side of Bunker Hill."

The Americans, in this passage, represent that portion of the American army that had fought the battle. How many Massachusetts men were with them that night we do not know, but it is quite certain the New Hampshire and Connecticut men were there, and the commander in the battle was there with them. No one seems to have any question about these acts of General Putnam. Even those who have made him a kind of mysterious and half-mythical personage during the battle of Saturday, hardly knowing where he was or what he was about, some keeping him very still and quiet in one place, and others making him the very embodiment of perpetual motion, these differing writers appear to have no difficulty in locating him with the American army on Saturday night, over at Prospect and Winter Hills. What a strange and curious man he must have been to have rushed in at the very last moment to snatch that defeated army out of the hands of its rightful commander! What a desirable moment that was to come into such a possession! How eagerly most men covet the glories of leadership under such conditions!

There can be no doubt (for we have many witnesses) that he spent that night with this discomfited army, and that Prescott did not. We have his own express statement on this point, made to the Committee of Safety not long after, at a time when he had the burden of some grievances

on his mind.   He says, " Pray, did not I take possession of
Prospect Hill the very night after the fight on Bunker Hill
without having any orders from any person ?   And was not
I the only general officer that tarried there ?"   There was
no time to consult or wait for orders.   He had to take the
responsibility and do the best he could.   And the very language he uses implies that what he did was generally acknowledged to have been wisely and well done,— an important step taken.

Daniel Putnam found him at Prospect Hill the next
morning, about 10 o'clock.   But before allowing him to tell
what his father was doing and how he looked, there is a
little story about this Daniel Putnam himself, which will
help to bring freshly before us the scenes and events connected with this famous action.   .

He wanted to go to the battle ; begged hard to be permitted to go.   His older brother was going, and he himself
would be sixteen years old the next November.   But his
father would not hear to it, told him he must go and stay
with Mrs. Inman and make himself useful.   This Mrs. Inman and her nieces lived in the house * which gave the

---

* It happened by a somewhat curious coincidence, that on the very day
while we were writing these words, a local celebration was going on in Cambridge on the occasion of the dedication of Inman Square.   We knew nothing of it until we saw the report in the next morning's paper.   From the historical address delivered by Mr. C. M. Hovey, as reported in the Boston
" Daily Advertiser " of February 4th, 1876, we cut the following passage, which
will very clearly explain the circumstances of this house and farm, and give us
a glimpse of their surroundings in 1775 :

"In 1775 the principal family in Cambridgeport was the Inman family.
There belonged to this estate about one hundred and eighty acres of land,
which was described as arable pasture and woodland.   It comprised nearly
one-half of what is now the Port.   The house, near the corner of Main and
Inman Streets, was approached from Milk Row, now in Somerville, by a pleasant lane, part of which was identical with the present Inman Street.   Ralph
Inman died in 1788, and by his direction the land was sold in 1802 for the
benefit of his heirs.   It brought ten dollars an acre.   Until 1793, when West

name to General Putnam's headquarters, in what is now
Cambridgeport, and one of the present streets of Cam-
bridgeport near this locality bears this name. Mr. Inman
was a Tory, and feeling quite uncomfortable where so many
American soldiers were about him, had himself gone into
Boston to share the protection of the King's troops. Mrs.
Inman and her nieces, who lived with her, had applied to
General Putnam for protection, and he had set a guard to
keep her premises from harm. General Putnam told Daniel
he must go and stay at Mrs. Inman's house during this
Bunker Hill business, and make himself as helpful to
her as possible. He felt a little as David did when his
elder brothers had gone to fight the Philistines, and he
was left with the sheep; but he obeyed, for some one has
well said of him that he dared do anything but disobey
his father.

On Saturday night, when the news reached Cambridge
that the Americans had been compelled to retreat, Mrs.
Inman, like others, fearing that the British would follow,
and she should find herself in the very path of the flying
and pursuing troops, determined to leave her house, with
such valuables as she could carry, and take refuge with
some friends at a place called *Brush Hill.* Putnam assisted in this hasty removal. They did not reach their destination till nearly midnight, but on the way young
Putnam's mind was greatly relieved from its load of pressing anxiety by hearing that his father was safe. The
next morning was Sunday. As soon as he could gain

Boston bridge was built, there was no way of reaching the estate except
through Charlestown. In 1809 Craigie's bridge was also built. In 1818 the
land lying between the college grounds on the west, Broadway on the south,
Prospect Street on the east, Cambridge and Hampshire Streets on the north,
was laid out as a racing park and used for that purpose for some years. When
it was given up, the land returned to bushes and trees again, till about 1840,
when population began to approach it."

permission he went in search of his father.   He tells the story thus:

"I was not long in retracing my steps of the last night back to Cambridge. General Putnam was not at his quarters; he had been there it was said for a few minutes only, and with fresh men was then fortifying Prospect Hill. There I found him about 10 o'clock on the morning of June 18th, dashing about among the workmen, throwing up intrenchments, and often placing a sod with his own hands. He wore the same clothes he had on when I left him thirty-eight hours before, and affirmed he had never put them off or washed himself since; and we might well believe him, for the aspect of all bore evidence that he spoke the truth."

General Putnam not only went to Prospect Hill that night, but he stayed there. It was a vital point to occupy. It controlled the path along which the British would have to move, if they attempted to march by the Charlestown road to Cambridge. They never attempted to march along that road. They had their fortifications on Bunker Hill, but they did not venture across the neck. Additional troops were detailed to be under Putnam's special command, and to help build his fortifications. But he went there directly from Bunker Hill and led the army there, as one entrusted with its destinies. In all this he is seen to have been their commander-in-chief, and Prescott is seen not to have been their commander-in-chief. We hold that the evidence to be derived from these circumstances immediately following the battle, is as vital as any that can be adduced from any quarter. The facts, too, seem to be admitted by all parties, though some have not stopped long enough to see the effect of the admission.

Through the kindness of Mr. A. W. Haskell of Boston, we have before us a neat and well kept diary, the work of his father, Caleb Haskell, who was a soldier at the battle of Bunker Hill in Colonel Little's regiment. A brief reference has already been made to this diary. Mr. Haskell was from Newburyport. This record will show us, in a natural and life-like manner, how those days in June, 1775, were passing.

" *June 17, Saturday.* — This day begins with the noise of cannon from the ships firing at our men intrenching on Bunker Hill. The firing continues all the forenoon of the day, but one man killed. We were alarmed at Cambridge, heard that the enemy were landing in Charlestown. The army set out, we found the town in flames, and the regulars ascending the hill, the balls flying almost as thick as hailstones, from the ships and floating batteries and Copp's Hill and Beacon Hill in Boston, and the ground covered with the wounded and dead. Our people stood the fire some time, until the enemy had almost surrounded us and cut off our retreat. We were obliged to quit the ground and retreat as fast as possible. In this engagement we lost the ground and the heroic General Warren. We had one hundred and thirty-eight killed and two hundred and ninety-two wounded. The loss on the enemy's side was ninety-two commissioners ; one hundred and two sergeants ; one hundred corporals, and seven hundred privates. Total loss, nine hundred and ninety-four. [This was probably an early report of British losses.]

" *June 18, Sunday.* — Early this morning were employed in making cartridges and getting in readiness for another battle. A large reinforcement came in from the country. At noon were alarmed again, marched to Prospect Hill, which we were fortifying, were ordered to halt and wait for orders from the General,* marched back again, had orders to hold ourselves in readiness to march at the first notice. The enemy keep a continual firing upon us at Prospect Hill, which we are fortifying. At 9 o'clock in the evening received orders to go down to the hill, march to headquarters, received new orders to go back to our quarters and hold ourselves in readiness.

" *June 19, Monday.* — The day comes on with noise of can-

---

* The General thus referred to was doubtless Putnam.

non from Bunker Hill, and floating batteries discharged at us on Prospect Hill, which continues all day. The enemy set the upper end of Charlestown on fire. We mounted picket guard.

" *June 20, Tuesday.* — On guard this morning, we passed muster in the afternoon, in the evening were relieved from guard. . . . .

" *June 23, Friday.* — This day were ordered to Prospect Hill, where we are stationed, went down, pitched our tents, went to intrenching. . . . .

" *July 2, Sunday.* — This day the Honorable George Washington, Esq., commander-in-chief of the united forces in America, arrived at Cambridge. This afternoon had rain."

In all these entries after the first, this soldier representing Colonel Little's regiment is circling about Putnam at Prospect Hill. The owner of the diary recollects an anecdote which his father loved to tell of General Putnam. Coming around one day to see how the works were getting on, he found some men that evidently had not bestowed much labor upon their section since he was last there.

" To what regiment do you belong ? " said the General.

" To Colonel Doolittle's," was the reply.

" Doo-little? do nothing at all ! " was the prompt rejoinder.

The anecdote shows that both Colonel Little's and Colonel Doolittle's regiments were there, and there were, as the records show, several other Massachusetts regiments intrenching under Putnam's orders.

CHAPTER XI.

TESTIMONY OF BUNKER HILL LITERATURE AND ART.

Art.— Three Pictures.— Mr. Dawson.— Early Notices of the Battle, American and English.— General Dearborn and the Controversy of 1818.— What was its Import ?— " Siege of Boston."— Frothingham.— Bancroft.— Irving. — The Question of To-day a new and modern one. — Mr. Frothingham's later Pupils.

IN this chapter, which will necessarily be long, we propose to bring together and set in order a mass of evidence which will certainly help to determine who was the commander at Bunker Hill.

We will begin with Art.

The first picture, so far as we know (and without much doubt it was the very first), designed to represent to the eye the battle of Bunker Hill was a rude sketch published in Philadelphia in the summer of 1775. This picture was variously used in the newspapers at the time of the late Bunker Hill Centennial. It may be found in the " Boston Herald " for June 17th, 1875, in connection with the able article prepared for that paper, from the pen of W. W. Wheildon, Esq., of Concord, and the brief history of the picture itself is there given in these words : " The larger map (or picture) was printed in the ' Pennsylvania Magazine ' in July, 1775, and the original, as may be imagined, was crude in form, conception and execution. So the *fac simile* is not put forward as the copy of the work of an artist."

It may be found also in the " Bunker Hill Times," and in several other papers. But the most curious and un-

looked-for place where it may be found is in the small volume prepared by Mr. Frothingham for circulation during
the centennial year of the battle, which volume is a valuable compendium, chiefly made from his larger work. By
what fortune this picture found its way into that little book,
we have never inquired, but have always been curious to
know; for the picture is in the most positive and direct antagonism with the theory of the book itself.

If the questions be asked, Why should a place so far off as
Philadelphia be the first to issue a picture? and what clear
information could the people there have at that time? the
answer is ready and obvious. The Continental Congress
was sitting at Philadelphia, and every item of information
of any importance to the common cause was carried there
as soon as the express riders could convey it. Ten days
after the battle, as sure and accurate information might
be gained in Philadelphia, as to the various details of the
action, as almost anywhere else in all the thirteen colonies.
Boston was in no condition then to indulge in pictorial
art. The town was occupied with British troops. In that
American camp about the town there was one man, at
least, who was equal to the task of producing such a picture, and a much better one; but he, with all the rest of
those officers and men, was occupied with very different
cares. Philadelphia was as natural a place as any in the
land for such a picture to appear, and there it was published
in July, 1775. This picture is peculiarly strong in its testimony. It is accompanied by a key, pointing out the features which are most important to be noticed. There are
nine points in the picture to which the eye is directed.
They are these: "(1) Boston; (2) Charlestown; (3) Breed's
Hill; (4) Provincial Breastwork; (5) Retreating Regulars;
(6) Frigate; (7) Somerset; (8) Broken officer; (9) General
Putnam." And there the sturdy old General is, on his

white horse, with his sword drawn, his steed on a half-leap, as in the act of cantering, the only person mentioned by name, and the commander-in-chief as clearly and distinctly as the pictorial art, with words accompanying, can make him so. Prescott is nowhere named or indicated. Is it likely they were all wrong about that matter in Philadelphia, in the summer of 1775, under the very droppings of the Continental Congress?

The next picture which we notice was published in London in September, 1775. To understand why this picture should be published there, let it be remembered that there were many officers in the British army, some of them on this side the water at that time, and some on the other, who were intimately acquainted with Putnam, by long intercourse during the French War, and who loved him like a brother. No amount of writing can destroy the fact that Putnam was a man to be loved. He won the hearts of those about him to a most remarkable degree. Let it be still further borne in mind that there were great multitudes of men in England at that time, as we shall hereafter see, who were intensely indignant at the course the British government was pursuing, whose sympathies were with us in all those trials, and who saw in that battle of Bunker Hill an outburst of provincial patriotism and courage that elicited their warmest approbation. There was, therefore, a natural demand, even in England, for a picture of the hero of Bunker Hill.* We know not how many copies of this picture are to be found in this country, but probably a goodly number. We know that Samuel Adams Drake, Esq., of Boston, has a copy. It was placed in the window of a book store in Bromfield Street, last summer, during the week of the centennial celebration, and was attentively studied by many a passer-by. We know that a copy of it

* Appendix C.

may be seen in Danvers, in the house already described, where General Putnam was born. We know that there is a copy of it hanging in the rooms of the Historical Society in Hartford, Connecticut. The picture bears the name of the artist, J. Wilkinson, and the name of the publisher, C. Shepherd (for the painting served as the basis for an engraving). This picture carries the following verbal inscription : " Israel Putnam, Esq., Major-General of the Connecticut forces, and commander-in-chief at the engagement on Bunker Hill near Boston, 17th June, 1775." This inscription is not technically correct, but on the point now before us its testimony is unequivocal.

In these two pictures we have the American testimony on the one hand, and the British testimony on the other, both exactly concurring, uttered in the plainest manner, in the summer of 1775. And is there one particle of historical evidence, that in those years nearest to the battle, when living men in great numbers knew the facts, any writer ever objected to those two pictures as bearing false witness?

But we come now to a far more celebrated picture than either of these, copies of which have been multiplied till almost everybody is familiar with it. There was in that American army about Boston, in the spring and summer of 1775, a youth of only nineteen years, a graduate of Harvard College, at first an Adjutant in General Spencer's regiment at Roxbury, but when Washington arrived he was taken into his family as one of his Aids. This was Colonel John Trumbull, youngest son of Governor Jonathan Trumbull of Connecticut. He was of frail constitution, but of exquisite tastes and sensibilities, and notable for a nice sense of honor. No man in the American army could have any better opportunity than he for knowing exactly what went on in those months of May, June and July,

1775. For in the first place, his father (the only Governor in the thirteen colonies on the side of the people
against the crown) had in his hands the entire organization of the Connecticut troops, and every important fact
with regard to the conduct of the officers and soldiers was
brought to his immediate notice; and any event so important as the battle of Bunker Hill would in after months
and years be familiarly talked over by that fireside at Lebanon, Connecticut. But more than this. Though not in
the battle, because Spencer's regiment did not partici-
pate in it, yet from the hills of Roxbury he watched it in
the distance, and was not wholly out of danger in so doing.
The British that day sent their cannon shot over Roxbury
Heights as well as over those of Charlestown. They
wished of course to keep up the impression that Roxbury
might be one point at which they were aiming, so that the
American troops would not dare to move from the right
wing to help their brethren at the centre. Trumbull saw
one man killed that day by a cannon shot in Roxbury. It
could not, of course, be otherwise than that he should hear
the facts of Bunker Hill all minutely talked over in those
days at General Spencer's headquarters. Then, early in
July, he passed over to Cambridge and was domiciled in
General Washington's family. At Washington's table,
Putnam by invitation dined once a week, and Washington
went once a week to dine at Putnam's headquarters. Colonel Trumbull therefore, without question, heard all the
details of the 17th of June freely talked over between
those two men. Can we doubt after all this that he knew,
if anybody knew, what took place on those Charlestown
Heights during the day of the battle ? The next year
Trumbull was appointed Adjutant-General. But his tastes
were not for war or military office. He was passionately
devoted to art, and after a time he resigned his commission

and went over to England, where in 1780 he became a pupil of the celebrated painter Benjamin West, who, it will be remembered, was also an American, a native of Pennsylvania, though passing the larger portion of his life in England. Under his tuition Trumbull studied the art of painting, and after he had acquired skill and independence, projected and executed a series of paintings illustrating some of the battle scenes of the American Revolution. Of all these pictures perhaps the favorite one alike with the artist and the public, has been the " Death of Warren" at Bunker Hill. All the other parts are made accessory to this central incident of Warren's death. But when an artist undertakes thus to give a battle scene, he will naturally group the chief figures to be represented according to his own fancy. He works upon a very small piece of canvas, and he cannot scatter the personages over a large territory, though as a matter of fact they might have been at some distance from each other at the time contemplated. No one, of course, supposes that the men shown in that picture stood in that exact attitude and relation at the moment of Warren's death. That is the work of the artist's own imagination. But back of these minor details, the law of historical truth will prevail, if the man who was commander-in-chief in the battle is so represented ; and the law of historical untruth will prevail, if the artist makes a man commander-in-chief who was not so. No matter, as we just said, whether that commander were exactly on that spot at that moment, or not. He might even have been in some distant part of the field. The artist is not trying to follow such details.

Trumbull, in painting that picture, made General Israel Putnam the American commander. He did it, not because he had any pet theory to maintain. There was no discussion on the subject. He did it naturally, as a thing of course, as a simple matter of fact, just as those who pro-

duced the other two pictures, already named, had done.
Any person, we care not who he may be, who would accuse
such a man as Colonel John Trumbull of attempting to per-
petrate a historical falsehood in painting that picture does
not know the character of the man against whom he brings
that charge.   His opportunities for exact knowledge were
certainly rare and peculiar.   And perhaps the chief reason
why this picture surpasses in interest some of his other
historical paintings, was just because of his intimate acquaintance with the persons and the facts.   He wrought
with his heart as well as with his pencil.*

But the men in these modern days who will have it that
Colonel William Prescott was chief commander in the battle desire very much to destroy the testimony of this picture.   Why they do not have an equal antipathy to the two
others already named it is hard to see, except that this one
is more widely known.   Referring to Trumbull's painting,
Dr. Ellis, in his "History," etc., says (p. 67), "The writer
was also assured by Judge Prescott — indeed he has it in
writing from his own pen — that Colonel John Trumbull,
the painter, in 1786, of the fancy piece of the 'Battle of Bun-

---

* "Colonel John Trumbull attempted to depict the events of the Revolution in a series of large historical *tableaux*, which are now chiefly valued for
the faithful portraits they contain of the soldiers and statesmen of that time.
His sketches and studies for these works show a vigor and grasp which are
wanting in the larger canvases.   His 'Death of Montgomery,' the 'Signing
of the Declaration of Independence,' and the 'Battle of Bunker Hill,' and
others of his important works, exhibit considerable skill in grouping and composition, but it would have been better for his fame had nothing remained
but the original sketches and portraits.   His talent is displayed to greater
advantage in the 'Trumbull Gallery' at New Haven than in the National
Capitol.   An Aid-de-Camp to General Washington, in the early part of the
Revolution, Colonel Trumbull enjoyed peculiar facilities for studying his
character and features under the most varied circumstances, and his portrait
of him, now in the gallery at New Haven, is full of soldierly spirit.   By contemporaries, to whom it recalled the leader of the American armies, it was preferred to Stuart's." — S. S. Conant in "Harper's Monthly" for April, 1876,
p. 701.

ker Hill,' in which Putnam appears as the commander of the redoubt, at Judge Prescott's dinner table, expressed his sincere regret at the error he had committed, and his desire and purpose to rectify it!"

There is one little item here that needs a passing remark before we come to that which is of main interest. We do not understand that Trumbull makes Putnam the "commander of the redoubt." The scene is at the redoubt, because the death of Warren, which is the central idea of the picture, was there. But Trumbull would have admitted what everybody, so far as we know, admits, that Prescott was the commander of the redoubt in the same sense that Stark was commander down by the shore of the Mystic, or as Knowlton was commander of the Connecticut men behind the rail fence, nearer to the fort.

But letting this pass for the present, we have long heard of this rumor, viz., that Trumbull expressed to Judge Prescott his regret at the error he had committed, and his purpose to amend it. We have always believed that the story, if traced, would be found springing from a very small germ. Colonel Trumbull was a strictly polite man, and under the circumstances might very naturally have expressed a regret if he had not duly honored Colonel Prescott in that picture. Whether a topic so intensely personal to both was a happy one to be introduced at Judge Prescott's table, when Trumbull was a guest there, would be open to consideration.

But the artist lived on to the advanced age of eighty-seven, dying in 1843. He was buried from the house of Professor Silliman of New Haven, where for many years he had lived. (Professor Benjamin Silliman, the elder, married Colonel Trumbull's niece.) It must have been many years before his death that Colonel Trumbull made the promise (if he ever did make it) that he would rectify his mistake. He probably was not expected to paint his picture over again, but to come out with some public statement or acknowledgement. Those who have known Colonel Trumbull would say that he was a man exceedingly apt to keep his word. His sense of personal honor was unusually high. And yet he seems at last to have died and made no sign, though he had had so many years in which to make it. This circumstance alone seems to render it doubtful if the rumor, in the form in which it has circulated, had any good foundation. We do not doubt there was a germ and starting-point for this story, but probably it has grown out of its true shape by transmission. The most natural place to go for exact information seemed to be to the family of Professor Silliman. The elder Professor Silliman has been dead for a number of years, but his son, the Professor Benjamin Silliman of the present, inherits the reminiscences, the traditions, the writings, and many of the pictures of Colonel Trumbull. To him we looked for information. What he has furnished will be found more fully in the Appendix.* But for our present purpose, it is sufficient to quote the following sentences:

"For more than ten years I was almost daily in intimate communication with Colonel Trumbull, and hold in memory many vivid statements respecting the early events of our national history. If he had ever said anything supporting the theory of a change of view on his part as to the parts borne by Putnam and Prescott at the battle of Bunker Hill, I should certainly remember it. He never said anything of the kind in my hearing, though he often dwelt in detail, and always with enthusiasm, upon the composition of his picture of the 'Death of Warren,' which he justly esteemed as on the whole the most remarkable of all his battle pieces. He was always strenuous on the authenticity of his records and the fidelity of his reputation, and explained the

* Appendix D.

unwearied pains he took to secure, in every possible case, authentic portraits. The only Americans in the Bunker Hill picture, of whom the portraits are marked by him as *likenesses*, are the heads of Warren and Putnam. The last he drew from the life, and I now own his original pencil sketch, from which the head in the picture was taken." *

Colonel Trumbull, then, did not intend to make Putnam the "commander of the redoubt," and did not paint *primarily* to make him anything, but in his grouping, as incidental to his main design, he made Putnam what he had to make him, in order to be true to history, viz., commander-in-chief on the general field.

The painter introduces two incidents † in his verbal description of the battle, and one of them is also introduced into the painting itself. This is the attempt of Major Small to parry the thrust of the soldier who is about to plunge his bayonet into the dying hero, Warren. Upon this incident we will not dwell. In the other, it is stated that when the British forces came up the second time, and their front lines were terribly cut down by the American musketry, Putnam saw some muskets aimed directly at his old friend, Major Small. Springing forward, he exclaimed, "Don't kill that man, I love him like a brother," and so stopped the discharge of those particular muskets. Mr. Frothingham says, "These incidents wear too much the air of romance to be implicitly relied upon." But Colonel Trumbull claims that they are authentic, and that he had

* "It is not with an array of names, with loose, incoherent, hearsay testimony, nor evidence of a nature purely negative, that an intelligent public can or will be satisfied on a point not affecting the character of one man only, but of many men and of the nation. The correctness of historical facts is felt to be important. If Mr. Trumbull's picture of this battle is erroneous and false, we ought to know it and to banish it from our parlors." — Hon. John Lowell, 1818.

† Appendix B.

15

them from Major Small himself. Concerning this last, which we have given more fully, it makes some difference whether it be implicitly relied upon or not. If it is true, then Putnam at that moment was not far from the redoubt, and at any rate at the very forefront of the battle, when it would be just as convenient to have him over on the back side of the hill, out of the way of danger, and doing nothing but vainly urging forward the reinforcements.

Turning over the voluminous pages of Force's "Archives," the eye fell upon a letter which a certain John Stuart (probably belonging to the English army and stationed at St. Augustine) wrote to Major Small. The opening of the letter is as follows :

"St. Augustine, October 2, 1775.

"Dear Sir : I was extremely glad to learn by our old friend, Captain *Barker* of the 16th [regiment], who arrived here yesterday, that you was well when he left *Boston*. I congratulate you upon a very narrow escape where so many fell." *

The words "where so many fell" prove that the sentence had reference to the battle. The words "a very narrow escape" would not have been naturally chosen if the writer was thinking of one who had simply come out alive and unharmed from the battle, as some two thousand other men had done. The language would certainly seem to point to something particular, some special deliverance. It is altogether natural to suppose that Captain Barker had just been telling Mr. Stuart how Major Small had been saved by Putnam's interposition, and so had "a very narrow escape." While no one can absolutely assert that this is the interpretation to be given, it is at least very highly probable. Mr. Frothingham ("Siege of Boston," p. 172) says, "That Major Small felt grateful for an interference at some time in his behalf is undoubtedly true. It might might have been the incident given on page 79."

* "American Archives," 4th Series, Vol. IV. p. 317.

Now, the incident related on page 79 is the following:

"The late Dr. Prince of Salem used to relate, that as he was standing with a party of armed men at Charlestown Neck, a person enveloped in a cloak rode up on horseback, inquired the news and passed on, but he immediately put spur to his horse, and the animal started forward so suddenly as to cause the rider to raise his arms, throw up the cloak and thus reveal a uniform. The men instantly levelled their guns to fire, when Dr. Prince struck them up, exclaiming, 'Don't fire at him! he is my friend Small, a fine fellow.' It was Major Small, an express from the army, who got safe into Boston."

The reader will see at a glance that this anecdote does not meet the conditions of the letter we have quoted from Mr. Stuart. That language evidently belongs to the battle of Bunker Hill, and cannot apply to anything else. It looks as though Colonel Trumbull's testimony as to this incident would stand secure against all attempts to discredit it, and that General Putnam was near the redoubt, in the very midst of the conflict, when the British made their second assault. Added to all these proofs and suggestions is a circumstance mentioned by Daniel Putnam in his reply to General Dearborn, which to most readers will be convincing and weighty. He says, "I shall make no comment on the first anecdote by Colonel Small, except that the circumstances were related by General Putnam without any essential alteration soon after the battle, and that there was an interview of the parties, on the lines between Prospect and Bunker Hills, at the request of Colonel Small, not long afterwards."

We have, then, three pictures, prepared very soon after the battle, all pointing to General Putnam as the chief commander at Bunker Hill. Are there any ancient paintings or engravings that bear a like testimony in favor of Colonel Prescott?

We turn now to the Literature of Bunker Hill, and strike a far more extended field. But it will not be wise to go over again the thousand and one testimonies and affidavits which constitute a part of this literature. All we can do is to make a rapid analysis of what has been accumulating for a hundred years. In the course of it we shall introduce at least one witness who, so far as we are aware, has never before spoken.

In the review we are now about to make, it might seem to some an intended *slight*, and to others a *sign of timidity*, were we to take no notice of the remarkable theory respect- · ing General Putnam advanced by Mr. Dawson in his fa- mous number of the "Historical Magazine" for June, 1868. We have no wish to neglect a writer who has performed such large and valuable services in gathering together the authorities on this topic, and whose study of the battle itself is usually so correct, and we certainly have no fear that should keep us from reporting the worst things he has written. The public shall have the full knowledge of his theory, so far as this volume is concerned. Mr. Dawson thinks Putnam was acting the part of a traitor in this battle, and trying to sell himself for British gold; but the price he named was too high, and the bargain was not com- pleted. He speaks (p. 335) of a kind of double record which has come down to us through English and American channels, which "confirms the terrible suspicion of some- body's 'treachery,'* and fastens upon the same General Putnam a secret desire, about that time, to return to the peace of his sovereign, as well as an offer of terms for that purpose to the royal general-in-chief, and their qualified rejection."

* Peter Brown's letter to his mother, June 25, 1775, quoted in " Historical Magazine," June, 1868, p. 396, as follows :

" The danger we were in made us think there was Treachery, and that we were brot here to be all slain ; and I must and will venture to say, there was Treachery, Oversight or Presumption in the conduct of our officers."

Again, in a note, after quoting a passage showing what hardships Putnam went through in the French War, and what wounds he received, he sympathizingly remarks (p. 355), "After having lost his scalp, and endured the pain resulting from *fifteen* wounds, it seems to us that this officer would have been as useless to the King as he was to the Congress; and General Gage may therefore be entitled to more credit than he has received, for refusing to purchase him at the price demanded."

Again, "General Putnam, after safely resting at Cambridge until the next morning, returned to the peninsula a little before noon, and blustered as was his habit, without rendering any service to the fatigue parties, until his eyes fell on the tools which the weary workers, still unrefreshed, had recently laid down near the works."

Still again, "It is also evident that the greater number were skulkers, who sneaked back to the eastern [western?] side of Bunker Hill, and there assisted General Putnam in waiting for the result of the action, and in joining in the retreat."

We might quote other passages, but these will be enough to show the nature of Mr. Dawson's theory, the quality of his opinions on this particular point, and the style of his expression. One tries to imagine in what condition of mind and body the writer penned such sentences. There is a bitterness, a vindictiveness in them, especially as written against a man who had been sleeping in his grave almost a century, that seems to call for special explanation.

But certainly this is a remarkable discovery about General Putnam. A distinguished man, yet living among us, but not noted for early rising, got up one morning in uncommon season. A friend, surprised at seeing him stirring at that time of the day, asked him how he managed to wake up, and wished to know if any one called him. "No, sir," was the sardonic reply, "I woke up by my own ingenuity and vivacity." Mr. Dawson, in like manner, appears to have roused himself to the construction of this theory purely by his own "ingenuity and vivacity," without any one to wake him or help him in any manner. His English forefathers, men who fought alongside of Putnam through the French War, and against him in the war of the Revolution, never understood his character and designs. Putnam's own countrymen did not understand them. Even Washington did not understand them. Mr. Dawson found out exactly what they were, only a very few years ago. It is truly remarkable. Mr. Dawson is well known for his historical learning. His pages are richly freighted with notes and references, such as are usually quite valuable. But the word *reference* and the word *inference* are very much alike in mechanical structure. They have the same number of letters, only one has four e's and the other three e's and an i. It is curious to notice that the foot notes supporting this theory in Mr. Dawson's pages contain no *direct* evidence or testimony in its favor; his *references* all turn into *inferences*.

Some of the men on that hill during that long forenoon suspected "treachery," and of course it was General Putnam who was the traitor. It could not possibly have been General Ward out at Cambridge, who promised to send reinforcements and refreshments early in the morning, and never sent the latter apparently at all, and the former not till afternoon. It could not have been *his* course of conduct which occasioned the feeling that some one was playing false with them. No; it was General Putnam; there is no doubt of it. If those men suspected treachery somewhere, General Putnam was the traitor. It is a remarkably brilliant discovery, and Mr. Dawson shall have all the honors belonging to it and springing from it. But it is very natural to remark, that a man who *could* play the traitor that day to any purpose must have been one who stood at the head of the action on the field. A subordinate officer or a volunteer could not easily have guided that battle into the British hands, if he wished to. The whole theory is so preposterous that we are sure many of our readers will be utterly surprised to know that any man ever thought of such a thing.

Leaving this aside as a mere episode, we turn now to the work which we propose in connection with the literature of Bunker Hill.

At the outset, it is to be borne in mind that immediately after the battle, the official authorities were careful in all their publications not to mention the names of the leaders. In the account which the Massachusetts Provincial Congress prepared (June 28th) to be sent to the Committee of Safety at Albany, they speak only of a "body of men," and mention not a name connected with the battle. In the statement prepared by the Massachusetts Committee of Safety (July 25th) to be sent for publication to England, they mention only the names of the dead, already removed out of the way of British vengeance, such as General Warren, Colonel Gardner, Colonel Parker, Major Moore and Major McClary. It was the opening of a great and uncertain contest, and the authorities would not needlessly expose men who had taken their lives in their hands for the common good. But after a little time this habit of silence began slowly to disappear. The strife had assumed national proportions. The Continental Congress had acted. Washington was commander-in-chief of the American army, and his higher officers were grouped around him. The thing could no longer "be done in a corner."

It is also to be borne in mind that the news of the death

of Warren — a man greatly beloved — was instantly carried in all directions, and the first natural conclusion of men was that he was the commander.

Rev. Andrew Eliot of Boston writes two days after the battle (June 19th) to his brother in London, "Dr. Warren is among the slain. It is said he had the chief direction of the defence; if this is true, it seems to me he was out of his line."

With the British officers and soldiers there was of course no principle of secresy as to the facts on our side. They were at liberty to tell all they knew or suspected. An officer of the British army, writing home, June 25th (" American Archives," 4th series, Vol. II. p. 1092), has the following sentences in his letter : " After the skirmish of the 17th we even commended the troops of Putnam, who fought so gallantly *pro aris et focis.*" And again in the same letter, " So very secretly was the late action conducted, that Generals Clinton and Burgoyne knew not of it till the morning, though the town did in general, and Putnam in particular."

Another of these British officers that give accounts of the battle is John Clarke, Lieutenant of the marines. His narrative may be found in Mr. Drake's book, entitled, " Bunker Hill : the story told in letters from the battle-field, by British officers engaged." The sentences we quote are on p. 50. The writer is speaking of General Warren. " The doctor's dress was a light-colored coat, with a white satin waistcoat laced with silver, and white breeches, with silver loops, which I saw the soldier soon after strip off his body. He was supposed to be the commander of the American army that day; for General Putnam was about three miles distance, and formed an ambuscade with about three thousand men."

We know of course that he was all wrong in this last

supposition, but this sentence is an intensely interesting and instructive one for this reason : It throws a distinct ray of light over some of the obscure things of that day. The British officers knew, probably, that Putnam was stationed at Inman's farm, and that he had there a regiment of one thousand men, and they may have known that he had also two other regiments under his command, which might be just as large. Now, this Lieutenant Clarke's theory of the battle is seen to be that Putnam was lying back at Cambridgeport, expecting the British would break through the lines on Bunker Hill and pursue the flying troops towards Cambridge ; and he, the old, wily French and Indian ranger, would suddenly spring up with his three thousand men, and confront them, and possibly cut them all to pieces. They were not to be caught in that trap. But *we* know that trap was never set, though it was fortunate for us, perhaps, that some of the British officers thought it was.

To show that this was not Lieutenant Clarke's theory alone, but was to some extent current on the British side, we give a few lines from the poem of George Cockings, printed in London, and happily included in Mr. Drake's book, p. 62. In this poem General Warren is represented as commander, and the poet says,—

> "With sage precaution Howe the chase declined,
> With circumspection mov'd, and wou'd not dare
> To hazard a defeat in Putnam's snare."

And again the poet says,—

> " Each eminence was fortified around,
> And ambuscades possessed the lower ground ;
> Here Putnam, Pribble, Ward, and Thomas stayed
> To check pursuit, and pour in friendly aid."

With what we know of the battle, it is easily seen that

everything is at "sixes and sevens" in these minds. But be it noted, that the reason why Lieutenant Clarke supposed Warren was commander was because Putman was three miles off with an ambuscade. It seems not to have occurred to him that a *Colonel* was chief commander.

That fact about the ambuscade failing him, he would doubtless return to the other opinion, and say Putnam *was* commander. It is a somewhat impressive fact that in all these British accounts of the battle published in Mr. Drake's book, we do not discover that Colonel Prescott is mentioned in any connection whatever. He is mentioned once in the poem, but not in any association with the redoubt or with any command that day. It stands simply in a list of nineteen names, when, by the poet's fancy, General Warren is represented as telling over the elements of American strength. The first name in this list is Putnam, and the seventeenth is Prescott. With this exception we discover no reference to Prescott in these British accounts embraced in Mr. Drake's book. These English officers, thoroughly acquainted with the constitution of an army, if they thought of Prescott at all, thought of him only as a subordinate officer, as they would of any other Colonel or Major.

But we will turn now from the early English literature of the battle to the American. When that battle was fought, Dr. Ezra Stiles (two years later made President of Yale College) was the Congregational minister of Newport, Rhode Island. He was a native of Connecticut, and was then forty-eight years old. He was most intensely patriotic, and burning with desire to hear the news from Boston. He kept a diary, which is now in manuscript in the library of Yale College. Mr. Dawson obtained leave to have that diary transcribed and published, so far as it relates to the matter before us. This portion was first brought out by him, and we are very much obliged to him for this service.

One of the most curious and interesting features of that diary is, that it shows us exactly how news would reach a man seventy miles away, after travelling over the hills and passing through the mouths of men intensely excited. June 18th, he hears that a battle has been fought, and among the items that reach him, this is one : " That Colonel Putnam is encamped at Charlestown on Bunker Hill, and has lost one of his best Captains, but is determined to stand his ground, having men enough."

Being a little one side, he has not kept up with passing events. He calls him " Colonel Putnam," the title he wore when he came home from the French War, and the common title by which he was known to the people before 1775. He has not heard, apparently, or forgets for the moment, that the Connecticut Assembly has made him a Brigadier-General.

By June 19th he hears some more news. He says, " We have various accounts, some that General Putnam is surprised and taken by the King's troops, some that he repulsed them, and had, by assistance of others coming up, placed the regulars between two fires. At 10 o'clock at night the news was that General Putnam was forced from his trenches on Bunker Hill, and obliged to retreat." This time it is General, and not Colonel, Putnam.

On the 20th he hears more news. " General Greene says General Putnam, with *three hundred* men, took possession and intrenched on Bunker Hill, on Friday night, 16th inst." Then on June 23d, some visitors, who had been to Boston, returned and reported that "They spent one hour with General Putnam in his tent on Prospect Hill, about half-way between Cambridge and Charlestown. The General gave them an account of the battle last Saturday."

But we cannot linger on these details. At first, with Dr. Stiles, it is all the while Colonel Putnam or General

Putnam. By and by Prescott's name begins to come in, and the diarist is evidently in a kind of confusion as to the relations of the two. He is trying hard to find out how many of the British were killed and wounded, and he takes evident pleasure in recording large numbers under this head. For some days he inclines to the idea that about one thousand of the regulars were actually killed.

Mr. Frothingham quotes this same diary on the Prescott side. We do not think this can fairly be done, especially when we notice that some of Dr. Stiles's early information came directly from General Greene himself, who we know was in Rhode Island at that time, and who doubtless understood what he was talking about. One good clear word from General Greene in those exciting hours was worth any number of mixed and wandering rumors.

If any one wishes to know the men who were uppermost in Dr. Stiles's mind eight years afterwards, in 1783, when the war was just over, he may find some of their names in the Election Sermon which he preached that year before Governor Trumbull and the General Assembly of Connecticut. There is one passage where he brings out our indebtedness to France. After a high rhapsody over the beloved name of Washington, he goes on as follows: "None but Americans can write the American War. They will celebrate the names of a Washington and a Rochambeau; a Greene and a Lafayette; a Lincoln and a Chastellux; a Gates and a Viomenil; a Putnam and a Duke de Lauzun; a Morgan, and other heroes who rushed to arms and offered themselves voluntarily for the defence of liberty."

Then he adds the names of the illustrious dead, "Warren, Mercer, Montgomery, De Kalb, Wooster, Thomas, Pulaski." The name of Prescott does not stand on this honored roll, but the name of Benjamin Lincoln, a Massachusetts man, is found there. He was a Colonel, like Prescott, in 1775. He was a Major-General of militia in 1776, a Continental Major-General in 1777, chief commander of the southern department in 1778, received the submission of Cornwallis's troops in 1781, and in the same year was made Secretary of War. That was a record which entitled him to have his name on that roll.

There is one document which we must not pass by, and which belongs to the very early days. We refer to the letter which Colonel Prescott wrote to John Adams on the 25th of August, 1775. It is a very remarkable letter, and we quote it in full. We have already several times taken short sentences from it, but its very extraordinary character makes it deserving of careful consideration. This was written more than two months after the battle, and the secresy as to names was no longer needful. We do not discover that much use was made of this letter by the newspapers and orators on the centennial 17th of June.

"CAMP AT CAMBRIDGE, August 25th, 1775.

"SIR: I have received a line from my brother, which informs me of your desire of a particular account of the action at Charlestown. It is not in my power, at present, to give so minute an account as I should choose, being ordered to decamp and march to another station.

"On the 16th of June, in the evening, I received orders to march to Breed's Hill in Charlestown, with a party of about one thousand men, consisting of three hundred of my own regiment, Colonel Bridge and Lieutenant Brickett with a detachment of theirs, and two hundred Connecticut forces, commanded by Captain Knowlton. We arrived at the spot, the lines were drawn by the engineer, and we began the intrenchment about twelve o'clock; and plying the work with all possible expedition till just before sunrising, when the enemy began a very heavy cannonading and bombardment. In the interim, the engineer forsook me. Having thrown up a small redoubt, found it necessary to draw a line about twenty rods in length from the fort northerly, under a very warm fire from the enemy's artillery. About this time the above field officers, being indisposed, could render but little service, and the most of the men under their command deserted the party. The enemy continuing an incessant fire with their artillery, about 2 o'clock in the afternoon on the 17th, they began to land a north-easterly point from the fort, and I ordered the train with two field pieces to go and oppose them, and the Connecticut forces to support them ; but the train marched a different course, and I believe those sent to their support followed, I suppose to Bunker Hill. Another party of the enemy landed and fired the town. There was a party of Hampshire, in conjunction with some other forces, lined a fence at the distance of threescore rods back of the fort, partly to the north. About an hour after the enemy landed, they began to march to the attack in three columns. I commanded my Lieutenant-Colonel Robinson and Major Woods, each with a detachment, to flank the enemy, who, I have reason to think, behaved with prudence and courage. I was now left with perhaps one hundred and fifty men in the fort. The enemy advanced and fired very hotly on the fort, and meeting with a warm reception, there was a very smart firing on both sides. After a considerable time, finding our ammunition was almost spent, I commanded a cessation till the enemy advanced within thirty yards, when we gave them such a hot fire that they were obliged to retire nearly one hundred and fifty yards before they could rally and come again to the attack. Our ammunition being nearly exhausted, could keep up only a scattering fire. The enemy being numerous, surrounded our little fort, began to mount our lines, and enter the fort with their bayonets. We was obliged to retreat through them, while they kept up as hot a fire as it was possible for them to make. We having very few bayonets, could make no resistance. We kept the fort about one hour and twenty minutes after the attack with small arms. This is nearly the state of facts, though imperfect and too general, which, if any ways satisfactory to you, will afford pleasure to your most obedient humble servant,   WILLIAM PRESCOTT."

"To the HON. JOHN ADAMS, Esq."

Now, we pronounce this to be, under the circumstances, and in whatever way it be looked at, a most extraordinary production. Knowing what we now do of the battle, what everybody knows who has made any study of it, what the special friends of Prescott most fully admit and publish in all their writings, it is almost inconceivable that Prescott should have sent such a letter to John Adams as giving any adequate account of the action. Even as a local commander at the redoubt, if he told *substantially* all he knew, the fact must stand as a marvel. But if he were general commander on that field, and could give no fuller and better account of what transpired there, the military and civil authorities of that day certainly had very good reasons for never promoting him.

Let us look at this matter in detail. Any reader, who knew nothing of the battle otherwise, would say that Prescott here conveys the impression that the battle was fought mainly by those one hundred and fifty men that he had with him in the fort, and the two detachments which he sent out.

But this letter is remarkable in many other respects. There is not one generous word here for anybody but himself, except a modified compliment for his own Lieutenant-Colonel and Major, and a compliment to them was in some sense a compliment to himself.* General Putnam † is not even named or remotely hinted at, and no one would know from this letter that there was such a man in existence.

---

* In one of the sarcastic accounts from an English pen, which will be found in the Appendix, there is this sentence respecting Gage: " With all the vanity of a military man, be praises the conduct of his officers."

† " It is a noticeable fact that this remarkable paper (the Prescott Manuscript) . . . . (nor yet Colonel Prescott's letter to John Adams, soon after the battle, each of them giving an account of the engagement) does not contain the name of Colonel [General] Putnam, an omission hardly to be expected in these papers, or in any respectable account of the battle." — W. W. Wheildon, Esq., in " New History of the Battle of Bunker Hill," p. 16.

"The engineer forsook me." This was the brave, noble, skilful Colonel Gridley, afterwards one of the Major-Generals of the Continental army. Prescott does not condescend to tell us that Colonel Gridley, a man already sixty-four years old, who had been up all night, was in the thickest of that fight simply as a *volunteer*, was carried off the field severely wounded, and came near being shot through and through after he had received his wound, by a concentric fire from the British muskets. All that he had to say of him was, "The engineer forsook me." Next, "Colonel Bridge and Lieutenant Brickett * .... could render me but little service, and the most of the men under their command deserted the party." Did Colonel Prescott think that just in proportion as the men he was set to command ran away, so much the more would his own military heroism shine out? Then he sent the artillery to oppose the enemy, and the Connecticut men to support the artillery; but the artillery cleared out, and he implies that the Connecticut men did too, or at least that they went where they were of very little use. We know how those Connecticut men built and manned that fence line and defended it, never stirring from their post of duty till the redoubt was carried, after the British had beaten ineffectually against the fence, and could not carry it. *We* know all this; but Colonel Prescott knew nothing of it, as would appear by this letter. "There was a party of Hampshire!" What a diminutive idea this expression conveys of the part New Hampshire played in this battle! They might be a company of forty or fifty men; the reader would hardly suppose from this letter that there were more than some such number. And

---

* One would naturally infer from the letter that Colonel Bridge and Lieutenant Brickett, who "could render me but little service," went off,— "deserted the party," when their men did. But Colonel Bridge and Lieutenant Brickett were both, like Colonel Gridley, wounded in the battle, though not so severely. And what is equally important, this Lieutenant-Colonel Brickett, as already stated, was the next year promoted to the rank of Brigadier-General.

yet that "party of Hampshire" contained six times the number of men that *he says* he had with him in the fort. He knows something about their being behind a fence " in conjunction with some others," but he is inclined to think he "believes" that the Connecticut forces went off to Bunker Hill. Now, to show what kind of service this "party of Hampshire" rendered, we quote a brief passage from the British officer, Lieutenant John Clarke, to whose narrative we have already referred. He says (see Mr. Drake's volume, p. 49), "Another remarkable circumstance of the heat of this action is, that all the grenadiers of the 4th, or King's own, regiment were killed or wounded except four; and of the grenadiers also of the 23d, or Royal Welsh fusileers, only three remained who were not either killed or wounded." Now, those two companies of grenadiers, in the first attack, were the front companies in the British column moving close by the shores of the Mystic, that was expected to break through the fence and flank the redoubt. This movement brought the column directly in the face of this "party of Hampshire," and the result is told above. In the "Life and Letters of John Stark," it is stated that the regiment of Welsh fusileers of seven hundred men could muster only eighty-three the next morning.

But we must not linger on these details. We pass to note another item in this letter. The friends of Prescott are very fond of making him the man who before the action told his men, and sternly commanded them, and sent the order all along the line, not to fire a musket until the enemy were close at hand; and in some accounts he is represented as moving along the lines, and threatening with death any man that should discharge his musket before the order to fire was given.* Now, Prescott tells no such story,

* "The advancing columns, however, having got within gunshot, a few of the Americans could not resist the temptation to return their fire without

16

but a very different one. He says there was "a very smart firing on both sides," and then adds, "After a considerable time, finding our ammunition was almost spent, I commanded a cessation till the enemy advanced within thirty yards." We are satisfied that this order to withhold the fire was passed along the fence line and was there acted upon from the first, but if we are to believe Colonel Prescott, the ammunition was mostly spent at the redoubt before that order was given; and we may add that it was fired away at long range, for the British did not seriously attack the redoubt in the two first assaults.

We think it perfectly fair and legitimate at this point to raise the query whether a man that had no more generous emotions than are shown in this letter, no fund of magnanimity out of which to give others their due meed of praise, could by any possibility ever become a great military leader. Personal courage he might have in a high degree, and we do not doubt that Prescott possessed this courage, but magnetic power over other men with this spirit he did not have and could not have. Contrast this conduct with that ascribed to Putnam, even by such a man as General Heath, who was not a friend over fond of Putnam. General Heath wrote to John Adams, October 23d, 1775 (the passage may be found in the "Siege of Boston," p. 396), and told him of an account which had been published in a Connecticut paper of the battle of Bunker Hill, in which Prescott and other prominent Massachusetts names had been wholly omitted. But said General Heath, "this account was detested by the brave Putnam and others of that colony." In that brief sentence, one can see the movings of a great soul that scorns to take from another man his due; and the

waiting for orders. Prescott indignantly remonstrated at this disobedience, and appealed to their often expressed confidence in him as their leader; while his officers seconded his exertions, and some ran along the parapet and kicked up the guns."—" Siege of Boston," p. 141.

secret of that power which Putnam had over other men was largely in this noble quality of his character. He asked no man to go where he was afraid to go himself, and in the honors of any action he often distribûted to others even more than their rightful portion. · A man may be personally as bold as a lion, but if he will have everything to himself, and leave others to cold neglect, he cannot bind men in any heroic devotion to his leadership.

And just here, as it appears, was the weakness of Prescott, even as local commander of the redoubt. He ought not to have lost so large a portion of those eight hundred Massachusetts men. He ought to have infused them with the patriotic fire which would have enabled them to bear a little hunger and thirst and weariness, and almost criminal delay in Ward, the commander-in-chief. The men of Connecticut endured all these things, and stayed faithfully on the field to the last. Moreover, there ought to have been such magnetism in Prescott as to have drawn naturally to his help his own Massachusetts brethren, who were scattered to the number of many hundreds around those hillsides and about the neck, doing little or nothing, yea, worse than that, a mere hindrance and source of bad contagion to others. From the very best lights we can gain, out of all the records of this first great action of the Revolution, we say unhesitatingly that Prescott was then for the first time thoroughly tried in his military capacity, and did not equal the hopes entertained of him, and consequently he was never promoted. If he had held in his grasp that first number, eight hundred, as Stark and Reed held their men, to the battle line, and as Captain Knowlton held his, the day, glorious as it was, would have had a still more illustrious issue. With those eight hundred doing such service as the "party of Hampshire" did, the rest of the Massachusetts regiments might have stayed in their camps at Cambridge, and the victory would have been ours.

There are a good many bits of literature lying about, which, like that just noticed, when brought out and fairly confronted, do not impress one as great intellectually, while at the same time they are sadly wanting in magnanimity. We may notice one more of these at this point. General Ward also wrote a letter to John Adams in the October following the battle, in which he said, " Some have said hard things of the officers of this colony and despised them ; but I think, as mean as they have represented them to be, there has been no one action with the enemy which has not been conducted by an officer of this colony, except that at Chelsea, which was conducted by General Putnam." (A part of this sentence has been quoted before in another connection. We give it here in full.) This sentence has been allowed to lie quietly in the background (not much used, but never forgotten), to impress the reader that General Ward meant in this way to say that Prescott was the chief commander at Bunker Hill. But as the sentence was written in 1775, and we have shown, and shall still further show, how the people of 1775, British and American alike, spoke of the leadership in that battle, we find no evidence whatever that General Ward once thought of Colonel Prescott while he was penning those words. We look at these sentences, on the other hand, chiefly as an attempt on the part of General Ward at self-justification ; for his conduct, in a military point of view, had been sorely criticised, as it was right and proper it should be. We have evidence enough of that in the first words of the sentence. He meant to say, so far as Bunker Hill was concerned, that he was the general director of that affair, as he was. If it had been Napoleon Bonaparte out at Cambridge doing the same class of things (though they would have been done in a very different style), no one would have hesitated to call him the commander-in-chief. General Ward was here trying to tell John Adams something like what the centurion in the Gospels said — Was not I a man under authority, having soldiers under me, and did I not say to this man, Go; and to another man, Come; and to my servant, Do this? Undoubtedly he did, and he did it in such a way that it was best for him to retire from military life upon those laurels, in the following spring. He went back to civil life, where, as we have already said, he was a good man and true,— honorable alike in character and conduct. But he was wholly out of his place as a military officer, and especially as chief commander of the American army.

They who can find in those words of his to John Adams any theory as to Prescott's being chief commander in the battle, must read them with minds fixed only upon one favorite idea. As to this matter of chief command, there was precisely the same problem on the British side as on ours. Howe was the chief commander on the field, but General Gage was the real commander-in-chief, and was held strictly accountable as such by the British people. Ward opposed the movement itself beforehand, so that the American people never held him so blameworthy for his conduct as they otherwise would; but strictly he occupied the same relations to the battle on his side, that General Gage did on his, and that is what he quietly claims in his letter to John Adams. By the time he wrote that letter, the great advantages secured to us by the battle were acknowledged on both sides the water.

In sharp and striking contrast to the spirit of these two letters, and their utter silence about General Putnam, we propose now to introduce a witness that is doubtless impartial, and whose utterances cannot but have weight with any unprejudiced mind. There was belonging to Boston, in

1775, a newspaper called "The New England Chronicle, or Essex Gazette." A year or two later it was named "The Independent Chronicle." For short, when we have occasion to mention it by name, we will call it the "Chronicle." It could not of course be published in Boston in 1775, but it was "printed by Samuel and Ebenezer Hall at their office in Stoughton Hall," Cambridge. It was therefore close to the headquarters of the American army, and had every advantage for obtaining military news. But for two or three months it acted upon that policy of silence as to the leaders which we have elsewhere noticed. Some of the very first items which we find, indicating who was the chief commander in the battle on the American side, are in little paragraphs of English news, or clippings from English papers, — in other words, we see at first, through English eyes, who was at the head of this Bunker Hill army.

In the issue of October 19th, 1775, is the following, which, though not true in point of historical fact, is just as good for our purpose as though it were true:

"*London, July 22d.*—It is reported that a letter from Boston brings an account that General Putnam had sent a message to General Gage, wherein he informed him that if he did not quit that place and embark with his troops, he would lay siege to it with thirty thousand men, when neither he nor his troops were to expect any quarter."

If this passage needs any commentary, the explanation is simple. The battle of Bunker Hill had passed, in which Gage had met with great losses. The writer of the above embodies the American fighting interest in Putnam as the head man, and considers Gage's condition very critical. It will be seen in reading these items that we had, as already suggested, warm friends in England.

October 26th, the "Chronicle" has the following:

"*London, August 9th.* Yesterday the right honorable

the Lord Mayor invited the freeholders of Middlesex to dine with him at the George at Cheswick, when upwards of three hundred honored him with their company. Several toasts were drank, among which were the following: 1. General Putnam and all those American heroes who like men nobly prefer death to slavery and chains."

At Dublin there was a Society of Free Citizens. At one of their meetings we have this record of a toast drank, as reported in the " Chronicle," November 2 :

"*Dublin, July* 19*th.* — General Putnam and his brave provincials — Governor Trumbull. May the military ever be subservient to the civil power."

The friends of America over in England were doing the same thing that the Philadelphians were doing, according to Silas Deane's account, quoted in a previous chapter. It was the day for drinking toasts, and men expressed the sentiments which were uppermost in their hearts in this way; and so Putnam was the " second or third toast at almost all the tables " in Philadelphia.

All those items from Mr. Deane's letters, written in 1775, which are placed in Chapter VI. of this volume, to show Putnam's popularity, might just as appropriately stand here as evidences of his leadership in the battle.

Here is another item from the " Chronicle :"

"*Cambridge, December* 14*th.* — A letter from London dated September 1st, mentions that the day before a gentleman of that city, a sincere friend to America, had his newborn son baptized by the name of PUTNAM."

Why all this excitement in England over Putnam?

Another item in the same paper :

"*Cambridge, December* 14*th.* — The fort on Cobble Hill was completed the latter end of last week, without the least interruption from the enemy. It is allowed to be the most perfect piece of fortification that the American army has constructed during the present campaign, and on the day of its completion was named *Putnam's impregnable fortress.*"

This last item proves nothing except the fame and reputation of Putnam at that time in the American army.

In the record of the court-martial to try Colonel Scammans, as published in the "Chronicle" for February 19th, 1776, occur little sentences in the testimony of witnesses, of which the following may be taken as examples :

"After which General Putnam came up and ordered the regiment to advance, within hearing of Colonel Scammans."

"I was sent by Colonel Scammans to General Putnam to know if his regiment was wanted."

For some items that follow, a little explanation is needed. On the 13th of June, Colonel John Whitcomb was chosen first Major-General of Massachusetts troops, by the Massachusetts Provincial Congress. He was reluctant about accepting. On the 16th, the Congress appointed a committee to write what it calls a "complaisant letter" to him on the subject. That letter seems to have prevailed, for on Friday, June 23d, a committee was sent to him to "desire him to attend this Congress and receive his commission."

On the day of the battle, therefore, he had not received his commission. He was in this respect in the same condition as Warren, who was chosen second Major-General, June 14th. Whitcomb, however, did not, like Warren and Pomeroy, go to the battle-field. Still he was in the vicinity, and was partially recognized as a *general* officer. His name often occurs in this trial of Colonel Scammans, and he himself is one of the witnesses called to give testimony. To show how his name is used, we give the following passage from the "Chronicle" of February 21st, 1776 :

"Captain Jeremiah Hill deposed and said, that down by the bridge near Lechmere's Point we met General Whitcomb, who told Colonel Scammans that he had better go round to the little hill and wait their motions there ; we accordingly went and stayed there half an hour. *Colonel* John Whitcomb, who is styled by the foregoing deponents *General*, deposed and said : I met Colonel Scammans with his regiment about fifty rods from Lechmere's Point ; I asked him what brought him there ; he replied by asking me where he should go ; I told him where he could do the most service ; I am positive I never ordered him to the little hill, if my memory serves me, because men could be of no service in such a place except in the night."

Upon this testimony the editor, who, as already suggested, was probably Colonel Scammans, himself, bases some remarks of his own, which are inserted into the midst of the narrative in this wise : " [N. B. Colonel Whitcomb then acted as a general officer, and as there was no general officer that commanded at Bunker Hill, was it not his duty to have been there ?]" We copy only this single sentence. The editor, whoever he may be, calls him *Colonel*, because he had not been commissioned. But in what he said and did that day he *acted* as a *General*, on the ground that he had been chosen Major-General by the Congress. And acting so, at and near Lechmere's Point, the editor's opinion is, that he ought to have gone on to Bunker Hill, where there was "then no general officer that commanded." Now, the hasty reader might conclude that this was testimony by this writer against General Putnam, and those words are quoted and allowed to carry this meaning by some writers. But if he will study the passage carefully, and consider its connections, he will see the meaning to be this : At that point of time, while the battle was in progress, General Putnam was fully occupied at the front, a third of a mile away from this scene of confusion. Bunker Hill was the path over which all the regiments were compelled to go, if they would reach that front line where the battle was then raging. This hill was crowded with these regiments that were sent on at the last moment, and here was that scene of utter disorder described in a previous chapter. What the editor meant to say, therefore, was, that if Colonel Whitcomb acted as a General at all, he ought to have gone over to Bunker Hill and exercised his authority in trying to heal those gross disorders, to disentangle that snarl, and send the halting regiments forward to their post of duty. The very testimony into which these remarks are projected shows at various points (as in the passages we have selected) that Putnam was the recognized commander in the battle; and it is the editorial opinion that Whitcomb ought to have gone to his help, and urged forward, by his authority, the reinforcements.

And now there is one general remark to be made, which in its way is quite significant. We have looked over with a considerable degree of care the pages of the "Chronicle," for the years 1775-79, and we have not found the name of Colonel William Prescott mentioned in any connection whatever. Several times we thought we had run against it, but upon examination it always proved to be Colonel Richard Prescot, afterwards General Richard Prescot of the British army. We will not say the name is not there, for in that fine and faded type the eye might overlook it; but we have honestly tried to find it in those pages, and could not. They are seemingly just as silent in that respect as was Colonel Prescott in his letter to John Adams about General Putnam.

We turn now from the "Chronicle" to similar bits of contemporary literature gathered from various quarters.

A letter written by a gentleman in Providence to his friend in New York (June 20, 1775), and which may be found in "American Archives" (4th series, Vol. II. p. 1036), opens as follows: "On the evening of the 16th, Colonel Putnam took possession of Bunker Hill with about two thousand men, and began an intrenchment."

The "Pennsylvania Packet" of June 26th says, "General Putnam, who commanded the continental troops, is a veteran soldier of great experience. He served during the whole of the last war against the French. . . . . Such a man is every way qualified to command a set of virtuous provincials. General Gage, with a mercenary handful of troops, will stand an excellent chance against such a man as Putnam, who abounds in bravery, good sense and honor."

Here it is directly stated that "Putnam commanded the continental troops," but in many of the items given this statement is not made in *form*, but in *substance*. When a man is talking with his fellow-men about deeply exciting and passing events of wide-spread interest, their common knowledge and emotion make it unnecessary that certain words should be used, which would otherwise be natural and requisite.

A week after the great fire which consumed so large a part of Boston, two citizens of Massachusetts, talking together upon the subject, would not be apt to remind each other that this fire was in Boston. In like manner, when the men of England and the men of Philadelphia, and doubtless of many other places, in the summer of 1775, were drinking toasts in honor of "General Putnam" or "General Putnam and his brave provincials," it was not necessary for the living hearers or readers of 1775, that one should stop to add with each repetition of his name, "who commanded at Bunker Hill." That was the underlying basis of common knowledge on which the toast itself was built, for it is preposterous to suppose that they were so largely engaged in drinking Putnam's health for what he did in the French War, or simply because he was generally known to be a brave and able military man.

The following items are taken from a report made to the Massachusetts Provincial Congress, Friday, June 23, 1775 :

"The committee who were appointed on the 20th instant, to inquire into the misconduct in the late engagement, reported as follows, viz., ... Your committee proceeded to *Cambridge*, waited upon the General [Ward] and made him acquainted with their business. He informed your committee that General *Putnam* had made complaint of an officer in the train, etc. . . . . We applied to General *Putnam* and other officers who were in the heat of the engagement for further intelligence. General *Putnam* informed us that in the late action, as he was riding up Bunker Hill, he met an officer of the train drawing his cannon down in great haste ; he ordered the officer to stop and go back ; he replied that he had no cartridges. The General dismounted and examined his boxes, and found a considerable number of cartridges, upon which he ordered him back. He refused, until the General threatened him with immediate death. . . . . The relation of this matter from General *Putnam* was confirmed by several other officers of distinction." *

There is, of course, no absolute proof from this passage that Putnam was in chief command; but its suggestions point strongly in that direction, and one can hardly read it without receiving that impression.

We find some very strong evidence in the same direction in a letter written from Philadelphia, September 26, 1775, by Samuel Adams to Elbridge Gerry. ("Wells's Life," etc., Vol. II. p. 323.) He says,—

"Some of our military gentlemen have, I fear, disgraced us [Massachusetts officers he means] ; it is, then, important that every anecdote that concerns a man of real merit among them, and such I know there are, be improved as far as decency will permit of it to their advantage, and the honor of a colony, which for its zeal in the great cause, as well as its sufferings, deserves

* "American Archives," 4th Series, Vol. II. p. 1438.

so much of America. Until I visited headquarters at Cambridge, I never heard of the valor of Prescott at Bunker Hill, nor the ingenuity of Knox and Waters in planning the celebrated works at Roxbury."

This passage may need a word of explanation. During the summer of 1775, Mr. Adams had been at Philadelphia, a member of the Continental Congress. He reached his home in Massachusetts August 11, and now, September 26, he has just reached Philadelphia on his return. He wants Mr. Gerry and others to be particular in forwarding promptly to that city all important news. But it is natural to remark, that if he had not, between June 17th and August 11th, "heard of the valor of Prescott at Bunker Hill," it had not probably been much noised abroad, and certainly it is not likely that he had heard of him during that time, as the chief commander in the battle. Turn this sentence over again, for here is testimony in point from one of the foremost men of the revolutionary period. Mr. Adams did not of course mean to say that he had not heard of the battle of Bunker Hill. In a letter written to James Warren, July 2, 1775, and found in the same volume (p. 317), he says, "We know nothing of the disposition of the army, not even who commanded in the late important engagement." But this was July 2d, and Mr. Adams had even then doubtless heard what other people in Philadelphia had heard. We have seen that Silas Deane, another member of Congress, had considerable information by that time. We have seen that the editor of the "Pennsylvania Packet," as early as June 26, was able to talk quite intelligently upon the subject. But Mr. Adams means to say, probably, that he had received no reliable official intelligence showing who commanded, whether it was Warren or Putnam, for both names, as we have seen, were floating on the air. But of "Prescott's valor" he did nor hear until he reached his home in Massachusetts on the 11th of August.

The evidence presented in the last few pages is of a kind hard to be resisted. These items, gathered out of the newspapers and letters and records of 1775, tell their own story, and one item confirms another. There can be no possible collusion among the men who pen these paragraphs. The three hundred guests of the Lord Mayor who are drinking General Putnam's health at the George at Cheswick, in England, had no knowledge of what Silas Deane had written in his letters to his wife that same summer. Samuel Adams, even though reliable news from Boston was scarce, did not get his information from the Society of Free Citizens at Dublin.

Such items as these might be greatly extended, no doubt, by a wider and longer search among the writings of 1775. But enough of them has been given probably to satisfy the candid reader, and we do not wish to overload this branch of the testimony, because other very important evidence yet remains to be unfolded.

In this analysis of Bunker Hill literature we now make a leap forward to the year 1818. After a little time the siege of Boston was ended. The British took their departure, satisfied that they were not to enter the interior parts of the country through the Boston gateway. The clouds which had so long hung over the chief town of New England rolled away, and drifted toward New York, Philadelphia and the more southern portions of the country. In that incoming tide of exciting events, the memories of Bunker Hill in some measure slumbered, though the record of that brilliant day could not be forgotten.

The long war at last closed, and the nation turned to its great work of reconstruction and the making of constitutions. General Putnam died in 1790, and slept "with his fathers" in an honored grave, — his services acknowledged almost universally by his countrymen, as among the most important of the revolutionary period. Years passed on. The distressing and unpopular war of 1812 came to disturb the country for three years. Captain Dearborn, a man to whom we have already been introduced as having charge of a company in Stark's regiment, had risen to the rank of Major-General in this war of 1812. He was a man of no mean abilities, and had served with honor in both civil and military affairs. He it was who first gave vent to the old pent-up envies and jealousies which had been engendered among certain military men in that army about Boston, in 1775. His own Colonel Stark had doubtless ministered in an evil way to a mind not kindly disposed in itself toward General Putnam.

In March, 1818, in the "Port Folio," he opened his hostile batteries, and uttered many hard and cruel words against this old revolutionary hero, which we do not propose at any great length to repeat. Our purpose is simply to call attention to the characteristic feature of this Dearborn literature,— its main drift or design,— which has often been strangely overlooked. General Dearborn was not trying to prove that Colonel Prescott was the general commander at Bunker Hill. His chief point is, that General Putnam *was, or ought to have been*, chief commander, but skulked away and did not do his duty. He expressly says that "No general officer except Putnam appeared in sight; nor did any officer assume any command, undertake to form the troops or give any orders in the course of the action that I heard, except Colonel Stark." Now, be it noticed that there were two general officers on that field besides Putnam, viz., Pomeroy and Warren. If Putnam was there, as some contend, just as *they* were there, as a volunteer, trying individually to help all he could, why should Dearborn launch his thunderbolts at him any more than at them ? No ; his underlying philosophy all the while is that Putnam was in nominal command at least, but was ineffi-cient, and did not do his duty. General Dearborn's strong assertion that he heard no one give orders except Colonel Stark, and therefore General Putnam did not really command, reminds one of the Irishman, who was confronted in a court of justice by two witnesses, who swore that they saw the prisoner commit an act of theft. " May it please your honor," said the Irishman, " I can bring fifty witnesses that will swear they did not see me do it." When one con-siders that Stark's troops came upon the field just as the action was beginning, that they were down by the Mystic River, at the farthest possible remove from the centre of operations, and that every man had his thoughts most in-tently pre-occupied by what was passing before him, how little could they know of General Putman's movements during the battle !

We will take one single passage from Dearborn, in which will be comprehended, as in a nutshell, the military phil-osophy which underlies his charges. He says,—

" I heard the gallant Colonel Prescott (who commanded at the redoubt) observe after the war, at the table of his Excellency James Bowdoin, then Governor of this Commonwealth, ' that he sent three messages during the battle to General Putnam, re-questing him to come forward and take the command, there being no general officer present, and the relative rank of the Colonel not having been settled ; but that he received no answer ; and his whole conduct was such, during the action and the re-treat, that he ought to have been shot.' " *

* It has been very seriously doubted whether Prescott ever made those remarks ascribed to him at Governor Bowdoin's table. We are willing to have the same doubt, and we quote them here only to show the nature of General Dearborn's attack on Putnam, and what he was aiming at.

How very differently Colonel Prescott appears in this passage from the man of the same name that figures before us in some of the modern books! So far from wishing or claiming to be commander-in-chief, he is a very humble individual, who does not quite know what his relative rank is even among the Colonels, and three times sends to General Putnam to come forward and take command at the redoubt. He would have him leave the general oversight, leave the eleven hundred men who were doing such excellent service along the fence line, and come and take special command of those "perhaps one hundred and fifty men" in the redoubt, over whom he was appointed local commander. But why did he not send this imploring cry to General Pomeroy and then abuse him for not coming? Why did he send for a man who "could not command Massachusetts soldiers on Massachusetts soil"? Why did he not call on General Warren, who was right by his side, if he had any serious doubt about his own rank and title? For the very obvious reason that Pomeroy and Warren were both *volunteers*, while Putnam was general commander. And while Prescott, on the one hand, thought Putnam ought to come and take special command of the fort, and Dearborn, on the other hand, wondered and complained because he was not at the other extreme of the line, giving orders down by the Mystic River, Putnam, as commander of the whole field, kept a central position where he could overlook all parts of the contest. General Dearborn says, "He [Putnam] remained at or near the top of Bunker Hill until the retreat." If he did so, as we have before suggested, he occupied a very dangerous position, for we will take from this same article of his a passage descriptive of the British style of firing. He says, "The fire of the enemy was so badly directed, I should presume that forty-nine balls out of fifty passed from one to six feet over our heads, for I

17

noticed an apple tree, some paces in the rear, which had
scarcely a ball in it from the ground as high as a man's
head, while the trunk and branches above were literally cut
to pieces." Now, though the balls going in that manner,
at the point where Dearborn was, would not have reached
the top of Bunker Hill, but would have lodged in its sides,
yet farther to the left, toward the redoubt, where the
ground was much higher, such firing as that from those
British muskets would have rendered a man extremely liable to accidents, "at or near the top of Bunker Hill." But
General Dearborn knew nothing of Putnam's movements.
He did not stay in any one place. He was here and there
and everywhere, as he thought his presence was needed.

But we will not enlarge. The one point which we wish
to show is, that this Dearborn literature is not at all concerned to prove that Colonel Prescott was general commander that day. It is positive on the other side of that
question. And so far as General Putnam is concerned, its
import is, that he was understood to be commander, but
that he failed in his duty.

But General Dearborn totally overshot his mark. The
American people in 1818 were in no mood to hear old
General Putnam, whose heroic bravery was of the most
unquestionable type, called a *poltroon* and *coward*, by a
man who confessed he asked Colonel Stark just to quicken
his pace a little, as they marched across that neck. The
publication of that article in the " Port Folio " roused a
storm of indignation which Dearborn little anticipated.
Men of the highest rank and character came forward to vindicate the memory of a hero who had been thus shamefully
abused. We shall place in the Appendix of this volume,
two of the seven articles of the Honorable John Lowell of
Boston, which this attack of Dearborn called out. They
will be good reading for this generation, and in these cen-

tennial days; and he that reads them will see that Mr. Lowell, looking at Dearborn's work as above described, is not discussing at all the modern question, as to whether Prescott or Putnam was chief commander.

Before proceeding farther, it may be well to recall to the readers of this generation who Honorable John Lowell was, and what were his qualifications for this kind of writing. He was born in Newburyport in 1769, six years before the battle of Bunker Hill. He had lived near the historic ground, and had brought with him from his early years the memories and associations clustering around that famous battle-field. He knew from all the conversations of men about him in his childhood whom they regarded as commander of the American forces on those heights of Charlestown. He was about fifty years old when he replied to General Dearborn's accusations. He was at that time one of the most able and active lawyers of Boston, inheriting in a good degree the legal abilities of his father, Judge John Lowell. He was therefore a man most eminently fitted to hear and weigh general evidence.

It was forty-three years after the battle when he took up his pen, and these Prescott claims had not yet come up in any such way as to attract attention from him. The question which he discussed was this : Did General Putnam act well his part as commander at Bunker Hill, or did he fail in his duty? The very first sentence of his first or preliminary article opens the field which his arguments are to cover. He says, " It is honorable to the moral feelings of the American people, that a general burst of indignation at the unwarrantable attack on the reputation of one of their earliest and ablest officers has compelled the accuser to put himself on trial." That style of language from one of the ablest men in Boston in 1818, comprehending in his own memory the things whereof he is writing, sounds strangely unlike some of the modern utterances. Judge Lowell says, at the opening of his last article, " It is a little extraordinary that at this late period of time we should find men disputing about the most essential facts relating to such a battle as that of Bunker Hill ; that even the important one, whether there was *any* commander-in-chief or not, is still the subject of controversy. For ourselves we think the evidence recently before the public settles that question satisfactorily ; and that General Putnam was undoubtedly commander in that action."

So important is the evidence contained in these articles of Mr. Lowell, that the writer had the seven copied in full to be placed in the Appendix ; but want of room compels him to give only a portion of them there, and it is desirable at this point to furnish a brief summary of a part of one of his articles, as showing his method of treatment, and what the subject was that he was discussing. In his *fifth* article he proposes to introduce what he calls "presumptions . . . . to support the character of a hero whose name will be as immortal as the history of that battle, or of the Revolution, of which it was the first and most glorious fruits."

"(1) The *first* presumption we introduce is, General Putnam's high character for valor acquired in Lord Chatham's glorious war for the conquest of the French Colonies in America. . . . .

"(2) The *second* presumptive proof we shall adduce is the silence of all contemporaneous and subsequent historians, as to such an infamous charge ; and the positive testimony of all such witnesses to his valor.

"(3) The *third* is, that when the delinquents in that battle were brought to trial, to wit, four Colonels, three Captains, and five Lieutenants, many of whom were *convicted* and *cashiered*, there should not have been a color of evidence, a surmise, a whisper, against the conduct of General Putnam. . . . .

"(4) The *fourth* presumption in favor of the utter falsehood of these charges against General Putnam is his appointment, immediately after this battle, by the Congress of the United States, to the second military office in the Revolutionary armies. . . . .

"(5) *Fifthly*, the next and highest presumption in his favor arises from the confidence which Washington reposed in him, immediately after the battle and during the whole war, until, by the act of God, he was compelled to leave the service. Washington was the most impartial man, both in his character and from his situation, that could be found in the nation. Yet Washington was the man who recommended Putnam to this appointment. Washington was the man who instituted the inquiries into the conduct of the battle of Bunker Hill. Washington was the man who entrusted Putnam with the forlorn hope, who were to land on Boston Common [on March 5th, 1776, if the British had attacked Dorchester Heights, as they did not] and carry the war into the very headquarters of the enemy. Washington was the man who selected Putnam, nearly a year after the battle of Bunker Hill, to defend New York against the whole forces of the enemy that he believed had gone there."

These are the five *presumptions* that Mr. Lowell introduces in one section of his long and diversified argument, and which, in its whole length and breadth, is designed to be exhaustive, and in our judgment is so. No man has ever answered it, nor can any man answer it, in any adequate way.

It would be well if some of our modern writers would give heed to the weighty words which Mr. Lowell introduces under one of the heads above given. He says, "Every honest and honorable man, indeed the whole nation, have a deep interest in the character of Putnam. His reputation constituted a part of the national property; it formed a large portion of its fame."

We cannot dwell longer upon these articles of Mr. Lowell. We have given enough so that every reader can see what one of Boston's most distinguished citizens, born

before the battle, and having, of his own personal knowledge, such materials for its history as no man can now
have, thought and said on this subject in the year 1818.
We repeat, the question he was discussing, and the only
great question then up for discussion was, whether General Putnam, as commander at Bunker Hill, did his duty
ably and faithfully, or did not. The modern question had
not then so arisen above the horizon as to attract attention from leading minds. The point to be decided was not
between Putnam and Prescott, but between Putnam doing
his duty or not doing it; between Putnam as commander
in the battle, or no proper commander at all, — "a headless
mob," as Colonel Swett calls it.

In the course of this fifth article, from which we have
made the above quotations, Mr. Lowell introduces the letter which John Adams wrote to Daniel Putnam, after reading his (Putnam's) reply to the slanders of General Dearborn, as also another letter from the same pen to President
Monroe.* Mr. Adams says,—

"Neither myself nor my family have been able to read either

* The following are the closing sentences of Mr. Lowell's last article :
"We now take our leave of this subject, happy in the conviction that
every generous mind, every man who knows the inestimable value of reputation, every fatherless son who cherishes the memory of one whom he laments,
will be convinced of the unguardedness of those charges against General
Putnam as well as of their untruth. In performing this pleasing duty of defending the virtuous and brave, we have as much as possible abstained from
all recrimination, inviting and open and easy of access as it was. We have
abstained partly because any comparison of the services of the accuser and accused would seem to presuppose some equality in desert, which would have been
an indignity to the memory of Putnam ; and partly because it would seem as
if there were some fault imputable to Putnam, which we wished to offset
against the defects of his calumniator. It is indeed extraordinary that a man
who has reason to fear that his actions may yet become the subject of bio-
graphical criticism should have become the accuser of one who was in possession of a nation's respect, and whose merit was so well able, as we have
seen, to endure the closest scrutiny. Is it that we are blind to our own fail-
ings, or is it policy, to bring the character of others into question to prevent a
too curious examination of our own? ˙ A FRIEND TO INJURED MERIT."

with dry eyes. They are letters that would do honor to the pen of Pliny. You ask whether any dissatisfaction existed in the public mind against General Putnam, in consequence of his conduct on the 17th of June. I was in Philadelphia from the 5th of May through the summer of 1775, and can testify to nothing which passed at Charlestown on the 17th of June. But this I do say without reserve, that I never heard the least insinuation of dissatisfaction with the conduct of General Putnam through his whole life."

In the midst of this controversy of 1818, an article appeared in the "North American Review" (in the July number of that year) which has been generally understood to have come from the pen of Daniel Webster. Perhaps some things said in that article may have afforded a slight foundation for the modern theories and speculations. It is important, therefore, that we should distinctly understand the end and aim of the article. It is a strong and bold defence of General Putnam against his slanderers. It is written with the same essential spirit and design as the articles of Mr. Lowell. Near the beginning it is said, " Every descendant and connection of General Putnam is bound to protect and preserve his character and fame from unmerited reproach. He has a *right*, it is his *duty*, to call upon the prosecutor to produce evidence in support of the charges, or to retract them." That sentence will be sufficient to reveal the current idea of the whole article. But in the course of it he says, " Properly and strictly speaking there was no commander-in-chief in the battle." It may be observed, in passing, that this remark does not enure to Colonel Prescott's benefit, whatever honor it may take from General Putnam. We do not credit Mr. Webster with his usual large-orbed wisdom in making such an assertion. We have no doubt whatever that the battle of Bunker Hill had a plan and a guiding head. Mr. Lowell, as we have just seen, was decided on that point. Mr. Webster may have just been reading John Adams's letter about "four armies," or some similar piece of writing, and had not taken time to straighten the tangle ; but certainly he was not trying to prove that Colonel William Prescott was the commander-in-chief, though his distinguished name is sometimes slipped in as authority in that direction. At a later stage he might perhaps be more fairly quoted on that side, but in 1818 it had not revealed itself to him that Prescott was chief. Forty-three years ought to suffice to give that revelation to him, if it was ever to be made.

This may be a place as appropriate as any other for introducing an item of evidence that has never before been presented to the public. Last summer the writer received a pressing invitation from Hon. Daniel Putnam Tyler of Brooklyn, Connecticut, to visit him at his home, as he was seriously ill, and had some things which he wished to communicate. Mr. Tyler was formerly Secretary of State in Connecticut, and will be well remembered by many in Massachusetts as an effective public speaker in political campaigns. He was much employed in this way, years ago, in various parts of New England. He was a great-grandson of General Putnam, and his home has long been near General Putnam's old residence. As a public speaker, he carried into his audience something of the energy and force and sympathetic contagion which his ancestor employed in matters of war. He had also a strong personal resemblance to General Putnam, so much so, that old men who had known the revolutionary leader were always reminding him of this resemblance. The story is told of his speaking once to a large audience in New Haven, and as the assembly was breaking up and scattering, an old man threaded his way through the crowd and took him by the hand most cordially, saying, " I need no introduction to you, sir ; you are the perfect embodiment of my old friend, General Putnam. My name is Noah Webster."

The visit above referred to was paid, and Mr. Tyler had more things to say than he had strength to say, for he was suffering greatly from heart disease, of which he has since died.* But he felt most acutely the wrong which had been done to his noble-hearted and generous ancestor, by certain modern writers. For long years he had borne in his memory an incident that greatly impressed and delighted him, and which he had often related to others. He felt now that his end was approaching; and he had taken pains to write out this bit of history, and go before a justice of the peace and make oath to its truth.

A word of explanation, before his statement is given. In some of the narratives of what transpired on the 17th of June, it may be remembered that when Warren was going upon the ground, just before the battle, he met William Eustis, then a medical student in his own office. Young Eustis was acting there that day as surgeon. He was afterwards Governor of Massachusetts, Member of Congress, and Secretary of War at Washington. The statement of Mr. Tyler runs as follows:

I, Daniel P. Tyler, of Brooklyn, Windham County, Connecticut, depose and say that sometime during the year 1822 or 1823, Dr. William Eustis, then a Member of Congress from Massachusetts, travelled with his family in his private carriage from Washington to Boston, and on the night next preceding the interview

* "Daniel P. Tyler of Brooklyn, who died on Saturday, November 6th, 1875, at the age of seventy-seven, was one of the leading men of the State a generation ago. He was a great stump speaker, and did particularly vigorous work in the 'Tippecanoe and Tyler too' campaign. When a young man he was Lieutenant in the United States army for several years, and after settling down at Brooklyn as a lawyer, held the offices of Clerk of Courts for Windham County for fifteen years, County Judge, and Secretary of State. He was a great-grandson of Israel Putnam." — "Tolland County Press."

of which I shall speak, he lodged at Canterbury, six miles south
of Brooklyn, and the weather being very warm, an early ride to
Brooklyn, to breakfast there, was determined on. While at the
breakfast-table he learned to his surprise that he was quite near
the house of General Putnam and the place where he died,— surprised, because he had always understood that Putnam lived and
died in *Pomfret.* Now, what was Pomfret became Brooklyn in
1786. On learning this, Dr. Eustis inquired whether any of the
descendants of Putnam lived near by, so that he could see them.
A messenger was thereupon sent for me, with a request from the
Doctor that I would come at once to the hotel. Being away
from home when the messenger came, it was some time before
I went to the hotel, and then I found the Doctor's carriage
already standing before the door, and the family ready to leave.
The Doctor introduced himself to me, and expressed regret that
I had not come sooner, for he had much that he was anxious to
communicate about the battle of Bunker Hill and General Putnam, but said that the heat was so great that he could not delay
his journey till later in the day, and consequently could not remain to make the statement he wished. The difficulty, however,
was overcome by sending in advance the carriage with the family,
while Dr. Eustis and I followed leisurely in my own humble
equipage. Our immediate destination was Thompson, distant
seventeen miles.

"The Doctor began the conversation by speaking of a pamphlet published by General Dearborn, purporting to give an account of the battle of Bunker Hill, which he said was inaccurate
in many respects, but more particularly in regard to what was
said of General Putnam, and what he (the Doctor) himself knew
to be incorrect. He said he was a student in Dr. Warren's
office, that early in the morning of the battle Putnam was there,
and with almost superhuman energy, acting as commander, and
so far as he knew was alone recognized as such. It was not till
many years after the battle that he heard it suggested that any other
than Putnam had the chief command on that occasion. He said
he knew that Colonel Prescott was intrusted with the defence of
the redoubt, that he was an intrepid and gallant soldier, and

defended that with great military skill and Spartan valor. The Doctor also said that he was absent from the country when General Dearborn prepared his pamphlet ; and that as General Dearborn knew of his acquaintance with the scenes enacted on Bunker Hill, and of his subsequent connection with the military affairs of the country, having himself succeeded General Dearborn as Secretary of War, he might, he thought, have presumed without arrogance that General Dearborn would have submitted to his examination the manuscript ; and that had he done so, he (the Doctor) would have strongly advised against its publication.

"The above is only a synopsis of the conversation, so interesting to me, which was held during our ride. The Doctor informed me that toward the close of the revolutionary war he was surgeon in the army at West Point when General Putnam commanded at that post. The foregoing is *memoriter*, but perfectly fresh in my recollection. The only written memorandum I made is on a blank leaf of Humphrey's "Life of Putnam," and is as follows: '1822. Went to Thompson with Dr. Eustis at his request, so that he could tell me about Bunker Hill and General Putnam, — said he was at the battle, surgeon, — that General Dearborn's account of the battle was not correct, that General Putnam was the commander, and he didn't know of any other nor see any other acting as such. He said he was there all through the battle.'   DANIEL PUTNAM TYLER.

"Dated BROOKLYN, July 9th, 1875."

"WINDHAM COUNTY, *ss.*

Then personally appeared Daniel Putnam Tyler, signer of the foregoing deposition, and made oath to the truth of the same, before me.   ELIAS H. MAIN, Justice of the Peace."

The value of this testimony.is enhanced by the fact, not only that it came from such a man as Governor William Eustis, but that it came from him as one burdened with a desire to deliver it, for the ends of personal justice and historical truth. It will be remembered by those who participated in the scenes of the Bunker Hill Centennial at Boston, that a unique and well preserved, but old-fashioned carriage of Governor Eustis passed in the procession. Mr. Tyler had read of this in the papers, and at the time of the writer's visit to Brooklyn, he was curious to know whether this might not be the identical carriage which he saw at Brooklyn in 1822. As Governor Eustis died in 1825, it is altogether likely that it was the same, though on this point we could give him no reliable information.

We have shown, we trust, to the satisfaction of the reader, that the questions so earnestly discussed in 1818 were totally different from those forced upon us to-day. The claim that Colonel William Prescott had the chief command in the battle was not urged upon the public attention at all. That is a later assumption, having its origin somewhere between forty-three and one hundred years after the battle. This fact, of itself, we hold to be utterly fatal to the doctrine. If there were nothing else to be said about it except this one thing, it would be enough. A theory on *such a subject* that has to wait more than forty-three years for its birth — wait till most of the actors in the battle are dead, before it dares to be born — is destined, sooner or later, to die and be forgotten. It has no chance for any immortal place in human history. Some historical questions are in their very nature secret and subtle, and hard to be resolved; but the man who led the American army that long, bright summer day, on the heights of Charlestown, was not shut up in a cell, and did not wear a mask. He was moving boldly and openly in sight of heaven and earth, and the living men of that generation did not require forty-three years to find out who he was.

And now we take another wide step and come down to the year 1849, when Richard Frothingham, Esq., published his celebrated book, the "Siege of Boston." Thousands will remember the pleasant impression which that book made upon the public mind. It was a delightful book. It charmed the reader. It gathered up the minute facts, the old legends, the romantic incidents, which had lurked away in obscure volumes and narratives, or in unpublished manu-scripts drawn from dusty pigeon holes. Mr. Frothingham arranged and set in order all this diversified material, in a manner quiet and scholarly, and when the book was issued, many a reader was ready to say, "There! that is the first book that ever gave us a complete history of Bunker Hill." He became at once an authority. Irving was writing his "Life of Washington," and Bancroft was going on with his "History of the United States," and it would seem, in both cases, that these able authors said to themselves, "Mr. Frothingham has saved us the labor of an independent investigation, as to this critical and important period of our national history, and we will give him full credit, and take the substance of what he has written for our own volumes."

Be it noticed, moreover, that Mr. Frothingham never in a single instance propounds this theory of Prescott's com-mand in any bold and defiant manner. It creeps in quietly in many passages, as though it were almost a matter of in-difference to him whether Prescott or Putnam shall be re-garded as chief commander. His style of argument is, that we have no express information that Putnam was ap-pointed to the command, and being from Connecticut, there would be serious difficulties (owing to the relations of the several States) in his taking command without an express order from General Ward; and it seems therefore most likely that Colonel William Prescott must be looked upon as chief commander. This, in general, is the way in which this scheme takes shape in Mr. Frothingham's delightful book,— very different from that rampant and audacious style of assertion in which we confront it in the pages of many later writers, who may be called Mr. Frothingham's pupils and followers.

Moreover, in the "Siege of Boston" General Putnam is nowhere abused and slandered. He is constantly recognized as a good and true man. There is not a single touch of the General Dearborn spirit and tone. His eminent services, his immense activities, his unquestionable bravery, are all acknowledged and dwelt upon. So predominant throughout the whole volume is this style of treatment, that Colonel Swett, in his second production (which will be soon noticed), was moved to say of Mr. Frothingham's method, " He has treated General Putnam's character with the utmost candor and kindness, as animals destined for the altar are pampered, to be sacrificed at the last."

We do not wish to deny that between the years 1818 and 1849, there had been, here and there, certain intimations and forerunners of this new theory of the command at Bunker Hill. There had been these droppings and suggestions along the way by one writer and another, on various occasions and at various times. It would unduly prolong this narrative if we were to stop and pick up these scattered instances. But there is some general law about them. They do not as a common fact come from men who are disposed to slander or undervalue General Putnam's services in the battle. They spring out of that confusion and entanglement of thought, to which even such men as the illustrious John Adams had ministered, in his talk about "four armies," and about Putnam's being as independent of Ward as Ward was of him. The orations and addresses in the great Bunker Hill gatherings in 1825 and in 1843 (at the completion of the monument), on the whole, ministered to the same idea.

It was not until 1849, when the "Siege of Boston" appeared, seventy-four years after the battle, that we had any fully constructed theory showing Colonel Prescott as chief commander in the battle; and even then the theory came forth in such a gentle and winning way, with so large and generous an appreciation of General Putnam's immense services, that the men who did not believe the theory at all could not be as cross and indignant as they wanted to be.

But with Colonel Samuel Swett of Boston, then a man of over sixty years, the case was different. He had put himself forth in authorship thirty years before, and his judgment as a man, and as a military officer, was impugned by the speculations of Mr. Frothingham. His memory reached back almost to the revolutionary days. He had been honorably connected with the army in the war of 1812, and he broke forth upon this new theory in a storm of indignation, and published his pamphlet to refute it; which led to a rejoinder on the part of Mr. Frothingham. We do not propose to dwell upon the merits or demerits of this controversy.

We are concerned at this point, simply to show that almost three-quarters of a century had passed away,— the men who fought the battle were in their graves,— the men who acted in the civil affairs of the nation had gone to their rest before this theory, in full form and shape, was launched upon the world. As already said, this circumstance alone is fatal to the idea. The living men of 1775 must have known the truth in the case, and in the earlier portions of this chapter we have recorded their verdict. That verdict will stand against all the waves and storms that may beat upon it. The history of this first great act of the revolutionary drama may abide for a time in this perverted form, incorporated as it is on the pages of some of our leading histories; but other historians will arise, as the years pass on, who will return to the "old paths," and walk in the ways in which the fathers taught them to walk.

In theological seminaries, where the dogmatic professor has any new and peculiar doctrines, theories or ideas to broach, his most dangerous enemies are his eager and admiring pupils. They will sound abroad his new discoveries without any of the checks, the qualifications, the safeguards, which the professor himself would throw around them. And something like this has been true in the present case. In the "Siege of Boston" the new discovery creeps forth very modestly. It is only the roaring of the "nightingale" and the "sucking-dove." It is not the bringing of the real lion upon the stage at all. General Putnam is still a most heroic, generous, admirable man. His services on that day of the battle are forever to be held in grateful remembrance. But there is a difficulty in seeing how he could be exactly commander-in-chief. He would have made a good one, no doubt, if he could have been one, but then we have no written paper showing that Ward appointed him to that place. He never produced before Colonel Prescott, or any other man, such a paper which would have entitled him to hold the chief command. There lies the difficulty. But let us never forget that General Putnam was a brave old hero. He was not the poltroon and coward that Dearborn said he was. Not by any means. He was ready to face the thickest dangers, and go where any other man dared to go, and to some places where hardly any other man did dare to go. We must all of us learn to love and admire brave old General Putnam.

That is the general spirit and temper of Mr. Frothingham, and it is also the spirit of some who have followed his lead. When Irving wrote his "Life of Washington," he acknowledged his great indebtedness to Mr. Frothingham, and he followed quite faithfully, altogether too faithfully, his version of this most important action of the revolutionary struggle. But Irving could not close that chapter without giving vent to his pent-up emotions, and he finds relief in a magnificent tribute to Putnam, which we quote.

" Putnam also was a leading spirit throughout the affair ; one of the first to prompt and of the last to maintain it. He appears to have been active and efficient at every point,— sometimes fortifying, sometimes hurrying the reinforcements, inspiriting the men by his presence while they were able to maintain their ground, and fighting gallantly at the outpost to cover their retreat. The brave old man, riding about in the heat of the action, on this sultry day, 'with a hanger belted across his brawny shoulders, over a waistcoat without sleeves,' has been sneered at by a contemporary as 'much fitter to lead a band of sickle men or ditchers than musketeers.' But this very description illustrates his character and identifies him with the times and the service. A yeoman warrior, fresh from the plough, in the garb of rural labor, a patriot, brave and generous, but rough and ready, who thought not of himself in time of danger, but ever ready to serve in any way, and to sacrifice official rank and self-glorification to the good of the cause. He was eminently a soldier for the occasion. His name has long been a favorite one with young and old, one of the talismanic names of the Revolution, the very mention of which is like the sound of a trumpet. Such names are the precious jewels of our history, to be garnered up among the treasures of the nation and kept immaculate from the tarnishing breath of the cynic and the doubter."

Bancroft, too, though he allowed himself to be led too obediently by another through this portion of his great work, does not go beyond his guide in any use of hard language.

But there are multitudes of lesser pupils who have not had this discretion of silence. By them Putnam begins to be jostled about as if he were a mere intruder on that hard-fought field — rather in the way than otherwise — interfering all the while with arrangements that would have been better without him ; while on the other hand, out of the mists of one hundred years, begins at last to loom up the stately form of a great military hero, Colonel William Prescott,—

18

the man that always stayed a Colonel, while some fifteen or twenty of his associates were advanced to higher military positions. When an object is thus seen through the mist, it often grows upon us as the mist thickens, until the proportions become perfectly gigantic. The man that figured before us last year, in the writings of some men about Boston, in certain of the newspapers, and in orations and speeches, was of this prodigious character. General Israel Putnam, second in military command to Washington, was nothing to him,—a mere child in military knowledge and force. What this man might grow to before another centennial, if no check were put upon his enlargement, it is painful to think of. What he has already grown to may be seen in the following:

"He [Prescott] was the hero of that blood-dyed summit, the midnight leader and guard, the morning sentinel, the orator of the opening strife, the cool and deliberate overseer of the whole struggle, the well-skilled marksman of the exact distance and the point of aim at which a shot was certain death; he was the trusted chief, in whose bright eye and steady nerve men read their duty; and when conduct, skill and courage could do no more, he was the merciful deliverer of the remnant. Prescott was the hero of the day, and wherever its tale is told, let him be its chieftain. Whose statue other than his should grace the monumental summit, beside, not beneath, that of Warren, the 'volunteer'?"

But it has been pleasant to observe, amidst all this noise and excitement, that there were men enough, Massachusetts men, who still read the old history correctly, and were not to be stirred from their moorings by the waves that were beating about them. Samuel A. Drake, Esq., besides the contribution to centennial literature already noticed (the testimony of the British officers), prepared a pamphlet on the battle itself, in which General Putnam still held his old and true position as commander. W. W. Wheildon, Esq., of Concord, wrote a " New History of the Battle of Bunker Hill," which is clear and excellent. He takes no extreme ground, but sums up his conclusion on the point now before us in the following words :

" After what has been said, perhaps it is unnecessary to express opinions on the specific question of commander. It is assumed that this question has been finally settled, and it is now very boldly asserted — the statement resting on a basis of assertions and opinions — that ' it is certain *and now beyond all question* that he [Prescott] had *the command of the day and the action.'* This statement ignores all the fact and argument on the other side, which have never been satisfactorily answered, and we think is distinctly untrue."

The italics used in this quotation are Mr. Wheildon's, and the passage may be found on p. 50.

In closing this extended review, covering in a rapid way the century which has passed since the battle, we cannot resist the general impression that the literary process, so far as regards Colonel Prescott, began with his near friends, and the first effort was to relieve him from the charge of not having played his part well in that action. Manifestly he did not show military capacity like the other local and subordinate commanders, Stark, Reed and Knowlton. The current conversation of men in the times immediately following, both in the army and out of the army, we have no doubt whatever, if it could be faithfully reported to us, would run largely in this wise : Prescott was brave and did all he could, but he was not equal to the occasion. He did not know how to command men, and nerve them up to their duty. If he had done as well that day as the other commanders, the result would have been different. It is in this way that we explain the ominous silence about him in the contemporary literature, for that " unbounded applause of his contemporaries," of which Mr. Frothingham speaks, is just the one thing which we do not find, and the historical student may be challenged to find it. He was not rudely treated by the men of his generation, for they saw in him a man of personal dignity and worth, who had shown a large measure of individual courage, had remained steadfastly at his post of duty, and had done the best he could. But what they said one to another in private, is made manifest largely in a negative way, by that oppressive silence which broods over the general literature of those times, and by the fact that he was not promoted.

Let it be understood, that when we speak of *contemporaries*, we do not mean Prescott's kindred and personal friends. We do not accept the literature that is stored up in the "Prescott Memorial" and such like compilations. Nor are the affidavits that were called out in 1818, from soldiers that were in the battle, of much consequence. Such as they were, they carry vastly more testimony for Putnam than for Prescott. But they were extremely contradictory and unsatisfactory. They show us clearly how little confidence can be placed, after a long lapse of years, in the recollections and impressions of men as excited and absorbed as were those soldiers at Bunker Hill. We could find hundreds of men to-day, who have lived their "threescore years and ten," who would be ready to go before a magistrate and make oath that the ordinary snow storms of sixty years ago were twice or three times greater than the ordinary snow storms of these passing years.

When we talk of "contemporaries" and of contemporary literature, it is meant that one shall go out upon the broad field of the world, far away from circles of admiring kindred and local glory, and examine books, public records, newspapers, letters passing from man to man, in the large intercourse of society, all forms and varieties of testimony,

which the living men of that generation have left behind
for our instruction. And when we bring Colonel Prescott
to this broad and comprehensive test, the "unbounded
applause" is not found. In the case of General Putnam it
is most easily found. We have furnished evidence in this
volume to show this clearly, and far more testimony could
be brought were it needed. But we challenge any man to
hunt up a similar record, or one in any degree corresponding, for Colonel Prescott. So far from this, the silence
respecting him in those years that cluster immediately
about the battle is much more marked and significant
than was anticipated when we began this investigation.
Let us recur once more, by way of illustration, to the testimony of Samuel Adams. He actually had to come to the
camp at Cambridge, about the middle of August, before he
heard of "the valor of Prescott." * It is freely admitted
that Prescott exhibited valor at Bunker Hill. That fact
has been recognized again and again in this volume. But
it was in such connections and associations that it had
not reported itself to Mr. Adams at Philadelphia, in the
nearly two months intervening — to *Sam. Adams*, who
studied every fact of those days, who scrutinized every
movement and event, with a diligence almost unparalleled.
John Adams says of his illustrious cousin, "Samuel Adams,

---

* And here we have another instance of that significant silence of which
we have spoken. In the three large volumes of Mr. Wells's " Life of Samuel
Adams," containing the letters and many papers from the pen of him who is
sometimes called "the Father of the Revolution," the only reference to Colonel Prescott seems to be in the passage above quoted. When we consider
that Adams and Prescott were from the same colony, and that Mr. Adams
had laid it down as a rule, that every instance of merit belonging to a Massachusetts officer should " be improved as far as decency will admit of it," it is
remarkable that he should never again mention him in his letters and other
writings. If he were really the chief commander at Bunker Hill, and the
great man shown to us in the modern books and pamphlets, he would have
been "improved." Mr. Adams lived on to the year 1803, and was in public
life until 1797.

to my certain knowledge, from 1758 to 1775, that is, for seventeen years, made it his constant rule to watch the rise of every brilliant genius," etc. But he had not heard of Prescott's valor until he reached Cambridge, about two months after the battle.

In contrast with this, notice how Putnam moved across those years. On the 19th of June, 1775, at Philadelphia, when they knew nothing as yet of the battle of Bunker Hill, in the choice of the first four Major-Generals, he was *unanimously* taken by the Continental Congress, and lifted at once over David Wooster, Joseph Spencer, John Thomas, Seth Pomeroy, William Heath, John Whitcomb, Joseph Warren, Joseph Frye, all of whom were higher in military rank than he, *i. e.*, either higher in the nature of their office, or earlier in receiving their commissions for the same office. The Continental Congress indeed did not know of the three last-named as having been raised to the offices they held, for that choice by the Massachusetts Congress had just been made. Nor did it know of Warren's death. But of the five others the Congress knew all the facts, and some of these men were very able officers ; and yet Putnam was taken from a lower grade and placed above them all.

After the battle, we have seen how the men of England and the men of Philadelphia were drinking his health, how full the air was with his name and his deeds, how large were the trusts placed in his hands, and how nobly he met them. To talk of the "unbounded applause of his contemporaries" in his case brings *words* into some reasonable connection with *facts.* But in the case of Prescott it is like having a band of music to marshal a laborer to his daily toil.

We repeat, that the first efforts in a literary way, with regard to Colonel Prescott, seem to have been to excuse him, to apologize for him, to show how other men were more to blame than he; and from this earliest form of *apologetics*, little by little, one man taking up the pen where another laid it down, the process has gone on, until at length with a certain class of writers he is the great man of that day, overtowering Putnam, Stark, Reed, Knowlton and everybody else. But this is the "unbounded applause" of 1875, and not of 1775. If any student of history, working upon the broad field, can certify to this "applause" in the literature of the last century, or find any evidence, outside of a small circle of men, that Prescott ever received the high plaudits of his contemporaries as a military leader, he will confer a special favor if he will report his evidence as soon as may be.

We have made frequent references in our previous narrative to Daniel Putnam and his testimony, as contained in the "Connecticut Historical Collections" (Vol. I. pp. 229–250). In concluding this chapter, we will copy from that article the sentences which relate to the interviews between Putnam and Prescott, previous to the battle, and their conversations on the projected enterprise.

"One afternoon, as Putnam had been marking out a new line on which his men had just commenced work, Colonel Prescott and Colonel Gardiner came up. 'I wish, General,' said Prescott, 'your men were digging nearer Boston.' Putnam replied that he wished so too, and hoped ere long we should all be of one mind. . . . .

"Next day [after the exchange of the prisoners], there was quite a *levee* of officers at Putnam's quarters to talk about the exchange, etc. He related to them all the particulars, and turning to Colonel Prescott said, 'Colonel, I saw ground yesterday that may suit your purpose. I suppose you have not forgotten your remark of the other day about *digging;* but more of this another time.' . . . .

"It was further stated by Putnam that there had been an understanding between him and Colonel Prescott that the latter

should have a part in the expedition, if it should ever be under-
taken. General Ward was apprised of this, and Prescott and
all his regiment was ordered on that service. . . . . [Three
hundred went that night, and the rest were expected to come the
next morning with the reinforcements.]

"The day before the battle of Bunker Hill, I noticed an unusual stir among the troops at Cambridge. Putnam's regiment
was under arms, and I was informed by the Adjutant that a detachment had been made from it for 'secret service;' but what
at the time impressed my mind most strongly, was the preparation my father himself was making. With his own hands he prepared cartridges for his pistols, took out the old flints, and put in
new. While he was doing this, Colonel Prescott came in, and observing what he was about, said, in a low tone, 'I see, General,
you are making preparation, and *we* shall be ready at the time.'"

Now, this is a perfectly straightforward and circumstantial
story, from one who had the best opportunities of knowing
whereof he affirmed, and who approved himself in after life
an upright and honorable man. Has that story ever been
historically disproved? Is there a single well established
fact to show its falsity? We know of none. The story is
in entire harmony with all we really *know* of the events of
those days. We are satisfied that it will stand the test of
the closest examination. And the closer the examination
the better. There is nothing to fear in this matter, except
from loose, rambling statements. The only danger is, that
men will continue to talk and write out of their imaginations, out of their preconceived impressions, without going
to the records.

And by this story, what we have claimed is made plain.
It is not likely that Prescott would have had any prominent
part at all in the battle of Bunker Hill, except by favor of
General Putnam; and if Putnam had had the same business
to do over again a fortnight after, he would not probably
have chosen Prescott as his assistant.

CHAPTER XII.

FOUR YEARS MORE OF ARMY LIFE.

Putnam chosen to be near Washington.— Honored and Trusted by Him.— Operations during the Summer and Autumn of 1775, and following Winter.— Occupation of Dorchester Heights.— March 5th.— Evacuation of Boston, March 17th.— Putnam in full Command at New York.— Letters. — Battle of Long Island.— Sent to Philadelphia.— Headquarters on the Hudson.— Ride down the Stone Steps.— Struck with Paralysis, 1779.— Compelled to leave the Army.

IT is, of course, a very unusual circumstance in writing a man's biography, to spend so large a portion of the volume in unfolding the facts and events of some two months of a long life. But we ask no apology for doing this in the present instance. The work was made necessary for the ends of justice and truth.

It may seem a sudden transition to turn from this theatre of controversy and argument into the more quiet strain of simple narrative. But we shall soon find enough to interest us. The great war of independence has only just opened. Exciting events are to follow in quick succession for years to come. The siege of Boston has not yet ended. For months the American army is to be chiefly concentrated here.

On the 2d day of July, Washington reached the headquarters of the American camp at Cambridge. There was great rejoicing at his arrival. He brought with him the commissions for the four Major-Generals appointed by the Continental Congress (June 17th and 19th), viz., Artemas Ward, Charles Lee, Philip Schuyler and Israel Putnam.

There was lodged in his hands by Congress a certain discretionary power, as to the delivery of these commissions on his arrival. If he encountered rumors unfavorable to any of his appointees, he might delay or withhold the commissions. Almost immediately upon his reaching the camp, he gave to General Putnam his commission. He had no doubt or misgiving in his case. It is true, in his letter afterwards sent to Congress, explaining his action, it is implied that when he delivered the commission to Putnam, he expected to deliver them all; but he soon found such complaints as to the others, that for a time he withheld the commissions. There is, however, in this letter to Congress no expression of regret that he had given his commission to Putnam. His case appears to have been perfectly clear to his own mind.

The following extract from General Washington's letter to the Continental Congress, dated "Camp at Cambridge, July 19th, 1775," will explain these complications among the officers, in consequence of the appointments made at Philadelphia. This letter in full is in Force's "Archives," (4th series, Vol. II. pp. 1624–27).

"The great dissatisfaction expressed on this subject, and the apparent danger of throwing the army into the utmost disorder, together with the strong representations of the Provincial Congress, have induced me to retain the commissions in my hands, until the pleasure of Congress should be further known, except General *Putnam's*, which was given the day I came into camp, and before I was apprised of these uneasinesses. In such a step, I must beg the Congress will do me the justice to believe that I have been actuated solely by a regard to the public good. I have not, and could not have, any private attachments; every gentleman in appointment was an entire stranger to me, but from character; I must therefore rely upon the candor of the Congress for their favorable construction of my conduct in this particular.

General *Spencer* was so much disgusted at the preference given to General *Putnam*, that he left the army without visiting me, or making known his intentions in any respect. General Pomeroy had also retired before my arrival, occasioned, as is said, by some disappointment from the Provincial Congress. General *Thomas* is much esteemed and earnestly desired to continue in the service, and as far as my opportunities have enabled me to judge, I must join in the general opinion that he is an able, good officer, and his resignation would be a public loss. The postponing him to *Pomeroy* and *Heath*, whom he has commanded, would make his continuance very difficult, and probably operate in his mind as the like circumstance has done on that of Spencer." *

There is a large volume of testimony in this letter, if we will only search it out. Washington heard, in that American camp, no such insinuations against General Putnam, as certain men in modern times are fond of slipping into their narratives. On the contrary, he did hear, very speedily, such things said of General Artemas Ward that

---

* In "American Archives" (4th series, Vol. II. p. 1114) we have the order and rank of those higher officers of the army, appointed in June by the Continental Congress, out of which appointments such hard feelings were raised among some of the officers. The list stands thus :

" *George Washington*, Esq., General and commander-in-chief of all the forces raised or to be raised for the defence of American liberty.

" *Artemas Ward*, Esq., First Major-General.

" *Charles Lee*, Esq., Second Major-General.

" *Philip Schuyler*, Esq., Third Major-General.

" *Israel Putnam*, Esq., Fourth Major-General.

" *Seth Pomeroy*, Esq., First Brigadier-General.

" *Richard Montgomery*, Esq., Second Brigadier-General.

" *David Wooster*, Esq., Third Brigadier-General.

" *William Heath*, Esq., Fourth Brigadier-General.

" *Joseph Spencer*, Esq., Fifth Brigadier-General.

" *John Thomas*, Esq., Sixth Brigadier-General.

" *John Sullivan*, Esq., Seventh Brigadier-General.

" *Nathaniel Greene*, Esq., Eighth Brigadier-General.

" *Horatio Gates*, Esq., Adjutant-General, and with the rank of Brigadier-General."

he hesitated. His commission was at length delivered, and he was removed to Roxbury to take charge of the right wing of the army, while General Lee was placed in charge of the left wing, and Putnam was put in command of the reserves at the centre, near the person of the commander-in-chief. During the centennial scenes in Boston last year, there was one writer at least, who ventured to insinuate that Putnam was placed over these reserves near General Washington, to keep him out of mischief; and that the other Major-Generals had more honorable and responsible positions assigned them than he. But he was evidently a man who knew how to read military history to suit his own purposes. The general understanding is that Putnam, in this American camp, held the highest post of honor and trust under Washington.

Daniel Putnam, who still remained with his father, and was with him in the scenes of his daily life, tells us on what terms Washington and Putnam stood to each other during that summer of 1775, and the winter of 1775-76.

"From the arrival of Washington at Cambridge till the enemy left Boston, his and Putnam's families [General Putnam's second wife was now with him] were not only on the most friendly terms, but their intercourse was very frequent. Not a week passed but they dined together at the quarters of one or the other. One day in the month of September, General Washington at his table gave for a toast, '*A speedy and honorable peace,*' and all appeared to join with good will in the sentiment. Not many days after, at Putnam's quarters, addressing himself to Washington he said, 'Your Excellency, the other day, gave us "a speedy and honorable peace," and I, as in duty bound, drank it; and now I hope, sir, you will not think it an act of insubordination, if I ask you to drink one of rather a different character; I will give you, sir, *A long and moderate war.*' It has been truly said of Washington, that he seldom smiled and almost never laughed; but the sober and sententious manner in which Putnam delivered his sentiment, and its seeming contradiction to all his practice, came so unexpectedly upon Washington that he did laugh, more heartily than ever I remember to have seen him before or after; but presently he said, 'You are the last man, General Putnam, from whom I should have expected such a toast; you, who are all the time urging vigorous measures, to plead now for a *long* and, what is still more extraordinary, a *moderate* war, seems strange indeed.' Putnam replied that 'The measures he advised were calculated to prevent, not to hasten, a peace, which would only be a *rotten thing*, and last no longer than it divided us. I expect nothing but a *long* war, and I would have it a *moderate* one that we may hold out till the mother country becomes willing to cast us off forever.' Washington did not soon forget this toast; for years after, and more than once, he reminded Putnam of it."

There was another occasion in the autumn of that year when Washington laughed. The story is pleasantly told in the recent "Life of General Nathaniel Greene" (Vol. I. p. 120). Dr. Benjamin Church, who in April, May and June had been specially put forward as a true and earnest patriot, who had been a member of the Massachusetts Provincial Assembly and a member of the Committee of Safety, was found at length to be consorting with the enemy. At first it was only known that *some one* in the garb of a friend must be doing this, — that an evil influence was abroad, and the authorities were trying to trace it to its source. There was a woman in the case, but it was not known exactly who *she* was. A woman had been known to deliver a letter written in cipher, which letter had been detected and stopped, and was in the hands of the authorities; but who the man was that wrote it, or who the woman was that carried it was not known, though they had some signs and marks by which to trace her. Great had been the efforts to find the woman. Finally Putnam was commissioned to undertake the business. One day, as Washington was looking from the chamber windows of the Cragie House,

Putnam came in sight on horseback, riding somewhat furiously, with a woman behind him. The sight was so comical that Washington burst into laughter. Putnam dismounted, and with strong arm brought the woman into the
house, and they both so vigorously threatened her that she
revealed the secret on the spot, and the man was no other
than Dr. Benjamin Church. Here was an element of danger, new and unexpected. Church was arrested, tried before the Massachusetts Congress, and afterwards imprisoned
in Connecticut.

No very active military movements on either side were attempted during that summer and fall. The British were shut
up in Boston, or at least inside of Charlestown Neck, and they
were in no mood to try the experiment of coming out from
that retreat. On the other side Washington was introducing military discipline into the American camp, and preparing the men to act as true soldiers. The cares that
were rolled upon him when first coming into his responsible office were many and various, and some of them very
burdensome, and it was best to get ready before any great
offensive movement should be attempted.

But while no battles were fought, and no great enterprises
attempted on either side during those months of summer
and autumn, hardly a day passed in which little collisions
of one sort and another did not occur along the skirmish
lines, and the drums often beat to arms, that the men might
be ready for such emergencies as might arise.

Mr. Frothingham, from Chapter IX. of his "Siege of
Boston," onward for some chapters, has traced with minute
care this course of daily events. It is inconsistent with
the purpose of this volume that we should linger long upon
this period; but it may enliven our work, if we pick out a
few entries here and there from the diary before mentioned
and quoted. It is not without interest for us to know what

kind of sermons were listened to by those American soldiers gathered about Boston. Mr. Haskell has indicated
many of these texts, and we shall, in a few instances, place
in brackets the words of Scripture corresponding to his
figures. It is commonly understood that the text will
point to the subject of the sermon, though this is not an
invariable rule in our day.

" *July 4th, Tuesday.* — This morning our people took four
horses from the British. In the afternoon a party were ordered
to Lechmere's Point to intrenching. . . . .

" *July 6th, Thursday.* — This day Rev. Mr. Cleaveland, our
chaplain, came into the camp. Attended prayers at our barracks. In the evening a man deserted from our army to the
enemy. . . . .

" *July 8th, Saturday.* — This morning at 3 o'clock our people
at Roxbury went down upon the neck, and rushed upon the
guard. They retreated. Our men set fire to the guard-house.
They made a heavy fire upon our party, which was returned. A
smart engagement ensued upon both sides. Our lines manned
for two hours.

" *July 9th, Sunday.* — This morning our chaplain came and
preached in our regiment, from 2 Chronicles, vi. 34. [" If thy
people go out to war against their enemies, by the way that thou
shalt send them, and they pray unto thee' toward this city which
thou hast chosen, and the house which I have built for thy name ;
then hear thou from the heavens their prayer and their supplication
and maintain their cause."] In the afternoon from Deuteronomy
xxiii. 9. [" When the host goeth forth against thine enemies,
then keep thee from every wicked thing."] A flag came from the
enemy with a packet by General Lee. A man in a neighboring
regiment was whipped twenty stripes for striking an officer. . . . .

" *July 12th, Wednesday.* — This morning our troops at Roxbury went down to Long Island, took eighteen men that were
tending cattle on the island, and brought off nineteen head of
horned cattle and one hundred sheep. In the afternoon had a

smart shower of rain with heavy thunder, were something wet in our tents. . . . .

" *July 16th, Sunday.* — This morning heard a sermon from Ephesians, v. 16 [" Redeeming the time, because the days are evil "]; in the afternoon from Judges, v. 23 ["Curse ye Meroz, said the angel of the Lord, curse ye bitterly the inhabitants thereof, because they came not to the help of the Lord, to the help of the Lord against the mighty."] "

July 18th was something of a high day on Prospect Hill. The statement which the Continental Congress had prepared and issued, justifying themselves and the Colonies for the steps taken, was first read in the hearing of the soldiers. Then a new flag was unfurled, with appropriate exercises. Mr. Haskell thus describes the scene :

" *July 18th, Tuesday.* — This morning at 6 o'clock the grand manifest from the Continental Congress was read to the forces in and about Prospect Hill (which were assembled on said hill) by the Rev. Mr. Leonard, chaplain to General Putnam's force. On the hill our standard was presented with this motto : ' Appeal to Heaven with the American arms.' After it was read Mr. Leonard made a short prayer, then we were dismissed with three cheers, the firing of a cannon, and a war-whoop by the Indians.* . . . .

" *July 20th, Thursday.* — This day is a fast appointed by the Continental Congress. [It was appointed by the suggestion of Governor Trumbull of Connecticut, in a letter to Washington, who recommended it to Congress.] . . . . Heard a sermon in the morning from Psalms, l. 15 [" And call upon me in the day of trouble: I will deliver thee and thou shalt glorify me "] ; in the afternoon from Ecclesiastes, vii. 14, [" In the day of prosperity be joyful, but in the day of adversity consider : God also

---

* " Apart, in a thick wood, near where the Charles enters the bay, stood the wigwams of about fifty domiciliated Indians of the Stockbridge tribe. They were armed with bows and arrows as well as guns, and were accompanied by their squaws and little ones." — Bancroft, Vol. VIII. p. 43.

hath set the one over against the other, to the end that man should find nothing after him.] " . . . .

" *July 24th, Monday.* — To-day all the troops under command of Brigadier-General Putnam, except Colonel Little's regiment, were ordered to march from Prospect Hill to be stationed elsewhere. Their vacancies are to be supplied with troops from Cambridge, Winter Hill, etc., under the command of Brigadier-General Greene."

The entry just copied marks the beginning of the new arrangement of the troops, under General Washington's order. It caused great changes in the location of the various military bodies. It brought General Nathaniel Greene over from Roxbury to be put in command of this important post of duty at Prospect Hill.

The diary runs on for a year, but perhaps we have quoted sufficiently from it to give the reader a taste of military life in 1775. It is strictly a *diary*, for hardly a day passes without its record, longer or shorter.

We have now reached a time when General Putnam has been taken out of all the entanglements of Bunker Hill jealousies, and has reached a fair and open field for the illustration of his character and military abilities. We shall have an opportunity to study him, not only in the light of the weighty enterprises which his fellow-men living in his daily companionship saw fit to entrust to him, but (what is also important in making up our estimates) we shall have the privilege of reading and criticising the letters which he wrote touching the enterprises which he had on his hands. If he is a noisy, coarse, boastful, blustering man, we shall find some evidence of it in his letters. If, on the other hand, he is a man of strong and sound understanding, clearly comprehending the matters he has in charge, and treating them with solid dignity and uniform propriety, we shall have opportunities for the discovery of these qualities.

19

We cannot undertake to go minutely through the whole of his remaining military life. It would make our work too voluminous. But now that he is setting off upon an important career, the chosen companion of Washington, we will, at least in the earlier periods, furnish facts and materials enough whereby he may be fairly and fully judged.

We have freely conceded that he was not a man of literary culture ; and for the honor of the country which he served, he would not be guilty of bad penmanship and bad spelling in his public communications. He employed an amanuensis to write for him the letters which he dictated. But the real life in any piece of writing is to be found in its thoughts and ideas. Some of the identical letters which he sent from the military camp may still be seen in the twenty manuscript volumes of the " Trumbull Papers," * which repose in great dignity and security in the library of the Massachusetts Historical Society. That he did not furnish the *ideas* for those letters, we are not aware that any one has ever charged. When we read them, we shall find it hard to convince ourselves that they did not emanate from a modest, clear-headed man, who perfectly under-

* The " Trumbull Papers," so called, are a part of the State papers of Connecticut, belonging to the period of Governor Jonathan Trumbull's administration, 1769–83, covering and more than covering the whole revolutionary era. Near the close of the last century, a Mr. David Trumbull, acting as administrator of an estate, found these documents on his hands, and gave them to the Massachusetts Historical Society, without duly considering the question whether he had a right to send out of the State such papers as these, or whether any society out of the State had a right to receive them. If they were only printed and published as they ought to be, because of their great importance, then historical students might have access to them, and it would not matter so much who owned the manuscripts. But they are still kept in their original form ; and any one going to consult them is met by such conditions, that he is likely to turn back at the very portals. The Massachusetts Historical Society has so hedged itself about with rules, that practically it holds these State papers of Connecticut for its almost exclusive use and interpretation.

stood what he was writing about, and knew how to express himself in few words, but in a style everywhere marked by courtesy and dignity. But first of all, to show that General Putnam still kept up some of his old activities about Boston, we have the following extract from a letter written about him from Cambridge, December 18th, 1775, and published in Force's "Archives" (4th Series, Vol. IV. p. 313) :

"Yesterday being dark and cloudy, General Putnam broke ground with four hundred men on *Lechmere's* Point, at 10 o'clock in the morning. The mist was so great as to prevent the enemy from discovering what he was about until 12, when it cleared up, and opened to their view our whole party at the point, and another at the causeway throwing a new bridge over the creek that forms the island at high water. The *Scarborough* ship-of-war, which lay off the point, immediately poured in upon our men a broadside. The enemy from *Boston* threw in many shells, and obliged us to decamp from the point, with two men badly wounded. The bridge, however, was raised by the brave old General, and was completed last night. The garrison at *Cobble Hill* were ordered to return the ship's fire, which they did, and soon obliged her to heave tight upon her springs and to cease firing."

The first letter* which we find of his, illustrating this particular period, was one written a little before the time of the above-named expedition, and is as follows :

"CAMP IN CAMBRIDGE, Dec. 1st, 1775.

"SIR: I shall esteem it a particular favor if your Excellency will be so obliging as to recommend my worthy friend, Colonel *Henry Babcock*, to the Honorable Continental Congress, to be appointed to the rank of Brigadier-General in the Continental army. I have been upon service with him several campaigns in the last war, and have seen him in action behave with great spirit and fortitude when he had command of a regiment. He has this day been very serviceable in assisting me in quelling a mutiny, and bringing back a number of deserters.

* "American Archives," 4th Series, Vol. III. p. 182.

"Your Excellency well knows I am in great want of a Brigadier-General in my division, and such a one as I can put confidence in and rely upon. I know of no man who will fill the vacancy with more honor than the gentleman above named.

"I have the honor to be, with great truth and regard, your Excellency's most obedient, most humble servant,

"ISRAEL PUTNAM, M. G.

"His Excellency General WASHINGTON."

To show how the British found themselves situated in Boston during this same month of December, take the following "Advices" received in England from America to December 14th, 1775:

"General *Howe* has barely six thousand effective men at *Boston*. The fortifications begun to be erected from water to water, within the *Neck of Boston*, he has been obliged to abandon for want of men sufficient to perform the work.

"General *Clinton* preserves his post at Bunker Hill. The provincials have abandoned *Ploughed Hill*, but the regulars have not taken possession of it. The situation of the troops at *Bunker Hill* is truly deplorable; much snow, north-east winds, etc., no fire, poor clothing, salt provisions, etc., etc.

"The distress of the troops and people at Boston exceed the possibility of description. There are advices in town of *December* 14th; not a coal ship was then arrived. The inhabitants and troops literally starving with cold. They had taken the pews out of all the houses of worship for fuel; had pulled down empty houses, etc., and were then digging up the timber at the wharves for firing; very poor clothing, and so scarce of provisions they have been eating horse flesh for some time."*

That winter of 1775–76, like this its centennial sister of 1875–76, set in with great severity of cold, but in its later stages was rather an open and mild one. There was gradually maturing in the mind of Washington a scheme for driving the British out of the town. He had some ear-

* "American Archives," 4th Series, Vol. III. p. 266.

lier schemes which the winter probably did not enable
him to carry out. It was so cold in November and December, that he began to lay some plans, founded upon the idea
that the inland waters would be covered with solid ice, in
which he was probably disappointed. The following letter*
to General Artemas Ward will explain what was passing in
his mind in November:

"CAMBRIDGE, November 17th, 1775.

"SIR: As the season is fast approaching when the bay between us and *Boston* will, in all probability, be close shut up,
thereby rendering any movement upon the ice as easy as though
no water was there; and as it is more than probable that General
Howe, when he gets the expected reinforcements, will endeavor
to relieve himself from the disgraceful confinement in which the
ministerial troops have been all the summer, common prudence
dictates the necessity of guarding our camps wherever they are
most assailable. For this purpose I wish you, General *Thomas*,
General Spencer and Colonel Putnam, to meet me at your quarters to-morrow at 10 o'clock, that we may examine the ground
between your work at the mill and *Sewall's Point*, and direct
such batteries as may appear necessary, for the security of your
camp on that side, to be thrown up without loss of time. I have
long had it upon my mind that a successful attempt might be
made, by way of surprise, on Castle William. From every account there are not more than three hundred men in that place.
The whale-boats, therefore, which you have, and such as could be
sent to you, would easily transport eight hundred or one thousand, which with a very moderate share of conduct and resolution might, I should think, bring off the garrison, if not the stores.
I wish you to discuss this matter, under the rose, with officers on
whose judgment and spirit you can rely. Something of this sort
may show how far the men are to be depended upon. I am with
respect, sir, your very humble servant,

"GEORGE WASHINGTON."

"To Major-General ARTEMAS WARD."

* "American Archives," 4th Series, Vol. III. p. 1593.

It will be noticed in this letter that Washington mentions Colonel Putnam, as a man whom he would like to have invited to this interview. This was the Rufus Putnam before mentioned, a cousin of Israel, and a Lieutenant-Colonel when the battle of Bunker Hill was fought. He has already been promoted, and has become one whose practical judgment is greatly relied upon in the laying out of fortifications and the like. On the 11th of February following, this Colonel Putnam submitted, at General Washington's request, plans for the operations which were soon to be set in motion.

In Force's "Archives" (4th Series, Vol. III. p. 1194) we have the record of a council of war, held at headquarters in Cambridge. The heading reads as follows :

"At a Council of General Officers held at headquarters in Cambridge, February 16th, 1776, Present, his Excellency George *Washington;* Major-Generals *Ward, Putnam;* Brigadier-Generals *Thomas, Heath, Spencer, Sullivan, Gates.*"

We have here a clear illustration of what was regarded as a council of war after General Washington came to Cambridge. None but Generals were present at such a meeting. We have spoken in a previous chapter of the council of war held at Cambridge, June 16th, 1775. From the example here before us, is it likely that any but general officers were present at that earlier council ?

This council of February 16th reached the following result :

"*Resolved:* That a cannonade and bombardment will be expedient and advisable, as soon as there shall be a proper supply of powder, and not before ; and in the mean time, preparations should be made to take possession of *Dorchester Hill,* with a view of drawing out the enemy ; and of Noddle's Island, if the situation of the water and other circumstances will permit."

The nights of March, 2d, 3d, and 4th, were memorable
in the history of the siege of Boston, for on those nights
a process was begun which, when finished, summarily ended
the occupation of the town by British troops.   Before
March 2d, the "proper supply of powder," spoken of in
the above resolution of February 16th, had been secured,
and on that night the Americans opened a bombardment
upon the British camps.   It was renewed upon the night
of the 3d, and with still greater earnestness on the night of
the 4th.   This bombardment, however, was purely secondary to another very important movement.   It was probably
kept up for two nights before the intended movement, in
order to make the British think it was only a bombardment.
But it was really meant simply to divert attention, and by
its noise to drown other noises that might be raised.   In
the night between March 4th and 5th, military possession
was taken of the heights of Dorchester, easily commanding
the town.   The British woke on the morning of March
5th, to find those heights in the possession of the Americans.   They were quite as much surprised as when they
found Breed's Hill fortified on the morning of June 17th,
in the previous summer.   This enterprise at Dorchester
was attended with greater labors and difficulties than that
at Charlestown.   The ground was frozen to quite a depth,
and the men could not use their spades for intrenchments.
The materials for the fortifications had to be brought from
a distance.   Three hundred teams went back and forth in
the light of a moon, just past the full, their operations being
upon the back side of the hills, and the noise of the rum-
bling carts being drowned by the almost incessant thunders
of the cannon, throwing balls and shells from various points
upon the town.   Colonel Rufus Putnam was the engineer
of these night works, and early in the morning the British
found themselves overlooked and commanded.   General

John Thomas was the military chief of this expedition, and
acted his part nobly.

It was naturally expected that the British would made
an attack and attempt to carry these works, as they had
carried Bunker Hill. They *must* do this or leave the place.
It was rather confidently expected that they would make
an assault, and it was hoped they would, for the plans had
been so laid that heavy damage and loss would most likely
have been inflicted upon them.

There were two main parts to the American plan. In
the first place, these works at Dorchester had been so built
and arranged, that it would have required a strong and resolute force to carry them, even though this force had nothing to disturb or interrupt it. The other part of the plan
we give as shown in Washington's letter to the Continental
Congress.

"When the enemy first discovered our works in the morning
they seemed to be in great confusion, and from their movements
to have intended an attack. It is much to be wished that it had
been made. The event I think must have been fortunate and
nothing less than success and victory on our side. . . . .

"In case the ministerial troops had made an attempt to dislodge our men from *Dorchester Hill,* and the number detailed
upon the occasion had been so great as to have afforded a probability of a successful attack being made upon *Boston,* on a signal
given from *Roxbury* for that purpose, agreeably to a settled and
concerted plan, four thousand chosen men, who were held in readiness, were to have embarked at the mouth of *Cambridge River*
in two divisions ; the first under the command of Brigadier-General *Sullivan,* the second under Brigadier-General *Greene,* the
whole to have been commanded by Major-General *Putnam.*" *

The British planned and intended an assault, but a violent
storm with wind coming on, they were obliged to desist, and

* "American Archives," 4th Series, Vol. V. p. 106.

the second sober thought, with some additional information probably gained, convinced them that any such assault would be only to their own damage, and that their best course was to leave the town. As this expedition under General Putnam did not take place, it is impossible to say how it might have terminated; but that he was entrusted with the care of a movement so very imporant as this, shows us at least what Washington thought of him, after a few months' acquaintance. Though Washington and Putnam had both been in the French War, yet their fields of operation lay wide apart, and they had never met, till they met in Cambridge in July, 1775.

And now all things betokened bustle and preparation in the British camps. Just at this point we will give two views, one an *outside*, and one an *inside* view of matters, such as concerned the British. Stephen Moylan, Aid to General Washington, writes the first letter, and a British officer the second. Moylan was an Irishman, gallant, brave, and well educated; and Washington made him one of his Aids. The letter, as will be seen, was written by Washington's direction to Lord Stirling, so called, at the head of two or three thousand Americans at New York.

"CAMBRIDGE, March 9th, 1776.

" SIR : I have it in command from his Excellency General *Washington* to inform you that, in consequence of his determination to possess himself of the Heights at *Dorchester*, a cannonade and bombardment was begun on *Saturday* night last, on the town of *Boston*, continued on *Sunday* night and *Monday* night. A vast number of shot and shell were thrown into that town, under cover of which the intended purpose was effected. On the enemy's perceiving next morning that we had taken post, they were all hurry and bustle, embarking their troops, as was expected, and wished to attack us ; but the violent storm which came on that day prevented them, and disappointed us, who were prepared to give them a warm reception.

. . . . "If they do not move off he (Washington) is determined to force them to a battle, by making that town so hot that
they will have little rest therein.

"His Excellency has good reasons to imagine that *New York*
will be the place of their destination. He therefore desires that
you will exert yourself to the utmost in preparing for their reception. . . . . If they steer west, you may expect a large reinforcement from this camp, and in all probability the main body
will soon follow." *

And now comes the second letter, which gives the *inside*
view. The following is from a letter written by an officer of distinction in the British army, to a person in London, dated Boston, March 3–17, 1776:

"For these last six weeks, or near two months, we have been
better amused than could possibly be expected in our situation.
We had a theatre, we had balls, and there is actually a subscrip-
tion on foot for a masquerade. *England* seems to have forgot
us, and we endeavored to forget ourselves. But we were roused
to a sense of our situation last night, in a manner unpleasant
enough. The rebels have been for some time erecting a bomb-
battery, and last night began to play upon us. . . . .

"*March 4th.* — Bad news from New York this morning. A
man who calls himself *Lord Stirling* . . . . put himself at the
head of three thousand men, in conjunction with that arch-rebel,
Lee, and has driven all the well-affected people [*i. e.* the Tories]
from the town of New York. . . . .

"*March 5th.* — This is, I believe, likely to prove as important a day to the *British* empire as any in our annals. We un-
derwent last night a very severe cannonade, which damaged a
number of houses, and killed some men. This morning at day-
break we discovered two redoubts on the hills *Dorchester Point*,
and two smaller works on their flanks. They were all raised
during the night, with an expedition equal to that of the genii
belonging to *Aladdin's* wonderful lamp. From these hills they

---

* " American Archives," 4th Series, Vol. V. p. 166.

command the whole town, so that we must drive them from their post, or desert the place.   The former is determined upon, and five regiments are already embarked. . . . . Adieu balls, masquerades, etc. ; for this may be looked upon as the opening of the campaign.

"It is worth while to remark with what judgment the leaders of the rebels take advantage of the prejudices and work upon the passions of the mob.   The 5th of *March* is what they call the bloody massacre, when in (I think) 1769 [in 1770], the King's troops fired on the people in the streets of Boston.   If ever they dare stand us, it will be to-day, but I hope by to-morrow to be able to give you an account of their defeat.

"*March 6th.*—A wind more violent than anything I ever heard, prevented our last night's purposed expedition, and so saved the lives of thousands.   To-day they have made themselves too strong to make a dislodgement possible. . . . . We are now evacuating the town with the utmost expedition, and leaving behind half our worldly goods.   Adieu ! I hope to embark in a few hours. . . . .

"*Nantasket Road, March 17th.*— According to my promise I proceed to give a brief account of our retreat, which was made this morning between the hours of 2 and 8. . . . . We kept a constant fire upon them from a battery of four twenty-four pounders.   They did not return a single shot.   It was lucky for the inhabitants now left in Boston that they did not, for I am informed everything was prepared to set the town on a blaze, had they fired one cannon." *

This man addressed as Lord Stirling was William Alexander, a native of the city of New York, honorably descended, and regarded by many as the rightful heir to an earldom in Scotland.   He could never, however, get possession of his estate.   Out of this belief in his rightful heirship he was commonly called Lord Stirling.   He was a man of fine military ability, and became a Major-General.

* "American Archives," 4th Series, Vol. V. pp. 425-26.

We find the following account, showing how Putnam stood at that time in Washington's estimation, in the "New England Chronicle," March 21st, 1776:

"The command of the whole being then given to General Putnam, he proceeded to take command of all the important posts, and thereby became possessed, in the name of the thirteen United Colonies of North America, of all the fortresses in that large and once populous and flourishing metropolis which the flower of the British army, headed by an experienced General, and supported by a formidable fleet of men-of-war, had but an hour before evacuated in the most precipitate and cowardly manner." *

Bancroft, in his "History," etc. (Vol. VIII. p. 302), has given us a description of the hurry of the British in their departure, and a catalogue of the spoils left behind.

"Everywhere appeared marks of hurry in the flight of the British. Among other stores they left behind them two hundred and fifty pieces of cannon, of which one-half were serviceable; twenty-five hundred chaldrons of sea coal; twenty-five thousand bushels of wheat; three thousand bushels of barley and oats; one hundred and fifty horses; bedding and clothing for soldiers. Nor was this all. Several British store-ships consigned to Boston, and ignorant of the retreat, successively entered the harbor without suspicion, and fell into the hands of the Americans; among them the ship Hope, which, in addition to carbines, bayonets, gun-carriages and all sorts of tools necessary for artillery, had on board more than seven times as much powder as Washington's whole stock when his last movement was begun."

Now, the man whom General Washington selects out of all the military men immediately about him, or from those

---

* "Last Sabbath, a few hours after the enemy retreated from Boston, the Rev. Mr. Leonard (Putnam's chaplain) preached an excellent sermon in the audience of his Excellency the General, and others of distinction, ... from Exodus, iv. 25: ' *And took off their chariot wheels, that they drove them heavily; so that the Egyptian said, let us flee from the face of Israel, for the Lord fighteth for them against the Egyptians.*'"

more distant, to proceed at once to New York and have
the supreme control of the military operations there to be
opened,— to be the commander-in-chief on that important
field until his own arrival, — must be one of good sense
and large capacity, else we impugn the good sense and capacity of Washington himself. Whom did he select for
this most responsible and delicate post? No other than
General Putnam. He actually made choice of that very
man whose "furious ardor may or may not have needed
the control of a cool, deliberating judgment." Here are
some words from the instructions given to General Putnam
in a written order, dated March 29th, 1776 :

"You will, no doubt, make the best despatch in getting to New
York. Upon your arrival there you will assume the command,
and immediately proceed to execute the *plan* proposed by Major-
General Lee for fortifying that city, and securing the passes of
the East and North Rivers. If, upon consultation with the Briga-
diers-General and Engineers, any alteration in that plan is thought
necessary, you are at liberty to make it ; cautiously avoiding to
break in too much upon his main design, unless when it may be
apparently necessary so to do, and that by the general voice and
opinion of the gentlemen above mentioned. . . . .

"Devoutly praying that the POWER which has hitherto sustained the American arms may continue to bless them with the
divine protection, I bid you FAREWELL.

"Given at headquarters, in Cambridge, this 29th of March,
1776.   G. WASHINGTON."

Immediately upon Putnam's arrival in New York he
wrote a letter * to Congress, of which the following is the
copy, with the answer received :
"NEW YORK, April 4th, 1776.

"SIR : Since my arrival at this place I have had abundant
reason to be convinced that the army here is in the highest need
of an immediate supply of cash. I therefore now send Major

* "American Archives," 4th Series, Vol. V. p. 787.

Sherburne to *Philadelphia*, and I hope the Congress will dispatch him as soon as possible, with at least three hundred thousand dollars for that purpose.

"I am, with great regard and esteem, your most humble servant, ISRAEL PUTNAM."

"To the Honorable JOHN HANCOCK, Esq."

"PHILADELPHIA, April 10th, 1776.

"SIR: In consequence of your letter, I laid the application before the Congress, who were pleased, in addition to the one hundred thousand dollars sent by Captain Faulkner, on *Monday* last, to order two hundred thousand more, which I have the pleasure of forwarding by Major *Sherburne.*

"Should the paymaster be at *New York*, please to order it to his care for the use of the troops ; if not, you will order the money to be improved for the same purpose, and send a receipt for it.

"I have the honor to be, sir, your most obedient and very humble servant, JOHN HANCOCK, *President.*"

"To Major-General PUTNAM, at New York." *

He also sent the following letter to the New York Committee of Safety:

"NEW YORK, April 5th, 1776.

"GENTLEMEN: The Continental Congress, imagining the new levies in this Province to be in a great state of forwardness, and finding, on inquiry, that none of the four regiments to be raised in it are properly regimented and completed, I must request of you, as the service absolutely requires it, that you exert yourselves to the utmost to accomplish this necessary service ; and that the troops already raised be ordered to the city without delay.

"I am, gentlemen, with respect, your humble servant,

"ISRAEL PUTNAM.

"To the Chairman of the Committee of Safety of the Province of New York."

A few days after his arrival at New York, he published an order regulating the conduct of the inhabitants, which we quote entire.

* "American Archives," 4th Series, Vol. V. p. 843.

"HEADQUARTERS, NEW YORK, April 8th, 1776.

"The General informs the inhabitants, that it is become abso-lately necessary that all communication between the ministerial fleet and the shore should be immediately stopped ; for that pur-pose he has given positive orders, the ships should no longer be furnished with provisions.   Any inhabitants or others, who shall be taken, that have been on board after the publishing this order, or near any of the ships, or going on board, will be considered as enemies, and treated accordingly.

"All boats are to sail from Beekman Slip.   Captain James Alner is appointed inspector, and will give permits to oystermen. It is ordered and expected that none attempt going without a pass.   ISRAEL PUTNAM,
"Major-General in the Continental army,
and commander-in-chief of the forces in New York."

So implicitly was he trusted, that while Washington was called away to Philadelphia from the 21st of May to the 6th of June, General Humphreys, in his "Life of Putnam," tells us (p. 107) that "General Putnam, who commanded in that interval, had it in charge to open all letters directed to General Washington on *public service*, and if important, after regulating his conduct by their contents, to forward them by express."

In the month of July he had occasion to write a letter of a peculiar character, and which we present as a rare speci-men of noble manliness and instinctive delicacy.   Few men could have composed a more admirable letter under the cir-cumstances.   The Miss Moncrieffe to whom the letter is addressed was, as we understand, the daughter of an engineer in the British army.   She is anxious to get access to her father, but finds herself sadly hindered by the military lines. A letter has been sent to General Putnam before by her father on this business, and she has heard that her father did not address him by his proper title, and is afraid that is the reason General Putnam has not answered the letter.

But he sets that suggestion aside as a man far above all small ideas. Take it all in all, the letter is one which shows General Putnam to the very best advantage. He little knew what was to happen by taking her into his family. This is that Margaret Moncrieffe that was thus brought across the path of the notorious Aaron Burr, then one of General Putnam's Aids. Of this General Putnam did not dream when he wrote the letter, and the subsequent fact can have no influence in changing our opinion of the letter itself, which is as follows: *

"NEW YORK, July 26th, 1776.

"I should have answered your letter sooner, but had it not in my power to write you anything satisfactory.

"The omission of my title in Major *Moncrieffe's* letter is a matter I regard not in the least, nor does it in any way influence my conduct in this affair, as you seem to imagine. Any political difference alters him not to me in a private capacity. As an officer he is my enemy, and obliged to act as such, be his private sentiments what they will. As a man, I owe him no enmity, but far from it, will with pleasure do any kind office in my power for him or any of his connections.

"I have, agreeably to your desire, waited on his Excellency, to endeavor to obtain permission for you to go to *Staten Island.* He informs me that Lieutenant-Colonel *Patterson,* who came with the last flag, said he was empowered to offer the exchange of —— for Governor Skene. As the Congress have reserved to themselves the right of exchanging prisoners, the General has sent to know their pleasure, and doubt not they will give their consent. I am desired to inform you if this exchange is made you will have the liberty to pass out with Governor Skene, but that no flag will be sent solely for that purpose.

"Major *William Livingston* was lately here, and informed me that you had an inclination to live in the city, and that all the ladies of your acquaintance having left town, and Mrs. Putnam and two daughters being here, proposed your staying with them.

* "American Archives," 5th Series, Vol. I. p. 471.

If agreeable to you, be assured, Miss, you shall be sincerely wel- come. You will here, I think, be in a more probable way of ac- complishing the end you wish, that of seeing your father; and may depend upon every civility from, Miss, your obedient ser- vant,   Israel Putnam."

The kindness of Putnam's heart toward any woman in dis- tress is most beautifully exemplified in a story told by General Humphreys, relating to the French War. A Mrs. Howe, a woman of uncommon graces and personal beauty, a widow now for the second time, had been carried captive with her seven children by the Indians, after her husband had been killed before her eyes. She had been separated from her children, and had suffered manifold mental tortures, not the least of which was the importunity of a young French officer, who persecuted her with his attentions, and who was extremely uncivil in doing so. She at length sought the protection of Colonel Schuyler, who took her under his care, and rescued for her her five youngest children, while the two eldest, daughters, the Indians had permitted to go into a convent. Colonel Schuyler had to leave the army and turn the widow and her children over to Major Putnam, and the rest of the story may be told by General Humphreys.

" She had just recovered from the measles when the party was preparing to return to New England. By this time the young French officer had returned, with his passion rather increased than abated by absence. He pursued her wheresoever she went, and although he could make no advances in her affection, he seemed resolved, by perseverance, to carry his point. Mrs. Howe, terrified by his treatment, was obliged to keep constantly near Major Putnam, who informed the young officer that he should protect that lady at the risk of his life.

" In the long march from captivity, through an unhospitable wilderness, encumbered with five small children, she suffered in-

20

credible hardships. Though endowed with masculine fortitude, she was truly feminine in strength, and must have fainted by the way had it not been for the assistance of Major Putnam. There were a thousand good offices which the helplessness of her condition demanded, and which the gentleness of his nature delighted to perform. He assisted in leading her little ones and in carrying them over the swampy grounds and runs of water, with which their course was frequently intercepted. He mingled his own mess with that of the widow and fatherless, and assisted them in obtaining and preparing their provisions. Upon arriving within the settlements they experienced a reciprocal regret at separation, and were only consoled by the expectation of soon mingling in the embraces of their former acquaintances and dearest connections."

Putnam knew how, with his strong hand, to take a woman, corrupt and traitorous, before the commander-in-chief, and to overawe her by the majesty of his wrath, so she dare no longer conceal the part she was acting ; but he knew how, on the other hand, to treat a true woman, who was in trouble, with all the kindness and delicacy imaginable. And there was that in his strong, robust, manly nature and honest heart which was exactly fitted to draw the confidence, the admiration, and the love of a woman.

We pass on now to the month of August, and to the somewhat unfortunate battle of Long Island, in which General Putnam is represented by Bancroft as showing military "incapacity," and in which certainly he did not secure his ordinary measure of success. But the circumstances under which this action took place deserve to be considered. The battle was fought on the 27th of August. The American army on Long Island was under the command of General Nathaniel Greene. On the 16th of August he was reported to be ill of a fever. He himself sent word to Washington to this effect, and also that the Hessians were landing in considerable numbers on Staten Island. On the 18th, General

Greene was reported better, and he hoped in a few days to be about. But the sickness continued, and he was worse again. August 23d, General Sullivan was appointed to take his place in the command ; and it was becoming more and more apparent that the British meditated an attack. August 24th, General Putnam went to take charge of these operations. He had not made the previous dispositions, and was not in a condition of knowledge to do as well as he might otherwise have done. The British forces also greatly outnumbered our own. They had accumulated their troops in that vicinity to the number of some twenty-four thousand, while the active forces on our side were far less. The British losses in killed and wounded were equal to our own, but they captured more than a thousand prisoners, and the victory was clearly with them.

Sparks, in his " Life and Writings of Washington" (Vol. I. p. 193), puts the case thus :

"It was unfortunate that the illness of General Greene deprived the commander on the spot of his counsel, he being thoroughly acquainted with the grounds and the roads ; whereas, General Putnam took the command only four days before the action, and of course had not been able from personal inspection to gain the requisite knowledge."

When Bancroft charges Putnam with " incapacity," it is one of those general assertions about as far from the exact balances of truth, as when in Volume VII. he makes William Prescott the chief commander and hero of Bunker Hill.

Lord Howe reported a loss of sixty-one killed, two hundred and fifty-seven wounded and twenty-nine missing, but at the same time reported one thousand and ninety-seven American prisoners taken. The result of the battle was that we had immediately to evacuate Long Island, and not long after the city of New York itself.

By the middle of September Washington had left New York and established himself with the army on Harlem Heights. The retreat of the American army from Long Island, and soon after from New York, was successful under the conditions of the case beyond all that could have been hoped. New York was a small affair then in comparison with its present dimensions. It was built on the lower end of Manhattan Island, and that large domain above, stretching on for miles, now covered by the great metropolis, was open country, and much of it half wild and unbroken country, with here and there some gentlemanly mansion, making a bright and cultivated spot amid the general waste. In 1776, the traveller passing up Broadway from the Battery, by the time he reached the vicinity of the City Hall Park and the Astor House, would find himself passing out into this country region. In the military occupation of the city by the American army in that spring and summer of 1776, Putnam's division was at the extreme southerly end of the island. His headquarters were at No. 1 Broadway, close by Castle Garden, and in a house which is said to be still standing. A description of it is given in "Scribner's Monthly" for February, 1876; also a picture showing it.

When the British troops came over from Long Island, and the American army was obliged to leave the place, there was imminent danger that Putnam's division would be cut off and fall into the hands of the enemy. The story of his escape is so admirably told in the number of "Scribner's Monthly" just referred to, that we cannot forbear quoting it. The passage is in an illustrated article, entitled "New York in the Revolution," from the pen of John F. Mines.

"Drawn from the field of battle by one of his Aids, he (Washington) at once sent word to Putnam to retreat to Harlem, and take measures to concentrate his entire forces on Harlem Heights. General Putnam was forced to abandon his heavy cannon and many of his stores, and even thus his flight was impeded by a throng of fugitives, men, women and children, with their baggage. Guided by Aaron Burr, he made a rapid march along the Hudson, happily escaping discovery until he had reached the Bloomingdale Road, and finally reaching camp with a comparatively insignificant loss. The day was hot, the fugitives were fairly panting with thirst and fatigue, but Putnam on his foaming charger flew from one end of the line to the other, entreating, urging, and dealing in stout objurgations until his charge had passed, at night-fall, the American pickets on the heights of Harlem.

" Neither soldier nor fugitive knew how narrow had been the escape of Putnam's army that day. When Sir William Howe, accompanied by Clinton and Tryon, had landed at Kip's Bay with the main body of the British army, they struck across to the Middle Road, intending to make their camp on the heights of Inclenburg, midway between New York and Harlem. They reached the road at a point just opposite to where Putnam was stealing along, under cover of the woods that skirted the Hudson to rejoin Washington. There was a house near by, from whose upper windows they might easily have discovered the dust created by the rapid march of the 'rebels,' and from its cupola the gleam of bayonets would have been plainly visible. The Americans were not distant, indeed, but there was another and more insidious foe near at hand. Close to the Middle Road, at a point now designated by the corporation as Fifth Avenue and Thirty-seventh Street, stood the unpretentious but exceedingly comfortable mansion of Robert Murray, a Quaker merchant of approved loyalty to the crown, as well as of large wealth. Fortunately the shrewd merchant could not control the feelings of his household, and his wife and daughters were ardent patriots. When Lord Howe and his staff reached the end of the Quaker's gardens, they were enraptured to find Mrs. Murray and her beautiful daughters ready to greet them with a warm welcome. The parties had once met in more peaceful days.

"'William,' said the fair Quaker matron, 'will thee alight and refresh thyself at our house?'

"'I thank you, Mrs. Murray,' said the pleasure-loving commander, 'but I must first catch that rascally Yankee, Putnam.'

"The Yankee General was not to be caught this time, if woman's wit could save him, even if the truth must be tortured into a shape that should deceive, in order to save life. Very demurely the lady rejoined, in that plain language of her sect which always carries with it such an emphasis of truth, —

"'Didst thou not hear that Putnam had gone? It is late to try to catch him. Thee had better come in and dine.'

"The invitation was seconded by the brightest smiles of the daughters, and Howe wavered. Promising to pursue the hated Yankees after he had dined, the British commander alighted and entered the house, where the fascinations of the charming hostess made him forget for hours the object of his expedition. Putnam meanwhile was flying up the Bloomingdale Road, never daring to draw breath until he caught sight of Washington's tents. Thacher, in his 'Military Journal,' writes that it became a common saying among the American officers that Mrs. Murray had saved Putnam's division."

When we bear in mind that the American army was making this retreat in the immediate neighborhood of some twenty thousand British troops, it was indeed fortunate that they escaped the entanglements of such a situation with only a very trifling loss. Hardly had they taken possession of the heights of Harlem, when a British force of three battalions, with cannon, came upon their skirmish lines with a bold audacity, as though acting against frightened fugitives. This body was very severely punished for its temerity. It had to withdraw, after a loss of seventy killed and two hundred and ten wounded, and this sudden success on our side, following immediately upon disaster, put new life and courage into the American troops. The victory, however, cost us the precious life of Lieutenant-Colonel Knowlton, an officer greatly admired and beloved. Another young and heroic life was sacrificed on the altar of war only a few days later. Nathan Hale, a young man of twenty-one, a native of Coventry, Connecticut, a graduate of Yale College, volunteered to go within the British lines as a spy; was detected and executed, dying with those memorable words upon his lips, "I only regret that I have but one life to lose for my country."

The American army, having now been brought into a position where it was hazardous to attack it, and General Howe, being in possession of Long Island and New York city, with a large army on his hands, determined to try his fortunes in making movements with a portion of his forces into New Jersey (or the Jerseys, as they were then called) and on toward Philadelphia. This necessitated a corresponding movement on the part of Washington; but this fall campaign of 1776, in New Jersey and vicinity, was attended with various fortunes upon which we will not dwell. After these operations had been mainly brought to an end, General Putnam was despatched from New York to Philadelphia, as he had before been from Boston to New York, to act as commander-in-chief about this central city, where the Continental Congress was sitting,— to superintend the fortifications in process of erection, and provide for the security of the inhabitants. General Humphreys has preserved for us in his "Life," etc. (p. 129), one of the military orders which Putnam issued after his arrival at Philadelphia.

"HEADQUARTERS, PHILADELPHIA, Dec. 14th, 1776.

"Colonel Griffin is appointed Adjutant-General to the troops in and about this city. All orders from the General, through him, either written or verbal, are to be strictly attended to and punctually obeyed.

"In case of an alarm of fire, the city guards and patrols are to suffer the inhabitants to pass unmolested at any hour of the night;

and the good people of Philadelphia are earnestly requested and desired to give every assistance in their power, with engines and buckets, to extinguish the fire. And as the Congress have ordered the city to be defended to the last extremity, the General hopes that no person will refuse to give every assistance possible to complete the fortifications that are to be erected in and about the city. ISRAEL PUTNAM."

After General Putnam had fulfilled his mission at Philadelphia, he was stationed during the winter at Princeton, and by the various little expeditions which he set on foot, and which were superintended by himself or his agents, it was estimated, according to the statement of his biographer, that he captured in the whole season not far from one thousand prisoners.

In the early part of this chapter, it was stated that for a time such letters and military orders as were sent forth by Putnam would be given in so full measure that we might have before us the means of judging of his character and capacity. These have been given in sufficient numbers for such an estimate. We have taken them just as we found them, have suppressed nothing which would be of assistance for this purpose. And have we found anything in these products of his mind which seem to make him in any degree unworthy of that high confidence which Washington all along is seen to have reposed in him? From the day when Washington handed him his commission at Cambridge in July, 1775, to the close of 1779, when he was obliged by failing health to leave the army, he was always near to Washington, in the management of military affairs, and we know not the slightest evidence that Washington ever wished him to be displaced from that high position, and have another substituted in his stead. On the other hand, the chief commander early gave him his heart and his confidence to a very remarkable degree; and a letter written

to Putnam by Washington, after the war was over, and
which will be given in another chapter, will testify to the
strength of this regard. These things being so, can it ever
be edifying to the people who know them to be so, to read
articles in newspapers, or listen to long and elaborate orations, or study carefully prepared pamphlets and volumes,
in which Colonel William Prescott is made proudly to over-
top this man, even to such a degree that the Major-General
sinks into comparative insignificance ? We have been sub-
jected to these trifles and follies long enough. Let the little
fictitious eddies of local narrative cease their play, and let
the stream of veritable history flow on.

In the concluding portions of this chapter we will give
the most rapid outline of General Putnam's closing years in
the army. Some disasters had overtaken the northern army,
and he was moved up the Hudson, to make his headquarters
at Peekskill. This was in May, 1777.

In the month of August a Tory spy was caught in Putnam's camp, and put under arrest. The British officers
at once sent a flag of truce with a message demanding his
release. Only a few months before they had summarily
hanged Nathan Hale, when he was caught in the British
camp, and now they sent a message, haughtily demanding
that this Edmund Palmer (the name of the spy) should be
restored. Putnam promptly sent back the following reply :

HEADQUARTERS, 7th August, 1777.
" SIR : Edmund Palmer, an officer in the enemy's service,
was taken as a spy lurking within our lines. He has been tried
as a spy, condemned as a spy, and shall be executed as a spy ;
and the flag is ordered to depart immediately.

" ISRAEL PUTNAM.
" P. S.— He has been accordingly hanged."

The account given in General Humphreys' " Life," etc.,
is somewhat different, but substantially the same.*

* "General Putnam, whose exploits on the Upper Hudson have made

That is certainly using the King's English and the King's subjects to some purpose.

Hostile armies facing each other often find the means of diversion in their interchanges during the pauses of the fight. Rivington, in New York, the newspaper publisher, was a conspicuous Tory, and all news in his paper had a high Tory coloring. Putnam had known the British Major-General Robertson (now in his vicinity) in the French War, and one day he sent to him some American newspapers with the following note: "Major-General Putnam presents his compliments to Major-General Robertson, and sends him some American newspapers for his perusal. When General Robertson shall have done with them, it is requested they be given to Rivington, in order that he may print some truth." *

It was while thus occupied on the Hudson that General Putnam, being requested by General Washington to canvass the localities along the river, and fix upon the best place for the building of fortifications to command the

that region famous in history and tradition, was in command there. A young man, a scion of a good family in Westchester County, was arrested on suspicion of being a spy, and was brought before Putnam. On his person were found enlisting papers signed by Tryon, and other evidences of his guilt. Sir Henry Clinton sent a note to Putnam with a flag, claiming the culprit as a British officer, and making insolent threats of wrathful retaliation in case the young man should be harmed. Putnam replied in writing [as above]. No spy was ever found in Putnam's camp after that."—Benson J. Lossing in "Harper's Monthly" for April, 1876, p. 647.

* Putnam was fond of these little diversions. The following, which we find in the "New England Chronicle" for September 28th, 1775, will give another instance in point:

"An officer in Boston writes thus to his father in London: ' Why should I complain of hard fate. General Gage and all his family have for this month past lived upon salt provisions. Last Saturday, General Putnam, in the true spirit of military complaisance, which abolishes all personal resentment and smooths the horrors of war when discipline will permit, sent a present to the General's lady of a fine fresh quarter of veal, which was very acceptable, and received the return of a very polite card of thanks.' "

PUTNAM'S ESCAPE AT HORSENECK.

river, made choice of West Point for this purpose. It is claimed by General Humphreys that this spot, which has such a famous connection with our military history as a people, was first pointed out and chosen for military purposes by General Putnam, and we find this statement corroborated by other writers.

During the winter of 1777-8, for the better overlooking of all the interests entrusted to him, the headquarters of Putnam were removed to Reading, Connecticut, one of the western towns of the State, bordering New York, where he still kept himself in connection with the same general field of observation as when at Peekskill, though that field was now enlarged. It was not long after establishing himself at Reading that his famous ride down the stone steps occurred. General Sherman, in his Bunker Hill speech at the Centennial, was a little uncertain where this adventure occurred. But the writer has several times stood on the brow of that hill and looked down this famous declivity.

It was in the centre of the town of Greenwich, Connecticut. The traveller, passing from New Haven to New York, on the railroad, goes by this Connecticut town on his route, just before reaching the New York line, but the centre of the place lies on the high land about a half or three-fourths of a mile north of the railroad line. Here Mr. Tweed had his palatial residence in the days of his evil prosperity. Reaching the main village on the hill, the wide central street, running easterly and westerly, encounters at the eastern extremity of the village a steep declivity. Many years ago, the upper part of this hill was cut through to quite a depth, and the materials taken down to build up a high causeway on the lower slopes, and across the meadows, so that now the main road from Greenwich to Stamford passes directly over this declivity. In the revolutionary days, there was no such thing as a carriage or horse road there, and if it had been suggested that there ever would be, the idea would probably have been regarded as preposterous. But to save foot-passengers coming from the direction of Stamford a long roundabout journey, the steep descent had been furnished with steps, up which the esstern dwellers climbed to meeting on Sundays, and for the common transactions of life on week days. The declivity reaches on some distance to the north, and the carriage or horseback road to Stamford from Greenwich in the old times had to make this northerly circuit.

General Putnam had gone out from Reading, with a reconnoitering party and some pieces of cannon. He was trying to find out what was going on among the British in the direction of New York; when in the centre of Greenwich, he was met by a force far exceeding his own, under the command of Governor Tryon. He tried to make a stand, and did succeed in giving a few discharges from his artillery. But the opposing force was numerous, and there was no escape if he offered longer resistance. Bidding the men on foot seek shelter in the swamp below, he turned his horse's head down these steps, receiving a bullet through his military cap in the descent, but reached the bottom of the hill in safety, when he turned and waved his sword to the British dragoons, who stood wonder-struck at the top. Governor Tryon, in admiration of his adventurous daring, pleasantly sent him a new cap for the one which the bullet had spoiled. The story is told in Greenwich, how one of the citizens took an Englishman to show him this place, and to tell him the tradition connected with it, when the visitor complacently remarked that it was nothing very surprising. "Our English hunters," said he, "often ride down worse places than that." "But," said the citizen, "your English dragoons did not follow General Putnam down that hill."

In 1779, General Putnam's headquarters were removed to Buttermilk Falls, about two miles below West Point. When the summer campaign was over, and the troops were going into winter quarters, Putnam with his family (which means his son, Major Daniel Putnam, and his Aids) went home to spend a few weeks in Connecticut. We will allow General Humphreys to give the account of what happened during this visit, thus:

"Upon the road between Pomfret and Hartford [he had been to his home and was now on his return], he felt an unusual torpor pervading his right hand and foot. This heaviness crept gradually on, until it had deprived him of the use of his limbs on that side in a considerable degree, before he reached the house of his friend, Colonel Wadsworth. Still he was unwilling to think the disorder of the paralytic kind, and endeavored to shake it off by exertion. Having found that impossible, a temporary dejection, disguised under a veil of assumed cheerfulness, succeeded. But reason, philosophy and religion soon reconciled him to his fate."

This was the end of his army life. He was forced to leave a service which he loved, and in which he had gained such high distinctions.

CHAPTER XIII.

CLOSING YEARS.

A STRONG will often bows before the inevitable with a docility that a feeble will never exhibits. A person of weak and vacillating mind will fret and beat against those walls which he can neither break down or overleap; while the man of strong and resolute force will often bow before the power that is higher than he with the meekness of a little child. When the full conviction came upon the mind of General Putnam, at the end of that journey to Hartford, as he was on his way again to headquarters, in the winter of 1779–80, that his activities must cease, there was doubtless a great struggle of soul. How could he stop short, in his work of helping to deliver the land from the oppressor, and establish the fair heritage of freedom? But when he saw that this must be, he accepted the situation like a Christian man, and retired to his quiet home at Pomfret to linger out the remainder of his years.

Happily this paralytic stroke had not invaded his mind, which remained still wakeful and active. From his lonely watch-tower of observation, he followed with the deepest interest the chances and changes of the revolutionary struggle, during its remaining years, till at length, in 1783, the end was reached, and the land was delivered. The Dec-

318

laration of 1776 was made good, and the United States constituted a new and independent nation among the peoples
of the earth.

In this year 1783, but before the war had fully closed,
Putnam received, in answer to a letter which he had written,
a communication from the honored and beloved Washington, which must have deeply moved him, in the depths of
his retirement. The opening and closing passages of this
letter we will give, as follows :

"HEADQUARTERS, 2nd June, 1783.

"DEAR SIR : Your favor of the 20th of May I received with
much pleasure. For I can assure you that among the many
worthy and meritorious officers with whom I have had the happiness to be connected in service through the course of this war, and
from whose cheerful assistance and advice have received much
support and confidence in the various and trying vicissitudes of
a complicated contest, the name of a PUTNAM is not forgotten ;
nor will it be but with that stroke of time which shall obliterate
from my mind the remembrance of all those toils and fatigues
through which we have struggled for the preservation and establishment of the *Rights, Liberties,* and *Independence* of our country. Your congratulations on the happy prospects of peace and
independent security, with their attendant blessings to the *United
States,* I receive with great satisfaction ; and beg that you will
accept a return of my gratulations to you on this auspicious event,
— an event, in which, great as it is in itself, and glorious as it
will probably be in its consequences, you have a right to partici-
pate largely from the distinguished part you have contributed
towards its attainment. . . . .

"I anticipate with pleasure the day, and that I trust not far
off, when I shall quit the busy scenes of a military employment,
and retire to the more tranquil walks of domestic life. In that,
or in whatever other situation Providence may dispose of my
future days, the remembrance of the many friendships and connections I have had the happiness to contract with the gentlemen
of the army, will be one of my most grateful reflections. Under

this contemplation, and impressed with the sentiments of benevo-
lence and regard, I commend you, my dear sir, my other friends,
and with them the interests and happiness of our dear country, to
the keeping and protection of Almighty God.

"I have the honor to be, etc.,   GEORGE WASHINGTON."

"To the Honorable Major-General PUTNAM."

Rev. L. Grosvenor, his great-grandson, from whom we
have several times quoted in the earlier parts of this volume, thus describes General Putnam's personal appearance,
as also his manner of life after his return from the war :

" Putnam, in personal appearance, was of medium height, of a
strong, athletic figure, and in the time of the revolutionary war,
rather fleshy, weighing about two hundred pounds. His hair
was dark, his eyes light blue, his complexion a florid Saxon, and
his broad, good-humored face marked with deep scars, received
in his encounters with French and Indians. A portrait of him,
taken in his younger days, when he was a provincial Major, gives
him rather a slim but muscular figure, dressed in scarlet coat
and breeches, and a light vest, with buff gloves and black cra-
vat. He is described by those now living, who frequently saw
him in his old age, as being very large around the chest, showing what we should expect from his habits, a great amount of
the sanguine vital temperament. Even after his final return from
the wars, when one side of him was so paralyzed that his right arm
clung close and useless to his side, and he had to be assisted to
mount his horse, he rode almost every day on horseback, sitting
up as straight as a boy.

" Many anecdotes are related of his energy and perseverance
in the days of his bodily feebleness. Those who are old now,
but boys then, remember, and tell with delight, about the General's spirited bay mare, and the perfect mastery which he maintained over her, bringing her at any time to a dead halt by shaking
the head of his ivory-headed cane. He was frequently seen at the
houses of his sons and daughters in Brooklyn and Pomfret, and at

the raisings and other gatherings and merry-makings in the neighborhood. There, seated in some arm-chair, promptly brought forward by the young men for his comfort, he, leaning like another
old patriarch on the top of his staff, surrounded by a crowd of
children and grand-children, and friends and neighbors, related
abundant anecdotes of the olden time, while his happy audience
greeted with loud laughter the outpourings of his ready wit and
his kindly and genial humor."

Putnam was sixty-one years old when this stroke of paralysis fell upon him. He was not therefore a very old
man. But the immense physical strain that for so many
years taxed his system doubtless caused this calamity to
fall earlier than it otherwise would. When we consider
the scenes which he passed through in the French War,
the exposures of those northern winters, the terrible marches
through the wilderness, the fierce encounters which came
in his way as a ranger, when every faculty of mind and
body were taxed to their utmost ; or when we reflect upon
such a continuous ride over rough roads as he took when
he left Pomfret on the morning of the 20th of April, visiting
first the neighboring towns, then coming to Cambridge,
thence to Concord, and probably bringing up again at Cambridge on the night of April 21st ; or what he passed through
between Friday morning, June 16th, and Sunday evening,
June 18th, 1775, no wonder that a system, though naturally
built and compacted like iron, began to give way under such
almost superhuman labors. From his early years the horse
was his companion, till by long use he almost realized the
old fable of the Centaurs. The horse and the man became
but parts of one whole. The horse loves a bold and generous ruler, and in Putnam's hands the animal became obedient to the rider's every impulse. Even paralysis could
not shake him from his horse. It is related that only a
short time before his death he went back to the home of

21

his ancestors in Danvers, making the whole journey both ways on horseback, though by easy stages.

Perhaps the most graphic description ever given in few words of General Putnam — his personal appearance and character — comes to us from the pen of one of his grandsons, a man eminent in his generation, Judge Judah Dana, formerly United States Senator from Maine.

"In his person, for height about the middle size, very erect, thickset, muscular and firm in every part. His countenance was open, strong and animated ; the features of his face large, well-proportioned to each other and to his whole frame ; his teeth fair and sound till death. His organs and senses were all exactly fitted for a warrior ; he heard quickly, saw to an immense distance, and though he sometimes stammered in conversation, his voice was remarkably heavy, strong and commanding. Though facetious and dispassionate in private, when animated in the heat of battle his countenance was fierce and terrible and his voice like thunder. His whole manner was admirably adapted to inspire his soldiers with courage and confidence, and his enemies with terror. The faculties of his mind were not inferior to those of his body ; his penetration was acute ; his decision rapid, yet remarkably correct ; and the more desperate the situation the more collected and undaunted. With the courage of a lion he had a heart that melted at the sight of distress ; he could never witness suffering in any human being without becoming a sufferer himself. Even the operation of a blood-letting has caused him to faint. In viewing a field of battle his distress was exquisite, until he had afforded friend and foe all the relief in his power. Once after a battle, on examining a bullet wound through the head of a favorite officer, Captain Whiting, who died upon the field, he fainted and was taken up for dead. Martial music roused him to the highest pitch, while solemn, sacred music sent him into tears. In his disposition he was open and generous almost to a fault ; he never disguised, and in his social relations he was never excelled."

In reading such a description we cannot but think of Martin Luther. Among all the characters of history we can hardly remember any one with whom Putnam, by his natural gifts and qualities, had more in common. There was the same large, robust, animal nature, with its immense treasuries of strength and courage. Placed in Luther's position, it would have been just like Putnam to say, " I will go to Worms, though there are as many devils as tiles on the roofs of the houses." There was the same whole-souled generosity by which he touched and swayed the common people as with the wand of the enchanter. There was the same deep-seated mirth and jollity ; as for example, when the British officer challenged Putnam to fight, and he having the choice of weapons, chose that they should sit together over a keg of powder, to which a slow match was applied. The officer sat till the match drew near the hole, when he ran for his life, Putnam calling after him that it was only a keg of onions, with a few grains of powder sprinkled upon it. When Luther could not carry his audience in any other way, he could do it by a joke or the most comical anecdote. Both were men who touched our common humanity at many points, and both were men who did not indulge in mirth for its own sake merely, but they had a great moral purpose in their lives, which lifted them in-infinitely above all triflers.

Another striking characteristic of Putnam, and this he inherited largely from his ancestors, was his love of the soil. He took delight in the ownership of land, and not in the mere ownership, but in the subjugation of it to man's uses and wants. Like the first father of the race, he felt himself sent into the garden " to dress it and to keep it." There was wealth in that soil, the wealth that God gives to the " sweat of the brow." He would look with immeasurable contempt upon that unhealthy and ignoble crowd which throngs our great

cities to-day, hoping by cunning and fortunate ventures to
abstract wealth from other men's pockets, without any productive industry whatever on its own part.   He would perhaps sit over a real keg of powder with a man of this stamp
till he was blown up and the earth rid of him.   His idea of
accumulation was only as the fruit of honest service and
hard toil.   And he had his reward.   Through these last
years of his life, his farming operations still went on under
his eye as of old.   He kept adding to his lands, year by
year, through his whole life.   Mr. Grosvenor tells us, that
when he died, "he left by will about a thousand acres of
land in Pomfret, Brooklyn and Canterbury, divided between his sons Israel, Daniel and Peter Schuyler; and
£1,200 in money, divided equally among his four daughters.   He bequeathed also to his grandson Elisha Avery
£150; also to his son Peter Schuyler all his live stock,
farming tools and provisions." *   His wealth, such as he

* The following, which we cut from the Boston "Journal," though the
record is not brought down to the present time, will convey general impressions that are correct :

"GENERAL PUTNAM'S BOYS AND GIRLS. — A correspondent in the Rut-
land 'Daily Globe' takes exceptions to a statement in a recent item in the
'Journal.'   In describing the 76th birthday party of Mr. Lewis Putnam Glea-
son of Bedford, it referred to him as being 'a grandson of the *only* daughter
of General Israel Putnam,' whom, we know, ranked next to General Washington.   It should have read thus : ' A grandson of *one* of the daughters,' etc.
The descendants of 'Old Put' in Vermont felt a little agitated to have the
printer shut them out of so distinguished a family circle with the little word
'*only*,' and during the centennial year too !

"The descendants of Putnam are numerous, for seven of his children lived
to be married, and to increase and multiply after the fashion of their worthy
ancestor.   He had as many daughters as sons, that is, five of each.   We give
the names of his boys and girls : Israel, Jr., born Jan. 28th, 1740; David, born
March 10th, 1742, died young ; Hannah, born Aug. 25th, 1744 ; Elizabeth,
born March 20th, 1747, died young ; Mehitable, born Oct. 21st, 1749 ; Molly,
born May 10th, 1753 ; Eunice, born Jan. 10th, 1756; Daniel, born Nov. 18th,
1759 ; David, born Oct. 14th, 1761, died young ; Peter Schuyler, born Dec.
31st, 1764.

"Israel, Jr., removed with his family to Ohio, and his descendants are found

had, was real and solid; not of that spongy stuff, of which
a man can say that he is worth $200,000 to-day, and noth-
ing at all to-morrow. It was wealth that based itself on
God's enduring foundations.

In Rev. Mr. Grosvenor's delineations of Putnam's life
and character, he introduces a brief letter from Dr. Jared
Sparks, written in January, 1844. President Sparks, who
did so much with his pen to illustrate American history,
was a native of Willington, Connecticut, and was born in
1789, the year before Putnam died. Willington is only a
little way from Pomfret, so that Sparks, working upon the
soil, in his childhood and youth, was not far removed from
the traditions and associations circling around the name of
the old revolutionary hero. The air of Connecticut was
full of the stories which Putnam's career had set in motion.
In this letter to Mr. Grosvenor, he says, —

"That he [Putnam] never made mistakes I would not say, for
it cannot be said of a single officer of the Revolution; but I am
sure it may be safely affirmed, that there was not among all the
patriots of the Revolution a braver man, or one more true to the
interests of his country, or of more generous and noble spirit."

To measure the real extent of Putnam's services in the
revolutionary struggle, a few simple things are to be borne
in mind. There was, first of all, that perfect *abandon* with
which he threw himself into the breach, as a *leader*. It
was a fearful undertaking. A feeling widely prevailed
among the people, which found expression in such words

all over the Buckeye State. Peter removed to Williamstown, Mass. Molly
married a Waldo, and Hannah a Dana, and their descendants number many
of the best families of New England. Eight of Putnam's grandchildren were
known to be alive about fifteen years ago, viz., Captain David Putnam, Mari-
etta, Ohio, son of Israel, Jr. ; General Wm. P. Tyler, Brooklyn, Ct., son of Mehitable ; Colonel L. P. Grosvenor, Pomfret, Ct., son of Eunice ; Mrs. Har-
riet Grosvenor, Hartford, Ct., and Mrs. Emily Brown, Brooklyn, daughters of
Daniel Putnam, and three sons of Peter in New York and Ohio."

of Scripture as these: "We have no might against this great company that cometh against us; neither know we what to do; but our eyes are upon thee." To see a man like Putnam, at his age and with his military experience, without the least precaution or disguise, with no effort whatever at concealment whether in the presence of British officers, or among his fellow-citizens, throwing himself with his whole soul, with all his powers of mind and body, into the thick of the strife, from the very outset, this was worth more to the popular cause than can possibly be estimated.* Such a man, so acting, becomes a source and fountain-head of courage to a whole nation. We have seen that Sparks, and Washington himself, by the language quoted from their letters, have this in their minds, and they freely assign to Putnam a very large share in the securing of American independence.

Is there any other man (Washington only excepted) whose agency and service in this direction will rank alongside of those of General Putnam? We can think of no one. France sent us a most graceful, brave and chivalric helper in the person of Lafayette. His example was most inspiriting, and his services highly valuable; but Lafayette did not come till the first difficulties had been surmounted, and the nation fully organized for resistance. When Putnam plunged without reserve into this strife, it was all uncertain how the remoter colonies would act. The land was full of Tories. If the Middle and Southern States held back and failed New England, a traitor's doom was almost certain to await him at the end. The common sol-

---

* "Some of those persons who signed the Declaration of Independence in 1776, described themselves as doing it ' as with halters about their necks.' If there were grounds for this remark in 1776, when the cause had become so much more general, how much greater was the hazard when the battle of Bunker Hill was fought!"—Daniel Webster, in "North American Review," July, 1818, p. 227.

dier and the under officers might be spared, but a man moving in so high a sphere, and exerting such an immense influence, would be a sure mark for vengeance. Yet he halted not at the first, and never wavered to the end. Twice at least the British approached him, in the early days of the struggle, with the promise of great honors and rewards, if he would leave the patriot service and come over to their side ; which offers he scornfully rejected. Then the fighting of the battle of Bunker Hill broke, at the outset, the spell of British invincibility. The conflicts at Lexington and Concord had done something, but this was only guerilla warfare, and not a pitched battle. When the British army, on Saturday night, June 17th, found one-third of the men taken into that action lying dead or wounded on those Charlestown slopes, the day of their idle boasting was over, and the awful dread of the "regulars" was removed, in a large measure, from the minds of the American people. The consequences of that battle were immense ; and it becomes all lovers of their country to see to it that the glory of that action shall not be taken away from the man to whom it belongs. It was only by immense force, activity and persuasion, that General Putnam succeeded in getting the battle fought at all; and when it was fought, it was with such hindrance of his plans, such impediments thrown in his way, such a hang-back spirit on the part of many of the Massachusetts regiments, that he deserves a double glory for bringing it to so successful a completion. We shall ever contend, in the clear light of contemporaneous and subsequent history, that the *plan* of that battle was his, and the *conduct* of the battle was his.

But the time drew near when the hero of many conflicts, and the conqueror on many a field, was himself to die. Through all those eleven years after his separation from the army, he had been continued in the use of all his mental faculties, though his body could no longer render the service of the earlier days. He was of an eminently happy temperament, and the enjoyments of his life were such as we have seen.

His death, at last, did not come in a repetition of the paralytic shock, as might naturally enough have been expected. On the 17th of May, 1790, he was attacked with an inflammatory disorder which did not yield to medicine, and which was rapid in its march. He died two days after, May 19th, 1790, having entered in the previous January upon his 73d year.

His death stirred the entire population in the country towns of his neighborhood. They knew that a brave and noble-hearted patriot had fallen, and they desired to do honor to his memory. General Humphreys says in this connection (pp. 165–66), —

"Much of his life had been spent in arms, and the military of the neighborhood were desirous that the rites of sepulture should be accompanied with martial honors. They felt that this last tribute of respect was due to a soldier, who from a patriotic love of country had devoted the best part of his life to the defence of her rights and the establishment of her independence, and who, through long and trying services, was never once reproached for misconduct as an officer ; but when disease compelled him to retire from service, left it, beloved and respected by the army and his chief, and with high claims to the grateful remembrance of the country.

"Under these impressions, the grenadiers of the 11th regiment (of Connecticut troops), the independent corps of artillerists, and the militia companies in the neighborhood, assembled each at their appointed rendezvous early on the morning of the 21st, and having repaired to the late dwelling-house of the deceased, a suitable escort was formed, attended by a procession of the Masonic brethren present, and a large concourse of respectable citizens, which moved to the Congregational meeting-house in Brooklyn ; and after divine service by the Rev. Dr. Whitney, all that was earthly of a patriot and hero was laid in the silent tomb, under the discharge of volleys from the infantry and minute guns from the artillery."

The following is a brief extract from the sermon of Dr. Whitney, in which he delineated the marked traits of General Putnam's character :

" He was of a kind, benevolent disposition, pitiful to the distressed, charitable to the needy, and ready to assist all who wanted his help. In his family he was the tender and affectionate husband, the provident father, an example of industry and close application to business. He was a constant attendant upon the public worship of God from his youth up. He brought his family with him when he came to worship the Lord. He was not ashamed of family religion. His house was a house of prayer. For many years he was a professor of religion. There is one, at least, to whom he freely disclosed the workings of his mind — his convictions of sin — his grief for it — his dependence on God through the Redeemer for pardon, and his hope of a future happy existence whenever his strength and heart should fail him."

At the grave a brief address was made by Dr. A. Waldo, a physician, from which we copy these few words :

" Born a hero, whom nature taught and cherished in the lap of innumerable toils and dangers, he was terrible in battle. But from the amiableness of his heart, when carnage ceased, his humanity spread over the field like the refreshing breezes of a summer evening. The prisoner, the wounded, the sick, the forlorn, experienced the delicate sympathy of this soldier's pillar. The poor and the needy of every description, received the charitable bounties of this Christian soldier."

The monument that covers his tomb is now a structure of brick work, built up two or three feet from the ground, on which a stone slab was laid, bearing this inscription, prepared for the purpose by Dr. Timothy Dwight, President of Yale College :

SACRED BE THIS MONUMENT
to the memory
of
ISRAEL PUTNAM, ESQUIRE,
Senior Major-General in the armies
of
the United States of America,
who
was born at Salem,
in the Province of Massachusetts,
on the 7th day of January,
A. D. 1718,
and died
on the 19th of May,
A. D. 1790.

PASSENGER,
if thou art a soldier,
drop a tear over the dust of a Hero,
who
ever attentive
to the lives and happiness of his men,
dared to lead
where any dared to follow ;
if a Patriot,
remember the distinguished and gallant services
rendered thy country
by the Patriot who sleeps beneath this marble ;
if thou art honest, generous and worthy,
render a cheerful tribute of respect
to a man
whose generosity was singular,
whose honesty was proverbial ;
who
raised himself to universal esteem,
and offices of eminent distinction,
by personal worth
and a
useful life.

Within a few years, a more befitting monument has been erected, which the State of Connecticut bore a part in building.

Mr. George Canning Hill, who a few years since published a life of General Putnam, designed more especially for youth, but fitted to readers of any age, in his closing paragraph, gives the following picture of the old tomb-stone and its surroundings:

"The brave old man, who never knew the meaning of fear, sleeps quietly in this humble grave. A devious path has been worn among the hillocks of the little yard, by the feet of those who have come, year by year, to look upon his last resting-place. On the still summer afternoons the crickets chirp mournfully in the long grass, and the southerly breeze wails in the belt of pines that neighbor upon the spot. The associations are all of a thoughtful sadness. But it is good for one to visit the graves of the heroes who have departed, where he may kindle anew the sentiment of patriotism, without which he can become neither an estimable citizen nor a noble man."

PUTNAM'S TOMB.

CHAPTER XIV.

THE BUNKER HILL CENTENNIAL.[*]

Spirit of the Day. — Commendable Action on the Part of Massachusetts and Boston. — Efforts of Individuals to make it a Day for Prescott's Glory. — Outward Beauty of the Day. — The Military Review in the Morning. — The Procession. — Incidents.

IT has been made sufficiently apparent, perhaps, by the course of the preceding narrative, that if there had been no battle of Bunker Hill, June 17th, 1775, except what Colonel Prescott and the Massachusetts regiments fought, there would have been nothing which we should have cared particularly to celebrate June 17th, 1875. The centennial day therefore was not a Boston day or a Massachusetts day. It was a New England day in especial, and an American day in general; and we are happy to say, so far as the organic action of the State of Massachusetts is concerned, or the corporate action of the city of Boston, every thing was conceived and carried out on the largest and most catholic scale. There was no attempt on their part, so far as can be discovered, to fly in the face of history and attempt to make this day exclusively their own. So far from this, they did not even seek by their arrangements to make it a New England day, though it was alone by

[*] Hither came that way-worn " Pilgrim," in the " New Pilgrim's Progress," published at Hartford, Connecticut. Setting out at Plymouth in 1620, by devious and sometimes forced marches, but with rapid progress, he brought up in these parts on the 17th of June, 1875. The last record we have of him and his travels, is the following : " Goes to Bunker Hill to pay his respects to the illustrious men who commanded General Putnam."

332

the sons of New England that the battle was fought. Their thoughts were not circumscribed within these narrow boundaries. They made the occasion one of a broad national character, as was fit and becoming. They invited their guests from the east and the west, the north and the south, as having, all of them, a common interest in that first great battle which marked the nation's struggle and movement towards liberty and independence. The largeness of view and of plan with which the State and city took action, to make this centennial day a grand and noble occasion, has been most widely and justly commended.

But as the time drew on, and the bustle of preparation began to be heard, it became apparent that certain individuals, here and there, either acting separately or by concert, were disposed to seize this occasion to consummate a special and peculiar object, and put the great crown of leadership upon the head of Colonel William Prescott. Some of the Boston newspapers had almost daily droppings, "here a little and there a little," in the service of this particular idea. Larger periodicals wrought in the same direction. Books began to appear, to educate the public mind up to the required standard. One of Boston's favorite and bright-minded poets, to aid the general jubilee, chimed in with the following historical line in a graceful and effective poem :

"It was PRESCOTT, one since told me, he commanded on the hill."

The "one" that "told" him was probably the same man that has been largely employed in furnishing the modern evidence. But to any one who had studied the real history of this battle, all this wore a very peculiar aspect, though it was amusing to watch by how many processes and agencies the name of Prescott was made to fill the air in the early days of June, 1875.

It was of course something of a shock to the finer feelings, a kind of rude invasion of all the proprieties of the time, when the famous New York Seventh Regiment came into Boston, singing their regimental song composed for the occasion, every one of whose nine stanzas ends with the following chorus :

> "We won the victory at that fight,
> We knew we should, for we were right ;
> Old Putnam led the men that night,
> At Bunker Hill, at Bunker Hill."

It was evident that those young men had not received a good Boston education. It jarred a little, too, upon the sensibilities to have General Sherman, after the oration under the great tent on Bunker Hill, get up and say of General Putnam, "He was a glorious old soldier, and his services and examples are worth a dozen monuments like this on Bunker Hill, even if made of pure gold." But then some latitude of speech must be allowed to so distinguished a guest as General Sherman. And because he had said before, "Prescott was the actual commander on this spot" (*i. e.*, where the tent stood, and where the monument stands), one of the Boston papers immediately seized upon that remark, and quoted Sherman as having sanctioned the notion that Prescott was commander-in-chief. In that remark he said only what all writers say, what has been freely and constantly said throughout this volume. Of course, Prescott was the local commander at the redoubt on Breed's Hill. Who ever denied it ?

But notwithstanding all this care and precaution on the part of individuals, to give a Prescott turn and a Prescott flavor to everything, the city itself went on its way with dignity. There was a practical common sense in its action, showing that it did not propose to go against the old established history. There were coarse paintings executed to be put upon the front of the City Hall in School Street, at each corner of the front entrance to the building, well up on the walls, where they would be visible to every passer by. General Joseph Warren, the volunteer and martyr, was chosen as the subject of one of these pictures, and General Israel Putnam, the chief commander in the battle, was chosen for the other. The corporate body that ordered this work done was evidently impervious to the new ideas. Its action was in the spirit of the fathers. These were not very good pictures, it is true. They were not prepared as works of art. They were made for a temporary use, and were designed to speak, not to the æsthetic eye, but to the imagination and the heart. The picture of General Putnam was taken from the painting by Wilkinson in London, in 1775, which we have described in our chapter on the Literature and Art of Bunker Hill.

A communication, however, soon appeared in a Boston paper, the opening part of which was devoted to this topic of the pictures placed upon the City Hall, and read as follows :

" You have already expressed emphatically your sense of the wrong done in the omission of any recognition of the claims of Colonel Prescott to any share of the honors of Bunker Hill in the display on the front of the City Hall. If we try to put a charitable construction upon that seeming slight upon the commander of the provincial forces, we might infer that when those who provided for that display had taken note of the skill of the artist in the figures labelled Warren and Putnam, they kindly concluded to spare Prescott, as he had already suffered enough in the caricature of him by Trumbull. Happily, however, that omission and slight, which might have had some significance as indicating the judgment of a committee in the distribution of the awards of fame, are more than compensated by the decided and well-sustained utterance of the orator of the day, giving to Prescott the honor which belongs to him."

Soon after, the Bunker Hill Association met, and took action toward erecting another monument on Breed's Hill (now commonly called Bunker Hill), to the honor of Colonel William Prescott. This association in their action at this meeting did not name Colonel Prescott as commander-in-chief. So far as their vote is concerned, that point is left indefinite, and the enterprise may base itself, if it will, upon Colonel Prescott's personal merits and services, without regard to his exact military standing.

But leaving these things aside, we turn to the day and the occasion itself. It was a morning of summer splendors without oppressive summer heat, — very different in this respect from the day when the battle was fought. On this centennial morning the sun shone in full glory, but a gentle breeze was stealing in from the ocean, which tempered the heat to the point of comfort. As the military host, gathered from every part of Massachusetts, and from many other States, — their dress clean and their weapons bright, — passed in their morning review before General Sherman and many other distinguished men, civil and military, standing upon an extended platform erected for the purpose in front of the State House yard, the scene was extremely brilliant. It took the military bodies an hour and three-quarters to pass before that stand (and there were no long delays in the marching). As the regiments came up on the bend of Beacon Street and neared the stand, their own marching bands ceased playing, and the music for the review was supplied by two of the best bands that could be selected, who were kept stationary near the stand, and played by turns. All this morning review passed before the procession for the day was formed, and never was there a summer morning better fitted to give *eclat* to such a military march. General Sherman, in his speech on Bunker Hill, meant of course to include what happened later in the day with this scene of the morning, when he pronounced the whole "one of the most gorgeous pageants that has ever occurred on this continent." The military display was finest in the morning review. The men were fresh, the sun was sparkling, and the enthusiasm of the soldiers had not become jaded by weariness. As they passed before that stand, where so many searching and distinguished eyes were looking at them, and the band was playing its high festal music, they moved like men with wings to their feet. There was a springiness, an elasticity in their step, of which they were half unconscious. But they were lifted out of themselves and were blended with the great forces of feeling and emotion around them. Any one who looked upon that morning march from the vicinity of the State House steps will never forget it.

The procession was not ready to move till about 2 o'clock, and it had a route of six miles to travel. It may give one some impression of the length of the procession itself, if we say that the head of that military column leading the procession had completed its march of six miles, just as the last half of the procession began to untangle itself to set out on its journey; in other words, the procession was twice as long as the route was. Before this procession moved, the easterly breeze which was quiet in the morning, had increased its force, bringing in a half-haze from the ocean, making the air very invigorating for those who were on the march, and quite as cool as those sitting or standing as spectators wished it to be. But for the military, and all the pedestrian bodies and associations, that long march was performed under circumstances as favorable as a day in June could ever be expected to give. To those who rode in carriages, or who looked on from streets and open windows, before the day ended extra shawls and wrappers were not uncomfortable. Through the night that followed, this

22

sea-breeze increased and brought on a chilly rain, and the next morning was as dismal as the morning of the 17th was brilliant.*

Of the crowds that witnessed this spectacle, all attempts at enumeration would be comparatively idle. There was no place along the line where the crowd was not. But probably the most exciting point in the route, was in the wide open spaces of Columbus Avenue. The soldiers who marched in the procession, all seem to declare that the effect here was most exciting and half-bewildering. Especially toward the farther end of the avenue, where the procession turned toward Washington Street, and where the children were massed in great numbers on upraised seats, tier above tier, waving flags, and filling the air with cheers, the effect was almost overpowering, and some of the officers and soldiers on that march, could hardly tell "whether they were in the body or out of the body."

The day was eminently successful. Many a man and woman went home that night, never expecting to see such a spectacle on earth again.

But happiest of all was the blending of hearts long estranged, bringing men together from the ends of the land, and making them feel like brothers, sharers in one common country and heritage.

As we lay down our pen, at the close of this volume, we are moved to say that if we have ever written under a profound conviction of the truth of what we were writing, it has been in the preparation of this book. Nothing but the clear belief that history has here been turned aside from its true purpose would ever have moved us to this task.

* One of the mottoes on the wagons of the "Great Atlantic and Pacific Tea Company," loaded with chests of tea and bags of coffee (the motto applying especially to the latter), caught the spirit of the occasion on the General Putnam side. "We are all *Colonels* here, and one *Colonel* is as good as another."

The writer has no family relationships or friendships on either side, nor was he moved to this labor by any one having such relationships. No descendant of General Putnam ever knew of the enterprise until long after it was on its way. The appeal was made by the facts of the case to the sense of general justice and historical truth.

More and more clearly is it seen that the man who contrived and executed that Bunker Hill battle struck a blow of immense consequence for his country and for posterity. That the honor of this achievement should be taken from its rightful owner, and especially from one so noble, generous and self-denying as General Putnam, that he should be robbed of this hard-earned glory, and that it should be given over to those who are, to some extent, the natural successors of the very men that failed him in the time of his sorest need, that Massachusetts and her sons should claim the peculiar honors of a victory, which, under bad leadership, she helped rather to prevent, — this is using history for an unworthy purpose. And it is because we believe this that we have written this book. If at any point we have spoken unjustly or too warmly, we ask pardon of the reader; and if we never live to see this error taken out of American history, we have the full conviction that the time will come, when the whole nation will give the honors of the battle of Bunker Hill largely to the common soldiers of New Hampshire who, more than any other men, fought it; and to brave old General Putnam, who conceived the plan, and was chief commander on the field. The two hundred men from Connecticut performed extraordinary services, but they were few in number. Their heroic faithfulness has always been spoken of in terms of highest praise. The men at the redoubt who patiently endured and suffered to the end, are worthy of all honor. But the battle was fought chiefly by the soldiers of New Hampshire, whose muskets killed and wounded probably two out of three in that list of ten hundred and sixty-four, which General Gage reported to the home government.

If a monument is to be erected upon that battle-ground to any Colonel, it should be to Colonel Stark of New Hampshire, whose services in the strife were more important than those of any other man bearing that title.

APPENDIX.

APPENDIX.

A.

ADDRESS OF HON. HENRY C. DEMING, 1859.

The battle sword of Major-General Israel Putnam was presented, last night, to the Connecticut Historical Society, in the presence of a vast assemblage, in Dr. Bushnell's Church. The Hon. Henry C. Deming delivered the address, a portion of which is copied below. No outline could do anything like justice to the speaker's masterly analysis of the evidence by which Putnam's title to the honor of having commanded, as general-in-chief, throughout the fight on Bunker Hill, was settled as we believe for ever. Connecticut owes a debt of gratitude to Mr. Deming for this laborious but successful refutation of the attacks which Bostonians have made upon General Putnam's fame. Henry Barnard, LL. D., President of the Connecticut Historical Society, being in the chair, Mr. Deming took his position at a table in front of the pulpit, and said, —

"Mr. Lemuel Putnam Grosvenor, late of Pomfret, having inherited from his grandfather, General Israel Putnam, the sword which he wielded in the battles of the Revolution, and bequeathed it to the Connecticut Historical Society, I have been deputed to deliver it into your hands, and not informally, but with all the honors, not briefly, but with suitable prelude, to introduce this relic and emblem of Connecticut's noblest soldier to an imperial seat in this assemblage of Connecticut's worthiest historic numbers. In discharging this duty, on the one hundred and forty-first anniversary of his birth, after the battles in which he fought

343

have all been finally passed upon by history, and the foes who dared assail him in the grave have proved that he could vanquish still, it hath seemed proper to me to place in your archives, in company with the sword he wore in war, a careful and deliberate *estimate of his military career and services.*"

[Here follows the passage quoted in Chapter IV.]

" Let it not be supposed, however, because Israel Putnam was shaped thus by the times in which he lived, and the circumstances in which he was placed, because he was not made and trained to lead great armies and conduct great campaigns, that he was unequal to the grander emergencies which sometimes try the genuineness of heroism. There was enough in him of the unalloyed, heroic metal to have stamped his name conspicuously on any epoch, and have contended successfully on any field of adventure. If it had been the mission of his generation to have purged Connecticut of Nemean lions and boars and other devouring monsters, before it could have become a suitable dwelling-place for man, he might have been our Hercules, for he would have faced a hydra as soon as a wolf ; if posted at the gates of empire in its last extremity, there was enough in him for another Leonidas ; with lance in poise, and battle-axe in hand, against overwhelming infidel hosts, a Cœur de Lion might have been reproduced in our history ; or hurled against the Austrian centre by some remorseless Napoleon, he would have moved steadily forward, another Macdonald between an enfilading fire of artillery, strewing his path with dismantled guns and slaughtered battalions, straight to his mark, with the inflexibility of a thunderbolt, and the weight of flying hills slung by Jove's right hand. . . . .

"Putnam entered the military service of the colony at the commencement of the seven years' war with France, and if a decisive war is one in which a contrary issue would have essentially varied the drama of history in all its subsequent scenes, then this war deserves to be classed among the decisive wars of the world. If France had succeeded in her schemes of American conquest, the whole course of civilization on this continent would have run in a different channel and have assumed another char-

acter. At its commencement the English colonists held the sea-
coast from Nova Scotia to Florida, and the French held the interior, and had drawn around us on the north and west, from
Cape Breton to New Orleans, a cordon of settlements which
could rapidly be converted into garrisons, for every lay French-
man in America owed military service. At its close the French
had surrendered all these possessions except the island of Orleans,
and the Anglo-Saxon race could roam undisturbed, from the Gulf
of Mexico to where the frozen barriers of the north arrest the
march of civilized man. The question determined in the narrow span of time between 1756 and 1763 was whether French
colonization should transfer to this hemisphere the effete mon-
archy of Versailles, the dilapidated feudal edifice of Europe, with
its successive layers of privileged classes built upon crushed and
suffering labor, with its castes, fatal to the manliness and growth
of the unprivileged majority, its hierarchy, intolerant of a free
conscience and hostile even to intellectual enfranchisement, its
servile tenures baffling by antiquated fines and encumbrances
the easy transfer of leaseholds and lands, its reactionary spirit
indifferent to enterprise or social progress, and its despotic tendencies unchecked by local parliaments, or courts of law, or the
outspoken remonstrances of indignant freemen ; or whether English colonization, leaving behind the crown, the mitre and the
peerage, should plant on this virgin soil constitutional rights,
freeholds, common law, personal independence, schools, free
churches, printing presses, colonial legislatures, town organiza-
tions and municipal self-direction.

" In this connection, too, we should never forget a secondary
effect of the seven years' war, in many respects more important
and manifest even than the primary one to which I have briefly
adverted. More than twenty-five years ago, Mr. Everett, I believe, was the first to observe the manner in which the colonial
wars were interwoven with the Revolution, and that no 'thought
of independence could suggest itself, and no plan of throwing
off the colonial yoke could prosper, while a hostile power of
French and Canadian savages, exasperated by the injuries inflicted and retaliated for a hundred years, was encamped along

the frontier. On the contrary, the habit so long kept up of acting in concert with the mother country against their French and
savage neighbors, was one of the strongest ties of interest
which bound the colonies to the crown.' It is this systematic
connection of events in which the links of the great chain are
visible, and the providential meaning of war rendered intelligi-
ble to finite comprehension, that imparts such a grandeur of interest to our historic evolution. We can almost see the mighty
arm which marshals the movement, and as the ordered eras un-
fold their meaning, discern at least the shadow of God in our
history. Each billow as it rolls is not self-impelled or independent, but is moved by the one which precedes, and moves the one
which follows, and all with consenting voices proclaim that society here shall be free, free from barbarism, free from the European colonial system, free from kings and caste, free from re-
strictions on its commerce, industry and thought, free to drop its
worn-out feudal carcass, and be transfigured into a more erect
and shining presence, and tread with firm footsteps a loftier
plane, and cherish nobler theories, and speak with a bolder
tongue, and carry its head nearer the stars.

" By the light of the present we are able to translate the myste-
ries of the past, and to detect that philosophic relation of events
which defied contemporaneous scrutiny, and to see that Pepperell
at Louisburg, Wolfe at Quebec, Amherst at Montreal, as well as
Putnam at Bunker Hill, and Gates at Saratoga, and Washington
at Yorktown, were all striking blows for the independence of the
States. When the last French forts surrendered, and the last
French regiment embarked, the lion and the unicorn began to
fade from our national escutcheon, and to the prophetic eye the
eagle of liberty was seen grasping the spears and unfolding the
scroll.

" To the decisive struggle which threw the western continent
into the arms of English colonization, and prepared the way for
the American Revolution and for the American Union, with all
its self-directing vitality and progressive system of incorporation,
no provincial, not even Washington, no regular, not excepting
Wolfe, contributed more steadily and efficiently, or exhibited

more resolution and gallantry, than Israel Putnam of Mortlake.
He fought it through, from the first tocsin sound till the treaty
of Paris terminated the most glorious war England ever fought
by the most honorable treaty she ever signed.   He plunged with
Williams into the bloody defile where that dauntless philanthro-
pist fell ; he struggled with Lyman for his dearly bought victory
over Dieskau ; he received the dying Lord Howe in his arms before the fatal breastwork of Ticonderoga ; he marched with Amherst to Montreal, and with Bradstreet to Presque Isle, and when
Spain became a party to the strife, he served under Abercrombie
in the West Indies.   He waded with frost-bitten feet through
Canadian snows ; he was bound to a stake, and the fire kindled
around him in the wilderness of the Horicon ; he was wrecked in
midsummer under the burning sun of the tropics, and escaped
from a watery grave only to encounter, before one of the most
formidable fortresses in America, as frightful a mortality as ever
battened on human life, and while the hardiest frames were dropping by his side in the agonies of thirst, or gasping their last in
the gripe of the pestilence, this iron provincial, under that scorch-
ing sky, scratched from the crevices of the rock the earth on
which the siege artillery was planted, and finally joined the forlorn hope who carried Moro Castle by storm.   In the forest fast-
nesses of Michigan, he confronts Pontiac, whose war whoop could
arm against our settlements every copper-colored warrior of the
northwest.   Putnam was one of the ten thousand victims sent by
ministerial fatuity from Crown Point to Montreal by the roundabout way of the New York wilderness and Lake Ontario and
the River St. Lawrence,— an approach, one would suppose, more
circumambient than any circumlocution office could devise.   Toil-
ing through the forests and Serbonian bogs that then separated
Albany from Oswego from the opening of June to the close of
August, and crossing the lake in open galleys, he at length
reaches the egress of the St. Lawrence, where the adventurous
parts of the monotonous march commenced.   Sailing down the
river in bateaux, Putnam leads the boarding party that, with
nothing but side arms, and a beetle and wedge to pin the rudder,
carries two French vessels of war that were disputing the pas-

sage, and contrives an ingenious engine of bullet-proof boats with upright planks twenty feet long in their prows to fall as a bridge for the scaling party upon the overhanging stockade of an inaccessible island fortress. The spirit of Putnam exults in such new dilemmas, in the impracticabilities and impossibilities of war, and if an adventure is once pronounced foolhardy by the martinets he feels challenged to execute it. View him paralyzing the bloodthirsty Hurons on his track by his audacious escape adown the roaring rapids of the Hudson. See him, against the protest of his commander, dashing the water on the flames of Fort Edward, when the fire was licking the combustible sides of the cracked powder magazine ; leading a detachment to Noddle's Island in the face of his enemies, up to his waist in mud and water ; precipitating himself down the declivity at Horseneck, 'impracticable' to the British troopers in pursuit. Recall these and forty other similar exploits of hairbrained knight-errantry, if you would learn his contempt for impossibilities and how parsimoniously prudence was employed in moulding him. It was quite uniformly the case, as upon the St. Lawrence, in emergencies that were entirely novel, in difficulties unprecedented, in front of obstacles which engineering had provided no rules for storming, when military science halted in despair, and all the resources of experience were exhausted, for the officers of his Majesty graciously to surrender operations to the untaught leader, who held a commission from the hand of nature, and drew only upon original genius for his plans and expedients. And even in our revolutionary war his Continental superiors in similar straits were not slow in imitating the judicious deference of the British regulars to his ingenuity. When a thing was to be done by a mad temerity alone, or with grossly inadequate means, and at the grievous risk of life and reputation, Putnam, as a special favor, was always permitted to do it, both in the French War and in the Revolution, and it is but fair to say that so far from requiring great urging to undertake such an adventure, he always leaped into it as into the arms of blooming joy.

"The part of this large field, thus hastily sketched in outline, which Putnam most bountifully filled in with his peculiar and

characteristic audacity, was that region of unsurpassed natural
beauty where, on the side of France, Ticonderoga and Crown
Point, and on that of England, Forts William Henry and Edward, stand as sentinels at the gateway of the Canadas and Lake
George, and the head waters of the Hudson lie in the embrace of
mountains. To say that for five campaigns in summer and winter, these crimsoned acres were his dwelling-place and home,
that he rushed into battles and skirmishes which were the daily
exercise of this bloody ring, as if he had forty lives to spare,
would be but a meagre epitome of this chapter in his biography.
Every ravine of this broken region was his ambush, every brake
or outlook upon these frowning mountains his bivouac ; scarcely a
rod of its soil was unimpressed by the foot, or a reach of its water
uncut by the oar, of one who was not only the soldier but the engineer, laborer, scout and spy of a great natural amphitheatre
where the two rival nations of Europe were in hand-to-hand
fight for the mastery of America. A warfare in which the out-
posts of the two armies were within hailing distance, and hostile
picket guards and scouting parties were constantly crossing and
intersecting each other, and the woods were alive with scalp-
hunting Indians, was precisely the kind of warfare for Putnam's
cool judgment, desperate courage, and fertility of resource. A
Turenne, or Marlborough, or Wellington, with their marches and
counter marches and grand movements and learned strategy,
would have been useless as carpet knights in the rough and tum-
ble attacks and defence that were hourly improvised here.
Science and tactics availed nothing, but a foot that never wea-
ried, an arm that never failed, an eye that could decipher the
hieroglyphics of the trail, an ear that could distinguish the ordinary voices of nature from the concerted signals of wily foe, a
cunning that could circumvent infernal ingenuity in mischief, a
courage that could not only brave death but roasting by a slow
fire. It was his romantic exploits on this conspicuous field in
reconnoitering the enemy's lines, gaining intelligence, cutting off
straggling parties, beating up the quarters and capturing advance
guards, scouring the woods, outlying on Indian war-paths, leading
forlorn hopes, succeeding in retreats and escapades that were

scarcely less than miraculous, in danger the most desperate yet
never yielding to despair, in perils the most terrific without losing
self-command, in ambuscades yet facing the foe, hopeless but
not helpless, cast down but not destroyed, defeated but not van-
quished, often entrapped and but once caught, falling into clay
pits with fourteen bullet holes in his blankets, diving into chasms
and down rapids amidst a shower of balls, standing bound to a
tree without the power of dodging, between two sharp-shooting
war parties, and with his head the target at which expert Indians
practised with the tomahawk in the brief intervals of the fray, —
it was such adventures, with his prowess in single combat and remarkable good fortune, that won for Putnam the almost superstitious confidence of his associates ; for there were many whose
skins were not red that held that he was invincible by mortal foe,
and that no bullet was ever run which could touch him in a mortal part." . . . .

From this point Colonel Deming goes on at considerable length,
in a minute examination of the proofs which go to establish the
fact of Putnam's command at Bunker Hill.

———

B.

LETTER OF COL. JOHN TRUMBULL TO COL. DANIEL PUTNAM, AND COL. PUTNAM'S REPLY.

This letter of Colonel Putnam has probably never before been
published :

"New York, March 30th, 1818.

"Dear Sir : Mr. Hall has just shown me 'The Port Folio' of
last month, containing an account of the battle of Bunker Hill,
which appears to have been written for the mere purpose of introducing a most unjustifiable attack upon the memory of your
excellent father.

"It is strange that men cannot be contented with their own
honest share of fame, without attempting to detract from that of

others ; but after the attempts which have been made to diminish the immortal reputation of Washington, who shall be surprised or who repine at this unenviable attendant on human greatness ?

" In all cases like this, perhaps, the most unquestionable testimony is that which is given by an enemy.

" In the summer of 1786, I became acquainted in London with Colonel John Small of the British army, who had served in America many years, and had known General Putnam intimately during the war of Canada, from 1756 to 1763. From him I had the two following anecdotes respecting the battle of Bunker Hill. I shall nearly repeat his words. Looking at the picture which I had then almost completed, he said, ' I don't like the situation in which you have placed my old friend Putnam ; you have not done him justice. I wish you would alter that part of your picture, and introduce a circumstance which actually happened, and which I can never forget. When the British troops advanced the second time to the attack of the redoubt, I, with the other officers, was in front of the line to encourage the men. We had advanced very near the works, undisturbed, when an irregular fire, like a feu-de-joie, was poured in upon us. It was cruelly fatal. The troops fell back, and when I looked to the right and left, I saw not one officer standing ; I glanced my eye to the enemy, and saw several young men levelling their pieces at me. I knew their excellence as marksmen, and I considered myself gone. At that moment my old friend Putnam rushed forward, and striking up the muzzles of their pieces with his sword, cried out, " For God's sake, my lads, don't fire at that man ; I love him as I do my brother." We were so near each other that I heard his words distinctly. He was obeyed ; I bowed, thanked him, and walked away unmolested.'

" The other anecdote relates to the death of General Warren.

" ' At the moment when the troops succeeded in carrying the redoubt, and the Americans were in full retreat, General Howe (who had been hurt by a spent ball, which bruised his ancle) was leaning on my arm. He called suddenly to me, " Do you see that elegant young man who has just fallen ? Do you know him?" I looked to the spot towards which he pointed, "Good God, sir, I believe it is my friend Warren." "Leave me, then, instantly; run, keep off the troops, save him if possible." I flew to the spot. "My dear friend," I said to him, "I hope you are not badly hurt;" he looked up, seemed to recollect me, smiled and died! A musket-ball had passed through the upper part of his head.' Colonel Small had the character of an honorable, upright man, and could have no conceivable motive for deviating from truth in relating these circumstances to me; I therefore believe them to be true.

"You remember, my dear sir, the viper biting the file. The character of your father for courage, humanity, generosity and integrity is too firmly established by the testimony of those who *did know him*, to be tarnished by the breath of one who confesses that he *did not*.

"Accept, my dear sir, this feeble tribute to your father's memory, from one who *knew* him, *respected* him, *loved* him, — and who wishes health and prosperity to you and all the good man's posterity. JOHN TRUMBULL.

"DANIEL PUTNAM, Esq."

"BROOKLYN, 5th May, 1818.

"MY DEAR SIR: It was not until the 29th of April that I saw General Dearborn's 'account of the battle of Bunker Hill,' and it was the same day that Mr. Hall gave me your friendly and obliging letter of the 30th of March.

"I need not tell you how grateful it was to me, after reading such a tissue of falsehood and malignity, to find that my father's friends partook somewhat of my feelings on the occasion.

"Mr. Hall told me I was at liberty to make what use of your letter should be necessary; and I *have* used it to support truth and detect falsehood. I hope you will not be displeased that it occupies a prominent place in the defence of General Putnam's slandered character, which I have written very hastily, and now forward to you; with a request that it may be published in the 'Port Folio,' whose pages have been stained with the malicious representations of General Dearborn.

"The editor, if he possess a particle of that impartiality which ought always to characterize the conductor of a public journal, cannot, I think, refuse this act of justice to the memory of the insulted dead.

"With much respect, I am, dear sir, your obliged and grateful friend,   D. PUTNAM."

"Colonel TRUMBULL."

C.

BRITISH ACCOUNTS OF THE BATTLE.

At what precise time the news of the battle of Bunker Hill first reached England it may be difficult to determine. From certain items which we have given in Chapter XI., it would seem that the reports had reached that country as early as July 19th. Gage's official report was not dated until June 25th, eight days after the battle, and that report was published in England near the last of July. But it was charged in England that "the ministry received this account several days before it was announced." It will be seen by one of the following papers that Gage's account was published before the end of July, notwithstanding the delay on this side before sending, and the delay on the other side before publishing. At that season of the year, vessels were passing and repassing quite frequently, and the news, if started from our shores immediately after the battle, would have reached England by a little after the middle of July.

It would be easy to copy English articles on this subject upon the government side, showing great bitterness of spirit, and treating the people of this country with contempt; but in such selections as we here make we wish rather to illustrate what has been several times stated in this volume, viz., that we had many warm friends among the English people of that day who were not afraid to utter their thoughts freely against the course of the British government.

23

GENERAL GAGE'S FULL ACCOUNT.

Annexed is a copy of a letter written by General Gage to the Earl of Dartmouth, describing the event. It is taken from an English magazine, published in July, 1775, at London.

" BOSTON, June 25th, 1775.

" MY LORD : I am to acquaint your Lordship of an action that happened on the 17th inst., between his Majesty's troops and a large body of the rebel forces. An alarm was given at break of day on the 17th inst., by a firing from the Lively ship-of-war ; and advice was soon after received that the rebels had broke ground and were raising a battery on the heights of the peninsula of Charlestown, against the town of Boston. They were plainly seen at work, and in a few hours a battery of six guns played upon their works. Preparations were instantly made for landing a body of men to drive them off, and ten companies of the grenadiers, ten of light infantry, with the 5th, 38th, 43d and 52d battalions, with a proportion of field-artillery, under the command of Major-General Howe and Brigadier-General Pigot, were embarked with great expedition and landed on the peninsula without opposition, under the protection of some ships-of-war, armed vessels and boats, by whose fire the rebels were kept within their works. The troops formed as soon as landed (the light infantry posted on the right, and the grenadiers upon the left ; the 5th and 38th battalions drew up in the rear of those corps, and the 43d and 52d battalions made a third line). The rebels upon the heights were perceived to be in great force and strongly posted. A redoubt thrown up on the 16th at night, with other works full of men, defended with cannon, and a large body posted in the houses in Charlestown, covered their right flank ; and their centre and left were covered by a breastwork, part of it cannon-proof, which reached from the left of the redoubt to the Mystic or Medford River. This appearance of the rebels' strength, and the large columns seen pouring in to their assistance, occasioned an application for the troops to be reinforced with some companies of light infantry and grenadiers, the 47th battalion and the 1st battalion of marines ; the whole, when in conjunction, making a body of something above two thousand men. These troops advanced, formed in two lines, and the attack began by a sharp cannonade from our field-pieces and howitzers, the lines advancing slowly, and frequently halting to give time for the artillery to fire. The light infantry was directed to force the left point of the breastwork, to take the rebel line in flank, and the grenadiers to attack in front, supported by the 5th and 52d battalions. These orders were executed with perseverance, under a heavy fire from the vast number of the rebels, and notwithstanding various impediments before the troops could reach the works, and though the left under Brigadier-General Pigot was engaged also with the rebels at Charlestown, which at a critical moment was set on fire, the Brigadier pursued his point, and carried the redoubt. The rebels were then forced from their strongholds and pursued till they were drove clear off the peninsula, leaving five pieces of cannon behind them. The loss the rebels sustained must have been considerable, from the great numbers they carried off during the time of action, and buried in holes, since discovered, exclusive of what they suffered by the shipping and boats ; near one hundred were buried the day after, and thirty found wounded in the field, three of whom are since dead. I enclose your Lordship a return of the killed and wounded of his Majesty's troops. This action has shown the superiority of the King's troops who, under every disadvantage, attacked and defeated above three times their own number, strongly posted and covered by breastworks. The conduct of Major-General Howe was conspicuous on this occasion, and his example spirited the troops, in which Major-General Clinton assisted, who followed the reinforcement. And the success of the day must in great measure be attributed to his firmness and gallantry. Lieutenant-Colonels Nesbit, Abercrombie and Clarke ; Majors Butler, Williams, Bruce, Spendlove, Smelt, Mitchell, Pitcairne and Short exerted themselves remarkably ; and the valor of the British officers and soldiers was at no time more conspicuous than in this action.

"I have the honor to be, etc., THO. GAGE."

"The attack was begun by a most severe fire of cannon and howitzers, under which the troops advanced very slowly toward the enemy, and halted several times to afford an opportunity to the artillery to ruin the works, and to throw the provincials into confusion. Whatever it proceeded from, whether from the number, situation, or countenance of the enemy, or from all together, the King's forces seem to have been *unusually staggered in this attack.* . . . . The provincials stood this severe and continued fire of small arms and artillery with a resolution and perseverance which would not have done discredit to old troops. They did not return a shot until the King's forces had approached almost to the works, when a most dreadful fire took place, by which a number of our bravest men and officers fell. Some gentlemen who had served in the most distinguished actions of the late war declared that, for the time it lasted, it was the hottest engagement they ever knew. It is, then, no wonder if, under so heavy and destructive a fire, our troops were thrown *into some disorder.* It is said that General Howe was, for a few seconds, *left nearly alone;* and it is certain that most of the officers near his person (who were picked out by the sharpshooters) were either killed or wounded. . . . .

"Thus ended the hot and bloody affair of Bunker Hill, in which we had more men and officers killed and wounded, in proportion to the number engaged, than in any other action which we can recollect. The whole loss in killed and wounded amounted to one thousand and fifty-four, of whom two hundred and twenty-six were killed ; of these nineteen were commissioned officers, two Majors and seven Captains. Seventy other officers were wounded. . . . . The event sufficiently showed the bravery of the King's troops. . . . . The battle of Quebec, in the late war, with all its glory, and the vastness of the consequences of which it was productive, was not so destructive to our officers as this affair of an intrenchment cast up in a few hours. . . . . The Americans said that though they had lost a host, they had almost all the effects of a most complete victory, as they entirely put a stop to the offensive operations of a large army sent to subdue them, and which they continued to blockade in a narrow town. They now exulted that their actions had thoroughly refuted those aspersions which had been thrown upon them in England, of a deficiency in spirit and resolution."

OBSERVATIONS ON THE GOVERNMENT ACCOUNT OF THE LATE ACTION NEAR CHARLESTOWN.

"LONDON, Aug. 1st, 1775.

" There are two sorts of persons who always persevere uniformly, and without shame, in one unvaried line of conduct, regardless of the contempt and detestation of mankind. The sorts I mean are the thorough virtuous and the thorough scoundrel. To one of these classes most evidently belong the ministers, who settled the account they have given us in last Tuesday's 'Gazette.'

"The action near *Boston* happened on the 17th of June, yet General Gage's letter is dated eight days after, on the 25th of June. By this letter it appears that it cost one thousand and sixty-four of the troops, killed and wounded, to destroy a redoubt thrown up only the overnight, *i. e.*, on the 16th of June. The loss of the provincials, the letter says, must have been considerable, yet eight days after the action, the General, though completely victorious, can tell us only of one hundred buried and thirty wounded. But 'they had carried off great numbers during the time of action.' Did they so? That is no great sign of flight, confusion and retreat. But 'they buried them in holes.' Really! Why, are our soldiers buried in the air? But 'the King's troops were under every disadvantage.' So truly it seems, for we are told in the same letter that they had a proportion of field-artillery, and landed on the peninsula without opposition, and formed as soon as landed, under the protection of some ships-of-war, armed vessels and boats, by whose fire the rebels were kept within the works.

" But 'this action has shown the superiority of the King's troops.' Has it, indeed? How? Why, they, with a proportion of field-artillery and with the assistance of ships, armed vessels and boats, and with the encouragement of certain and speedy reinforcements if necessary, attacked and defeated above three times their own number. What! three times their own numbers? Of whom, pray? Of *French* or *Spanish* regulars? No! of the *Americans*. Of the *Americans?* What! of those dastardly, hypocritical cowards, who (Lord *Sandwich* knows) do not feel bold enough to look a soldier in the face? Of those undisciplined and spiritless *Yankees*, who were to be driven from one end of the continent to the other with a single regiment? What! of those skulking assassins, who can only fire at a distance from behind stone-walls and hedges? Good *God!* Was it necessary, to defeat these fellows, that the troops should be spirited by the example of General *Howe*, assisted by General *Clinton?* And can it be that Lieutenant-Colonels *Nesbit, Abercrombie* and *Clarke;* Majors *Butler, Williams, Bruce, Spendlove, Smelt, Mitchell, Pitcairne* and *Short* should be forced to exert themselves against such poltroons? Is it possible that this could be an affair in which 'the valor of the *British* officers and soldiers in general was as conspicuous as at any time whatever'? and notwithstanding all this, that the success in a great measure should be attributed to the firmness and gallantry of General Pigot?

"Good *God!* is it come to this at last? Can the regulars, with all these exertions, only defeat three times their own number of undisciplined cowards, and that too at the expense of one thousand and sixty-four (*i. e.*, more than one-half) killed and wounded out of 'something above two thousand'? Is every redoubt which the Americans can throw up in a short summer night to be demolished at this expense? How many such victories can we bear? Alas! when I read in the General's letter the regular and formidable preparations for attack, 'ten companies of grenadiers, ten of light infantry, with the 5th, 38th, 43d, and 52d battalions, with a proportion of field-artillery, under the command of Major-General *Howe* and Brigadier-General *Pigot;*' and these 'landed on the peninsula under the protection of ships-of-war, armed vessels and boats,' and their dreadful fire; when I read this, I concluded that the next lines would tell me of the immediate and precipitate retreat of the *Yankees*.

Judge then of my surprise when I read that (instead of being at all dismayed with the *Sandwich* panic) 'large columns' of these cowards 'were seen pouring in to their assistance.'

"Well, but then comes 'an application for the troops to be reinforced with some companies of light infantry and grenadiers, the 47th battalion and the 1st battalion of marines.' They will certainly, thought I, scamper away now. Alas, no! They stay and fight. And to complete my astonishment, I cannot find in General *Gage's* letter where our troops were when he wrote, nor what became of them after the action; whether they have returned to *Boston*, or have ventured to encamp without the town ; what prisoners they have taken; what advantages (besides five pieces of cannon) result from this bloody action; whether the war is now at an end, or what the troops propose to do next.

"To be serious, I am, for my own part, convinced that the event of this execrable dragooning is decided, and that before winter there will not be a single soldier of Lord *Bute's* and Lord *Mansfield's* mercenary troops left upon the continent of *America*.

"With what consolation those noble lords will wipe away the tears of the widow and orphans (as well *English* as American,) which these bloody *Stuart* measures have occasioned, I cannot tell ; but I know that my eyes will gush out with joy when they see the authors of our domestic miseries receive (what I believe they will soon receive) their just reward."

FURTHER OBSERVATIONS.

"I have the highest idea of General *Howe's* military character, yet cannot help wondering how he came to suffer the provincials to escape, and even carry off their dead, when drove from their strong lines ; for I conceive it very easy to have destroyed the whole body, after dislodging them so suddenly from their intrenchments, if Mr. *Gage* is suffered to tell the story right ; I can't help observing also, that I never before heard of so many men, in proportion to the number, being killed and wounded from redoubts made in four hours, and from six pieces of cannon only in the redoubts, to oppose one hundred pieces. I therefore suspect that the disagreeable scene is not unfolded.

"One or both of the following conclusions must be drawn from this narration : The *Americans* are either the cleverest fellows in the world at making strong lines in three or four hours, or the most desperate enemy in defending them ; for by Mr. Gage's account, they killed and wounded near half his army, in marching up about three hundred yards under a complete train of artillery, and all the fire of the navy to cover them ; which, by this account, is a new instance of successful defence from one night's labor. Hah! *Gad!* By this rule the *Americans* will put our whole army into the grave or hospitals in three or four nights' work and an hour's fire in each morning. I do not remember precisely, but am apt to believe that there were not so many officers killed and wounded at the battle of *Minden,* though the *English* regiments sustained the force of the whole *French* army for a considerable time. A six-gun battery, the production of a night's digging, had there been ten thousand men to protect it, could never have made such havoc against a vast train of artillery, and the irresistible fire of our ships, which would sweep on before them from every acre of the peninsula. But the true story is not told. A Methodist secretary and a Scotch printer can do more than our people. They pay off the sins of omission and commission of the day by a long prayer at night, and thus settle the account between *God* and the people by an hour's devotion."

"LONDON, Aug. 8th, 1775.

"The account of the late action between the *Americans* and the troops of General *Gage* is one of the most evasive and unsatisfactory that ever yet obtruded on the public, even through the channel of a ministerial paper, and yet it is every way worthy of the victory which it affects to describe. The General sent out 'something above two thousand men,' of whom something above half (*i. e.*, one thousand and fifty-three) are either killed or wounded. The General, however, takes care not to mention how many hours were employed in this hopeful business, but nevertheless pretends to tell us that great numbers of the enemy were destroyed, and seems to have employed his soldiers in digging up such as were buried in holes, that he might have power to tell the value of his conquest.

"With all the vanity of a military man, he praises the conduct of the officers under his command ; but prudently omits to say whether any such advantage has been gained, as may make up for the loss of one Lieutenant-Colonel, two Majors, seven Captains, nine Lieutenants, fifteen Sergeants, one drummer, one hundred and ninety-one rank and file, killed ; and three Majors, twenty-seven Captains, thirty-two Lieutenants, eight Ensigns, forty Sergeants, twelve drummers, and seven hundred and six rank and file, wounded, and unfit for service. In short, if every time the General sends out his brace of thousands, the one-half of them should either drop or be rendered useless, we shall soon see an end to the war in *America*, but it cannot be expected to terminate in our favor.

"The ministry received this account several days before it was announced, but were either unwilling or unable to cook it up for the public till after their despatches had been sent away. The printer may rely on this assurance from one whose private letters will always reach him unexamined and uncastrated by the spies of government. General Gage is but too well convinced that such another victory would oblige him to re-embark his troops and sail immediately for *England*, without attempting any further reduction of the *Americans*.

"The Captain who brought these despatches from *Boston*, was commanded to declare he had great news of the defeat of the *Americans*, though he had assured many people in the towns through which he passed on his way to London that he was afraid the accounts he brought would throw the whole nation into disorder, and direct its vengeance on the advisers of hostile measures in *America*."

D.

EXTRACTS FROM COMMUNICATIONS FURNISHED BY PROF. BENJAMIN SILLIMAN OF NEW HAVEN.

"I see no reason whatever for the statement that Colonel John Trumbull, in his memorable picture of the *'Death of General Warren at Bunker Hill,'* misrepresents the action of General Putnam. This officer is represented by Trumbull as at the close of the action and in the background valorously leading the retreat which had then become inevitable. The true motive of this picture seems to have been lost sight of in the pending controversy as to who commanded the forces in that action. The artist's design was to commemorate the noble patriotism of our ancestors, and to convey to posterity a feeling testimony of the price they paid for our liberties. This price was paid in the life-blood of our noblest and best, and General Warren's death, which is the 'eye' of the picture, is made to stand forth in token of these sacrifices. It was not with the artist a question of *command, but of sacrifice and valor.* That Trumbull could not have been ignorant of any important matter touching the events of June 17th, 1775, is evident from his personal 'Reminiscences,' Chapter II. He was Adjutant of Spencer's Connecticut Regiment, then stationed at Roxbury, and witnessed the battle from his position. He soon after made for General Washington a sketch map of 'Boston and the surrounding Country and Posts of the American Troops,' which is reproduced in his 'Reminiscences,' etc., about the time that he became a member of the military family of the commander-in-chief as his second Aid-de-Camp.

"I have before me a narrative statement by Colonel Trumbull (in his own handwriting), the substance of which has been printed but not published in his 'Description of the four Pictures from Subjects of the Revolution,' etc. I copy a paragraph or two which pertains to the question in hand. . . . .

"'Little was or could be done during the sixty days which elapsed between the 19th of April and the 17th of June to reduce this assemblage to order or discipline. Yet such was the zeal of the moment, that the determination was taken to advance from Cambridge and to establish a post on Breed's Hill, the nearest point of approach to Boston, distant little more than half a mile from the north part of the town; and on the evening of the 16th of June a detachment of twelve or fifteen hundred men, commanded by General Putnam and Colonel Prescott, marched for this purpose, arrived at the spot selected at 10 o'clock (at night), and commenced throwing up a small redoubt, traces of which were visible a few years since. . . . .

"'The British had no knowledge of this movement, until daylight exposed to their view the progress which had been made. From the moment of this discovery they opened a heavy fire from ships and batteries, which was continued incessantly through the day, until the attack was made in form by the troops under command of General Howe in the afternoon of June 17th. Thus, from 10 o'clock in the evening until 4 o'clock in the morning, *six hours,* was all the time which this gallant detachment had to prosecute their work without interruption. They were not relieved in the morning, but remained all day under the fire of the enemy, laboring to complete their work, which they valiantly defended, under the immediate orders of the gallant veteran Prescott, with the most unflinching bravery; and quitted their post only when their ammunition was entirely expended.

"'In the course of the day other troops were ordered down from Cambridge to support this first detachment, some of whom were deterred from attempting to cross Charlestown Neck by the fire of the hostile floating batteries, while others fearlessly dashed on and took up positions on the left of the redoubt; thus forming a line which extended from the redoubt on the right to Mystic River on the left, securing their front, at least in appearance, by throwing together fences, new mown hay, and whatever else was moveable, and could afford some show of shelter.

"'Joseph Warren, an eminent physician of Boston, had for some time been distinguished as an ardent and eloquent supporter of the rights of his country; at this time he was a very influential member of the Provincial Congress, assembled at Watertown, near Cambridge, and a few days preceding the battle (June 14th) had been elected a Major-General, but as yet had assumed no command. He was dressed, and going out to dine, when the increasing din of the action impelled him to gallop to the scene, where he arrived almost at the moment of defeat, and was killed by a ball through the head.

" ' This is the moment chosen for the painting, which of course is limited to that part of the scene which was near the redoubt, and where the death of General Warren, and the obstinate resistance of men almost unarmed to well armed and disciplined troops, is meant to be shown.

" ' In a scene of such extent and confusion as the entire battle, half-hidden of course by smoke, it was impossible to represent the equal gallantry of these brave troops who formed the line of defence between the redoubt and Mystic River, where Major Knowlton and many others distinguished themselves by the coolest bravery and the soundest judgment. . . . . The artist was on that day Adjutant of the 1st regiment of Connecticut troops, stationed at Roxbury, and saw the action from that point.'

· " These extracts plainly show that Trumbull's object in composing this picture was as has been already stated. He took the liberty of a painter to choose the critical moment of an action by bringing Major-General Warren to the front to meet his death, while both Prescott and Putnam are thrown into subordinate positions in the melee. If this artistic license is what is meant by a misrepresentation of the part borne by Putnam on this occasion, I can only say I think an expression less open to criticism might have been used.

" If anybody has stated, or can state, the date or authority for the conversation attributed to Trumbull, as taking place at the dinner table of Judge Prescott, or who the guests were at that dinner, I shall be glad to know it.

" But until we have the positive testimony of a competent authority who was present at the dinner, when Trumbull is reported to have said at Judge Prescott's table that he regretted he had made the position of Putnam as it is in his picturè (or words to that effect), I shall hold the whole story as an unfounded and mischievous rumor, born of the party spirit which animated General Dearborn's attack on Putnam in 1818.

"I can say, with the knowledge of an original witness, that I know from Trumbull's repeated discourses to me on this picture, that the one prominent event he intended to signalize was the glorious death and sacrifice of Warren, the noble friendship of Major Small of the English force, who parried the bayonet thrust of an English grenadier, crying out at the same time, 'Spare the fallen brave, he is my friend.' This Small told to Trumbull himself, as the latter delighted to relate. As I said before, this action is the 'eye of the picture' (Trumbull's own phrase in describing it). Next he intended to record the valor and heroism, the unquenched enthusiasm of the Americans, by several subordinate and yet prominent actions. This is especially seen in the heroic stand of Colonel Grosvenor in the foreground, who, though wounded in the shoulder and in the sword hand, turns again on the enemy as he retreats, supported by his black servant, as if he would have 'one more shot:' an action full of fire and dauntless bravery, which Rogers has again reproduced in one of his charming models of the late war, under the same title, 'One more Shot.' Sculpture and painting were never more in harmony than in the expression of this sentiment in those two distinct actions. Then the same sentiment of determination and valor is seen in the clubbed muskets, the empty guns held at half pose, and more than all in the fiery determination of Putnam, who, *on foot*, rallied the forces for a retreat in the last moments of the action. But all these skilfully blended actions are held in complete subordination to the main action of the whole scene,— 'The Death of Warren.' One can hardly restrain a feeling of surprise, bordering on a less respectful sentiment, when the whole soul and pathos of such a picture as that of Trumbull's 'Death of Warren' is lost sight of, and is viewed through the false colors and distorted medium of a provincial prejudice. . . . .

"If any man lived at the time who, from his position, his military knowledge, and his perfect impartiality of character, was

able to judge Putnam aright, it was George Washington He
was on the ground within three weeks after the action. He at
once initiated the Courts-Martial which investigated and dealt
with the cases of alleged unworthy conduct growing out of that
battle. He brought from the Continental Congress the commissions for four men destined for promotion to the rank of Major-
Generals, and of these commissions the only one he awarded
was to Putnam ! toward whom he ever after extended his unqualified confidence, and again and again entrusted with the most important commands. Could these things have been, if there had
existed any, even the least probable, grounds for impugning either
the valor or the patriotism of Putnam ? To suppose the reverse
is to assail the judgment and fair-mindedness of the commander-
in-chief, by whose act General Putnam was made his second in
command in the Continental armies. Trumbull, in the manuscript from which I quoted in my former letter, speaks of the
'valor of the veteran Prescott.' But Prescott continued in service only two years after, and was never, if I am correctly informed, advanced beyond the rank of Colonel. While this fact
may not be in the least to his discredit, certainly no one will be rash
enough to say that the rapid promotion of Putnam, and the undi-
minished, nay, constantly increasing confidence with which he
was regarded by Washington, is any ground, at this late day, for
an attempt to degrade him from his lofty position, as the bravest
man of his time, in favor of any other man, however deserving
he may be. As President John Adams eloquently remarked as
to the slander on the character of James Otis, 'It is mortifying,
it is astonishing, it is humiliating, to reflect how long a slander
will be continued and repeated, and how difficult it is to refute
it ' (Mr. Lowell's 'Review'). Truly, ' Slander runs a mile while
truth pulls on its boots.' It is a curious characteristic of a certain class in this world, that nothing gives them more pleasure
than to assist in the iconoclastic raid which topples over the people's idols. Every hero since the time of Agamemnon has passed
this ordeal, and I have no fear that 'Old Put' will be brought to
grief by the raids of this day any more than have some of his
worthy associates, not excepting Washington himself.

"NOTE. It may be worth while to note the fact that General Warren, in Trumbull's picture, is represented in full dress and with a ruffled shirt, conforming in this respect to Trumbull's statement that Warren was dressed for and on his way to a dinner, when the 'increasing din' led him into the fight, and the fact of his late arrival on the field, 'almost in the moment of defeat,' is testified to by many others. Putnam is spoken of by several witnesses who were in the battle, as mounted, and as urging his horse impetuously over the field. Trumbull represents him (misrepresents, shall we say?) as *on foot.* It is not necessary to reconcile these unimportant discrepancies, but it is quite probable that by the middle of the afternoon he had worn out his horse, and possibly the *unities* of action required of Trumbull to unhorse Putnam, not to give him too much prominence, and so detract from the prominence given to Warren's central figure."

E.

ARTICLES BY HONORABLE JOHN LOWELL, PUBLISHED IN "COLUMBIAN CENTINEL," BOSTON, JULY 4TH-15TH, 1818.

The author, as stated in the body of the book, had copied the whole of the seven articles by Mr. Lowell, with the design of placing them in this Appendix. They would, however, occupy so much space that only two are given, the *first* and *third*, with two brief extracts from others. These will show what a Boston man, of the first quality for character, intelligence and ability, thought of General Putnam in the year 1818. They will show, also, what questions were then discussed, and that the modern question as between Putnam and Prescott was not then up for discussion.

ARTICLE I.—OF THE AUTHORITY EXERCISED BY GENERAL PUTNAM
IN THE BATTLE OF BUNKER HILL.

"As to the first point, it is a little, and indeed very, curious, and shows the utter want of judgment in General Dearborn and his friends, that they have endeavored to make it out that Putnam had no *legitimate command* on that great and memorable day. If this fact, which they have endeavored to prove in the loose and unsatisfactory way in which they have conducted the whole of this defence against the charge of calumny be true, then General Putnam ought not to have been on the ground to take away the command from Colonel Prescott. It will be observed that we do not admit the fact to be so ; but it goes to the credit of the defence ; and shows of what weak and discordant materials it is composed. Let us now hear the witness to this point.

"First, Major Stark, in his letter to Wilkinson, states that he never could learn that there was any officer appointed to the general command. He further remarks that there ought to have been a simultaneous occupation of Bunker Hill as well as of Breed's Hill, in order to protect the retreat of our troops. If Major Stark is a judicious military man, and this opinion is sound, why undertake to censure Putnam for retaining his forces on Bunker Hill? We deny the fact that he did, but to those who censure him for it, it is surely a sufficient answer to say that his very accusers assert that it was a very suitable measure, and might have prevented what Major Stark says would have been the ruin of the detachment, the occupation of Bunker Hill, in the rear of our troops. Judge Parker, a New Hampshire Judge of Probate, a very flippant witness, says there was never any proof to his mind, that Putnam was ordered to take the command, and that he was only a volunteer, and, of course, in his ideas of military law, not subject to a trial. In this way he accounts for no notice having been taken of the subject during the last century, and until the present is very considerably advanced. The very respectable gentlemen of the clergy of Groton and Pepperell also confirm, from the testimony of their parishioners who were in the action, that General Putnam was not present, *either the night before* or during the action.

"Now, though this *is directly opposed to the fact, sufficiently and perfectly proved* (not, however affecting their veracity, as their testimony is derived from channels which may be incorrect), yet, *if true,* and General Dearborn adduces it as such, it proves that

.

Putnam could not, without a dereliction of duty and violating the rights of others, have advanced from his position on Bunker Hill.

"We have shown the gross inconsistency of the General's *evidence* with his *charge* against the venerable Putnam. In his 'Account of the Battle,' he considers Putnam as having shamefully deserted his duty, *and as deserving to be shot,* or, rather, he represents Colonel Prescott as having said so ; and, in his *defence,* he proves by two witnesses, that Putnam had no command on that day, and of course could be liable to no censure for not undertaking to command Prescott and Stark, of the Massachusetts and the New Hampshire lines. It is certainly true, as suggested by President Adams and Judge-Advocate Tudor, that there could not, in the nature of the case, have been any authorized commander. The troops were volunteers from three different States, under probably royal commissions, perhaps no commissions at all. The latter was certainly the case with Stark, who was chosen by his troops after their arrival at Medford. But, although Putnam could have no *legal* right to command, we shall show, in the sequel, that he was, *in fact,* the commander of that detachment, and by *his* orders were the works executed ; that they were obeyed as if he were the rightful commander ; and that Dearborn's own regiment (that of Colonel Stark) acted and fought under his immediate command, and in his presence, that day. In short, before the evidence is half through, it will be seen that there is at present more proof of General Putnam's active, bold, courageous exertions in the hottest of that battle, in the very front of danger, than there is that Dearborn, or even Colonel Stark, were in it.

"It would not be in the power of Washington's friends to prove that he was at the battle of Monmouth, by stronger or more complete evidence than General Putnam's friends can produce, to establish his audacious gallantry and coolness on Breed's Hill. But this evidence I shall reserve till I take up the third point of Putnam's *personal conduct.*"

24

ARTICLE III.—ON GENERAL PUTNAM'S PERSONAL CONDUCT AT THE BATTLE OF BUNKER HILL.

"Already we have arrayed the formidable mass of testimony in the depositions and statements of Judge Grosvenor, Abner Allen, Josiah Hill, and our venerable friend,— whose account is not anonymous because he is well known, and its authenticity may be settled by reference as above proposed. We shall pass by, for the present, the unanswerable evidence of Colonel Trumbull as to Colonel Small's declarations, because, although we feel, as President Adams does, a sort of instinctive feeling of the truth of that anecdote ; although it bears on the face of it, evidence which thrills in the heart of every honorable man ; yet there is a weakness too much cultivated in our country, which leads them to value less the testimony of an enemy, although no assignable motive could be invented for such a tale on the part of Colonel Small.

" But let it pass, in order to introduce some of General Dearborn's own comrades, in his own regiment, fighting by his side, whose eyes were not so blinded but that they could see Putnam in the hottest of the fight, even ordering Dearborn's troops. Perhaps Putnam came there at the unlucky moment when Captain Dearborn, *quitting his soldiers, had retreated for the strange purpose of gathering up the scattered fragments of powder to recruit their ammunition,*— a prudent and overflowing caution, which savors at least as much of discretion as of zeal. We take only his own account of it, that in the face of the enemy, and while actually pushed by them, he sauntered into the rear, inquired into the fate of Warren, and attempted to collect powder, leaving his troops without the example of his own determined and desperate courage.

" Reuben Kemp, now of Brooklyn, in Connecticut, but formerly of Goffstown, State of New Hampshire, deposeth on oath, —

" 'That, in 1775, he was a soldier in Captain Samuel Richard's company and Colonel Stark's [Dearborn's] regiment ; that, being quartered at Mystic, on the 17th of June, an alarm was given, and the regiment ordered to parade at the Colonel's quarters, when ammunition was distributed, namely, ten bullets and a *gill-cup of powder.* We sorted our bullets as well as we could ; and marched to Charlestown Neck. After we arrived at the high ground, over the neck, we were ordered to parade our packs and guns, and put sentries over them. Here we were furnished with intrenching tools and began to throw up a breastwork ; but we had not been more than ten or fifteen minutes at work before the drums beat, and we were marched immediately. An officer whom I had *never seen [he was in the condition of* Dearborn *and all* Stark's *troops, who never had seen Putnam*], and whom they called General Putnam, seemed to have the ordering of things. He charged the men not to fire till the enemy came close to the works ; and then to take good aim, and make every shot kill a man. But there were a few pieces discharged before the order was given to fire. General Putnam appeared very angry, and passed along the *lines quickly,* with his sword drawn, and threatened to stab any man that fired without order. The enemy kept firing as they advanced, and when they had got pretty near the works we were ordered to take good aim and fire. *At this time* General Putnam was *constantly* passing backward and forward, from right to left, telling us the day was our own if we would stick to it ; and it was not many minutes before the enemy began to retreat.

"'Upon being questioned whether he had afterwards known Putnam, and recognized him to be the same officer who so gallantly distinguished himself, he said, "I saw him often after, for he commanded on Prospect Hill ; and I knew him to be the same that was in the fight." REUBEN KEMP.'

"'Sworn to before me, JOHN PARISH, Justice of the Peace.'

"Pray, where was Captain Dearborn, that he could neither see this gallant officer nor hear his orders to Dearborn's own regiment ?

"To the host of unanswerable witnesses, already adduced, we add the following :

"'Isaac Bassett of Killingly, in the county of Windham,

and State of Connecticut, deposeth, that he was a private soldier in General Putnam's regiment, in 1775. The day previous
to the battle of Bunker Hill a detachment had been made from
that regiment, and, under the command of Captain Knowlton,
composed part of the force that *first occupied Breed's Hill.* On
the morning of the 17th of June, another detachment from the
same regiment, under the command of Ensign Sprague, marched
from Cambridge, either to relieve or reinforce the party which
went on the hill over night. To this last detachment the deponent belonged, and arrived on the hill at the *redoubt and breastwork*, just as the *action commenced.* Here *he saw* General Putnam with his sword drawn, encouraging and animating the troops.
One of the company, Benjamin Grosvenor by name, was wounded
in the shoulder ; and the deponent's father, who *was also a soldier*
in the same regiment, was leading him from the field of action.
General Putnam stopped him, and, pricking him with his sword,
told him the wounded man could walk off himself, and not a soldier should leave the ground. This happened at the *breastwork
leading from the redoubt*, where our *party took post. I saw* General Putnam in the *hottest* of the fight, calling on the men to
stand their ground ; and I *am sure* he was at *this post* when the
enemy *scaled* the walls of the redoubt. I did not myself hear
the order given, but it was often said by the soldiers of our regiment, that General Putnam ordered them "not to fire on the enemy till they should see the *color* of their eyes, and then for
every man to make sure of his mark." Isaac Bassett.'

" ' Sworn to before me, James Danielson, Justice of the Peace.'

" These orders were precisely in the character of the fire-de-
vouring Putnam, of whose desperate valor and almost more than
human courage so many anecdotes have been for half a century
told. Here also is another positive eye-witness, who knew Putnam and could not be mistaken.

"We have also a deposition of another of Dearborn's comrades in Stark's regiment, who volunteered his testimony. Ebenezer Bean of Conway, New Hampshire, says, —

" ' The following are the most prominent facts which came under my observation, at the battle of Bunker Hill, relative to the conduct of General Putnam in that action. I was a private in Captain Kinsman's company, in Colonel Stark's regiment. A detachment under Captain Kinsman was ordered on to the hill, in the fore part of the day. We arrived at the redoubt about 12 o'clock, and continued there through the action. The rest of Colonel Stark's regiment arrived on the hill just before the action commenced. When we arrived at the redoubt, General Putnam was there, and very *active;* he was urging the men on, giving orders, *riding* from one end of the line to the other, as far as I could observe, and continued active *through the action*, and in my opinion fought with great bravery.

" ' EBENEZER BEAN.

" ' CONWAY, N. H., May 29th, 1818.'

" Here is another contradiction of General Dearborn, by *his own soldiers*. This disproves two assertions: 'that Putnam remained *inactive* during the battle,' and. that 'no officer was mounted on that day.'

" Amos Barnes, of the same town, swears that he was in Captain Abbott's company, in Stark's regiment. 'When we arrived at Charlestown Neck, we passed Gerrish's regiment. Colonel Stark marched in front, over the neck, and I was the third man from him. Captain Abbott marched next to Colonel Stark, and no other officer. [*This, though unimportant, contradicts General Dearborn, who says he marched in front with Stark. One of the witnesses must be mistaken. We may, hereafter, learn which, but it serves to show the confusion of the accounts of such battles.*] When we got on to the top of the hill, I saw one or two field-pieces which had ceased firing. Putnam was on his horse near them, and when we passed him he urged Colonel Stark to urge on his men as fast as possible. [Dearborn says they were moving at a very moderate pace, which did not suit the impatient temper of Putnam. These pieces were on Breed's Hill, as will appear by future evidence, particularly that of the Hon. James Winthrop.] We marched down the hill, by the redoubt, and after firing fifteen or twenty minutes, as nearly as I can recollect, at this distance of time, Major M'Cleary ordered us to retreat. I continued in service till 1777; and in 1778 entered again and continued till 1780, and never in my life heard a word said *against* the military character of General Putnam, till I saw General Dearborn's statement.   AMOS BARNES.

"'CONWAY, N. H.'

"Thus it seems that Colonel Stark's or Dearborn's *own soldiers* do not make so much of their exertions as their officers; and that this jealousy of Putnam's fame did not pervade *the ranks* so freely as in other places, in the New Hampshire line. But private soldiers are not so apt to feel humiliations and disappointments. They expect only to bleed and suffer for their country.

"We have another piece of direct testimony from an eye-witness, Benjamin Putnam, Esq., of Dixmont, Maine, and postmaster in that place, going to show the great energy of Putnam on the day of Bunker Hill; but as he only saw him 'pushing on the men with great activity' (to use his own words), 'and then *galloping* on towards Breed's Hill, the scene of action, from Bunker Hill,' we shall not insert it at large, though it is ready for the inspection of the curious."

BRIEF EXTRACTS FROM OTHER ARTICLES OF MR. LOWELL.

"It is said by President Adams that there could be no commander, because there was no general or national authority. But is this conclusive? or was it the fact? Were not the troops of Connecticut and New Hampshire acting as allies of Massachusetts, which was then engaged in a war *de facto*? And when allied armies are assembled, is there not generally a commander-in-chief? And if detachments are made *partly from each*, do not the officers retain their ranks, and command inferior officers of *allied troops*? Did not General Ward assume the command of all the troops at Cambridge? Dearborn states this fact; and it was by the orders of a Massachusetts General, that Colonel Stark of *New Hampshire* appeared on Bunker Hill. If Putnam, then, was in the battle at all, except as a volunteer, he must have had the command. That he had so is proved by his own history of the battle, as detailed by his son. General Putnam is certainly as good and credible a witness, at the least, as any one who has been cited. He is not to be viewed as an accused person defending himself; for it is admitted, even by his mortal enemy (and a man cannot have a more bitter one) General Dearborn, that he never was *accused*, and he thinks it unaccountable that he escaped. So far from being accused, he was instantly promoted for his conduct in that battle. . . . .

"We have already stated that all the historians of our war have done ample justice to the valor and enterprise of this veteran; nor have our poets forgotten him. What General Dearborn could mean by his 'ephemeral popularity having faded away,' we are ignorant. He retained that popularity to the hour of this atrocious calumny; and he will retain it long after the name of Dearborn and all his services and various fortunes shall have been forgotten.

"We have heard two officers of high rank in the army, who enjoyed the confidence of Washington, near his person or under his eye, declare since this charge, that they never heard a word nor an insinuation against the reputation of Putnam, till General Dearborn's 'account of the battle.'"

F.

EXTRACTS FROM ARTICLE IN THE "NORTH AMERICAN REVIEW," JULY, 1818.

Reference has already been made to this article on pp. 263–264. But for the purpose of showing more clearly its spirit and aim, we here give several extracts from it. We do this, not only for the marked ability displayed, but because one would not be likely to know the real purpose of the article from references often made to it at the present day. We have in Chapter XI. quoted the sentence in which the writer says, " Properly and strictly speaking, there was no commander-in-chief in the battle."

As has been fully explained in Chapter V., that may be a *legal* truth, a *rhetorical* truth, but is not a *historical* truth. It sets *form* above *fact.* But letting this pass, it will be seen that the article is a stout defence of Putnam against his slanderers. The very title plainly indicates the intent of the writer. It is the "Battle of Bunker Hill, — General Putnam." The writer, though not named in the "Review," was undoubtedly Daniel Webster. He was at that time thirty-six years old, and two years before had removed from Portsmouth to Boston. As a lawyer, it was but natural enough that he should look at the legal aspects of this "question of command." But it is quite apparent that the men of 1775 who fought the battle took a practical and, common-sense view of the matter, and left legal technicalities to take care of themselves.

"Were it not for the extremely unpleasant nature of the discussion to which the first of the pamphlets [General Dearborn's] has given rise, we should not regret the occasion of recurring to that distinguished and ever memorable opening of the revolutionary contest. No national drama was ever developed in a more interesting and splendid first scene. The incidents and the result of the battle itself were most important, and indeed most wonderful. As a mere battle, few surpass it in whatever interests and engages the attention. It was fought on a conspicuous eminence, in the immediate neighborhood of a populous city, and consequently in the view of thousands of spectators. The attacking army moved over a sheet of water to the assault. The operations and movements were of course all visible and all distinct. Those who looked on from the houses and heights of Boston had a fuller view of every important operation and event than can ordinarily be had of any battle, or than can possibly be had of such as are fought on a more extended ground, or by detachments of troops, acting in different places and at different times, and in some measure independently of each other. When the British columns were advancing to attack, the flames of Charlestown (fired as is generally supposed by a shell) began to ascend. The spectators, far outnumbering both armies, thronged and crowded on every height and every point which afforded a view of the scene, themselves constituted a very important part of it. The troops of the two armies seemed like so many combatants in an amphitheatre. The manner in which they should acquit themselves was to be judged of, not as in other cases of military engagements, by reports and future history, but by a vast and anxious assembly already on the spot, and waiting with unspeakable concern and emotion the progress of the day. In other battles the *recollection* of wives and children has been used as an excitement to animate the warrior's breast and nerve his arm. Here was not a mere recollection, but an actual *presence* of them, and other dear connections, hanging on the skirts of the battle, anxious and agitated, feeling almost as if wounded themselves by every blow of the enemy, and putting forth, as it were, their own strength and all the energy of their own throbbing bosoms, into every gallant effort of their warring friends.

"But there was a more comprehensive and vastly more important view of that day's contest than has been mentioned, a view indeed which ordinary eyes, bent intently on what was immediately before them, did not embrace, but which was perceived in its full extent and expansion by minds of a higher order. Those men who were at the head of the colonial councils, who had been engaged for years in the previous stages of the quarrel with England, and who had been accustomed to look forward to the future, were well apprised of the magnitude of the events likely to hang on the business of that day. They saw in it, not only a battle, but the beginning of a civil war, of unmeasured extent, and of uncertain issue. All America and all England were likely to be deeply concerned in the consequences. The individuals themselves who knew full well what agency they had had in bringing affairs to this crisis, had need of all their courage, — not that disregard of personal safety in which the vulgar suppose true courage to consist, but that high and fixed moral sentiment, that steady and decided purpose, which enables men to pursue a distant end, with a full view of the difficulties and dangers before them, and with a conviction that before they arrive at the proposed end, should they ever reach it, they must pass through evil

report as well as good report, and be liable to obloquy, as well
as defeat. . . . .

"Nearly half a century has elapsed from the commencement
of the Revolution, and in this flight of years, a great majority of
those who acted prominent parts in it have been carried to the
tomb. A small number survive, yet enjoying the fruit of their
services, and rejoicing in the prosperity of their country. We
cannot conceive what motives should induce any one of those
who are still living to venture rashly in an attack on the fame of
the dead. How long can he who is the youngest of the survivors expect to live to vindicate his own claims to his country's
gratitude? And which of them can expect that those who come
after him, and are of another generation, shall pay a more tender and sacred regard to his fame than he may have been
found to manifest to the fame of one of his own associates and
companions in arms? The last man who should bring forward,
at this day, an accusation against one who has long been dead,
and who died in the full possession of his country's regard and
gratitude for his services in our Revolution, is he who has himself claims on that regard and gratitude for similar services.
Even the common feelings of self-interest would seem sufficient
to repress such an undertaking by such a hand. What is the
value of revolutionary merit, if, forty years after the actions on
which it rests were performed, and twenty years after he who
performed them has gone to his grave, this merit may be denied
in terms of bold and unqualified assertion, and the country informed that imbecility, cowardice, want of patriotism and neglect
of duty, were the true characteristics of those to whom it has
uniformly ascribed a generous devotion to the public interest,
inflexible virtue and dauntless courage? And especially what is
to be the value of this merit, if such attacks are to be made upon
it, not by the temerity of the striplings of the rising generation,
but by one who was an associate and fellow-laborer? There are
occasions, it is true, in which great sacrifices must be made to
the truth of history, and to a desire of disabusing mankind of
their prejudices and false opinions. But such necessity, we have
flattered ourselves, has not existed in relation to the public men

of the United States.   We cannot persuade ourselves that it existed in the case of General Putnam, and we cannot, therefore, but feel the deepest regret for the occasion that has produced these remarks. . . . .

" A very ordinary degree of candor would induce the belief, that if there had been grounds of complaint against any officer, at that time, not of a shadowy and unsubstantial nature, they would have been attended to and investigated.   That was certainly a *jealous* period.   Every officer was watched, because it was the beginning of a civil war, and dangers were to be apprehended not only from cowardice but from defection.   If those who knew General Putnam's behavior at that time found no fault with it, the presumption is that no fault could be found with it.   And those whose lips were silent then, when well-founded complaints would have been a duty, must, long afterwards and after the death of the party, be heard not without much abatement and allowance. . . . .

" Taking the evidence together, we apprehend the following to be a true general account of General Putnam's conduct on this occasion: He came over from Cambridge with a party of the Connecticut troops, the night before the battle, and directed and assisted in throwing up the redoubt.   He was on the field of battle at or about the time the action commenced at the rail fence.   At some period, during the battle, he probably went back to bring up the residue of his own regiment.   [The writer is evidently mistaken in this suggestion.   There appears no evidence that General Putnam ever tried to move his regiment into that battle, except the one hundred and twenty men detailed the night before.   He sent his son, Captain Israel Putnam, just before the battle, for the rest of Chester's company, and perhaps Coit's, but it is sufficient proof that this call did not apply to the eight hundred men or more that still remained of his regiment, at Inman's farm, that we have no account of their movement that day.   Putnam in this paid respect to Ward's orders.]   He may possibly have gone back more than once for this purpose.   He was encouraging the troops, giving command, passing along the lines, and partaking of all the danger of the occasion, in the heat of the engagement at the rail fence. When the British made the last attack, which was confined principally to the redoubt, he might have been gone back to bring up the other troops. If so, this would explain a fact, which has been asserted, that Colonel Prescott on his retreat met General Putnam. He was not in the redoubt at any time during the battle. That post was Prescott's. His command and operations were confined to the troops which lined the rail fence, and perhaps the breastwork. It should be understood that the redoubt and breastwork were on a line. But the rail fence was not on a line with these, but considerably in the rear, and much nearer Bunker Hill. If General Putnam had been at the rail fence itself when Colonel Prescott retreated, the latter might be said to have met with, or, in more correct terms, to have passed, the former. The contiguity of the rail fence to Bunker Hill may explain the passing, even perhaps more than once, of General Putnam from the one to the other. It has little tendency to prove the absence of General Putnam from the field at the time of the battle, that troops passed him as they went to Breed's Hill or as they returned from it. They went *before* the battle and returned *afterwards ;* and an officer on horseback certainly is able to move with more velocity than a corps of infantry. It was an open field, not a strait and narrow path, that led to the redoubt, the breastwork and the rail fence. Officers no doubt traversed the field, sometimes meeting troops, sometimes passing them in various directions, as their duty required. No part of the fight was hotter or more fatal than at that part of the line occupied by Knowlton's company. . . . . In order to understand the operations of the day, it should be borne in mind that the object of the British was to dislodge the troops from the redoubt. . . . . The first operation of the British infantry was a movement on the flank ; and it was to prevent the success of this movement that the rail fence was thrown up. Being repulsed in this attempt the British, on the arrival of the reinforcement, changed their mode of operation and proceeded to a direct assault of the fort itself, in which they succeeded. . . . .

"The fact is, that the troops at the rail fence, a part of which belonged to Putnam's regiment and were more immediately under his command, never were repulsed and did not retreat, till the fort itself, the whole original object of the battle, was abandoned. *The deficiency of force was in the redoubt, and if Putnam had been able to have reinforced Prescott there, it would have been in the highest degree advantageous.* [We desire to call special attention to the sentence just copied. The writer of the article, though he has before said that "strictly speaking there was no commander-in-chief," yet in this very sentence treats Putnam as chief commander. What had Putnam to do with reinforcing Prescott, except as having the general oversight and command? Why should not Prescott, through his subordinate officers, reinforce himself.] . . .

"General Putnam was an uneducated man. In the science of his profession he could not, of course, be greatly accomplished. He made his way by the force and enterprise of his character, and his devotion to the public interest. He was suited to the times, and the times were suited to him. Habituated from early life to an acquaintance with the *militia*, trained in the school of Indian and colonial warfare, of integrity above suspicion, and of courage not to be doubted, much esteemed by the people of Connecticut, and a warm friend to the Revolution, it could hardly be otherwise than that he should possess that weight and consideration which is called an unaccountable popularity."

NOTE.

In closing, we desire to emphasize a distinction which has been several times made in this volume, between the *civil* and the *military* capacity of General Artemas Ward. In the sum total of his character, he is not by any means to be spoken of contemptuously or even lightly. He was in public affairs a man of high standing and large service. S. A. Drake, Esq., in his "Historic Fields and Mansions of Middlesex," speaks in terms of high praise of his firmness and courage, as a Judge in Worcester, in the time of Shay's rebellion. As head of the American army at Cambridge, he was suffering under a painful disease, which prevented his riding a horse, and doubtless took away from his natural courage and force. We have only desired to show, whatever may have been the excuses for his slowness and timidity, that he was a very poor head commander in that summer of 1775.

Mr. Drake, in the work above referred to, on p. 260, gives the following anecdote of what happened years afterwards:

"It is well known that Washington spoke of the resignation of General Ward, after the evacuation of Boston, in a manner approaching contempt. His observations, then confidentially made, about some of the other Generals, were not calculated to flatter their *amour propre* or that of their descendants. It is said that General Ward, learning long afterwards the remark that had been applied to him, accompanied by a friend, waited on his old chief at New York, and asked him if it was true that he had used such language. The President replied that he did not know, but that he kept copies of all his letters, and would take an opportunity of examining them. Accordingly at the next session of Congress (of which General Ward was a member) he again called with his friend, and was informed by the President that he had really written as alleged. Ward then said, '*Sir, you are no gentleman*,' and turning on his heel, quitted the room."

INDEX.*

A.

Abercrombie, Gen., 56, 57, 62, 355.
Adams, John, 87, 88, 89, 95, 138, 175, 242, 245, 264, 270.
Adams, Samuel, 112, 252, 253, 254.
Agassiz, Prof., 80.
Allen, Ethan, 137.
Alner, James, 303.
Amherst, Gen., 166, 346.
Andrew, Daniel, 24.
Andros, Edmund, 36, 70.
Army at Cambridge, constitution of, 87–104.
Avery, Ephraim, 47.

B.

Babcock, Henry, 291.
Bailey, John, 113.
Bancroft, George, 4, 50, 51, 52, 77, 78, 81, 86, 122, 124, 125, 173, 269, 273, 306, 307.
Barker, Captain, 226.
Barnard, Henry, 343.
Beard, Edwin S., 4.
Belcher, Jonathan, 37, 46.
Belknap, Jeremy, 111, 121.
Bircham, Edward, 15.
Blackwell, John, 35, 36, 37, 39, 46.
Braddock, Gen., 51, 56.
Brewer, David, 92, 114, 162, 194, 206.

Brewer, Jonathan, 114.
Brickett, James, 115, 237, 240.
Bridge, Ebenezer, 113, 149, 237, 240.
Brinley, George, 87.
Brooklyn, Ct., 39.
Brooks, Eleazer, 115.
Brooks, John, 116, 155, 175.
Brown, Benjamin, 40.
Brown, Peter, 228.
Bruce, Major, 355.
Bunker Hill Art, three pictures, 216–227.
Bunker Hill Association, action of, 336.
Burr, Aaron, 304, 309.
Burr, Thaddeus, 200.
Bushnell, Dr., 343.
Butler, Major, 355.

C.

Chandler, John, 42.
Charles II., 36.
Chastellux, 236.
Chester, John, 116, 119, 135, 143, 144, 176, 179.
Cheever, Ezekiel, 24.
Church, Benjamin, 131, 285, 286.
Church, Thomas, 114.
Clarke, John, 200, 201, 232, 233, 234, 241, 355.

* This is mainly an index of names; but, from the very character of the work, certain names recur so frequently, that we have not been careful to repeat them in every instance. The index will be more useful for finding a large number of names not of so frequent recurrence.

25

Franklin Press: Rand, Avery, & Co., Boston.